The Serpent's Tooth

Also by Margaret Bacon

Going Down
The Episode
The Unentitled
Kitty
The Package
Snow in Winter
The Kingdom of the Rose
The Chain

Non-Fiction

Journey to Guyana

For Children

A Packetful of Trouble

The Serpent's Tooth

Margaret Bacon

Copyright © 1986 by Margaret Bacon

First published in Great Britain in 1987 by
Judy Piatkus (Publishers) Limited of
5 Windmill Street, London, W1

British Library Cataloguing in Publication Data

Bacon, Margaret
   The serpent's tooth.
   I. Title
   823'.914[F]   PR6052.A3115
   ISBN 0-86188-562-7

Phototypeset in 11/12pt Linotron Times by
Phoenix Photosetting, Chatham
Printed and bound in Great Britain by
Mackays of Chatham Ltd

Chapter 1

'I'm five years and five days old,' Jimmy told her. 'I shall soon be six.'

She glanced down at him, decided he was too young to argue with and instead took a firm grip on his hand and prepared to cross the main road.

It was the first time their mother had let them come home on their own. Polly took her responsibilities seriously, waiting now until the road was clear, watching to see that he didn't catch his feet in the tramlines, holding on to him until they reached the safety of the far pavement. Only when they had turned into their own street did she let go of his hand.

He rubbed it against his leg to show that she had held it too tightly, then transferred his painting to it from his left hand. It was the first he had done since he started in the Infants' class last week. He wouldn't let her look at it.

Theirs was a long narrow street, lined on each side with terrace houses. Although it was late September the afternoon was hot and the road dusty. She took off her cardigan and tied its arms round her waist, simultaneously kicking open the gate of number 135. Jimmy ran up the concrete path ahead of her but couldn't open the door.

'It sticks sometimes,' she said, and gave it an expert shove with her thin shoulder. It didn't move. She lifted the corner of the door-mat with her foot and stooped down to pick up the key.

It was very quiet indoors. Their footsteps were loud on the bare floorboards and even on the torn linoleum of the kitchen floor they still sounded noisy. There was bread and margarine on the kitchen table and a jar of jam. She lit the gas and put on the kettle.

'Where's our Mam?' Jimmy asked.

'Gone to the shops, maybe.'

'Perhaps she's been run over by a tram?'

'Don't be so soft.'

The first tear fell. It landed on his picture.

'You'll spoil it,' she warned, wiping it with the sleeve of her cardigan. 'All right, I'm not looking at it.'

'It's for Mam to see first. I wish she was here.'

'We'll have a picnic, you and me,' she said in her mother's cheerful voice. 'There now, you'll like that. I'll make jam sandwiches and we'll take it all out into the garden. You take those mugs and I'll bring the rest.'

They sat on the back doorstep, their tea arranged around their feet. The late afternoon sun slanted directly on to them.

'I like our garden,' Jimmy remarked, a smile of contentment on his baby face. She glanced at him and immediately the smile was reflected on her own sharp little features. Then she lay back against the warm, peeling green paint of the back door and gazed appreciatively down the garden, delighting in the sight of the long grass, the heap of coal, the pile of rubble which had once been a henhouse and was now overgrown with pink, flowering weeds. A length of much-knotted rope which linked the clothes post at the far end of the garden to the drain pipe by the kitchen window, seemed to tie it all together.

'Yes, it's a tip,' she said approvingly, using her mother's word. 'And it smells nice, too.'

'I like the noise it makes,' Jimmy added.

It was soothing, the distant hum of traffic, the occasional faint rattle of the trams, the sound of insects in the long grass, a bee buzzing somewhere and Mrs Biddle next door shovelling coal.

'She might know where our Mam is.'

'All right.'

They got up and squeezed through the gap in the scratchy bit of hedge.

'I thought you might be round,' Mrs Biddle said, watching them, shovel in hand. 'Come in. They're having tea. Sarah's been off school with her cold.'

They followed her indoors. The house was a replica of theirs, only everything was in reverse. It fascinated Polly seeing it all as if in a mirror. It always seemed bigger, but her mother said it couldn't be.

'Mum's not at home,' Polly explained.

'Well, yes, I did see her go out earlier,' Mrs Biddle said, rubbing her hands on her apron then busying herself with plates and cups. 'There now, you two sit down with the others.'

The four Biddle children were already at the table. There was cake, she noticed.

'She was carrying a suit-case,' Sarah Biddle said.

'That's enough,' her mother told her sharply. 'Have a biscuit, Jimmy. You can stay here until your dad's home.'

She knew that nobody carried a suit-case unless they were going on a train. Where had her mother gone? Her heart thumped. No good asking Mrs Biddle, she knew that, only had to glance at her face. Jimmy was quite unconcerned, busy with his second biscuit, his eye on the cake. It was iced.

Mrs Biddle, usually placid, was edgy. She kept running her fingers through her springy, yellow hair making it stick out all over the place. When she caught Polly's eye she pretended to smile, twitching her mouth and momentarily rounding her flabby pink cheeks, but her eyes stayed anxious. She was listening for the sound of their father coming home, Polly knew that.

After they had cleared away the tea things, Mrs Biddle pretended to read the newspaper.

'Well, there's not going to be a war,' she said. 'So that's one good thing.'

A gate clicked. Mrs Biddle jumped up. 'That'll be your dad,' she said. 'Don't you worry. I'll go and tell him you're here.'

She was away a long time.

'I've been helping your dad get tea,' she said when she came back. 'You'd best run along now. You must help your dad, Polly. You're a big girl now.'

It was true. She towered above the other seven-year-olds in her class. Last week somebody had thought she was ten.

'Come on then, Jimmy,' she said, taking his hand. 'Thank you for the tea, Mrs Biddle.'

Jimmy allowed himself to be pulled along home. Neither of them was particularly keen to meet their father. A tall, silent man, he never took much notice of them. He didn't tell them things, unlike their mother who was always chattering, laughing, telling them funny stories about when she was little. Sometimes Polly thought that perhaps he didn't talk because he couldn't breathe very well – he made a wheezing sound – or maybe it was just that he hadn't anything he especially wanted to say.

'Well,' he said now, 'your mother's gone.'

'Where?' Jimmy asked.

'Don't know.'

'But you *must* know.' There was panic in Jimmy's voice.

'It's all right,' she said automatically. 'She'll be back soon.'

'She's not coming back,' her father said.

She stared at him, feeling sick. It didn't make sense. Her mother would never leave Jimmy. She knew how much Mam loved Jimmy, always worrying about him because he was little. Yet, at the same time, she knew beyond any shadow of doubt that it was true. There had been all the little signs, all the ways grown-ups tell you things when they think they are keeping secrets.

'She must come back,' Jimmy said, beginning to cry. 'I've got a picture for her.'

'She's gone for good. That's the sort she is,' their father said. He had a fit of coughing, then went on: 'We'll manage without her and there's an end to it. Polly, you're in charge of the house now. Mrs Biddle's going to come in and clean through once a week and take the washing. I'll pay her something, of course. We can do most of the shopping on Saturday afternoons and the rest you can get on your way home from school.'

And so it was. They muddled through somehow. Despite Mrs Biddle's weekly ministrations, the house got steadily dirtier. Dust accumulated and the gas stove developed a smell of its own. Polly took it apart and washed it, but afterwards the gas wouldn't light and her father was angry. He was very grumpy that winter and had to be off work with a bad cough. When he was well he got the breakfast and she cooked the supper. Her mother did not come back.

Jimmy fretted. She wouldn't let him cry or tell anyone about it. They had to pretend that everything at their house was just the same as at everybody else's, she insisted. As long as nobody else knew, she could make herself believe, at least while they were at school, that it hadn't happened. But one winter morning in playtime, one of the big boys sidled up to her in the yard and said, 'I know something about you, Polly Adams. Your mum's run off.'

All the pent-up fury that had been inside her since her mother left rushed into her head and hands. She flew at him, butting him in the stomach with her head and at the same time lashing out wildly at him with her fists. Taken by surprise, he slipped on the ice and fell back against the wall.

'You shut up,' she shrieked at him, thrusting her face into his. 'Don't you go telling lies about my mam.'

Her green eyes were narrowed with rage, like a cat's. For a moment he thought she was going to scratch his face. He was scared. She was only a girl, but she was strong and had red hair.

'It was that Sarah Biddle told me,' he said, moving warily along the wall, trying to get out of range of her hands without making it too obvious. 'I expect she made it up.'

She stood eyeing him, for a moment, and then drew herself up and said grandly, 'All right. We'll say no more about it.' And nobody ever did.

Her father was off work again in the spring.

'He'll be better when the weather warms up,' Mrs Biddle promised.

But he wasn't.

'My bed shakes when he coughs,' Jimmy complained one night. 'Doesn't he ever sleep?'

She and Jimmy shared the bedroom on the other side of the landing at the top of the stairs. The thin walls and ill-fitting doors presented no barrier to the sound of the perpetual cough.

'I think he must be asleep when he's coughing,' she told him.

'He's lucky. I can't sleep when he's making that noise. What time is it, our Polly?'

'I don't know. Middle of the night some time.'

'I'm hungry.'

'I'll go and get some bananas, shall I? I bought some today.'

She crept out on to the landing. The noises from behind the other door were dreadful. She scuttled as quickly as she could downstairs, rummaged in the cupboard for the bananas and ran back upstairs with them.

'It's four o'clock by the kitchen clock,' she told him. 'We must settle down now.'

They ate their bananas and slept.

They got up too early the next day, misled by the brightness of the morning.

'It's going to be hot,' she told him, putting another slice of bread and margarine on his plate and pushing the jam pot towards him. 'You needn't take your jumper. There, you eat that while I make the tea.'

She warmed the teapot and took the milk out of the metal meat safe. She sniffed at it. 'It's gone off,' she said.

'Never mind. Oh, Polly, isn't it lovely having breakfast without him coughing all the time?'

'Yes. I'll take him up a cup of tea before we go.'

'Why not leave him? Mrs Biddle said he'd get better if he got more sleep.'

She shook her head. 'He said he wanted to get up to go to the doctor.'

She poured out the tea and stirred it vigorously, but the little white blobs of congealed milk soon reappeared on the surface.

He was sound asleep. She put the tea down by the bed and shook his shoulder. He didn't wake. He always slept hard when he wasn't coughing. She waited by the bed for a moment, then went downstairs.

'Perhaps Mrs Biddle was right,' she said. 'It might make him better to get his sleep.'

'He'll be mad at you if he said you were to wake him to go to the doctor,' he warned.

She hesitated, standing with one foot on the fender in front of the fireplace which hadn't been cleaned out since last used in the early spring. Bits of paper and orange peel littered the rusty cinders. On the other side of the grate they could hear Mrs Biddle, who had a fire on all the year round, raking out the ashes. Soon she would carry them down to the ash pit at the bottom of her garden.

'Let's ask her,' Jimmy said, going to the back door to summon her.

Mrs Biddle came in, wiping her hands on her apron. 'I'd let him have his sleep out,' she said. 'We can hear him coughing something terrible through the walls. Like paper them walls are. It sounds as if he's in the same room, he coughs that loud.'

Still talking, she made her way upstairs, the children following her. They waited on the landing. They heard Mrs Biddle exclaim. Then she reappeared, carefully shut the door behind her and stood against it, barring the way.

'Well, now,' she said. 'Well, now. That's all right. You two just get off to school. That's the best way. I'll see to everything. Just make sure that your bedroom's tidy. Leave everything tidy. That's the main thing.'

Mystified, they went obediently into their bedroom and made their beds, pushing their clothes out of sight in the cupboard.

'What about the banana skins?' Jimmy whispered.

'Best just hide them under our pillows for now.'

Mrs Biddle was still standing outside their father's bedroom door as if on guard. She looked uneasy. Mrs Biddle at bay. She told them to go on ahead, then followed them down the stairs.

'When you get home tonight, come round to us for tea,' she said. 'That's the best way.'

She gave them muffins for tea, and cake with icing. When they had finished, she sent her own children out into the garden to play. They went without arguing, as if forewarned.

Mrs Biddle asked them if they'd like more cake or biscuits, and when they refused, told them that their father had died.

They said nothing. Polly tried to understand what she meant, put some sense into the words, but they didn't mean anything. She wouldn't see him again or hear him cough. She didn't really believe it. His death lacked the finality of her mother's departure.

She tried to remember what he looked like, but couldn't. It was always like that. She never could remember what he looked like when he wasn't there. The only bit of him she could recall was his waistcoat with the shiny buttons. She had no picture of his face. Her mother's face she could remember very clearly, although she hadn't seen it for nearly a year. She could see it in her mind's eye, looking down at her in bed, close up to her for a kiss or a cuddle, screwed up and laughing, sometimes really red and cross, but always vivid. Now she stood in Mrs Biddle's kitchen feeling stupid as she struggled to remember what her father looked like and trying to believe in his death. But she could do neither. Worse still, she could think of nothing suitable to say.

'I've brought all your things round here,' Mrs Biddle said.

'But aren't we going home?'

'No, it isn't your home any more. It's rented weekly.'

Polly stared at her. She wanted to go home. She wanted to sit again on the back doorstep and look down the garden. She wanted to sit in the kitchen and eat jam sandwiches while their own kettle boiled. She wanted to lie down on her own bed.

'You'll go to your mother and your uncle now.'

'Mam? We'll go to Mam?' In Jimmy's voice there was wonder beyond joy. He had really believed he would never see her again.

'What uncle?' Polly asked.

'Well, the gentleman your mother's with, he'll be your uncle.'

'Oh, I see,' she said, but didn't.

'It'll be all right.'

'Why doesn't Mam come back and live here?'

'Because she lives at this address now,' Mrs Biddle said, taking an envelope from behind the clock on the kitchen mantelpiece.

'You knew where she was all the time?' Jimmy shouted, suddenly furious.

'No, love. And your father didn't know either. This morning I went down to the depot where your father worked and somebody there happened to know. They took a message and she's expecting you this evening.'

Later Mrs Biddle took them on two trams. They each had a case and Polly had a pillow slip of extras. There was quite a long walk at the end of the second tram journey, but Mrs

Biddle told them the way, gave them an envelope with the address on it, kissed them both, told Polly she was a big girl now, and left them.

For once it was Polly who walked slowly, dragging her feet, while Jimmy kept ahead. The road seemed endless, the suitcase handle dug into her fingers and the pillowcase was awkward to carry. Besides, she wasn't in a hurry to see her mother again. If her mother had wanted them, she wouldn't have left them in the first place. She was amazed that Jimmy didn't think of that as he hurried eagerly ahead, sure of his welcome. She wondered where her father was. Would they have buried him? Or was he still lying in the bedroom with the cup of cold tea on the floor beside him, its surface afloat with little white blobs of milk?

Their house would be very quiet now. She imagined the silence of it, their bedrooms emptied of all their belongings. Suddenly she remembered the banana skins under their pillows and went hot with shame.

Chapter 2

Their mother must have been looking out for them, for she opened the door before Polly could knock. She stood there in the little hall, and just behind her was a round-faced, tubby little man. Polly stared at them and didn't move. Her mother looked back at her and for once she seemed hesitant, nervous. She looked different, Polly thought, smaller.

'How you've both grown,' her mother said.

Then Polly felt herself pushed aside and Jimmy shot past her and hurled himself at his mother, who opened her arms wide. He leapt into them like a little wild animal and seemed to climb up her so that his arms were round her neck and his legs gripped her waist. She swung him round, hugging him.

Polly and the tubby little man watched them, embarrassed. Mother and son were half-laughing, half-crying. How can he, Polly thought, how can he?

Jimmy took to the house, too, in the same uncritical way.

'It's better than our old one,' he said, looking out of the bedroom window at the neat lawn like a strip of green cardboard at the back. 'And a bedroom each, just think!'

Their mother had prepared a special tea. There was tinned fish and salad followed by tinned peaches and tinned cream. The kitchen smelled of furniture polish and her mother was wearing lipstick. Polly felt like a visitor and couldn't think of anything to say. She thought longingly of bread and margarine on the kitchen table at home, and of the noise the kettle made as it boiled on the gas cooker.

The tubby man, whose name was Uncle Fred, was quiet, too. Now and then he smiled at her. They seemed the odd ones out.

'You're very quiet, Polly,' her mother said. 'Anything wrong?'

'No.'

'You don't need to start at your new school till next term.'

'New school?'

'Yes, it's too far to your old one.'

'But what about our friends?' she objected. 'And all our teachers? And I was in the middle of –'

'I don't mind,' Jimmy said obligingly. 'I'd like to have a new school. I didn't like the old one much.'

'That's my boy,' her mother said. 'You always make the best of things, don't you?'

'Of course you'll be evacuated if there's a war,' Uncle Fred said.

'Mrs Biddle said that there wouldn't be a war,' Polly remarked. She remembered very clearly everything that had been said or done that day, the day their mother left home.

'Well, we'll see. If there's a war, these industrial towns won't be fit places for kids.'

The conversation was strained. Everything was awkward. It went on being awkward the next day, too. It was having this strange man in the place that did it. Without him she might have had a go at her mother.

It wasn't that Fred was nasty. He was much more friendly

than their dad had been. He talked to them more and smiled a lot. But he wasn't their father and his presence was inexplicable. He was just an extra.

'I'm taking you for an outing this afternoon,' he said two days after they had arrived. 'Your mother has things to do.'

'What things?'

'Oh, just things.'

'It's nice of your Uncle Fred to take time off,' their mother pointed out. 'All the week he's taken off, just to get to know you.'

'Where would you like to go for an outing?' he asked them.

They didn't answer. They weren't sure what an outing was.

'We'll go to Hollies Park then,' he said. 'There are swings there, and roundabouts – you'll like that. And there's a pond, too, with ducks. We'll take bread for them.'

'We'd best have dinner early,' their mother said.

'I'll give them a treat out. There's a café there.'

'Thanks, Fred.'

They had reached the tram stop when they remembered the bag of stale bread for the ducks.

'It's on the kitchen table,' Polly said. 'I'll run back and get it.'

She ran back to the house and into the kitchen. The bag of bread was on the table, just as they had left it. Her mother was upstairs. It was very quiet. She stood quite still, taking it all in, realising that she was alone in the house with her mother for the first time. Suddenly she was overwhelmed with a desperate need to be close to her. She didn't know, as she dashed upstairs, if she wanted to hug her or hit her, only that she was frantic to be close to her and that she was going to cry.

The bedroom door was open. Her mother was standing in front of the mirror fastening her best coat. It was a dark grey cost. On the bed was a shiny black straw hat which Polly had never seen before. She stopped still in the doorway, staring at the scene. Her mother, concentrating on tying a purple silk scarf at the neck of her coat, suddenly saw her daughter reflected in the mirror and her expression changed to one of exasperation. Polly had not expected that look. She stood still, not daring to go into the room.

'Whatever is it, Polly? I thought you'd gone, all of you.'

'I'm sorry,' she muttered. 'I just came back for the bread.'

She turned and ran downstairs. As she left the house she slammed the front door behind her so hard that for a moment she was frightened at her own violence and waited, scared, for the roof to slide off.

It needed a tram and a trolley bus to get to the park. She stared in wonder at the leafy suburbs for she had never been so far out of the town. It was very clean-looking and quiet and the houses were like palaces.

The café was grand, too, with its tables covered with American oilcloth in red and white squares. There were bottles of sauce and of vinegar in the centre of each and a waitress came to see what they wanted to eat. She brought them a big plate of bread and butter and a pot of tea. Then she brought their fish and chips which they doused in vinegar and ate in silence. When they did speak, it was in whispers for they were overawed, Jimmy and she, by their first experience of eating in a public place.

Uncle Fred talked loudly and laughed a lot. He bought trifle for their pudding and encouraged them to ladle spoonfuls of sugar into their tea.

'We'll soon fatten you up,' he said.

'We're not thin.'

'Well, if you're not thin, I don't know who is. Skinny as beanpoles, if you ask me. It worries your mother,' he added reprovingly.

He didn't have the right to rebuke them, Polly thought resentfully. Besides, if their mother had cared about what they ate she shouldn't have left them. She sat in sullen silence and refused more food. Jimmy, eager not to be a worry, helped himself to another piece of bread and butter. There was no jam so he sprinkled it liberally with sugar.

As they came out of the café, they had to wait for a procession of cars to pass. Uncle Fred took off his cap.

'Why did you do that?' Jimmy asked.

'Because it's a funeral,' he said.

'Was there a body in that big car at the front?'

'Yes Jimmy, but never you mind. Come on, we can cross now. We'll go to the swings first, shall we?'

There was something about the way he didn't want to talk

about the funeral procession, or perhaps it was the glimpse she had had of men in dark suits and ladies in black hats that did it. Suddenly she knew for certain that her mother had gone to a funeral, too. A different one but a funeral all the same. That was it. She had gone to their dad's funeral and not told them. Uncle Fred knew and they didn't. He hadn't really wanted to take them out for a treat, it was just to get them out of the way. That's what her mother was doing now.

'I don't mind which we go to first,' Jimmy said. 'I like everything.' He took his sister's hand as they crossed the road and somehow that made it impossible to say anything that might upset him.

There were a lot of children at the Hollies playground. The roundabout was nearly full. They stood watching as it swung to a halt and its cargo of children climbed down.

'Want a go?' Uncle Fred asked.

'Oh, please.'

Jimmy had to be helped up. She refused to get on, determined not to cooperate in the deception that had been practised on them.

'As you like,' Uncle Fred said, and shrugged.

'You were sick when you went on a swing last year,' she warned Jimmy.

'I was only little then,' he shouted back as the roundabout began to move.

He let go with one hand and waved to them, then made a hasty grab at the horse's mane as it got up speed. They stood watching. He grinned at them when he passed the first time. Suddenly the horses began to go up and down as well as round and round. She hadn't expected that. Neither had Jimmy. The second time he passed them he was looking terrified.

'He's gone white,' she said. 'He might be sick.'

'Oh, no, he's loving it. You can see that he's loving it.'

She could see that he wasn't. He was easily the smallest one on the roundabout. She watched him anxiously. If she hadn't been so mad about the funeral she'd have been up there with him, looking after him. She should have stayed with him, she thought watching him as he clutched, terrified, at his steed. If he fell off and killed himself it would be all her fault.

The roundabout was going so fast now that she couldn't see

which horse he was on. Then it slowed suddenly as he passed them again. 'I want to get off,' Jimmy shouted at her. 'Please lift me off, our Polly.'

Impulsively she moved forward and grabbed at him. He let go and wrapped his arms around her neck, his legs still entangled in the horse's stirrups. She ran alongside, trying to disengage the rest of his body. The roundabout was gaining speed again. Then Uncle Fred suddenly had hold of them both, had lifted Jimmy clear. For a moment the three of them seemed entwined in an embrace and looking up she could see an expression of intense relief on Jimmy's face, as it swung above them. Then, prescribing a great flying arc on his way to the ground, he was copiously sick over both of his rescuers.

It was Hitler who brought all this awkwardness to an end. They were summoned back to school early to prepare for the evacuation. There was going to be a war, it was explained to them, and they would be going somewhere in the country called Reception Area where there would be no bombs.

They didn't have proper lessons at their new school. They were each given a gas-mask and spent a lot of time practising putting it on and taking it off. Wherever they went they had to take the gas-mask with them. It fitted into a little grey box which hung from a strap around their necks. Some people grumbled but Polly didn't. In fact she liked having this new possession. They also spent a great deal of time practising marching to the station and back. They had to take a case or bag full of all their belongings and a picnic for the journey and wear a label with their name on it. Thus equipped they set off every morning in a crocodile while people in the streets waved to them and occasionally gave them sweets. Afterwards they marched back to school again and ate their picnics sitting at their desks.

Then it all happened very suddenly. One day they were just practising marching to the station and back, and the next day they were told that this time it was real and that they were getting on a train and would not be coming home again. Everyone told them that it was just like going on holiday and one or two of the children even had buckets and spades. They were all very excited, waving and cheering as the train moved out of the station.

Polly had never been on a train before. She stared in wonder at the criss-crossing lines and at the other trains moving alongside, at the warehouses and old buildings that they passed with increasing speed and then at the back yards and gardens of houses. There seemed to be row after row of these houses. She had never realised that people lived on railway lines. She couldn't see any streets, just these yards and gardens, often with washing hanging out. She seemed to be seeing everything from the back.

The compartment was very hot; a boy who knew how everything worked, managed to slide open the window. Immediately soot and smoke from the engine blew in and covered them with smuts. She took a handkerchief, told Jimmy to spit on it and wiped his face. He was very quiet, much more upset than she was at leaving their mother and Uncle Fred. She was afraid he might cry. She comforted him and then added, 'I'll belt you if you blub,' after which she read comics to him.

Most of the others had brought comics, too. They read them in turns, passing them from hand to hand round the compartment, the big ones reading to the little ones. Then they sang songs and played noughts and crosses and ate their picnics early because they were bored. Soon Miss Tidy, who was in charge of them, came round and gave them each a postcard which they were to send home when they knew their address at Reception Area and tell their parents where they were and that they had arrived safely. If they liked their new homes, Miss Tidy suggested, they should tell their parents so, but if they weren't quite sure it would be better to say nothing. Then she told them to practise putting their gas-masks on.

The compartment was beginning to feel like home. There was something reassuring about its comfortable litter of comics and discarded clothing and remains of picnics. They all groaned when they were told they would soon have to leave it to change trains. Reluctantly they packed up their belongings and then waited in the corridor, clutching cases and bags and younger brothers and sisters while the train drew slowly into what seemed to Polly must be the biggest station in the world.

It was so thronged with people that it was quite difficult to find a place to stand on the platform when they jumped down from the train. There were soldiers in uniform everywhere and everybody seemed to be surging ceaselessly up and down platforms and across great bridges that arched over the railway lines. Trains kept coming in and out and sometimes the smoke and steam was so thick that they could scarcely see each other. They stood huddled together, the children from her school. Miss Tidy suggested that they might like to sing a hymn, but in the end they sang Ten Green Bottles. They were halfway through it when they were told they were on the wrong platform and their train was about to leave from the other side. Led by Miss Tidy, they rushed to the bridge whose metal stairs were so steep that Polly almost had to lift Jimmy up each step. All around them children were struggling with cases and boxes, panting and crimson-faced as they hurried to catch the train, for there seemed to be a great panic to get there quickly. She sensed that somebody thought that bombs might start falling very soon now and began to run, dragging Jimmy along the platform with her.

When at last they reached the safety of the train and the doors had been slammed behind them and the whistle blown, she was surprised that it didn't rush off quickly to Reception Area. Instead it made several false starts, moving out of the station and then shunting back again.

'I don't know *why* they've brought us here,' Jimmy said tearfully. 'It felt much safer at home.'

'It'll be all right when we get to Reception Area,' she told him. 'You'll see. Oh, look we're really going now.'

The train had set off in earnest and they all cheered, but it was a half-hearted cheer compared with the noise they had made when they left home that morning. The novelty was wearing off and they were hot and tired and dirty. She gave up the attempt to keep Jimmy looking clean. He leaned against her shoulder and fell asleep. So, gradually, as the long hot afternoon wore on, did all the others, drugged by the heat and by the rhythm of the train.

Polly didn't sleep. The view from the train windows had suddenly become very strange and exciting. She had never seen anything like it. Great green expanses unfolded before her very eyes, with huge grey rocks and stone walls that seemed to grow out of the ground. Animals looked up as the train passed by and stared back at her. There were no more rows of friendly houses, no more back yards hung with washing, no more warehouses and factories. This was wild country, uninhabited. She had had no idea that anywhere in England was like this. It was all right to travel through on a train, she thought, but she wouldn't like to have to get out into it, especially with those great animals loose everywhere. She watched fascinated from the safety of the compartment.

As evening drew in, great shadows appeared on the hillsides and raced menacingly alongside the train. It grew colder and soon the others began to wake and pull on cardigans and jackets and look anxiously out of the window.

Suddenly the door opened and there was Miss Tidy telling them they were nearly there now and please get ready to leave the train. She had gone and was opening the door of the next compartment before they had time to ask any questions. They looked at each other in consternation. Polly knew what they were all thinking: it was one thing to travel through this strange land, but a different matter altogether to get out into it.

'I expect,' she said to Jimmy, 'that we'll go round a corner in a minute and there'll be this nice town called Reception Area and it'll be just like home.'

But the train went more and more slowly and finally came to a halt by what seemed to be a wide pavement in the middle of a field. Evidently they had reached their destination. They were very quiet as they moved down the corridor to the single open door of the train, in front of which a man in uniform had placed a box for them to step down on to the platform far below. One by one they jumped down and then stood huddled together in this station which was so tiny that it hardly seemed like a station at all. Silently, they watched as the train, their last link with home, disappeared from sight around the side of the hill.

The country air struck very cold and sharp against their faces as they followed Miss Tidy to a yard where a bus was waiting for them. Jimmy was gripping her hand as if terrified of losing her. She could see that he was near to tears, but he held them back. He was very pale and had dark rings under his eyes. She remembered how he used to hate having to hold her hand to cross the roads when he first started school. Years ago it seemed now, before their mother had gone off and their father had died. But she could still remember the feel of his hand trying to escape from hers.

'Where'll we sleep tonight, our Polly?' he whispered now as he clung to her.

'Somewhere. Don't you worry. Give me your case while you climb on the bus.'

The bus was orange and had a very big step up to it. She had to give his bottom a shove with the case as he hauled himself up by the hand rail.

There weren't enough seats for them all, so she told him to sit on her knee. He didn't protest, just snuggled up against her as the bus, which was very old and rattly, lumbered along narrow, winding roads between grey walls. In the distance they could see what looked like huge barren mountains. Nearer, in the fields behind the walls, sheep and cows stared at them, nobody in charge.

'Are they all over the country?' Jimmy asked. 'Them great things.'

'I expect they chain them up at night,' she reassured him vaguely.

Suddenly there were houses, grey like the walls. They were not proper brick houses in streets, but seemed to be made out of piles of boulders like the ones she had noticed strewn about the barren green landscape. Then the road divided and there was a big triangle of grass with a huge tree in the middle. The bus slowed down. A black-robed figure walked across the grass to talk to the driver.

'Evening, Vicar,' she heard the driver say. 'Where do you want them?'

'In the village hall,' the vicar replied. Then they drove a few yards further on and stopped outside a big building like a school. Two adults were waiting in the wide doorway and watched in silence as the children got off the bus and filed past them into the hall, Miss Tidy counting them to make sure that none had got lost on the journey.

Chapter 3

Polly never forgot what followed. The hall was vast, bigger even than the one at her new school. It was very high, too, with great beams and rafters and smelled old and dusty. Grown-ups stood around the walls and the children huddled together in the middle of the room, their belongings piled up around their feet.

Miss Tidy talked to the two people who had been at the door and to the vicar, who had followed them in, an alarming figure with his great bald head and bony face and long black robes. Then she came across to talk to the children. Until now, she explained, she had not been able to tell them where they were going as the Government had said that it must be kept secret, so that the Germans wouldn't know where they were. But now it was quite safe to tell them that they were in the Yorkshire Dales and that this village, where they were going to live for the duration of the war, was called Sidgewick and all these kind people were going to look after them. She asked if they had any questions.

The biggest girl among them asked when they would get to Reception Area. Miss Tidy looked puzzled.

'But this *is* the Reception Area,' she said.

'But you've just said it was Sidgewick, Miss.'

'Ah.'

Polly realised, from the glances exchanged between the adults, that the girl had made a fool of herself. She knew it too from the excessively kind way Miss Tidy said, 'I'm so sorry, I should have explained better. Reception Area is just a general expression for our destination, it is not the name of a real place.'

The girl went red. Polly, who had very nearly asked the

same question herself, felt momentarily light-headed with relief that she hadn't.

Miss Tidy then explained that the two gentlemen with armbands were billeting officers who were in charge of making all the arrangements. The others were very kind hosts and hostesses who would now choose which of the children they would like to come and live with them. She smiled at them, the vicar smiled at them and the billeting officers smiled at them. Then, very slowly, the people standing around the walls moved forward and began to look at them more carefully and to talk to the billeting officers and to Miss Tidy. She heard them say things like 'We'd like a good strong lad to help on the farm, like', and 'Two nicely brought up little girls, please', and 'A *very* quiet one, if you can, because of Grandfather.'

Gradually the group of children dwindled. As each child was picked it was led away, out through the great big doors and into the night for it was dark now. She wondered what would happen if nobody wanted you. It reminded her of being picked for sides in games at school, except that she was usually picked early because she was quick and didn't mind a fight. Maybe it was Jimmy being so little that put them off. Also, with the hand that wasn't gripping hers he was clutching himself between the legs as if he wanted to go to the lavatory. He didn't. It was just a habit he'd got into over the past year, his way of comforting himself when he was tired or frightened. But strangers wouldn't know that. They probably thought he was going to wet the floor. Whatever the reason, she got used to the way their eyes looked first at her and then dropped to Jimmy and took on a vague look, floating away into the distance as if the pair of them had suddenly turned invisible.

The door slammed yet again, only this time it was somebody coming in, a little woman whose head looked too big for her body because she had thick plaits of hair wound round it. 'But you've been spared, Mrs Braithwaite,' she heard one of the billeting officers say. 'You were considered too remote from the village to take in evacuees. There's the problem of getting them to school and so on.'

'I know, but I thought I'd call in, just in case you were short of homes for any of them.'

'Well, yes, perhaps that *is* fortunate. I think we might be having one little problem – or rather two.'

He dropped his voice, so that she could only hear with great difficulty. 'The little pair over there.'

Mrs Braithwaite came straight over to them. She didn't smile or say anything soft. She just looked at Polly and said, 'I'm Mrs Braithwaite and I live up the dale, a bit out of the village. Do you want to come and live with us?'

It was a direct question, woman to woman.

'Yes,' Polly said.

'Right,' she said. 'Come along then. The trap's just outside.'

She picked up Jimmy's case, took his hand in hers and made for the door, Polly following them.

Outside it seemed at first pitch black. Polly stood for a moment, blinking, trying to adjust to the darkness after the light in the hall. Suddenly Jimmy wrenched his hand free of Mrs Braithwaite's and shrieked, 'I won't go in a trap. Polly, don't get into the trap.'

'It's not that sort of trap, love,' Mrs Braithwaite said calmly. 'It's just a little cart. Look, you can just see the pony. He's called Napoleon. Come and say hello to him.'

It was light enough for them to be able to see the outline of the pony and cart. Jimmy allowed himself to be led round it and then be lifted up into the trap. Polly climbed up beside him and they sat together on a bench, alongside their cases.

'There's a rug back there,' Mrs Braithwaite called to them from her perch at the front. 'Wrap yourselves up in it if you're cold.'

Then she talked to the pony with funny little clucking sounds and they began to move forward.

'Weren't you frightened when she said she'd got a trap outside?' Jimmy whispered, squeezing up close to his sister.

'No. I thought she said a tram.'

It seemed much lighter now. The road, the village green and the tree were all clearly visible by the light of the stars. Polly, who had never seen a road lit by anything except street lights before, found it very unnatural, this strange, silvery light. Jimmy shivered. 'It's ever so creepy,' he whispered.

It was very quiet, too, as they moved through the sleeping

village. There was no roar of distant traffic, no rattle of trams, not even the occasional shout or the bark of a dog. The silence was as eerie as the silvery light. She could see why Jimmy was scared. She wrapped the rug round him and held him firmly against her. She was scared, too, in a way, but it was with a kind of excitement, a nice kind of fear, like going to see something frightening at the pictures.

They were very soon through the village and out the other end, where they turned off up a steep hill. She could see the lane stretching before them, a pale line almost white between green banks topped with grey walls. Beyond the walls were fields and hills. They were going into the great wild countryside that she had watched from the train windows. The wind was fresh on her face. She threw back her head and suddenly noticed the moon. It was a huge, yellow thing and she stared at it in amazement, sure it hadn't been there before. She was going to show it to Jimmy but realised that he was asleep. She tucked the blanket more tightly round him instead. He'd done very well, she thought proudly. He hadn't cried once all day. Some of the other little ones had, especially the boys.

The lane was sometimes grassy, sometimes stony. She could tell by the sound of the pony's feet and the little noises the cart made. They had reached the brow of a hill. She felt as if she was on top of the world. She was wide awake now, entranced with it all. She wanted the ride to go on for ever. But Mrs Braithwaite called out, 'Nearly home,' and turned off down a track which led to a clump of trees.

As they drew nearer, she saw by the light of the moon that there was a house among them. Protected, it looked, and safe. Perhaps it was her underlying exhaustion, or confusion after travelling all day, or just a trick of the light, but it seemed to Polly that the cart was standing quite still and it was the house and the little wood that were moving slowly but steadily towards them. Closer and closer they came until she could see the front of the house clearly, with its little windows and stone porch.

'Wake up, our Jimmy,' she said. 'We've got there.'

As she spoke, Mrs Braithwaite jumped down, opened the farm gate and led the pony and trap into the yard. At the same time a great barking broke out and the door opened. Silhouetted in the light stood a man. He was so tall that he had to stoop in the porch and seemed to fill the doorway, so it looked as if he was carrying the house on his back like a great shell.

'I've got a surprise for you,' Mrs Braithwaite called to him.

'Aye, I was wondering. You're that late.'

His voice was deep and he spoke slowly. He didn't hurry when he walked either. He came slowly across the yard and stood by the trap, almost ceremoniously, to help them down. Polly felt suddenly very grand and grown-up as she took his hand and thanked him.

'What's your name then?' he asked.

'Polly.'

'And t'lad?'

'Jimmy. He's my brother.'

'Well, it's a shame to wake him,' he said, and picked Jimmy up, still wrapped in the rug. 'By, but there's not much of him, is there?'

'I'd carry him straight upstairs, Tom,' Mrs Braithwaite said. 'We'll bring the cases, won't we, Polly?'

So she followed as Mr Braithwaite carried Jimmy across the yard, into the house and up the stairs. Mrs Braithwaite showed her the bedroom and she undressed her brother, found his pyjamas and put him to bed, still sleeping.

'What about you, love? Are you hungry?'

She shook her head, suddenly too tired to speak. She seemed to have been travelling for weeks. Surely it couldn't have been only last night that she was in bed at her mother's house? She felt again the rhythm of the train, the shaking of the pony trap, and began to sway on her feet. She was hardly aware of Mrs Braithwaite catching hold of her and helping her into bed. She felt her nightie being slipped gently over her head but her eyes were already closed and she was asleep before Mrs Braithwaite had drawn the curtains and tiptoed out of the bedroom. So she did not see her turn and stand for a moment in the doorway shaking her head as she looked at the two children, nor hear her say savagely as she crossed the landing, 'That bloody Hitler. I could wring his neck.'

But Mr Braithwaite heard her and was shocked. He had been married to her for twenty-five years and had never heard her swear before.

She awoke to the sound of her father coughing. She lay for a moment, listening, then she remembered where she was. The sound must be coming from the farmyard. There were footsteps, too, and voices and always this coughing noise, sometimes little dry coughs, sometimes wet and rumbly. She got out of bed and crossed over to the window. Sheep! Hundreds of them, all over the place, being herded across the yard or lying about in the fields, and all the time baaing and rumbling and bleating.

It was a funny little window. The walls of the room were so astonishingly thick that she could sit right on the sill as if it was a real seat. She fitted herself comfortably into the space, drawing her knees up against her chest, tucking her nightie under her feet, pressing her spine against the wall. It was rough and little flakes of whitewash came away on her nightdress. She thought of the brick walls at home and the panes of glass, all rectangular and matching. Both windows of this bedroom were funny shapes and quite different from each other. One slid sideways. The door was a funny shape, too. It was cut away at one side to fit into the slope of the ceiling. She wondered if all the houses in the country were as odd as this, and why nobody had ever told her. They reminded her of houses in picture books at school, especially fairy tales like Hansel and Gretel. She had never imagined that funny-shaped houses existed in real life.

Jimmy stirred. She went and sat on his bed so that he would see her when he woke and not be frightened.

'It's only them old sheep,' she reassured him when he opened his eyes.

'I want to go home.'

'Well, you can't. Because of the bombs.'

'Polly –'

'Yes?'

'If everyone in the town's going to be bombed, what about our mam?'

She shrugged. She had worked that one out already. She

knew that all the children on the train had had the same thought, though they were too scared to put it into words. Besides, she wasn't sure what she felt about it. Sometimes she was terrified that her mother would be killed. Sometimes she thought that it would serve her right.

'Perhaps there are bombs that just kill children?' Jimmy said. 'Then it would be all right to leave the mothers behind?'

'We'll ask Mr and Mrs Braithwaite,' Polly said. 'They'll tell us.'

The Braithwaites were very definite about it.

'The Government's got to be precautious,' Mr Braithwaite said. 'That's all there is to it. And, then again, it's not so healthy in the towns. The air's better for children in the country.'

'There's no air at all in the towns,' Mrs Braithwaite agreed. 'And of course the food's much better in the country, too.'

The food was certainly different. The bacon they were eating now, which Mrs Braithwaite had cut in thick slices off a great grey slab which she unhooked from the kitchen ceiling, didn't taste like ordinary bacon at all, and the home-made bread didn't taste like proper bread either. Jimmy remarked politely on the funny taste the butter had, too, but Mrs Braithwaite said that that was because it was proper butter not that shop-stuff. Mrs Braithwaite didn't seem to approve of shops. Polly, who had thought that shops were the only place where you could get food, was baffled by the contempt with which she spoke of them. They didn't have a milkman either. When she asked where the milk bottles were and Mr Braithwaite said they got their milk straight from the cows, she thought he was teasing, because although he was big and slow and quiet, there was something about the way he spoke that sometimes made her not quite sure if he was serious or not.

'If Jimmy wants milk for that second cup of tea,' he said as they finished the huge breakfast, 'he'll just have to go and beg some off Daisy. She's very obliging.'

'That's enough,' Mrs Braithwaite said. 'You'll have them muddled and it's strange enough for them as it is. You come with me, Polly, and I'll show you where you can get milk any time from my larder, or next-door in the dairy.'

She realised at once that the larder was really Mrs Braithwaite's own private shop. It was stacked with bins of flour, great bags of sugar, huge round cheeses, bowls full of eggs, pats of butter. On a wide marble slab there was the promised milk, in jugs covered with little muslin circles, edged with lace and weighted down with tiny green beads which tinkled against the jugs when the breeze blew in through the netted window at the back of the larder.

'Father's going down to the village and he'll take your card to the post so your family'll know you're safe. And he'll call in at school and find out what the arrangements are there.'

'They're best to have a few days to settle in here, I reckon. Get some colour in their cheeks. It's a grand day for getting out.'

'Will you come with us?' Jimmy asked Mrs Braithwaite.

She shook her head. 'Nay, lad, I've work to do. Besides, I must wash all your clothes so you can have a clean start.'

'They could take a picnic down by the stream,' Mr Braithwaite said. 'It's nobbut in the next field.'

'Oh, it's safe to go anywhere here,' Mrs Braithwaite assured them. 'Not like them towns with traffic and all.'

'But towns *feel* safer, don't they, Polly?' Jimmy said later, as they closed the farm gate behind them and stood looking in awe at the vast green landscape all around. The hills towered in the distance, while near at hand sheep moved unpredictably about and made unexpected noises. Some of them had thick curly horns and mad eyes.

Keeping as far away from the sheep as possible, they made their way down to the stream. It was wide and shallow in the field below the farm, but soon divided into two. They stood, uncertain, at the fork. Finally they chose the branch which was further away from most of the sheep and followed it until it disappeared under the wall at the far side of the field. Then they retraced their footsteps, carefully following every bend in its course until they were back where they started. Emboldened by their success in not getting lost, they decided to follow the other branch which soon divided into two further tiny streams, leaving an island in the middle.

'I don't expect sheep can swim,' Jimmy remarked. 'We could live on this island all day.'

She knew what he meant. The island seemed somehow safe in the middle of this vast strange land. They jumped the narrow stream and took possession. It was just big enough for the two of them. She set about making them at home on it, putting the can of milk into the water to keep it fresh as Mrs Braithwaite had instructed, covering the picnic bag with the towel they had been given in case they paddled. Then they lay on their stomachs and gazed down into the water which flowed protectively around them.

'It's like glass,' Jimmy said. 'I can see my face in it.'

The water was so clear that they could make out the outline of everything in it very sharply. Each pebble seemed to shine separately. Some were very smooth and round, brown or grey or speckled. Some were almost blue. Some were mossy, covered all over with bright green slime. Others had long strands floating from them like green hair. They lay looking down into the stream, mesmerised by the flow of the water and the gentle rippling sound it made. They could see little animals crawling about among the stones and funny insects hopping on the surface of the water. Sometimes there were tiny fish.

'We could bring a jam jar and catch some one day,' Jimmy said. 'And Mrs Braithwaite could cook them for tea.'

'Yes, she'd be glad of them. I don't expect there's a fish shop here.'

'I'm hot. Let's paddle.'

The water, which had looked so inviting, was astonishingly cold. They shrieked at the shock of it, leapt out and then made themselves try again.

'Why is country water so cold?' Jimmy asked, his teeth chattering. 'It's like ice. And it's summer.'

Polly shook her head. It was beyond reason, like so many things up here. The water at home was always warm in the summer, even out of the cold tap.

They warmed themselves up by jumping from the island to the far bank of the stream, making marks to show how far they could leap, surprised that each time they managed a few extra inches.

After they had eaten their picnic, they lay back on the short grass, eyes shut, lulled by the ceaseless rippling of the water.

Even the gentle bleating of the distant sheep sounded friendly. She could feel the sun prickling her face. It would bring out her freckles. Jimmy was asleep, she could tell by the way he was breathing. She sat up and, screwing up her eyes against the glare of the sun, searched the hills beyond the farm for the source of the stream. For that was where it started, Mrs Braithwaite had said. It gushed out of the hillside and made its way, white and foaming, down to the lane where it disappeared underground only to reappear on the other side of the farm, mysteriously tame and shallow. One day she'd climb up there, to where it started, and have a proper look at it.

Jimmy was still asleep. He didn't usually sleep in the middle of the day. Perhaps he was sickening for something. She woke him up to make sure he was all right. He was, so they paddled again and this time the water seemed warmer.

They were surprised when they saw Mrs Braithwaite waving to them to come in for tea. They had lost all idea of time.

'I've been to see about your schooling,' Mr Braithwaite told them at teatime. 'And you can have a week's holiday to settle in if you want, before you start your lessons.'

That night, as she crossed the landing, she heard, as she paused outside their bedroom door, Mrs Braithwaite saying to her husband, 'They look better already, don't they, Father? Another week and they'll be right set up for the winter. By, but they're a peaky little pair and no mistake.'

Polly went quickly back to bed. She had taken to eavesdropping since her mother left. If grown-ups wouldn't tell you anything, it seemed the only way to find out what was going to happen to you.

So for the next few days they walked across the fields, picnicked by the stream, built dams, played on the island. Lower down the stream they found a slate bridge where they sat, the slab hot against the backs of their legs, throwing sticks into the water and watching them come out on the other side. Each day they wandered further from the farm, not worrying any more about the sheep or even the curious cows which sometimes followed them.

'Let's climb right up to where the stream starts on the mountain,' she said on their last free morning.

'I can't. I'm going to help Mr Braithwaite clean the midden today.'

'Oh, shall I help, too?'

'No,' Mrs Braithwaite said. 'It's man's work. You can help me with the ironing tonight. That's girl's work.'

Mrs Braithwaite had very strict ideas about boys' and girls' work. Until now Polly had always assumed that she should do the heavier and more difficult jobs because she was older, and leave easy things like washing-up to Jimmy. But Mrs Braithwaite's way of dividing up the work was quite different. It wasn't age but sex that counted, and the rules were unalterable.

So Polly climbed the steep hillside alone, determined to trace the stream to its source. As she climbed, toiling from rock to rock, resting sometimes on little ledges of grass, she realised that the stream wasn't the simple gushing thing it had seemed from a distance. In fact it sometimes flowed quite gently and even lay in quiet pools for a time, before dropping suddenly over a ledge, turning instantly white and frothy. Even at the top it was not as it had seemed from the valley. There were in fact three sources, two dribbling out of an unexpectedly marshy piece of ground and the third emerging from under a great rock, all joining into a wide, shallow stream which moved slowly towards a mossy ridge over which it slipped in a leisurely kind of way into the dark pool below.

Mrs Braithwaite had warned her that it was a steep climb. By the time she reached the top she was panting, the blood pounding in her face and her heart feeling as if it would burst. She threw herself down on the grass, gasping. Then she lay watching the water as it folded gently over the first mossy ridge. Over and over it seemed to roll, as if it was the same water going round and round. The more she watched the water the more she wondered at it, as it made its way, now calm, now turbulent, now a rushing stream, now a still pool, down to the lane at the bottom where it disappeared underground, to re-emerge, wide and shallow in their own field below the farm. How could there be so little water one minute and then suddenly so much? Was it really the same water? Was it possible that the calm water in fact stayed all the time in the pool, gently circulating, and it was another lot of water doing all that noisy hurrying?

Everything in the country, she thought, as she got up to look for a stick to throw in, was much more complicated than in the town. Nothing behaved naturally. She couldn't find a stick for there were very few trees up here, just thin grass and rocks. But above the crag where one of the streams emerged was an old bush, bent by the wind. She pulled at a dead branch and it came away, a great forked thing with rushes and some dead blossom tangled round it. She dragged it back to the stream and managed to hurl it in.

It hesitated on the brink and then moved clumsily over the mossy ledge to reappear in the pool below, where it drifted slowly round and round, turning on itself. But all the time it was being drawn gradually towards the outer edge of the pool where the waterfall suddenly snatched at it and dragged it down into the turbulent water below. She thought it must have sunk, but suddenly saw it again much further downstream and from there she watched its descent, now rapid, now very slow, until it reached the lane where the stream went underground. There it lodged itself at the entrance to the tunnel, where there must be some kind of grating. It showed up well now for the water had brightened the blossom on it. On her way back, she thought, she would free it so that it could make its way into the field below the farm.

Meanwhile she lay on her stomach on the warm grass and watched the top of the waterfall, noticing how the water splashed up into the air every few seconds like a fountain, catching the sunlight, so that it seemed as if the light and the water were playing some endless game, leaping towards each other, falling back, but always rhythmically like a dance. It was like a ball game that children might play in the streets at home, throwing and catching, throwing and catching. Or a skipping game when the rope whirled round and round and you darted in and under and out, in and under and out. Never let the ball drop, never trip over the rope.

Drops of water were falling into the grass where she lay. She was crying and she had not realised until then. She never allowed herself to cry. It might set Jimmy off if she did. Besides, there was nothing to cry about, she told herself, giving way to helpless sobbing. Everything was going to be all right. It was just thinking about the games they used to play, that was all. And lying in the sun here was like sitting in the back garden at home, the same sun on her face, except that it couldn't be the same sun. Anyway she would never sit there again. Other people lived there now. It wasn't her home any more. Maybe Hitler would drop a bomb on it.

Determined not to cry any more, she got up, brushed her skirt down and set off for the farm. She had thought it would be easier going down than climbing up, but in fact it was much more difficult and took longer. Slowly she made her way down to where, far below, pushed and pulled by this current and that, and finally stranded at the entrance to the tunnel, lay her forked stick. It looked, with its skirt of grass and flowers which the water had refreshed and made more colourful, like a doll or even a human child.

Chapter 4

The war didn't work out at all as the grown-ups had planned. No bombs fell nor was there any gas attack. But the war in the village between the local children and the evacuees was real enough. At school they sat apart from each other and there were occasional skirmishes in the playground. But it was in the evening, after school, that the real fighting began: in the village street, behind barns, in nearby fields. Polly only heard tales of it, for by that time of day she and Jimmy were away up the dale.

In fact the only fight she got involved in was against her own side, a gang of other evacuees. She came out at dinner time to find they had Jimmy pinned up against the lavatory wall while the biggest of them, Tom Bragg, was amusing himself by swinging his fist like a pendulum backwards and forwards in front of Jimmy's face, getting nearer to his nose each time.

Jimmy was watching the fist, mesmerised, as it swung forwards and backwards, his eyes flicking from side to side, his mouth open in silent horror. One glance at that terrified little face did it for Polly.

'You leave him alone, you great lout,' she bawled at Tom Bragg, crashing through the circle of spectators. Taken aback, they turned to stare at her. Simultaneously Miss Tidy appeared at the door, her cup of tea in her hand and said, in the exasperated voice of one who has come to seek fresh air and finds trouble instead, 'And *now* what's going on?'

They muttered and shuffled away, but it was the expression on Polly's face that had scared them, not Miss Tidy, for they didn't return to torment Jimmy even when the teacher had gone back indoors to drink her tea in peace.

'Jimmy,' Polly said on the way home, 'you must fight back, you know. Honest, you've just got to. I won't always be there.'

He looked at her in alarm.

'It's all right,' she reassured him. 'I don't mean I'll be dead, or gone away for ever. I just mean that I might be, well, somewhere else.'

'But they're bigger than me.'

'Yes.'

'And there's more of them.'

She couldn't deny it. Yet that wasn't the real way of it. After all, Tom Bragg was bigger than she was, too, and he had had his mates handy. It was something about the way Jimmy looked which made them want to bully him.

She sighed. 'Well, just try to keep out of their way,' she said.

They were walking home today for the first time, partly because the trap was being mended and partly because they must learn to be independent. It was almost twilight; the damp November air was cold against their faces. Mrs Braithwaite had knitted them scarves and showed them how to cross them over their chests to keep the cold out of their lungs.

'Anyway,' Polly said, 'some of them are going back home.'

Jimmy stopped. He peered into her face in the semi-darkness.

'You mean *home* – to their proper homes?'

'Yes. They say it's silly to stop here when there's no bombs falling at home.'

'I'm *glad* they're going. I like the village kids better,' he said.

'Oh, Jimmy, you shouldn't say that!' she exclaimed.

'Well, I do,' he insisted. 'They're not so rough.'

She agreed with him really; it was just that it was treachery to say it.

'Do you think,' Jimmy asked suddenly, 'that *we* might go home?'

'Oh, no.'

It was a cry of anguish. She stared around her, horrified by the thought. She couldn't bear to leave here now.

'I wouldn't mind,' Jimmy said.

'Anyway,' she said, 'she doesn't want us back. She said in her last letter that with Uncle Fred away at the war and her out at the munitions all day, she couldn't look after us and since we were happy here we'd best stay put.'

'Yes.'

'And we are happy, aren't we?'

'Yes, Polly.'

The weather was unexpectedly hot the following weekend. A bit of an Indian Summer, Mrs Braithwaite called it, and sent Polly out for a walk, letting her off the ironing which, she said, would keep better than the sun in late November.

So she climbed the hill opposite the farm and lay there by the stream, although she'd been warned not to lie on the damp ground. True, the grass was damp, but it was a lovely warm kind of moistness. The turf was short and springy yet firm, for she could feel the rock just below the surface, pressing up against her spine, bone to bone, as if there was nothing between the earth's body and her own. Over to one side lay the green slopes of Middle End and beyond that towered the grey mass of Old Bear. There were other hills, too, and distant mountains. She knew them all by name just as she had known the streets at home. In the few months she had lived here she had climbed all the nearby hills, and grown familiar with the rest. She knew where all their cairns were and their little copses, where ferns grew unexpectedly out of crevices in the rocks and where the streams would suddenly leap out from the hillsides. She knew where there were patches of scree, where there were rich green slopes because the soil was deeper, and she knew the sort of shadows the clouds would cast on them. She knew their individual characters, how in shadow some of them suddenly turned quite cold and remote while others kept their friendliness, the shadows rippling swiftly across them.

She lay back, eyes closed, filled with a contented feeling. What exactly was it that she felt here? She felt at home somehow. She felt safe. Suddenly she recognised it. It was the kind of feeling she used to have at home, sitting on the back doorstep in their old garden, or at the kitchen table. A relaxed sort of feeling because you were where you belonged. But it hadn't been safe, had it? It had been taken away, just like that, without notice. It had only been rented, like her mother. She crushed that thought down and went on thinking of the house and garden. But this was safer, she reasoned, because nobody could take it away. These hills had been here for ever, all of it had, and it belonged to everybody and always had. And since it belonged to everyone, it belonged to her and nobody could take that from her. She'd always belong here. Soon she would be walking back through her own countryside down to the farm.

It was suddenly cold. She shivered. Winter was coming.

'There's a letter for you and Jimmy from your mum,' Mrs Braithwaite said when she got back. 'She enclosed one for me, too. Jimmy's upstairs reading yours. You go along up and help him. I'll see to the tea. You don't need to help today.'

It was only when Polly had read the letter that she realised why Jimmy was looking guilty.

'What did you say to her?' she demanded, remembering the letter she had helped him with, spelling out words for him, addressing the envelope for him, but stupidly omitting to check the contents. 'What did you say to her?' she repeated, as angry with herself now as she was with him.

'I told her about Tom Bragg,' he muttered.

'And?'

He hesitated, frightened. 'And I told her Mr Braithwaite belted me.'

'But you deserved it,' she said furiously. 'You know you did, chasing the hens like that.'

'I'd seen Mrs Braithwaite chasing one that morning.'

'But she had to! You knew that. She has to catch them and put them under a bucket if they go broody. It's what farmers' wives do. *You* just chased them for fun. It was cruel.'

'He shouldn't have hit me all the same,' Jimmy said sullenly.

'Yes, he should. *And* he said he was sorry, *and* you said it was all right. *And* Mrs Braithwaite explained about how he hates animals upset and how his nerves are on edge because of the war. You understood all that and now you've sneaked off and told Mam so that she'll think you're unhappy and take us away.'

'I didn't ask her to take us away. Honest I didn't.'

'Well, she says that if you're unhappy you can go home. And if you do, I shan't go with you, so there.'

'Oh, Polly, I couldn't go without you. You couldn't make me do that.'

She stared at him. She knew it was true. She wouldn't be able to let him go alone. Oh, it was so unfair!

'Perhaps she won't come and we'll just go on as we are,' Jimmy suggested timidly.

But she did come. She came for what seemed to Polly a very long weekend, though in fact she arrived on Saturday afternoon and left on Sunday morning. She and Jimmy seemed pleased enough to see each other, but it wasn't ecstatic like last time.

Polly watcher her mother carefully, source of danger that she was. She didn't fit in here. She looked all wrong with her make-up and blue costume and high-heeled white shoes. Especially next to Mrs Braithwaite at teatime. Mrs Braithwaite wore her best tweed skirt and home-knitted jumper. She was going to teach Polly to knit this winter. A great lump came into her throat at the thought that she might not be here to learn. The fruit cake stuck and she choked, tears welling up. Mr Braithwaite rubbed her back, and Mrs Braithwaite poured her more tea. As Polly swallowed the hot, sweet comforting liquid she vowed that, whatever happened, she would still be here come winter, learning to knit. Yet she knew that all the vows in the world wouldn't let her stay here if the grown-ups decreed otherwise.

After tea they were sent into the parlour to play while the adults talked in the kitchen. She told Jimmy she was going to get a jigsaw from the bedroom, but went to listen at the kitchen door instead. She couldn't quite make out what they were saying. It was infuriating. She could hear their voices quite clearly, she could distinguish voice from voice and make out syllables but not sentences. She got the impression that the Braithwaites were trying to persuade her mother to let them stay and that her mother wasn't needing much persuasion. Then, quite clearly, she heard her mother say, 'They really do love it here,' and her heart lurched for joy. It was going to be all right, she was sure of it.

But she went on listening just the same for she enjoyed eavesdropping. It had started as a need for information, but now it was exciting. It gave her a wicked feeling, a sort of power over the people who did not know she was listening to them. Like a spy. Once when she had hidden, during a game of sardines, in a cupboard at school she had accidentally overheard a conversation between Miss Tidy and the school caretaker. It was a very boring conversation about fuel for the school boiler, but all the same it was exciting hearing their voices like a play on the wireless only these actors didn't know they had an audience.

She was so absorbed that she didn't notice Jimmy come creeping up behind her.

'What are they saying?' he whispered.

'I dunno,' she said casually. 'I was just going past and I dropped my hanky. I expect they're talking about the war or something. Anyway, come on back to the parlour. It's rude to listen to other people's conversations.'

The next morning, after breakfast, their mother asked them if they were happy here. They both said they were and she said, yes, she could see that, and they must be very good and do everything Mrs Braithwaite told them. A few minutes later Mr Braithwaite brought the trap round to the door to take her down to the village to catch the bus. It was so cold that her mother had to borrow Mrs Braithwaite's coat for the drive and even after that they had to wrap a blanket round her, too. It was her own fault, of course, Polly, thought, for wearing such silly townified clothes.

After they had gone, Mrs Braithwaite said, 'Come on, Polly, I've got the wool and needles upstairs. Sunday's a good day to start learning to knit.'

Polly liked the Braithwaites' bedroom which was next to hers and Jimmy's. It had the same sort of deep little windows and a funny door that fitted into the ceiling, but the floor was much more uneven than theirs. The dark, shiny planks of wood went up and down like the furrows in the bumpy field which Mr Braithwaite had just ploughed because the Government said he had to, even though it was better suited to grazing sheep. Mr Braithwaite grumbled a lot about the Government.

In the middle of the bedroom was a very big four poster bed with brass knobs. Polly stopped as she always did to admire the patchwork quilt that covered it.

'Could I learn to make one like that?' she asked.

'The war'd likely be over before you'd finished it,' Mrs Braithwaite said, smiling. 'It took me three years to make that, ready for my wedding.'

'We had a story in school yesterday about a lady called Penelope. She didn't want to marry really, so she said she'd get married only when she'd finished her tapestry. Then at night she unpicked it so she never got it finished and fooled the men she didn't want to marry. If you hadn't wanted to marry Mr Braithwaite you could have unpicked a little bit of patchwork every night.'

Mrs Braithwaite laughed. 'He's not daft,' she said. 'He'd have noticed.'

'Yes,' Polly agreed, wandering over to the marble washstand, where Mrs Braithwaite had put the knitting needles and wool. 'I think Penelope's men must have been very stupid not to notice. I mean it's bound to show where you've unpicked stitches, isn't it?'

Next to the washstand was a small table with a Bible and prayer book and a picture of a little child. She had often wondered who it was. What with the light shining behind the head like a halo and the Bible and everything, Polly had sometimes thought it might be a picture of Jesus when he was still a little lad and hadn't had his hair cut short.

'Who is it?' she asked now, standing in front of the picture.
'My little girl,' Mrs Braithwaite said briefly.

It suddenly seemed very quiet in the room. Somehow, she didn't know why, Polly was quite sure that the little girl was dead. It was partly, of course, that she knew that they only had one grown-up son who was away on a farm of his own in another dale, but mostly it was the way Mrs Braithwaite spoke. She wished she hadn't asked and was just turning to say something about being sorry when she saw that Mrs Braithwaite was staring straight past her, looking directly at the picture. Her face was all twisted as if something had gone wrong with it, every feature separate from the rest, so that it was all a horrible jumble, not like a face at all. Then, suddenly, it all shifted back to normal and Mrs Braithwaite said in rather a high voice, 'Yes, that's our Maisie,' and gave a little laugh.

Polly recognized the dreadful cheerfulness of that laugh and knew it was worse than tears, so that without thinking she reached out and took Mrs Braithwaite's hands and for a moment Mrs Braithwaite held her very close as if some grief bound them together, but not the same grief. It all happened so quickly and none of it was thought out so she didn't really understand what was going on, and after a moment or two they took up the wool and went downstairs where everything was normal.

Often in the weeks that followed Polly thought how lucky it was that her mother had come when she had. If she'd come just a few days later she might have been stuck up there with them all winter, in her little blue costume and high-heeled shoes. For the snow came less than a week after she'd gone. Mr Braithwaite, who always knew what the weather was going to do, had foretold it one night, but Polly had imagined just a thin layer of white, like at home, that made the streets pretty and, if it lasted, meant snowballs for an afternoon before it turned to slush.

She was quite unprepared for this Dales snow. She woke early one morning with the feeling that somethng was wrong with the light. It wasn't yet dawn but there was an odd brightness about the window. She got up, curious, and drew back the curtains. The very early morning light reflected brilliantly off snow which was so thick she could scarcely make out one field from the next, for the stone walls were just long white humps. The distant hills were blue, but where the sun caught their peaks they glowed with an unearthly orange light. She sat staring out, her nightie tucked under her haunches, oblivious of the cold though she could see there was ice on the inside of the windows. There was no sound. She seemed to have caught the world unawares in this deep white slumber. She felt as if she was eavesdropping on its dreams.

When at last she woke Jimmy he didn't share her wonder; he simply went mad with excitement and tore downstairs in his pyjamas to look at the show from ground level.

The Braithwaites' reaction was disappointing. They seemed more worried than anything else: worried about getting supplies, worried about lambing, worried about everything. 'Never mind, we'll help,' Jimmy said, and to Polly's great relief Mrs Braithwaite didn't decree that shovelling snow was man's work but happily let her and Jimmy go out and clear the yard with Mr Braithwaite. They piled up great mountains of snow and swept the yard with brooms and cleared a way up to the lane. Then they went with Mr Braithwaite to look for any sheep that might be huddled under the drifts, prodding and poking with his shepherd's crook.

Day after day they spent like that, dressed in their thickest clothes, with their scarves crossed across their chests and each wearing not only gloves but also matching mittens which went over the top. Mrs Braithwaite had knitted Jimmy a balaclava helmet, and for Polly a pixie hood which fitted tightly over her ears and tied under her chin. There was no question of going to school. The snow was so deep that even the village was cut off, let alone the farms up the dale. Sometimes there would be a thaw for a day or two and great avalanches of snow would come thundering down off the roof, but in no time it would be replaced by a fresh lot. There seemed to be an endless supply of it.

There was nearly a week's thaw in February and they managed to get to school for a few days They were surprised to find that nearly all the evacuees had gone home. Miss Tidy had gone, too, and an elderly lady from the village had taken her place. She was called Miss Capstick and was very tall and had plaits like Mrs Braithwaite's except that her were wound in great coils at each side of her head and were called earphones. She had a very posh voice like somebody on the wireless. A girl called Miss Meg took the little ones like Jimmy, helping them with their reading and telling them stories, while Miss Capstick taught the big ones. There were about ten of them and they sat around the stove and did all sorts of subjects that they hadn't done before, and held discussions. Miss Capstick was very keen on discussions. Polly enjoyed them though the others said they were boring and they'd rather have proper lessions. On their last morning she had a discussion on evolution and it seemed to Polly that Miss Capstick's ideas about men and women were very different from Mrs Braithwaite's.

'God intended men to do the heavy work,' Miss Capstick explained. 'He intended women to do the thinking. That is why he gave women quick minds and perceptions and made men physically strong and muscular. Thus we can easily see that women were intended by God to rule the world which requires mental, not physical, strength.'

'But,' Polly objected – she seemed to be the only one who ever argued with Miss Capstick – 'Why is it then that it's all men who are in the Governments, like Mr Chamberlain and all?'

'And Hitler,' one of the boys put in.

'And the Vicar, and Stalin, they're all men,' another said, emboldened.

Miss Capstick shook her head. 'Unfortunately,' she said, 'God's plans don't always work out. Things go awry. Men abuse their physical strength, using it to dominate instead of applying it to the heavy work. Not all, of course. Some men are quite content to do the labouring tasks for which they were quite obviously designed.'

The vicar also called in at the school. He taught them Scripture and How to Stop the Germans. The Germans were likely to land at any moment by parachutes out of the sky and would be sure to want to know exactly where they were. That was why all the names of villages and all signposts had been removed. The children must be very careful not to render these precautions useless by telling the Germans where they were. It wouldn't be obvious that they were Germans, of course, so if anyone asked them the way, whoever it was, they must give false directions. It was lying, but God would forgive them for they were fighting for His cause. They mustn't expect the Germans to have foreign accents. They would sound just like us, for they would only send over soldiers who could speak perfect English. This was very unfair as not many English people could speak perfect German so there was no way of getting our own back. Unfortunately, it was typical of the enemy to have no sense of fair play, but one must try to be forgiving.

They all listened intently. They always did, for the gaunt figure was impressive and there was something about the way the words came slowly from between his great teeth that made them seem especially important. Only once did Polly argue with him and that was when he was teaching them their catechism and said that God was a jealous god who visited the sins of the fathers upon the children. Polly thought that was very unfair, but the vicar said it happened every day and he knew drunken fathers whose children suffered in consequence.

That wasn't what she meant, she tried to explain. She didn't mean it *didn't* happen, she meant it wasn't fair that God *wanted* it to happen. She couldn't make him understand and he began to flap about like a great crow in his black cassock so she got scared and stopped arguing, afraid that perhaps her sins would be visited on Jimmy. But afterwards Miss Capstick had understood. She said that she herself had always tried to prevent a jealous god inflicting punishments on children because of the sins of their fathers and forefathers. After that Polly thought even more highly of Miss Capstick, not so much because she seemed prepared to defy God and the catechism but because she was prepared to take on the vicar.

That last day Mrs Braithwaite came early to collect them for the sky was leaden and they could see, even before she told them, that there was going to be more snow. She grumbled as she helped them into their layers of clothing that she couldn't remember weather like it, but Polly was secretly rejoicing. She couldn't bear to think of this magic white world melting away for ever.

Suddenly the Billeting Officer was in the cloakroom suggesting that perhaps these two might come and live in the village now that there were plenty of homes to spare. It would save them missing so much school if the weather was bad. Polly stood staring at him, utterly taken aback by this unexpected threat. But Mrs Braithwaite just thanked him and said it was quite all right and they were better left settled where they were. She would see that they did their lessons every day, and promised that Polly would help Jimmy with his reading and writing and sums. Then they collected a pile of books from Miss Meg and drove off in the trap, just as the first of the new snow began to fall in slow, fat flakes. Polly sat gazing into it and heaving great sighs of relief all the way back to the farm.

She knew that it was Jimmy they were most worried about, because he really wasn't very good at lessons. He struggled with his reading and his writing was bad. So all through the snowy weather, when they couldn't get to school, she sat with him for two hours every morning and again in the afternoon, teaching him. It was hard work but she reckoned that if it was the price she had to pay for being allowed to stay up on the farm, it was well worth it.

It was almost the beginning of the Easter holidays when the break came. 'This time it's a real thaw,' Mr Braithwaite told them. 'It'll be slow but sure, you'll see. You'll be able to get into Bingham by Friday, Mother, to get t'lad his new boots.'

Jimmy's feet had grown at least two sizes since their arrival. When his toes came through his slippers Mrs Braithwaite made him new ones, but even she couldn't make shoes. All the same Polly could tell she didn't like the idea of being obliged to go into a shop to buy anything, not even shoes.

'When we were children,' Mrs Braithwaite remarked as she got into the trap on Friday, 'my dad made all our boots. Now, are you sure you'll be all right, Polly? We'll be back before dark.'

Polly loved it, the feeling of being in charge, with them off buying shoes and Mr Braithwaite away up on the fells. She did all the tasks Mrs Braithwaite had written down for her. She even swept the kitchen floor for a second unnecessary time, using the besom and pretending to be Cinderella. Once an aeroplane flew over so low that she thought it would hit the hillside. By the sound of the engine she thought it was a German plane and suddenly worried about Mr Braithwaite.

She had asked him before what he would do if he met a German soldier face to face out there in all that lonely space. But he had just laughed and said he'd knock him over with his crook and then leave Jock to keep him prisoner while he went to fetch the Home Guard. They'd come marching up the lane and take him away to the prisoner of war camp. Then he added that on second thoughts it would take the Home Guard a week to march up so maybe he'd truss the German up with the clothes line and take him to the camp himself. Mr Braithwaite would never be serious, not like the vicar. But then the vicar had been something called a padre in the last war, so naturally knew more about the Germans than Mr Braithwaite who had stayed at home on his farm and never shot anyone.

As the afternoon drew on, she collected the eggs from the henhouse and then went back to give them their final feed and shut them in for the night. The main door was kept closed, of course, but she had to slide the little trapdoor shut. It didn't take long. The hens were all up on their roosts already.

It was as she turned back towards the house that she saw him: a German soldier. He was standing by the pump, his back to her. He couldn't have seen her. Her mind raced. She realised that if she tried to creep quietly behind him, he'd probably turn round and get between her and the farm door. But if she dashed, never minding about the noise, and hurled herself in, she'd get there before he realised, even as he turned round.

It worked. One dash, one glimpse of his startled face as he turned and she had slammed the door behind her, pulling first the big iron bolt at the bottom, then the one at the top. Then for good measure she heaved and tugged at the wooden bar that they didn't normally use but which Mr Braithwaite had once demonstrated to her.

She leant against the door, faint with relief.

'Hello,' a voice said outside. She was surprised she could hear him clearly through all the wood and the bolts.

'You're not very hospitable,' the voice continued.

His English was good. The vicar had been right.
There was a pause, then the voice asked suddenly, 'I say, do you think I'm a German or something?'
'I don't know.'
'Well, I'm not.'
'You would say that, wouldn't you?'
He laughed.
'You're no fool,' he said approvingly.
Polly loved praise. It pleased her now, even from the foe. She decided she would trick him with her cleverness.
'Tell me something to show you're English,' she said. 'Do you know this part of the country?' she added formally.
'Yes, I'm local. Ask me anything you like.'
'Who owns this farm?'
'My uncle.'
She knew for certain that Mr Braithwaite had no nephews. The soldier was a German all right. He must have dropped out of the plane she'd heard flying over. Her heart thumped. Thank goodness she had locked him out. Please God make the others come back home soon. It's nearly dark. They said they'd be back by dark. I'll never eavesdrop ever again, God, if you'll send them home soon.
'Well?'
'It's not true, what you said,' she whispered. 'I know who owns the farm –' her voice was shaking, but she added as boldly as she could '– and it's certainly not your uncle.'
'Are you staying here, then? Evacuee perhaps?'
She didn't reply. Give nothing away, the vicar said. The Germans want to know where everything is – armaments, aerodromes, evacuees, it's all the same to the Germans. They make a note and mark the place on a map with a little flag on a pin.
'I suppose you think the farm belongs to Mr Braithwaite? All right, let's say it does.'
'You've just said it belongs to your uncle,' she said, indignant at this duplicity.
'Actually Mr Braithwaite is the tenant. My uncle owns most of this area and he's the landlord. You may have heard Mr Braithwaite refer to him.'
'No, I haven't.'

'Probably calls him the squire.'

She tried hard to remember. Somewhere in the back of her mind was a memory of Mrs Braithwaite saying something about the squire. What was it? Something about the agent's wife being more stuck up than the squire's lady.

She repeated the remark and was astonished by a great guffaw of laughter from the other side of the door.

'Describe Mr Braithwaite,' she ordered.

'He's a big man, good-looking chap. Blue eyes. Grey hair, plenty of it still. His wife is small and has plaits round her head – and, praise be to Allah, she's coming up the lane in a trap!'

'On her own?'

'No, there's someone with her. A child. Oh, and I think I can see Mr Braithwaite coming down Little Fell. Yes, that's surely Jock with him, I can see the white bit on his tail. Honestly, I do think you might let me in. It's cold out here.'

She could hear the pony and trap. She heard the soldier call a greeting. She heard Mrs Braithwaite return it. Shame-faced, she drew back the bolts. They all came in together and she took herself off to the kitchen to put the kettle on.

He didn't say a word about how she'd shut him out. They all had tea together and the man, who was called Captain Quigley, talked to Mr Braithwaite about the hard winter and lambing and she was grateful to him for not telling on her. He said he'd walked over the top of the fells to get some exercise but was really on his way down to the village to visit his great aunt, Miss Capstick.

'You mean our teacher?' Jimmy asked. 'At least, I have Miss Meg, but Miss Capstick teaches the big ones.'

'That's right. She used to teach years ago, so when the school master volunteered for the army and then your own teacher went back, she offered to help out.'

'She's grand is Miss Capstick,' Mrs Braithwaite remarked. 'We could do with more of her sort.'

'And she's taken in two evacuees,' the man said. 'It's hard work at her age.'

'Oh, that's Jimmy Ackroyd and Bert,' Jimmy said. 'I know them, they're my friends. They've gone back now. They said she was a queer old stick, but all right.'

'Jimmy,' Mrs Braithwaite said sharply. 'Remember your manners. Miss Capstick is the captain's relative.'

Jimmy blushed scarlet, right to the roots of his fair hair. Looking at him, you'd believe the blush went right inside his head. Polly ached for him, but then she saw that they were all looking at him indulgently. Nobody ever got really cross with Jimmy. It didn't much matter what he did or said.

'It's all right, Jimmy,' the captain said, laughing. 'I'm very fond of my great aunt, but if ever there was a typical, eccentric Englishwoman, she's it. And, as your friend said, she's all right. She's a good sort. Now I must be off to visit her, or she'll be bolting the doors against me.'

As he said this he gave Polly a little smile, like a conspirator, and she smiled back, glad that they had a secret. Jimmy's blush was fading gradually.

That night, lying in bed, she heard the captain's name mentioned again by the Braithwaites, who were in the hall, seeing to the lamps. Their voices floated up the stairwell. She decided to go and listen on the landing. After all, her promise to God about not eavesdropping had been extracted under false pretences since she had been in no danger at all. God must have known all along that the captain wasn't a German.

'Of course it was all right for her to let in Captain Quigley, but if ever she's left on her own again, I think we should tell her not to open the door to anyone,' Mrs Braithwaite was saying.

'Yes,' her husband's slower voice agreed. 'I was thinking the same. Of course, you don't want to frighten children, but all the same there's always a chance it could be a bad 'un.'

'I'll have a word with her. Children are naturally trusting.'

The lamps were extinguished. The candles moved towards the foot of the stairs. Polly slipped back to bed. I'm always in the wrong, she thought miserably. If they knew what happened, they'd laugh at me. But if he had been a German, I'd have got into trouble for letting him in.

Mr Braithwaite was right about the thaw. But Polly didn't mind for the spring was astonishing, too. It happened so suddenly, like a declaration that couldn't be ignored. She tried to remember what spring had been like at home but could only remember that the house and streets got warmer until it was summer. But here it was something quite different. Everything burst into life. It was still cold; the tops of the mountains were still white and there were still patches of snow in sunless corners. Yet there could be no possible doubt that spring had come. Jimmy felt it, too. 'I feel all alive,' he shouted suddenly one day, dashing ahead as they set off for the fells.

'Spring's got into t'lad,' Mr Braithwaite said, 'like it's got into everything else.'

They went out with him every day of the Easter holidays, checking for stray sheep and lambs. He trusted them to go and look in certain places where he knew there would be drifts or other hazards. 'It's as good as having three dogs,' he told them.

Sometimes Jimmy forgot himself and called Mr Braithwaite Dad, but she never did. She loved him, all the same. She felt safe when he was there and happy, too, for he was big and strong yet teasing and funny. He bothered with her, even if it was only to have pretend fights. In fact, Mrs Braithwaite said he shouldn't be so rough with her. She was a girl, Mrs Braithwaite pointed out, and growing up fast. But Mr Braithwaite only laughed and said, 'You don't mind, do you, Polly?' and she shook her head and said, 'Course not.'

She was glad that she was allowed to go with him and Jimmy on the hills, afraid that Mrs Braithwaite might call it man's work. Mr Braithwaite was so strong he could lift her and Jimmy over a wall just as if they were as light as the new lambs. In fact when they sang, 'In His arms He gently bears us', at school, she used to picture Mr Braithwaite rather than Jesus doing the bearing.

For all his strength he was so gentle; that was what she liked about him. Once when she was lying by the stream he came upon her unexpectedly and lay beside her, holding her gently in his arms like the Jesus hymn. And when he found her crying in her bedroom because she'd been in trouble at school, he lay with her on the bed until she was better, just holding her. He had big gentle hands which stroked her all over, like she stroked Jock or the baby lambs. Her father had never caressed her so, but then he had been a strange man who never laughed. Just coughed. Probably Mr Braithwaite was more like a proper father, she thought.

Sometimes he would pretend to nurse her like a baby, just for fun. 'You're my baby,' he would say, taking her on his knee and rocking her, giving her a tickle. Or he would say, 'You're my prisoner,' and grip her bottom firmly between his thighs, and she would wriggle but couldn't escape because he was so strong. Besides, she didn't really want to; it was a nice feeling.

Sometimes he was a bit too rough, like Mrs Braithwaite had said. Once he had suddenly slipped both his hands up her skirt and put them on her stomach and she had kicked him quite hard and pushed him off. She was glad when Jimmy came in and they both attacked Mr Braithwaite until he lay on the floor, pretending to moan while they sat on him and kept him prisoner.

Suddenly he said, 'I'm Gulliver,' and jumped up so that they rolled off and Jimmy fell into the log basket and lay there helpless with laughter while Mr Braithwaite pretended he thought he was a log and picked him up to put on the fire.

They had burnt a lot of logs that winter; Mr Braithwaite had cut down the old pine tree which grew near the farm because the snow had weighed down its branches and he was afraid it might topple on to the corner of the roof. He said the logs warmed him twice: once when he sawed them up and again when they were burning. Mrs Braithwaite grumbled that the wood was too fresh to burn and certainly it did spit out sparks and then burn smokily, especially if the wind was wet and in the west which didn't suit the chimney. But Polly liked the warm smell of it, sharp but gummy.

There was a pleasant smell of pine logs and smoke now, as Mr Braithwaite taught them Ride-A-Cock-Horse. He was surprised that they had never played it at home. Polly loved it. He started off gently with a very ladylike ride and got rougher and rougher, rolling her down each leg in turn, and catching her just as she was going to fall, yanking her up on to his knee again.

'Grip my leg tight with your knees,' he told her, 'then you won't slip so fast.' It worked. She slithered gently down, perfectly controlled, enjoying the tingling sensation. Then he tipped her up with a jerk of his ankle and lifted her on to his knee again where she lay, red-faced and laughing, legs straddled across him.

'You shouldn't do that,' Mrs Braithwaite said, coming into the kitchen. 'She's too big for such games now, Tom.'

'Oh, she enjoys a fight, don't you love? And she hasn't had much playing when she was a little lass at home, I reckon. Nor Jimmy neither.'

She could see that Mrs Braithwaite was worried for her. She could see it in the protective look in the kind brown eyes. She could see it even in the way she was standing there, leaning forward towards her. She hastened to reassure her, 'Oh, I don't mind, Mrs Braithwaite,' she said. 'And I'm strong. I belted him one when he put his hands up my skirt.'

She didn't have any more fights or cuddles after that because the Billeting Officer once again suggested that they should go and live in the village. She waited confidently for Mrs Braithwaite to refuse like the last time, but instead she said, yes, perhaps it would be better for them as they wouldn't miss their lessons if the weather was bad, nor waste so much time getting to school and back. Besides, they could always come back and visit the farm, keep in touch, like.

So in a daze they packed their cases and left the farm to go and live with Miss Capstick.

It was dark when Mrs Braithwaite took them down in the trap, but Polly could see that she was crying. Jimmy cried, too. Only Polly was dry-eyed.

Chapter 5

'Well, I think she's a quite dreadful child, hard and stubborn,' Miss Capstick's cousin said. 'And I really don't know why you had to get involved.'

'I'm sorry, Emily. I know it's more work for you.'

'It's not that. I've only the housekeeping to see to, but you're teaching all day. There are plenty of younger women with children of their age who could have taken them in. Much more suitable.'

'There are fewer than you think – evacuees have gone out of fashion. The reality proved a little disappointing after all the rush to make them welcome last August. And even last August this pair weren't particularly easy to find a home for.'

'I'm not surprised. She's a sly little puss, that one.'

'No, you're being too harsh. She's wary, certainly. I suspect life has made her so.'

'Oh really, Vera! How can life have made her anything at her age? You talk as if she was a grown woman.'

'Furthermore,' Miss Capstick went on, ignoring the interruption, 'she interests me. She's clever.'

'Oh, she's sharp enough. And crafty. So unlike her brother. He has such an open little face.'

'He'll soon learn to trade on that look, if he hasn't already.'

'Vera! And you call me harsh!

Polly, hanging over the banisters, could not hear the next bit as the fire was noisily poked and stirred, coal shovelled, curtains drawn. She waited, straining to catch the next words, for the conversation was still going on despite the infuriating background noises. Then, just as they seemed to be settling down again, one of the women turned on the wireless and their high-pitched, refined voices were instantly rendered inaudible.

They had put it on in good time for the nine o'clock news. She might as well go and lie on her bed for a bit, she thought, straightening up and feeling for a moment quite dizzy. She left her bedroom door open so that she could just hear the distant droning of the wireless. When they turned it off she would go back and listen and surely she would find out why she and Jimmy had been moved here. If she knew the truth, she could bear it, but none of them understood that, she thought bitterly. They lied to you, like Uncle Fred had lied about her father's funeral, and now this silly tale about needing to live in the village. They made it all sound fair and sensible, so you couldn't argue with them, but it wasn't the real truth of it. It didn't make sense to move now when the winter was over.

And why did they always do these things to you just when everything seemed all right? A sunny afternoon after school with her and Jimmy happy in the garden, and her mother vanished from home. A lovely spring up in the dale and everything so beautiful and the people kind and loving, so you relaxed. Then they turned on you. It had all been pretence. Really they were traitors, waiting for the moment when they could hurt you most.

It seemed to Polly, lying there in her nightie on the eiderdown, that if she worried about something it didn't happen. It was only when she relaxed and trusted people that they were able to strike. So she must be on her guard always and make sure she was never caught like that again. She would never trust any of them, however nice they pretended to be. And she'd leave school as soon as possible and get a job and be independent. Then she could spit at the lot of them.

They had a bedroom each here, she and Jimmy, for it was a big house. It was old, like the farm, but much grander. It was managed by Miss Capstick's cousin, Miss Emily, but most of the real work seemed to be done by an ancient maid who lived in and was called Jessie, and a woman who came in every morning called Mrs Oliver. They all liked Jimmy, she could see that. Jimmy had cried when they came, but really he minded hardly at all compared with her. He liked having his own bedroom where he played for hours with an electric train set which had once belonged to Captain Quigley. In his room there were lots of picture books and Miss Capstick bought easy books for him to read. It didn't seem to occur to him that if she, Polly, hadn't made him learn to read, against his will, he wouldn't have been able to enjoy Miss Capstick's bounty now. 'It's all right here, Polly,' he said. 'Better just make the best of it. We can go back and visit the Braithwaites when we want. It's not as if they were dead.'

He missed the point. The Braithwaites hadn't died but had chosen to get shot of them, without warning, just as their mother had chosen to leave them without warning. That was the terrible thing, the evil thing, the black and cruel thing. That people could do such things. But Jimmy only saw the things from the outside, as if the reason didn't matter. It was stupid of him really because if you didn't work out the reason it would go on happening to you again and again. On the other hand, she reflected as she lay on the bed, straining to catch the sound of the wireless being turned off in the room below, since Jimmy didn't seem to care about reasons and just went along with things, he didn't get hurt in the same way as she did. Oh, he was so lucky! Why couldn't she have been made like that, so that she could just shrug her shoulders and help herself to the good things? It's not fair, she thought, suddenly beginning to cry. It was the first time she had wept since they'd come here a week ago. She cried bitterly until she exhausted herself and fell asleep, still lying on top of the eiderdown. When she awoke, stiff and cold, the wireless had been switched off long ago and everyone had gone to bed.

Polly was glad that Miss Emily had noticed that she was hard and stubborn. She had been determinedly uncooperative ever since she arrived, and had cultivated a blank look, an expression of dull-eyed insolence, calculated to infuriate grown-ups. She could see that it made Miss Emily really mad. Miss Emily was short and plump and looked more motherly than her cousin, but appearances were misleading. Polly soon decided that Miss Emily was unkind and stupid and that it was her tall, spinsterish cousin who should have looked kind and plump and pretty.

Unlike Miss Emily, Miss Capstick didn't seem to notice Polly's studied indifference, or if she did she didn't show it. At school Polly no longer joined in the discussions. Her response to the questions and ideas that Miss Capstick threw out was a bored stare, or even a shrug of her shoulders to show that she thought the topic of no importance whatsoever. Without her to encourage them, the others soon fell silent. Miss Capstick struggled to keep the debates going but they gradually turned into monologues.

Polly even managed to stifle her instinct to respond to praise. She had heard Miss Capstick call her clever. So what? She wasn't going to be clever just to please a teacher. She'd rather be stupid.

She practised her stupid look, her long unresponsive stare in front of the bedroom mirror, adding refinements like a slow yawn. It was a full-length looking glass fixed to the wall, so she could see not only the sullen face and unkempt red hair – which she had ceased to brush the minute Miss Emily, with heavy-handed tact, had said it was such a pretty colour that it was a pity not to look after it better – but also the rest of her long thin body, not enhanced by the lumpy tweed skirt which was already too short and revealed altogether too much brown woollen stocking. Her stockings always wrinkled round her ankles because her legs were too thin to hold them up properly. Her feet, in their heavy lace-up shoes, seemed too clumsy for the insubstantial limbs above, from which they dangled like the leaden feet of a puppet. 'You're a *sight*,' she told her reflection. 'That's why they all hate you.'

Meanwhile Jimmy became every day more cheerful and obliging. He was popular with the adults and getting better at his lessons, too. They said he read well for his age and his spelling was good. She heard Miss Emily say he might pass his County Minor and go to the Grammar. Nobody mentioned her chances, though she was due to take the exam next year. Not that she cared. The last thing that she wanted was to have her name inscribed on the roll of honour outside the cloakroom and hear the vicar say that the village was proud of her.

She didn't care for the village which had rejected her and Jimmy the night they arrived, and where she had ever since felt an outsider. She preferred to go off walking by herself on the hills, though she never visited the Braithwaites. The beck which ran through the village was a boring brown stretch of water, quite unworthy of the many rushing mountain streams that fed it. Besides, other people were always near it, fishing maybe or just messing about. She liked to have places all to herself.

Her nearest retreat was Thieves' Way, so called from the days when it was the route the cattle thieves took. It was muddy and steep and the packhorse bridge was broken, supposedly by the Devil, and the place was said to be haunted by the ghosts of cattle thieves. She would run up this unfrequented lane, climb a stile and then cross a boggy field, jumping from hummock to hummock to avoid sinking into the peaty soil between them until she reached the place in the stream where a great rowan tree had grown right across the water like a bridge, so she could walk across it horizontally and hide in its branches. She went there when her mother wrote to say Uncle Fred had been killed in the war, and tried to work out if it was good news or bad for her and Jimmy. Mostly she went there in the evenings when she was supposed to be helping or doing her homework.

She made a point of doing everything badly, not only her school work but also any task that was given to her. So naturally when Miss Capstick asked her to fill the ink wells one afternoon at the end of school, she made as much mess as possible, slopping the ink out of the enamel jug into the little porcelain ink wells and then dropping them into the holes in the desks so hard that the ink splashed out on to the surrounding wood. Silently Miss Capstick handed her a wet cloth and Polly dabbed at the wood without conviction.

'Polly,' Miss Capstick said suddenly, 'shall we have a truce?'

'A truce?'

She had taken to repeating words as if she didn't understand them; she knew how it irritated adults.

'Yes, a truce.'

Polly gave her a blank stare then yawned slowly.

'If you don't know the meaning of the word,' Miss Capstick said kindly, 'you may go and look it up in my dictionary, in the desk cupboard.'

Polly turned and looked at Miss Capstick's desk. It was a high one, with a seat attached at the back and a cupboard with two doors that opened to the front. The dictionary was inside. She thought about it. Borrowing dictionaries was a sort of cooperation.

'A truce means stopping fighting for a bit,' she said, without moving.

'Yes. You are fighting me and all of us. I don't want you to think it hurts me in any way. Even if it did, it wouldn't matter. But it isn't doing *you* any good, Polly, and that does matter – a great deal.'

Out of the high window behind Miss Capstick's head she could just make out in the distance the profile of Old Bear. She fixed her eyes upon it to give herself strength to resist these blandishments.

'Oh,' she said. 'Does it?'

'Yes,' Miss Capstick said, matter-of-factly. 'Because if you tie yourself into a hard little knot, you'll find it gets more and more difficult to untie yourself.'

She paused and then, when Polly said nothing but just went on staring out of the window, she took a deep breath and said, 'Polly, do please try to listen, for your own sake. We all need each other. We have an instinct to reach out to each other and yet we resist it sometimes. We reject the hand which would clasp our own if we would let it, and yet we want to feel that touch, don't we?'

It was true. She was surprised Miss Capstick understood the feeling. She felt tears pricking her eyes. Then something about the image of clasped hands took her back suddenly to Mrs Braithwaite's bedroom. They had taken each other's hands, they had clung together, and soon after that Mrs Braithwaite had got shot of them both. It was the day she had started to knit. Half a scarf, she'd knitted. Unravelled it was now, the wool all crinkly and knotted and pushed to the back of her drawer.

She clasped her own hands tightly together, kept her tears back and went on staring out of the window at the distant profile of Old Bear. She wouldn't trust anyone ever again, just hold on to herself.

Miss Capstick watched her, but said nothing. They seemed to stay like that for a long time. She could hear every tick of the clock on the wall above the stove.

Then Miss Capstick said almost to herself, 'It's not true about no man being an island. We are all islands. We are all on our own. Sometimes it seems that we can hurt each other, but never really help each other. We each have to manage to do that for ourselves. But I would help you, if you would let me.'

Then she turned and walked abruptly away.

Polly had never lived in a house with books in it before. She had thought that they were to be found only in schools and libraries but in Miss Capstick's house there were vast quantities of them. They lined whole walls of rooms, on open shelves, in glass-fronted bookcases. In a special little bookcase, hung from the wall in an alcove in the hall, was a set of Dickens. Once, last year, Miss Tidy had read them the first few chapters of *Great Expectations* by Dickens. Polly had been enthralled. She had sat, overwhelmed by the terror and pity of it, hardly able to wait for the next chapter. The only reason she had minded missing school because of the snow was not knowing what had happened to Pip, but when they got back to school Miss Tidy had left and presumably taken the book with her so Polly assumed that she would never know what happened next. And now she was standing in the hall, reading the titles of the row of books until she found the one she wanted. She looked carefully around her, made sure there was nobody in sight, then took the copy out. She moved the other books along so that the gap wouldn't show and then, hiding the book under her jumper, slipped quietly upstairs to her room. She knew she could have gone to Miss Capstick and asked if she could borrow it, and Miss Capstick would have been pleased to let her and there would have been smiling and conversation. It was simpler to steal it.

She hid it under the mattress until the next day when they were all supposed to be going for a picnic. She said she had a pain and couldn't go. They knew she hadn't a pain and she knew they knew, but they didn't argue, just left her behind. From the moment the door banged behind them and she settled down on the bed with the book, she entered a different world. It was a terrifying world, with its convicts and madness and cruelty, yet it seemed more real than this ordinary village and this house where she was temporarily lodged. She felt more at home in it than she did here. It took her two days and nights to finish the book and then she was suddenly lost and lonely, bereft of all those people she had been living with, until she realised that she could stay with them simply by going back and starting the book again.

By chance, at school the following week Miss Capstick began reading *David Copperfield* to them, and then gradually they read, either together or on their own, other books by Dickens that the school had copies of. They were ordinary copies, not the special leather-bound sort with gold edges and beautiful pictures like the one she had under her mattress. For she kept *Great Expectations* hidden and never returned it to the shelves. It was her favourite not only because it was the first she had read and she thought it the best, but also because she had stolen it and it was therefore more exciting than the ones she had read with Miss Capstick's official sanction. It had a special secret quality, like a conversation overheard. But she loved all the rest, too. She much preferred them to the other books on offer at school or those provided for her in her bedroom which were mostly schoolgirl stories especially for girls of her age. She never cared much for the people in them. The children seemed to lead such safe lives with rich parents and comfortable houses and sometimes even servants to look after them. There never seemed to be any great upsets or inexplicable happenings. Nobody went off or died or fought wars, or if they did it was just an adventure, too glamorous to be really frightening. Not like real life at all. Dickens was like real life. The children in his books were scared and they were pushed around, like she had been. She just wished they would fight back a bit more, but she knew it was hard for the grown-ups had all the power then as now. All the same she rejoiced when David Coperfield bit Mr Murdstone and Nicholas Nickleby belted Mr Squeers.

'It's a dreadful waste of talent,' Miss Capstick said to her cousin the evening they heard Polly had failed the exam to the Grammar School.

'She didn't try. She's nobody but herself to blame.'

'Not true,' Miss Capstick said sharply. 'A great many of us are to blame.'

'Anyway, too many of them are educated beyond their station nowadays,' Miss Emily said. Then, intending to be kind, she added, 'Perhaps Jimmy will pass when his turn comes, and that will make up for it. And being a boy it matters so much more, of course, that he should be educated.'

On the landing, Polly grinned to herself. Poor Miss Capstick, what a consolation to be offered! It occurred to her that there must be moments when Miss Emily could, without even trying, be much more irritating then she herself could ever manage to be. However, if she was irritated, Miss Capstick showed no sign of it. A gentle rustling of pages indicated that she was marking books.

'He really settles down and does his homework properly,' Miss Emily went on. 'Polly just doesn't bother. She's always got her head in a book or she's off walking somewhere by herself. She never applies herself to anything useful.'

Still no reply. Just the gentle rustling of papers.

'They'll teach her useful things at Bingham,' Miss Emily remarked. 'Sewing and knitting and cooking, much more use to a girl than all this academic stuff. I expect it'll turn out for the best in the end.'

There was another pause and then Miss Capstick's voice cut in, very controlled. 'I have just been marking the composition I set the class I took for a nature walk up Trackers' Lane. I said they could describe any aspect of it they chose. All except one are quite adequate accounts of fields and hills, or animals or flowers and so on. Polly's is quite different. She writes about the dry stone walls. Listen to this. "Some of them are encrusted with lichen. Look closely and you will see it is made of millions of tiny raised flowers and each one is like a snowflake turned to stone." ' She read more, but Miss Emily, evidently wishing to make clear her lack of interest, stirred the fire up very noisily and shovelled on more coal. When Polly could hear again, Miss Capstick was saying, 'She's different, she sees things her own way. It's direct and fresh – sometimes painfully so. She observes people too with real insight. I think she's a born writer.'

Miss Emily burst out laughing. 'What, with that spelling? And look now messily she presents her work. It's all blots and splodges. I'd hand it back unmarked if I were you. You're far too patient with her. She only does it out of insolence. She's her own worst enemy.'

'That, at least, is true.'

There was a pause and then Miss Emily said, suddenly and unexpectedly, 'I'm sorry, my dear. I know you care about her. I haven't helped. Forgive me.'

There was silence. What were they doing? Kissing and making up? She hoped not.

'I think I'll show that description to Tudor Bean,' Miss Capstick said thoughtfully.

Polly's heart thumped. The one person she liked in the whole village was Tudor Bean. Well, and Mr Potter who came twice a week to work in the garden, she liked him too. He had an earthy smell and used bad language. But Tudor Bean was different from everyone else and, like herself, he didn't really belong in the village either. He was quite an old man, about forty she'd heard them say, and he had left his job on a newspaper just before the war to start a country magazine up here. If he'd understood more about politics, everyone said, he wouldn't have chosen to do such a thing in 1938, but evidently the war took him by surprise. He hadn't expected there to be paper rationing, ink shortages, dearer postage, no staff and all sorts of other problems. He and his wife ran the office themselves, but really it was just part of their house. It was a rambling old place next to Miss Capstick's, which was how Polly got to know them as twice a week she had to go and collect the scraps for the hens from Mrs Bean and in return take back half a dozen eggs.

Mrs Bean always looked worried and people in the village said she was artistic. So for a while Polly thought she had something wrong with her legs, especially as she always wore long smocks. When she wasn't helping with the magazine, typing letters or designing its cover or illustrating articles, she painted pictures in the attic and let Polly and Jimmy paint, too. She showed them how to dye cloth and make lino cuts, never minding how much mess they made.

Every month the magazines were sent out by post and Mrs Bean let her and Jimmy help by sticking the stamps on hundreds of envelopes and then pushing them in a wheelbarrow down to the post office which was also the village shop. It was kept by Mrs Patmore, a very solid kind of lady who never moved out from behind the counter. On the back of her right hand Mrs Patmore had a big mole which was so round that it looked as if it might roll off. It wobbled like a jelly every time she thumped the rubber stamp down on an envelope to frank it, grumbling as she did so that a village post office wasn't equipped to deal with big business like this. Mrs Bean would look anxiously at her, say 'Oh dear', and hand her another bundle of envelopes to thump. Afterwards she would buy them sweets out of her own ration.

Mrs Bean was very tall and had long hair with streaks of paint in it, but Mr Bean was a little man, hunched up as if he was quite old. He had a funny sort of face that did unexpected things, as if it was made of rubber. He said unexpected things, too, and he teased a lot, yet he could look suddenly very sad. He was like a clown. People said he had taken a great risk and would lose all his money and that anyway he hadn't any. Miss Emily said that that was why poor Mrs Bean always looked so worried, but Polly didn't believe it. It was true she did stride around scowling when she did her shopping in the village but that was only because she didn't like shopping. She looked happy enough when they painted and did their lino cuts and would survey the mess they always made with a vague, contented sort of smile. It was quite obvious to Polly that they were both glad not to be working in the town any more, and that they loved their little magazine. They had no children and it sometimes seemed to her that they cared for it like a baby, planning its future and watching it grow.

One of the funny things about Mr Bean was that he pretended to be lots of different people. She loved to look at his post and take it into the sitting room which he had made into his office, though soon he spread into the dining room and gradually took over the rest of the house as well. The people who read his magazine used to think it came out of a proper office so they addressed letters to The Editor, and he of course was the editor so he opened them. But they also addressed letters to the Advertising Manager, the Features Editor, the Chief Reporter, the Head of Photography and all sorts of other people, and he opened them all because he was all those people. 'I'm Pooh-Bah,' he said to her and she didn't know what he meant, but thought that the name suited him.

She could hardly believe it when he said he was going to print the composition Miss Capstick showed him about the walk up Trackers' Lane. He told her it was as good as some of the articles proper writers sent him, and that her reward should be a visit to the printers. The magazine was printed at the offices of the *Bingham Advertiser*, a rambling building in a side street, in which they went along narrow corridors and up steep steps and watched words being turned into printed pages. She never forgot that day: the noise of the place, even the smell of it, the plates of type and the way the printers, mostly old men in thick leather aprons, could set the type all back to front. They could do it more quickly than she could have done it even the right way round. Down in the basement she saw the great press where the newspaper was printed and they showed her the paper, which they called newsprint, in great rolls going round and coming out with printed words wet upon them. That was the most exciting bit of all.

She had imagined that it would be wonderful to see her own words, written in private in her exercise book, all beautifully set out in black type on shiny white paper, and to know that strangers would read and enjoy them. But when the moment came it was not like that at all. After the magazines were posted, she took a spare copy and went to read her article quietly by herself and felt sick with disappointment that it was so bad. All she wanted to do was to write it again and make it much better, but it was too late now that it was printed.

Despite what they all said, Mr Bean didn't go bankrupt. More and more people asked to be sent his magazine and more shops agreed to sell it. Miss Capstick always went to the village shop and bought two copies, one for herself and one to send to Captain Quigley to keep him in touch, she said, now that he was serving abroad.

Polly spent more time helping in the office. Unlike Jimmy, who was now at the Grammar, she didn't have much homework so was free to go round in the evenings as well as the holidays and weekends. The work grew so much that Mr Bean had to get a proper secretary, who grumbled about the old typewriter and had to be bought a new one. Polly begged to be allowed to address some of the envelopes on the old machine and was so quick that they soon let her see to all the envelopes every month, in return for which Mrs Bean taught her to type properly out of a book which she herself had learned from years ago.

She used to take a short cut from the back of Miss Capstick's house, across the paddock and into the Bean's back garden. The Beans did not cut the grass in the paddock but let it grow until it was hay, ready for the roadman to come and scythe it down and carry it away for his cow. But before that, Mr Bean always got him to come and cut a path through the long grass so that Polly could still walk across the paddock. Nobody else used the path. It was specially for her. Mr Bean called it 'Polly's Way'.

She loved to walk along it when the grass was tall and the sweet summer smell of it, brushing against her bare legs, was somehow all mixed up with the happiness of the hours she was going to spend at the Beans' house. There were no secrets in that house. She supposed that it was because the Beans had never had any children that they had never developed the need to lie. Also there always seemed to be something interesting happening. Maybe they would be celebrating because Mr Bean had managed to get somebody famous to write an article for him, or maybe somebody unknown had sent in something really good. Then they would drink some of the dandelion wine or herb beer which Mrs Bean made in the cellar, and which occasionally blew up.

Once when she went round they told her, in whispers, that the dining-room ceiling was bulging from the weight of all the books and papers stored in the bedroom above and might fall down at any moment. They asked her to creep in very lightly, for they were too heavy to risk it, and gently move the papers towards the door, where they picked them up and carried them downstairs. It took all day but they got everything out and the ceiling didn't collapse. Afterwards the three of them stood in the dining-room looking up at it, and Mrs Bean said they'd have to get it repaired, but Mr Bean said he reckoned it wasn't worth the bother because it would probably be all right now they'd moved the papers out. So they left it like that, and it never did fall down. It just bulged over the dining-room table and looked interesting.

'What will you do when the war's over?' Mr Bean asked her one day.

'Will that be soon?' she asked, alarmed.

There had been so many years of people saying we were either just going to win or just going to lose the war, or just going to be invaded or just going to invade them, that she had given up trying to follow it. You couldn't believe anything they said anyway.

'Yes, I should think so,' Mr Bean said. 'Fairly soon.'

'Oh dear, I hope it lasts until I'm fourteen, next year.' She said.

Mr Bean smiled. 'You'd better go and arrange things with Adolf,' he said. Then he added as an afterthought, 'But they're thinking of raising the school leaving age to fifteen, aren't they?'

She went pale. Her green eyes blazed. 'Isn't that just the sort of mean underhand thing they would do?' she burst out. 'Just when I thought I was nearly there.'

'It's all right, Polly,' Mrs Bean reassured her. 'It can't go through Parliament in time to affect you. Don't go upsetting her, Tudor.'

'Sorry,' Mr Bean said. 'I didn't realise how much it mattered to Polly not to be educated.'

In fact it took until the following May for the war in Europe to be over. There were great victory bonfires and a torchlight procession through the village and dancing on the green. Polly had mixed feelings about all the celebrating. Of course it was lovely to be safe from the Germans and their bombs and to have no more black-outs, but on the other hand, though nobody actually said as much, it must surely mean that they would have to go back home and be sent to strange schools?

Then an unexpected thing happened. It seemed that the war with Japan still had to be won and that it might take some time. Her mother wrote and said that if Miss Capstick was agreeable, they had better stay where they were because you never knew with the Japs, did you?

'I'd never realised the other war was so important,' Polly admitted to the Beans. 'But isn't it lucky? It's bound to last till I leave school.'

'What will you do then, Polly?' Mr Bean asked.

'Dunno. But I don't want to be made to go to some strange school in town, not even for just a few weeks, I don't.'

'Do you have to go back to the town? There might be a job for you here. I might need an assistant. Or there might be a place for a trainee on *The Bingham Advertiser*, with the chance of coming here for a proper job afterwards. You could do worse than being a journalist.'

'A journalist? *Me*?'

If he had suggested she might be a film star and go and live in Hollywood, she couldn't have been more astonished.

He smiled, amused but sad.

'Yes, Polly, love,' he said. 'Does it seem so impossible to you?'

'But don't you have to have your School Certificate and go to university and all that?' Oh, why hadn't she bothered with the County Minor and gone to the Grammar and then to university?

'Not necessarily. You can work your way up the hard way – most do. I reckon there'll be opportunities after the war. We shall expand, certainly. Not that I ever want to be too big, but there'll be an end to all the restrictions, paper rationing and all the other bothers. We'll probably have to move into bigger offices before the house bursts. And all the newspapers will get back to their pre-war size and need more staff.'

'Oh, I do hope the war lasts till I'm fourteen,' she said earnestly. 'It's not long now. And maybe they'll let me stay here and learn to be a journalist.'

'Off you go and think about it,' he said, 'while I write my editorial.'

She was too excited to go home. She rushed up to Thieves' Way and sat on the packhorse bridge, then she jumped up and ran across the field with all the hummocks and down to the stream where the rowan grew right across like a bridge. She ran up it as far as she dared and then a bit further, and perched on the forked branch, looking through the leaves into the deep water below.

'I'm going to be a journalist,' she mouthed silently, afraid that even here somebody might hear her and mock her new ambition. She could see a trout lying very still just below her. She gazed down, her heart still throbbing. 'I'm going to be a journalist,' she mouthed at it in fish-language. Then she laughed loudly and nearly fell in. She made her perilous way down to the bank and, by a roundabout route, back to the village.

'There's a great big bomb been dropped,' Jimmy shouted at her. 'I've been looking for you everywhere.'

'Where? Where's the bomb? I didn't hear it.' She looked wildly around.

'Not here, silly, on Japan. So they'll give in now and the war'll be over. We can go home.'

'I'm not going.'
'Of course you are. I'll go to the Grammar at Monksheaton – it's one of the best in the country. Fancy that, and just near our house.'
'Our house! This is our house.'
'Don't be silly, this is Miss Capstick's house. I meant our mam's house.'
Miss Capstick wouldn't allow it. Surely she wouldn't. She went to find her. She poured out what Mr Bean had said. Miss Capstick listened.
'I'll do what I can,' she said, 'but of course it's up to your mother. She's your official guardian, naturally, whether you've left school or not. But I'll write to her immediately.'
Her mother wrote back saying she was looking forward very much to having her children back with her, all one happy family. She had missed them all these years. Besides Polly must be a big girl now, able to help in the house like a grown woman. She would be able to get a job, too, and it would all help, wouldn't it, because with Jimmy doing so well going to the Grammar they would need to earn enough for all his books and uniform and no doubt other additional expenses. With the war over, she said, rationing would stop and the shops would have more to sell and would need more assistants. Polly, she said, would make a good shop assistant.
She came up to get them. Her hair was dyed and she wore even more make-up than last time, all the little cracks in her face carefully filled in with powder. Dazed, Polly packed her case and tidied up her bed. Under the mattress was the copy of *Great Expectations*. She stood looking at it. She had had great expectations too. Stupid of her. She began walking downstairs to return the book to its shelf. By the landing window she paused and looked out. Mr Potter was busy in the garden, clearing beds. He had pulled up a lot of dead flowers. He had a bonfire going. She went to say goodbye to him. Then she threw the leather-bound book on the bonfire.

Chapter 6

'The war over three years and we're still having to cut out these ration coupons! Who'd have thought it, whoever would have thought it?' Mr Serpent asked rhetorically.

Polly, busy counting the little squares and triangles that had to be sent away to claim next month's supply of sugar and butter, didn't bother to reply. He didn't expect an answer. Besides, Mr Serpent, large, pink and benign-looking, didn't really want rationing to end. It had given him power. When rationing stopped, his customers would not need to grovel to him any more for extra bits of food in short supply and would be free to change to a different grocer if they wanted to. He would have to return to his pre-war servility.

She wasn't paid overtime for staying late to count up the coupons so got through it as quickly as possible, whereupon Mr Serpent gave her her pay packet, handing it over as slowly as he decently could for he hated parting with money.

Two pounds of her pay would go as usual to her mother, she thought as she walked home, and the remaining fifteen shillings, which she was allowed to keep for herself, she would put into her Post Office account together with the half crown she had found under the till. She suspected that it belonged to Mrs Hird who had released a great torrent of coins when she had upset her bag on the counter that morning. Mrs Hird was a show-off, dolled-up and actressy, forever carrying on about her next part in the amateur dramatics. She'd stood there making little shrieking noises while the coins rolled in all directions and Mr Serpent fussed about and ordered Polly to find them, every one, as if Mrs Hird might drop down dead, fur coat and all, if she lost sixpence. Polly had spent at least five minutes crawling about the floor hunting for the money, while Mr Serpent nagged at her not to forget to search under the fitments. So naturally when she was sweeping up at the end of the day and found the half crown, she felt as if she had earned it. It was hers by right, she thought, as she slipped it into the pocket of her overall.

'You're late,' her mother said when she got home. 'Tea's waiting,' she added, as she took the pay packet.

'Coupon counting,' Polly said, and handed her mother half a pound of butter.

Mollified, her mother said, 'Oh, he's really kind, isn't he? Sugar last week, butter this. Thank him very much, won't you? I really don't know how we'd manage if you didn't work in a grocer's.'

'Well, you're going to have to,' Polly thought to herself as she went to wash before tea. As soon as she could, she was going to enquire at *The Brigthorpe Chronicle* about being taken on as a trainee. She'd saved enough to manage even if she would be paid hardly anything on the newspaper. She was seventeen now. She reckoned she'd done her bit towards Jim's education. He had done well, distinctions in almost every subject in his School Certificate, and he'd taken it a year early, too. He was already in his first year in the Sixth form at the Grammar. If he went to university, he'd get a County Major scholarship and could manage on that. And, then it would be bye-bye Mr Serpent for her, Polly Adams. As for her mother's reaction, she just wouldn't think about that.

'Tell Jim, will you, Polly?' her mother called up to her.

She went into his room.

'Tea's ready,' she said.

He pushed his chair back and smiled at her, stretching his arms above his head. Then he got up slowly. He was tall now, and handsome. He reminded Polly of the man on Mrs Braithwaite's knitting pattern. A good-natured sort of face, a bit soft somehow.

'Oh, Polly, I'll be glad of a break,' he said. 'I've been at this essay all day. How's the shop been?'

'Oh, my dear, fascinating,' she said, imitating Mrs Hird. 'All that lovely sugar and the tea, you've never seen the like.' She rounded her eyes and pranced about the room. It never failed. Jim doubled up with laughter.

'Oh, I'm glad you're home,' he said. 'It's so *boring* all this stuff. Anything interesting happen? Go on, tell.'

She thought of telling him about the half crown and decided against it. 'Mr Serpent's spent the afternoon in the store room seducing the lady who travels for Heinz,' she said.

'Loony. Mr Serpent's far too fat to seduce anybody,' he said.

'Oh, the Heinz lady goes in in all the places he comes out. They'd fit all right.'

'Not in that store cupboard, they wouldn't. You forget I've seen it. Do you think he'll want extra help again at Christmas?'

She shrugged, thought of telling him she'd no intention of being there herself by Christmas but said instead, 'Tea's ready. Come on down.'

Her mother was just putting the teapot on the table. She covered it with the cosy and said 'All right, then?' She was speaking to Jim, of course, with that lingering look of concern with which she always regarded him when he had been working, as if afraid that the books might have wrought some damage invisible to the naked eye. Bookwork was something of a mystery to her, frightening in the way it seemed to weaken people, and yet ultimately bestowed such power. She shook her head, she didn't understand it. All she could do was provide comfort and nourishment to compensate.

'Have some bread and butter with your soup,' she said, handing the plate to him. 'It's real butter. And you can have more. Mr Serpent's given half a pound to our Polly. Oh, he is kind, that man.'

'He's not really,' Polly said. 'He's very mean. Really stingy. He only gave me the butter because he thought it had gone off. I told him it smelled rancid. He doesn't have a sense of smell, you know. He lost it in the First World War, he says.'

'Poor soul. Still, it's a small sacrifice, a sense of smell, compared to the sacrifices some had to make.'

She sniffed, and Polly and Jim both started talking at once, not wanting her to get on to the topic of Uncle Fred.

'Be fair, Polly,' Jim said, 'there was always the sugar. Sugar doesn't go rancid. And he gave you some of that last week.'

Actually she had helped herself to the sugar. 'No,' she said, 'but it gets mites in it.'

'Well, I never knew that,' her mother said. 'I didn't see any.'
'She's teasing you, Mum. He gives her stuff because he fancies her. She's a smasher, your daughter. You must have noticed,' he added, getting up and clearing away the soup bowls.
'That's enough of that sort of talk,' his mother said sharply. 'Anyway you'll turn her head.'
'She gets her looks from you,' he pointed out, pausing behind her chair and stroking her forehead. 'So it's not her fault.'
His mother smiled up at him and laid her hand on his as it rested on her shoulder.

Polly watched them. She could see, in a detached sort of way, that her mother had traces of beauty. She certainly looked a lot better now than she had when she had come to collect them after the war. It was only after they'd got back that Polly realised that the war had been quite different in the towns, that it had been a strain, a time of little sleep, constant worry and insufficient food. Her mother had worked at nights, too. No wonder she had looked so drawn and old. Since then she seemed to have gone into reverse and grown younger. It helped that she had stopped putting henna on her hair and let it revert to its natural mixture of brown and grey which suited her face better, for her skin was delicate and fair and had seemed too pallid under the harsh dye.

It was a lively face and sometimes there were flashes of that laughter and wildness which Polly dimly remembered from years and years ago, before she had gone off and left them. Sometimes she saw in her mother a reminder of that younger woman, laughing, swooping down on her, swinging her in the air when she was tiny, but it might have been a different person in another world, beyond her reach now. She saw it mostly when she came upon her mother by surprise, laughing with a friend or with Jim, maybe. With Polly she was always more reserved, cautious, as if she didn't want to invite criticism by being frivolous. But she was critical enough of Polly and everything she wanted to do. Neither of them would get back to being the person they had been before her mother deserted them; even if they did, they would never again be that person with each other.

Wednesday was early closing at the shop. So it was on a Wednesday afternoon that she walked into the *Chronicle* office, presented herself at the desk and asked to see the editor.

'Oh,' said the lady, who was busy counting money into a toffee tin, 'we're Notices and Small Ads here.'

Polly stood blushing, not knowing what to do, until the Small Ads lady took pity on her, stopped a young man who was passing, and said, 'Here, Randy, perhaps you can take her up to see Sir?'

Randy glanced at her and said, 'Will the chief reporter do?' and before she could answer led the way upstairs to a very smoky room where five or six men were sitting around a big table. He called to one of them, the oldest by far, that there was this girl here to see him.

'It's the editor I want to see,' she said.

The chief reporter shrugged, 'All right. On your own head, and all that,' and led her up some steep, uncarpeted stairs to a tiny landing.

'In there,' he said, nodding towards one of the two doors, and left her.

She didn't know what to expect but she hadn't expected quite such a messy little room with quite such a huge man in it. The impression his face made was mainly of thick black eyebrows, a jutting nose, turned-down mouth and a look of suppressed rage.

'Well?' he shouted at her, scowling furiously.

With a great effort, she made her feet stay exactly where there were and her voice say, 'Please, I want to be a journalist. I wondered if there might be a job for me here?'

'Oh, Christ! And on a Wednesday too!'

'Wednesday?'

He looked her up and down and when he spoke again the voice was quieter, but it was only sarcasm that subdued it.

'Before you came here asking me for a job, as if jobs were lying about in tins like biscuits which I could dispense on request, did you actually go and buy the paper and read it?'

'Yes. I read it nearly always, every week.'

'And did you observe the day it is published?'

'Thursday.'

'Exactly. Did you not deduce from that, that the worst possible day in the whole week to come badgering an editor with a request for jobs would be Wednesday, when we are, as we knowing ones say, 'putting the paper to bed'? In other words we're trying to get the bugger printed on time to be in the shops on Thursday morning.'

'I'm sorry,' she said. 'I didn't think of that.'

He glared at her.

'We've only once taken on a girl in this office,' he said, 'and she didn't think either.'

He turned back to what he had been doing when she came in, which was scribbling marks in a thick pencil all over something somebody had written. He took no further notice of her. She desperately wanted to run for it. But if she did, there was no other chance for her. It was the only local paper. This terrifying, grumpy man guarded the entrance to her only route into journalism and he had to be faced. She stood her ground.

'What? You still here?' he asked, when she didn't go.

'Shall I come back tomorrow? I could come in my lunch hour.'

'I've told you we go to press on Thursday.'

'But you've done all your work by then. You've just said so. It's the newsagents who are busy with it on Thursday. I don't want a job in a newspaper shop. I want one here.'

He gave a brief snort of amusement.

'You've got a nerve, young madam,' he said. 'Well, you need a bit of cheek it you're going to make a journalist. Actually Thursday's my hang-over day, if you want to know. Got shorthand?' he asked suddenly.

'No, but I can type a bit.'

'Much good that'll do you. There's only one typewriter in this office and it's mine.'

'Oh.'

'Tell you what, go away and learn shorthand – typing too, maybe, while you're at it. But you'll have to get your own typewriter. The comps'll love you if you type your stuff. They're always grumbling about the sort of handwriting journalists have. Come back in about a year. And make it a Friday, would you?'

'Oh, thank you.'

'Don't thank me,' he said. 'I haven't promised you anything.'

She waited in case he had anything further to say and, when

71

he hadn't, turned and found her way down the dark and rickety staircase, past the reporters' room, through the hall with the Small Ads lady and out into the blessedly friendly street.

She read the following day's edition of *The Chronicle* with particular interest. That was why she saw the notice about the new building society wanting a filing clerk. The pay was a whole pound more a week than she got in the shop and the work stopped an hour earlier so it would be much easier to get to the Tech in the evenings for her shorthand and typing.

'You realise,' young Mr Blenkinsop said to her after she had been given the job, 'that being a filing clerk is the lowest form of human life, don't you? If you get bored in two weeks don't say I didn't warn you.'

She couldn't make him out at all. He had sat in while she was interviewed by a small fat lady called Miss Porter who looked like one of those funny pouter pigeons she and Jim had seen in a bird show in the town, for her chest seemed to grow out of her chin so that she looked puffed-up and top-heavy on her thin little legs. She was middle-aged and in charge of the filing department but seemed to be in awe of this young man, who, it was explained, was familiarising himself with the work of each department in turn. Polly was surprised at how relaxed she herself was, not at all terrified like she'd been at the newspaper. She lied easily, telling them she wanted to have a business career and work her way up, and the young man laughed and said, 'She's after your job, Miss Porter,' and the old girl bridled and said, 'Oh, you are a *one*, Mr Blenkinsop.'

She was distinctly less affable when Polly started work two weeks later. There were five others girls in the department and Miss Porter watched as they clocked in then, curt and unsmiling, told Polly what to do. In front of her was a big revolving drum with pages containing the names and addresses of the subscribers. She had to go and collect little slips of cellophane-covered paper from the typists, superior beings who worked on the other side of a partition in an area which had carpet on the floor, and then sit on her stool and slot each slip of paper into the appropriate place on the pages of her revolving drum. It was much more repetitive and boring than she had imagined possible. Besides, she had no idea what it was all for.

They were not allowed to talk to each other: Miss Porter appeared at the slightest whisper. In fact she seemed to spend most of her time walking around in her curious strutting way, throwing her feet forward with jerky movements as if, being top-heavy, she might otherwise topple forward on her face. As she walked her head dipped up and down, her sharp little eyes glancing from side to side to check on the girls, or squinting down at the floor as if she might see something to peck at.

Polly tried various ways of whiling away the time. At ten o'clock she decided she wouldn't look at the clock for an hour and see how well she could guess when the hour was up. Diligently she kept her head down, picking up a slip of paper, turning over the folder until she found the right page, inserting the slip, then back to the little pile of slips and the same routine over and over again. When she judged the hour was over she looked up at the clock. Ten past ten.

'It *can't* be,' she said aloud.

One of the other girls looked up.

'All right?' she enquired, after glancing at the door through which Miss Porter had just vanished.

Polly blushed. 'Yes, sorry,' she whispered back. 'Just though it was later than that,' she added, nodding towards the clock.

The girl pulled a face.

'When you can't stand it, you go to the cloakroom,' she said.

She was amazed at how much time they spent there. They combed their hair, reapplied lipstick, talked about their boy friends, anything to delay returning to the little slips of paper. Golly, she thought, they ought to try working in a shop. It was ridiculous really. Work in a shop was much harder, on your feet all day, with customers in a hurry and Mr Serpent chivvying you and having to know the price of everything and where it was kept and how many coupons or points it needed and getting the change right and packing up the orders and everything. Here she just had to sit on a stool and didn't need to know anything except the alphabet. Yet she was paid more. It sounded better, too, working in an office than in a shop. She soon noticed the difference when she told people what she did. She reckoned that was why her mother had come round to it, after at first refusing to let her change jobs, though maybe it had quite a bit to do with the extra money which compensated for the loss of butter and sugar. She even came round to accepting that Polly would spend her evenings at the Technical college, so long as she bettered herself. Polly didn't tell her about *The Chronicle*. It was quite pleasant to keep things secret, just as her mother had once kept more important things secret from her. Besides she didn't trust anyone with her dreams, least of all her mother.

After a week of filing, it occurred to her that it would be quicker to save up a pile of slips, put them in alphabetical order and so work straight through the revolving pages, instead of jumping about among them. Before long Miss Porter came over, her little steel-bound body bustling as much as the tight corsets would allow. 'Whatever are you doing, Miss Adams?' she asked, her head jerking as if she might peck at the little slips Polly was arranging.

Polly explained. 'It's quicker, you see,' she ended. 'I mean, I often have three or four for one page and it's silly to put one in, then turn over four or five pages and then back again. Look, here are three Smiths. It's much more sense to file them at the same time.'

Miss Porter's face turned bright pink. 'It is not our system,' she said.

'But —'

'No "buts" if you please. Kindly do it as you were shown.'

It had gone very quiet. All the girls were listening hard, their hands moving desultorily about among the pages, achieving nothing.

'It's so silly,' Polly insisted.

The pink tide flooded downwards, filling the V-shaped gap in Miss Porter's crocheted jumper.

'I shall speak to Mr Blenkinsop about this,' she said.

Polly shrugged. 'All right, I'll do it the other way,' she said, 'but it's much quicker like this. You could manage with one girl less if you did it this way.'

Miss Porter walked away without replying and ignored her thereafter, but the other girls attacked her immediately they got her in the cloakroom at break time. Who did she think she was, they asked furiously, rounding on her, hair and lipsticks forgotten, and which of them would keep their jobs and which bloody one would get the sack?'

'I'm sorry,' she said humbly. 'I didn't think. At least I was just thinking that it made better sense of the filing.'

'No, you didn't think, did you? Not about us anyway.'

'I'm sorry,' she said again. 'I won't say anything more about it, ever again, I promise.'

'Even so, Ma Porter could still go and complain. And somebody up there might think it's a good idea. And we're warning you, Polly Adams, you'll be in trouble if they do.'

'If I lose my job, I'll scrag you,' a demure-looking girl called Diane promised quietly.

'If they say they can do without one of us,' Polly said, 'I'll give in my notice.'

Mollified, they began to get out their combs and make-up. For the rest of the day Polly worked slowly and deliberately, filing in the way she had been told.

All the same, she was sent for after work.

In front of Mr Blenkinsop an angry little Miss Porter had her say. Words like insubordination were used. Polly felt her temper rising. It took a great effort of will to control it. You want this job for the rest of the year, Polly Adams. Put up with them, with anything. Just until you've got your advanced shorthand, just until you've got yourself into *The Chronicle*. It doesn't matter. After that Miss Porter can go hang herself. But don't get yourself sacked after just two weeks here.

She was so busy suppressing her temper that she hardly heard what they were saying. They were both looking at her. She made sounds of agreement, compliance, goodwill, anything.

'I'm so glad that's all settled then,' Mr Blenkinshop said. 'You're sure you're quite happy about it now, Miss Porter?'

He had a very winning smile. He looked at Miss Porter as if the only thing that mattered to him in all the world was that she should be quite happy. She said that she was.

'Then I won't delay you,' he said. 'Miss Adams,' he added, severely, as they both prepared to move towards the door.

'Perhaps you would stay behind for a moment?'

He and Miss Porter exchanged glances and Miss Porter looked smug, assured that the girl was going to get a thorough trouncing. Polly waited, telling herself to put up with it, not to argue with anything he said.

'Well, Polly,' he began affably. 'In trouble already. I warned you.'

'Did you?'

'I told you it was boring. The real problem is that you're too bright for this job. Of course your system is better.'

She stared at him, stunned.

'Then why wasn't she pleased?' she asked.

He laughed. 'You may be clever but you haven't developed common sense yet. In business, anyway our business, power depends on how many people you have under you. The filing department is Miss Porter's little empire and you tell her how to cut her staff from five to four and expect her to be pleased? Really, Polly, take a bad mark.'

'I never thought,' she said miserably.

'Well, cheer up, it's not the end of the world. I've placated the old girl. Let's give the others time to get away and then go out for a drink.'

'I'll have to be quick. I go to the Tech of an evening. For shorthand and typing.'

He looked surprised.

'Why?'

'Oh, just to get better qualified,' she said cautiously.

'And by the way,' he added, 'do call me Simon when we're out of this place. Mr Blenkinsop sounds so formal.'

'All right,' she said. 'But I've never called you Mr Blenkinsop anyway.'

After that they often had a cider at the pub near the office either after work or later on in the evening when she came out of the Technical College. At least she had cider and he had beer. He was the nephew of some director or other and was going to end up working in Head Office in London but meanwhile was travelling about getting to know the different branches and departments. She hadn't realised he was so old. Twenty-seven.

He wasn't very tall, but thick-set and healthy-looking. He

made her laugh and yet he took her seriously, talking to her as an equal, encouraging her to try to get promotion at work, unlike her brother Jim who thought that all girls' jobs were trivial and just a way to fill in time before they got married.

'You could do well, Polly,' Simon said one evening. 'You could get on in the firm. Why didn't you do better at school?'

She shrugged. 'I didn't want to, I suppose. It all seemed pointless.' She couldn't explain; it had more to do with feelings and impulses than reasons. 'Anyway,' she said, 'I'm not going to try taking any more initiatives at work, not after that row with Miss Porter, I'm not.'

'Oh, that soon blew over. I didn't mean that. I mean long-term plans for you.'

He glanced at his watch. 'Time to go,' he said. 'We'll talk about it on the way home.'

That was another nice thing about him. He always made sure that she was home on time. It was a rule that she had to be indoors by half-past ten and prove it by calling goodnight in the direction of the light that showed under her mother's bedroom door. On Saturday she was allowed an extension until ten forty-five because the pictures come out later.

'You see,' he said, taking her arm as they crossed the road, 'I reckon there are going to be far more jobs for women in the firm than there were before the war. Things are really changing. I'm sure that you could work your way up to being a proper secretary and then perhaps private secretary to the head of one of the departments with real responsibility. But it does help if you have some paper qualifications.'

She felt mean, letting him think that the height of her ambition was to be someone's private secretary.

'Maybe I'll end up being chairman,' she said flippantly.

'I shouldn't. He's a real old misery. Do you know he's got all that money but he can't drink at all, eats scarcely anything because of his ulcer and never goes anywhere or enjoys anything?'

'That must be nice for his wife.'

'Oh, he's got through a few of those already. But it's you we're talking about, not him. Honestly, Polly, it's not too late to catch up on what you missed at school. You can take subjects like French and English at the Tech as well as shorthand and typing. You could get all the qualifications you didn't bother about at school.'

She shook her head.

'Otherwise you're letting life be unfair,' he insisted. 'It was all right for me. I got Higher Certificate and all that before the war. Afterwards they practically pushed us officers into university when we were demobbed. You just missed out, Polly. I'd like to help you put it right, truly. You're far better read than half the chaps I met at college.'

'Well, I'll ask about the English anyway. That was always my best subject at school.'

She was tempted to tell him her plans. She knew he wouldn't laugh at her. But some wariness prevented her. If nobody knew, then nobody could let her down. It was safer that way.

If it hadn't been for the 'flu epidemic she wouldn't have left the filing department, but the absence of most of the typists on sick leave, combined with the fact that the filing department seemed immune to infection, led to her being asked to go and type the little slips instead of filing them. It was only supposed to be a temporary arrangement but one of the typists didn't come back, so Polly stayed there, on the other side of the partition, where the carpet was. She earned fifteen shillings a week more.

'I told you,' Simon said. 'First step up the ladder. Let's go and celebrate on Saturday.'

He took her to a restaurant and she had a glass of wine, the first she had ever tasted. She pulled a face at the dryness of it.

'Don't you like it?'

'Mm. It's all right. Not as nice as cider.'

'Next time we'll have a meal in my room, and you can have cider. And sardines on toast. Meanwhile, congratulations on your promotion,' he said, raising his glass to her.

'Thanks. You know, there's something I can't make out about my new job. I'm paid just about double what I got in the shop and it's much easier. It's less tiring, and you don't need to think as much as you do in a shop, or know anything like as much. And I reckon shop work is more use, too. I mean I don't know what they do with all those bits of cellophane but I bet it's not as important as food.'

He laughed, but then shook his head. 'That's the fault of the management,' he said. 'They ought to see that all the employees understand what their work is for. It would make it so much more interesting for the girls if they knew why the files mattered and –'

'No, it wouldn't,' she interrupted. 'Nothing can make filing interesting. It's the money that's interesting, that's all.'

'That's very cynical,' he said, sounding genuinely shocked.

'No, it's not. You only think you can make it interesting because you've never done it. Oh, I know you've been round and watched them working and all that, but you haven't actually sat there yourself hour after hour, have you?'

He looked hurt and she was sorry, suddenly feeling that, although he was much older, he knew less about work and people than she did. He couldn't help it. He had been brought up soft and people like that often had theories; she'd noticed that before. Often when he talked about how he wanted to go in for modern management she felt uneasily that it was all right on paper but he overlooked things you only found out by doing, not thinking. So it was no good arguing.

Instead she said cheerily, 'Well, men get danger money sometimes, so why shouldn't girls get boredom money?'

He took her more seriously than she intended. 'You may have a point, Polly,' he said. 'Perhaps in these days of full employment we'll have to pay extra to get boring jobs done. We had an economics lecturer once who spent an hour explaining to us different factors in a man's wage – like, if he's producing something useful or of great value to the community, or if the work is hard or skilled or dangerous, he should be paid more. And at the end of all that he said quite casually, "And now I leave you with the thought that before the war a miner was paid less than a manicurist in a London beauty parlour." I shall always remember it. We sat there stunned because it made nonsense of all the notes we'd been taking.'

'But he was right, wasn't he? What people are paid has nothing to do with reasons, has it? Just traditions and what's the lowest people can get away with paying. I bet Mr Serpent would have paid less if he could have got anyone to work for less. It's got nothing to do with being of value to the community and all that stuff.'

'It's all going to change now,' he reassured her. 'The war taught us the real value of things. What I'd really like to do,' he went on thoughtfully, confiding in her in a way she would never have confided in him, 'is to study the whole of our industry and then to build up a personnel department in this firm and make everything more rational. That's what I'm aiming to do eventually.'

She shook her head, touched by his belief in rationality but unable to share it, just as she was unable to believe that people could be educated into thinking that filing was interesting.

'We've missed the pictures,' she said.

'Let's go for a walk instead.'

They walked, his arm around her, along the canal, following the towpath into the fields which opened out surprisingly quickly on this side of the town. There were barges tied up on the far bank, lights in their windows. She imagined the people inside. Cosy, like the farm had been. Lamps. Candles. Warm and safe, with the shutters closed against the cold harsh world outside.

A light drizzle began to fall. She put her scarf around her head and as they sheltered under a tree, he opened his raincoat and wrapped it round her so that it was like a rather inadequate tent sheltering their embrace. He held her close, her head on his shoulder. Then he kissed her wet cheeks.

'You're beautiful,' he said. 'But I expect you've been told that often.'

'No, I haven't,' she said.

It was true. She had had no boy friends. All Jim's friends seemed young and silly. Older men had made passes at her, but they were repellent. Boys of her own age were boring or embarrassed or both. One way or another there was always something wrong and she never got close to any of them.

'I can't believe that,' he said, smiling down at her. 'But you're so refreshing, Polly. No airs and graces. Most girls exaggerate the competition. Warm enough?'

'Yes, thanks. It's quite dry here.'

She looked up into the branches which, umbrella-like,

protected them from the rain which was falling quite heavily in a circle around them. Besides, his body kept her warm. He was strong, his arms felt hard and solid around her. She leaned back against them, as if to break away, but couldn't. Not that she wanted to anyway.

'Penny for them?'

'Well, I was just thinking I'm enjoying this.'

He laughed and covered her face with little kisses.

'Don't change, Polly,' he said. 'Don't let them spoil you.'

They stayed under the tree until it was time for the pictures to come out, then he walked her home.

She wore her new Horrockses cotton dress to go to supper at his digs. It had a full skirt, fitted bodice, no sleeves and tiny round buttons down the front. It cost three pounds and was the most expensive thing she had ever bought. It was beautiful and worth every penny. It rustled expensively as she climbed up the stairs to his room.

The hall and stairs were scruffy, she observed, and none too clean. The wallpaper was peeling off and the brown paint-work was all chipped and thick with dust. She'd expected something better. But his room came as a pleasant surprise. It was big and light and very tidy.

He hadn't seen the dress before.

'Golly,' he said, awe-struck.

He made her stand quite still while he admired her.

'I've never seen anyone suit a dress so well,' he said. 'Those autumn colours are marvellous with your hair and skin. It was made for you, Polly.'

'No, I got it at Dingley's.'

He laughed and kissed her. 'I meant it was *intended* for you, designed by fate – Oh, well, never mind. You look lovely in it.'

He had put everything ready for supper. There was a flagon of cider on the table and a row of tins by the gas-ring.

She looked at them with an expert eye.

'Sardines, tomato soup, peaches,' she said. 'Last year that would have been a month's points on the ration. Oh, and *bananas*.'

'Are they still a treat to you because there weren't any during the war?'

'Yes, the smell's still special,' she said, sniffing the fruit bowl. As always it brought back memories of the day her father died.

'When they came back into the shops, did you remember them from before the war?'

'Yes.'

She paused and then went on lightly, 'But our Jim didn't. It was ever so funny. He knew they were very special because everyone was fussing on about them in the shop and when our mam told him he could eat his on the way home, he just bit the end off, skin and all.'

'How much difference in age is there between you?'

'Two years,' she said. 'But he doesn't remember things before the war. At least, some things he forgets. He's lucky the way he forgets things, our Jim is.'

'You're quite protective about him, aren't you?'

'No, I don't think so. Well, I always used to look after him, I suppose. I mean you had to, didn't you?'

She began to wander round the room, examining things.

'You don't have a mirror,' she observed.

'There's one inside the wardrobe door,' he said, nodding towards it. 'Or you can go into the bathroom.'

'This'll do,' she said, opening the door and standing combing her hair. It was long now, more golden than red, less curly than it had been. All the same it still got tangled easily and she took her time combing it, while, at the other end of the room, he decanted the soup into a pan and stirred it over the gas-ring.

'Is that all you have to cook on?' she asked, coming back to him.

'Yes. It means I can only have one hot course. So it limits the cooking, thank goodness.'

'Can't you cook? Didn't you ever help at home?'

'No, I was sent away to boarding school when I was eight.'

'Oh.'

She looked at him with pity. It was bad enough to be sent away because of the war when you were little, but to be sent away by choice, that really was dreadful. At least she'd been able to blame Hitler.

'Were you home-sick?'

'Yes,' he said shortly. 'I loathed it. But I suppose it was a good preparation for the army.'

She handed him the soup bowls from the table. He waved them vaguely over the gas-ring.

'That's to warm them,' he explained. 'I always do that.'

'Oh,' she said, 'I thought you were going to do a conjuring trick with them.'

'I'm trying to impress you, Polly, with how domesticated I am,' he said, carefully filling the bowls and putting them on the table.

'I don't see why you didn't just have ordinary lodgings with a landlady to do for you,' she said as she sat down.

He cut bread for her and filled her glass.

'I did once, but I much prefer this. It's awful having to let them know when you'll be in and then having to talk to the other lodgers at mealtimes.'

'Yes,' she said, sipping the cider, 'I can see that. You're freer. And I expect some landladies are awful old bags.'

She glanced at the divan bed.

'And you can bring girls back,' she added.

'Polly! What a thing to say! What a suspicious mind you've got.'

'I didn't mean anything wrong. I just meant you didn't have to ask anyone's permission to have visitors, that's all.'

He shook his head at her. 'Sometimes I can't decide about you at all,' he said. 'You're all contrasts. Even your face changes from one minute to the next. Probably some of the things you say sound worse because you look so angelic.'

'Me? *Angelic*?'

'Maybe it's just the Titian colouring.' He looked at her critically. 'I'm trying to be as detached as I can,' he explained.

'I think you'd like to rationalise me like you'd like to rationalise the personnel department.'

'Heaven forbid! I'd just like to understand you better. You sometimes look so vulnerable and innocent, Polly. Then at other times you look quite wary. Surely other people must have noticed that?'

'Ye-es. Once somebody said I looked wary,' she said. 'But not innocent.'

Miss Capstick had said it of her. Miss Emily had used an uglier word. Sly. She heard it again as she remembered the sound of their voices, the feeling of dizziness as she leant over the banister. A lot of her childhood had been spent listening-in, she thought, sipping her cider while he removed the soup bowls and prepared the next course. It had gone on until the night before they went home when Jimmy had asked what eaves were and Miss Capstick had said that they were the projecting edges of the roof and asked if he knew of a word from them and neither of them could think of one, until Jimmy had said, 'Well, there's *eavesdropping*, but that's got nothing to do with the roof,' and Miss Capstick had explained that it had.

Then suddenly she'd said, 'I expect you've heard the expression "Eavesdroppers never hear good of themselves." What do you think that means?' and they hadn't known. Then Miss Capstick had looked directly at her and said quietly that she had always supposed that since it wasn't a very nice thing to do, nice things would not be heard about the sort of people who did it. And Polly had felt herself go very hot and never listened-in again. Somehow that conversation marked the end of an era, just as much as the end of the war did.

'You're very quiet,' Simon observed. 'Worried about something? I haven't upset you, have I?'

She laughed and shook her head.

'Of course not,' she said. 'I'm sorry. And after you've gone to so much trouble too,' she added, starting on the sardines on toast which he had carefully decorated with slices of tomato and sprigs of parsley.

'Pity about the toast,' he said. 'I don't know why it's so tough.'

'When did you do it?'

'This morning. I thought I'd do it in good time, so the room wouldn't be stuffy. I have to do the toast by the gas-fire, you see.'

She burst out laughing and then went and sat on his knee in case she had hurt his feelings.

'You're worse than our Jim,' she said.

She stayed there, sitting on his knee, sharing his plate as they ate cheese and biscuits, and drinking out of the same glass. When they had finished the flagon, he carried her over to the big armchair by the unlit gas-fire. It was a huge piece of furniture with plenty of room in it for both of them.

They lay comfortably together in the chair. He stroked her arms and his hands slipped easily inside the sleeveless bodice. It was unexpected, the feelings of his hands warm against her bare flesh. She had never felt so alive and tingling before. She snuggled up against him, just wanting to get as close as possible. His hands moved across her back, round to the side of her breasts, and then further. Automatically her body pressed closer to his, of its own accord really. They stayed like that, relaxed, hardly stirring, except that his hands moved gently as if by some telepathy they knew exactly what her body wanted.

She would like to stay like this for ever, she thought, it was the most perfect feeling. The only trouble was that as time passed the tingling grew more insistent and her body demanded to be closer to his, but bits of clothing and the chair got frustratingly in the way. By the same magic as before, just as she felt this, his fingers began to undo the little round buttons on her bodice. She had a moment of anxiety for the Horrockses cotton which had cost so much, but he was very careful and since the buttons went right down to the waist it folded back easily and became just a skirt.

She was glad she had put on her best bra, the one with the lace. She was glad too, in a different kind of way, when he took it off.

He eased her gently round so that she sat facing him, straddled across his knee, the full skirt enfolding them both. Then he took her long hair and gently drew it forward across her breast, speading it out like a bodice and she smiled at him because it was ridiculous to be perched there fully clothed from the waist down and mother-naked up above.

'It's all right, Polly,' he said, taking her face between his hands and kissing her. 'You're quite safe with me.'

'I know.'

'Quite safe, I promise you,' he said, smiling gently down at her and his hands moved slowly from her face to her neck, moulding her shoulders, playing with her hair, stroking her breasts, cupping them in his hands. And all the time she looked back at him, smiling with delight, suddenly aware that for the first time in her life she felt completely happy and carefree. Up till now, she realised, she had always had to be in charge, had always had to worry about something or somebody, but now she felt blissfully irresponsible as she relaxed and left everything to him.

'You're safe,' he said again later. 'I shall keep the rules.'

He did keep the rules, too. Typically he was the one, that first evening, who noticed when it was time to go. He rearranged her dress, fastening the tiny buttons of the bodice, combed her hair and walked her home in time for her to call goodnight to the light that shone under her mother's bedroom door, with a whole minute to spare.

After that they spent many hours together in the big armchair in his room. Sometimes she thought how odd it was that grown-ups didn't do this all the time. They were allowed to, after all. What were they thinking of, going out to the pictures and pubs, when they could be lying like this, for goodness' sake? But when she asked Simon he only laughed and said that perhaps they got used to it.

'I don't believe that. And when you think that they can go on, they don't have to stop like us.'

He sighed. 'I know,' he said and sounded so sad that she held him close, afraid that he might think her critical.

'I read the other day about aborigines in South America who chew some special roots that grow there,' he remarked, 'and don't have babies.'

'You mean they like chewing roots so much?' she asked, astonished.

He shouted with laughter.

'No, silly. It contains some kind of natural contraceptive and women don't conceive after chewing it.'

'Are you sure it said *chew*?'

'Yes. It sounds odd, but it would solve our problem.'

She shook her head.

'It's not just babies, is it?' she said.

'No, of course not. That's only part of it. I suppose it comes down to a matter of respect really. And if you care very much about someone you can't risk hurting them or ever taking advantage of them. At least that's how it seems to me. I mean, that's the logic of it.'

'There you go, rationalising,' she said, but softened the

words with kisses for he was not in the least rational about her and she loved being here with him in his room where they seemed to create their own little world, warm and safe from the outside world, shuttered in and timeless. Of course, you knew it would have to stop at ten o'clock, but while it lasted it seemed timeless, just as the world of snow had seemed timeless in the country during the war, although she had known that it would surely melt when spring came. Some things, while they lasted, seemed for ever. You forgot all about everyday life, like when you lost yourself in a book.

'I hate the outside world,' she said suddenly.

'Polly!'

'No, not really,' she recanted, realising she had spoken too vehemently.

'Maybe the outside world has been kinder to me than to you?'

'Perhaps.'

'Polly?'

'Yes?'

'One day – oh, not yet, I know you're far too young – one day I'd like to share it with you.'

'What?'

'The outside world.'

It was a funny sort of proposal but she knew what he meant. She understood it well enough to shake her head.

'Forget it now,' he said. 'Oh, my God, it's quarter past ten. Come on.'

They didn't meet again for more than a month as first of all she had exams, then he got flu, and after that had to go to London for a week.

It was from London that he wrote to her, just a brief note saying he was travelling back on Saturday morning, would meet her in the pub in the evening and had a lot to tell her.

'Such news,' he said, seizing her hands and almost dragging her towards the bar. 'I can't wait to tell you all about it.'

It was very crowded. He pushed his way ahead of her, emerged with two glasses and then shouldered his way through to a corner where there was an empty table. He was good at things like finding tables.

'I thought we'd just have a quick drink and then go back to my room, so we can talk properly. You can't really talk in a restaurant. I've bought in a few bits and pieces.'

He could scarcely sit still he was so excited. His hands gripped hers, his eyes raked her face, he kept grinning at her.

'Such news,' he said. 'Now listen.'

She had news too. It would have to wait. She could see that.

'First of all the bad news,' he said. 'Let's get that over and done with.'

She waited, tense now.

'I've got to go back to London, Polly. They want me in Head Office.'

'Oh, I'm sorry.'

'But I shall come back at weekends. None of that will change. Only I'll stay at some hotel or other. And you must come and see me in London.'

'Thank you. I'd like that.'

'And Polly, don't be proud. Let me pay your train fare. I can afford it better than you.'

'Well, we'll see,' she said.

He looked at her suddenly.

'You don't believe me, do you? You think I'll just vanish out of your life.'

She smiled, hesitating. 'No, it's not that,' she began.

'Come on,' he said, getting up suddenly. 'Back home to my room and I'll show you how much I want you. And I'll tell all the rest of it, too.'

She could hardly keep up with him. He was like a kid, he was so beside himself.

'They're really going ahead with the personnel department. A main board director will be in charge, but under him I'll be responsible for the actual day-to-day running of it. They seem to be offering me a free hand. It's really all because I did that management course. I mean it's not that I know a lot, it's just that nobody else knows anything.'

He stopped suddenly and turned to her. 'Oh, Polly, how awful of me,' he said. 'I never asked about your exams.'

'Oh, I got them all right.'

'How much all right?'

'Distinctions.'

'In French and English as well as the shorthand and typing?'
'Yes.'
They were almost at his digs now. He stopped in the road and hugged her.
'Clever, clever Polly.'
She was going to go on and tell him the rest, but he released her than grabbed her hand and began walking so quickly that she scarcely had breath to keep up with him, let alone talk.
'You just sit there,' he ordered, when they reached his room. 'I'll see to everything. Kettle on, fire for toast, here's cheese, here's soup, here's everything. Open the cider, there you are. Glasses.'
He rushed about and somehow or other got basic nourishment on to the table.
'Now listen, Polly,' he said carefully as they finished the soup, 'I can't promise anything, not really absolutely promise, but I can *almost*, well yes, dammit, I can actually –'
'Simon, do you think you could just explain, simply I mean, what you are on about?'
He beamed at her.
'How would you like a secretary's job? I don't mean a copy typist or the kind of thing you're doing now, but a real secretary. First of all here, and then in London?'
'Simon! Oh, Simon!'
He mistook her exclamation. 'I knew you'd be thrilled. Oh, my darling.' He leaned across the table and gripped her hands. She stared back. She felt like someone who has just been given a present and even as the donor beams with the pure joy of giving, knows that it must be handed back, the smile wiped away for ever.
'Simon, I wasn't going to tell you just yet. I mean I was, but later this evening. I can't be a secretary. It's very kind of you all the same.'
'I don't understand. What do you mean?'
She took a deep breath, but her voice came out in a whisper.
'Yesterday,' she said, 'I went to see the editor of *The Chronicle* and he's agreed to take me on as a trainee journalist for a trial period of six months.'

He stared at her in disbelief.
'But Polly –'
'Starting next week,' she added.
All the joy seemed to drain out of him, in front of her eyes.
'But why did you suddenly do that?' he asked. 'What's gone wrong?'
'Nothing. I've always wanted to be a journalist.'
'But you never said.'
'No.'
'Polly, why didn't you tell me?'
'Well, I couldn't be sure they'd take me, could I?'
He shut his mouth hard and she saw the muscles working there as if he was fighting not to say something. Then he said in a curiously flat and controlled voice, 'No, you couldn't be sure. But you could have told me what you were hoping, so at least I'd have known it was a possibility. You could have been straight with me, not led me on the way you did.'
'It wasn't just you,' she said. 'I didn't tell anyone. Not Mam or Jim or anyone.'
'Yes, but then I know you don't get on very well with your mother and Jim seems pretty self-absorbed –'
'Lay off our Jim,' she said unexpectedly.
'All right. But what I mean is, you could have trusted me, even if nobody else.'
It was true, she realised, seeing it all suddenly from his point of view. It did seem like deception. It would have been sensible and honest to have told him right from the start. Why shouldn't she have trusted him? What made her think her own dreams so special? They were, after all, only plans like anybody else's. She could have trusted him with them. He cared for her, she knew that. Once people cared for her, she always let them down, one way or another.
Tears pricked her eyes.
They looked at each other miserably across the table. Then he got up slowly and came round to her. He stood behind her, his hands on her shoulders. He turned her round to face him.
'You could have trusted me, couldn't you, Polly?'
She nodded.
'You trusted me in other ways,' he said, his hands slipping down from her shoulders. 'You let me –' He stopped and held

her close and then slowly began to unbutton her blouse. 'You trusted me like this, and like this, didn't you?'

He carried her over to the big armchair.

'Didn't you?' he insisted and this time there was bitterness in his voice.

'Yes,' she said, holding him close. 'Don't be angry. Don't let's talk about it. Let's just pretend it's an ordinary Saturday night.'

'But we must talk about it. If you'd told me, I'd have helped you. I'm not your enemy.'

'I didn't want your help.'

She felt him flinch.

'If you care for someone,' he said, 'you shouldn't mind taking their help.'

'In little things yes, but not in something like this. I wanted to do it myself. *You* wouldn't have wanted me to help *you* get a job in your personnel department.'

'That's different. You're a girl.'

She drew away from him, incensed. The mood of a moment ago was quite lost. She was cross with herself too. What was she doing sitting here on his knee, naked to the waist, nothing on her bare breast except the beads he'd given her for Christmas? She wasn't in a very dignified position for arguing man to man, as it were. All the same, she did her best. She put her bra back on for a start.

'I know you wanted to help me, Simon,' she said in her most reasonable voice. 'But I don't want the sort of work you think I ought to have. I'd die of boredom being your secretary or anybody else's. I want to work in my own way. No, I mean I *have* to work in my own way. I'm sorry it doesn't fit in with your plans.' She paused as she struggled to get her blouse back over her shoulders and then went on. 'And honestly I don't think I'd really fit into a big organisation.'

She'd got one sleeve inside out and the blouse was twisted across her back. He watched her efforts, his mouth suddenly quivering with suppressed laughter. Already furious with herself for getting her clothes all knotted up, she lost her temper completely. 'I'm sorry if you think I'm ungrateful,' she said sarcastically. 'I realise you saw me as a poor little filing clerk whom you could help and promote. Only you picked the wrong little filing clerk, that's all.'

'Shut up, you stupid girl.'

For a moment, she thought he might hit her or chuck her off his knee. But he only went on angrily, 'I never, never thought of you like that. I've always thought of you as special and talented.'

'Yes, but talented in the way your business needed. Clever enough to take a certain amount of responsibility on behalf of somebody else, but not really doing things in my own right.'

'That's not true. If I'd known what your plans were I'd have helped you just the same. *The Chronicle* gets quite of bit of advertising from us. One of the directors is a friend of the proprietor. I might have been able to help things along a bit, pull a string or two.'

Her anger ebbed away. It was quite simple really. He had been brought up in a world where you expected to know the right people, who pulled strings on behalf of each other and of each other's friends and children. She had been brought up in a world where you didn't expect help, trusted nobody and used your fists if necessary. So they spoke a different language. There was no point in arguing.

Chapter 7

They had both the lights on in the reporters' room although it was not yet noon. Even so they could scarcely see to read. No light came in through the big sash windows against which the fog pressed like a dirty brown fleece. Last week it had at least swirled about, green and watery, but now the dense smoke of the town had mixed with it, thickening and darkening it into smog. Nor did it stay outside, but found its way in, under doors and round windows, so that the rooms and corridors were filled with the taste and smell of it, and it was almost as difficult to see inside the office as outside.

Fred, the foreman compositor who was good with electrics, had done an emergency conversion job on the single overhead light so that now two unshaded bulbs hung down, one at each end of the table, linked by various bakelite connections, festooned together with a looping length of flex and kept in place by two cup-hooks screwed into the ceiling. Polly had commandeered the anglepoise lamp and put it on a pile of books on her side of the table so that it shed its pool of light on to the shorthand notes she had taken at last night's performance of *Dear Octopus* by the Brigthorpe Thespians. Next to her, Randy, the other junior, two years older than she, was editing reports which had come in from local correspondents; every now and then he spluttered with laughter and read a piece out to them.

Meanwhile, at the other side of the table, Sid was reading copy to Jeff, who was peering at the proof, turning the paper to catch what light there was. Sid intoned the words flatly and without meaning, as they all did, so that it sounded like a religious incantation. At first she had found it distracting, this proof-reading that went on all the time, but now it didn't disturb her at all. It was just another background noise, like the traffic in the streets or the clattering of the typewriter.

Magnus Pratt, the chief reporter, was crashing away on the typewriter now, two-fingered but incredibly fast. They smashed down rhythmically, those two fingers, like pistons, and the letters leapt up in response, never jamming as they did when she used the machine. It was a second-hand Remington acquired last year. Magnus said that the editor had found it in an archeological dig at Coalbrookdale and it was certainly antique. But they all seemed to manage it better than she did, although she had been properly taught. She realised it was a disadvantage to have learned on a modern typewriter with two shift-locks and whose keys did not have to be thumped into action. But she was determined to keep up her typing and crashed away at it as hard as the rest of them whenever she got the chance.

Magnus looked up now, yawned and stretched.

'How about some tea, Polly?' he asked.

She got up willingly, glad of the excuse to rest her eyes from trying to decipher the pale strokes of shorthand. The corridor was very dark; as she groped for the light switch the wall was wet against her hand for the fog lay cold and damp on every surface. Then she realised that the light was already on and made her way slowly along the passage to the long narrow room, part kitchen, part cloakroom, part general store, which housed the sink and the gas-ring. Bales of old newspapers lined the walls and narrowed the doorway. She filled the kettle and lit the gas, washed up the thick white cups in the sink and stood, blowing on her fingers, trying to peer through the brown rectangle of glass which was the window.

It was strangely quiet this morning; the fuzzy beige fluffiness not only hid the sight of the traffic but also blanketed the sound of it, as it crawled slowly along the main road outside. Even the rattle of the trams was muffled. Dear old trams, how would they have got to work without them? The buses had been taken off. Odd that in all the arguments since the war about getting rid of the trams nobody had ever mentioned how safe they were in fog. Well, not in the *Brigthorpe Chronicle*, they hadn't.

For all its nastiness and the dirt of it, she couldn't really dislike the fog, she thought as the kettle began to boil. Somehow it combined with the gentle hissing of the steam and the warm smell of the gas flames to make the little room feel safe and cosy. There was something about the way it enclosed them in the office which reminded her of being cut off by the snow in the Dales' farmhouse of her childhood. She smiled to think how inept the comparison was, how utterly unlike this dirty old fog, that pure snow had been. Yet the feeling persisted: both had made her feel that her little citadel of happiness was protected from the outside world by nature's encircling arm.

For she was happy here, happy as she had never been in all her adult life. She shivered as she remembered the tedium of the shop and the awful boredom of filing and the pettiness and squabbles of office life. Here there was always laughter, a feeling of working together as equals and an excitement which built up as publication day approached. Though the others teased her and gave her all the odd jobs to do because she was the junior, they would patiently explain things to her, lend her a hand when she was stuck with a report or a heading and give up hours of their time to help her, even though they were all over-worked. They would come in at about nine or ten in the morning, work all day, go to meetings or functions in the evenings, spend all their Saturdays at fêtes or bazaars or race meetings or matches and their Sundays writing up reports. There was no question of working by the clock as she had before; she simply worked until she was too exhausted to go on. Everyone grumbled but in a good-humoured way; their loyalty to the paper was total.

She hadn't expected it to be so much fun. In fact she had been very nervous that first day as she walked towards the office, clutching her shorthand pad like a talisman, stepping out as jauntily as she could to show she wasn't scared. *The Brigthorpe Chronicle* presented an impressive façade to the High Street: above the massive portals its name was picked out in Old English lettering. It was much more awe-inspiring than the building society had been. So she was amazed that the atmosphere inside was so relaxed, with everyone on Christian name terms, except the editor. Even the building was more friendly than she had expected; it was only the front that was grand. Behind that the offices extended back from the High Street in a succession of passages and little rooms until they reached almost to the canal. The editor said that the reason his staff was so fit was that they took so much daily exercise by walking miles from one department to another.

James Dinsdale, the editor, wasn't at all as she had imagined either. When she heard the staff call him Sunny Jim, she thought that they were doing it out of sarcasm, remembering the thunderous expression on his face that first time she had come to see him. But she soon realised that had only been his Wednesday face. He wasn't too good on Thursday either. It was a pity that he had to pore over the paper, groaning at every printing error, talking grimly of readers' complaints being inevitable and even hinting that he might be sued, for he lived in dread of libel actions. But for the rest of the week he was, if sharp, nonetheless sweetness and light compared with, say, Miss Porter or the surpervisor of the typing pool.

All the same, she hadn't expected he would keep her on when her trial period came to an end after six months. That week, of all weeks, she had been guilty of the crime of causing a reader to complain. She had reported a wedding – only a small one, for Sid and Magnus did all the important ones – and had worked on it thoroughly, even going to see the bride's mother when it was all over to make sure she got every detail right. She had spent a long time writing it up, but when it came out the report stated that the bride wore a short veil belonging to her grandmother, and carried a bouquet of mixed flowers. Somehow the lines about the wedding dress got missed out and she hadn't noticed. Mrs Spittle, the bride's mother, stormed round to the office and said it was indecent, that *The Chronicle* had made her family a laughing stock, especially it being winter and all. Polly had apologised, but Mrs Spittle had insisted on seeing the editor, who had offered to print a full apology but pointed out that it would only draw attention to something others might not have noticed in the first place.

After the woman had gone, mollified but still muttering, Polly was sent for. She was sure he was going to say that what with one thing and another she couldn't stay on. Miserably she crawled up the stairs to his little room.

'Well, Polly,' he said. 'You can take good shorthand notes and make a decent cup of tea. I think we might make a reporter of you yet. If you want to stay on I'll put your salary up to £1 a week.'

She stared, unbelieving.

'But what about Mrs Spittle's daughter's wedding?'

He shrugged.

'Next time you're going to present a verbal picture of a bride naked except for a short veil and a bunch of flowers, don't do it in February, there's a dear,' was all he said. 'It conjures up such a fearful vision.'

So she was still here. And after three years still felt the excitement growing each week, never got over the fear that they wouldn't get the paper to bed on time, still felt the same thrill as she had done years ago as a child as she watched the great printing press in the basement rolling out the sheets of warm paper, still sniffed with pleasure the special smell down there, a mixture of ink and hot lead and leather aprons.

So she couldn't hate the fog which cocooned this little world, she thought as she ladled the tea out of the old wooden box that must have been there since the paper was established in 1858, poured the scalding water and carried the tea with the cups and the milk and sugar on a tin tray out into the damp and misty corridor.

The editor followed her into the reporters' room.

'More cancellations,' he said. 'Where's the Bible?'

Magnus pushed towards him the big desk diary which contained all the events of the week, each initialled with the name of whichever one of them the editor had decided must cover it. He took a rubber out of his pocket now and made some erasions.

'It's a funny thing,' he said, 'but whenever I come into this office Polly is occupied in making tea, drinking tea or removing cups of tea.'

'Would you like some?' she asked, unabashed.

'Yes, please. Bring one up to me, would you?'

He was his charming self again, the roarings of last Wednesday and the denunciations of Thursday quite forgotten – until next week.

'Thanks, Flinders,' he said, when she put the cup of tea on his desk. She paused, for he only used her nickname when he was feeling conversational. 'What are you busy on now?'

'My piece about *Dear Octopus*.'

'Ah, yes, let me see it when it's done. It's your first review on your own, isn't it? Coming along all right?'

'Well, it's a bit difficult. You see, I couldn't actually see them very well on the stage because it was all so misty with the fog and the cigarette smoke mixed in with it. Their voices seemed swallowed up, too, so I couldn't hear either.'

He waved all this aside.

'Never mind that, Flinders. Just plenty of praise and don't miss out a single person. Every name must be in the write-up. Not just all the cast, but everyone back-stage, front-stage, management, the lot. The golden rule to remember is that every name mentioned is an extra newspaper sold. Whatever the function, it's the names that matter. Were there refreshments?'

'Yes. They sold tea and coffee and biscuits upstairs in the interval.'

'Find out who organised that, who served, get every name in.'

'You don't think something about how the fog created difficulties –'

'No. That sounds like criticism.'

'But –'

'Keep to the names, there's a good girl. And make sure you spell them right. We'll make a reporter of you yet.'

'Oh, yes, I wanted to ask about that. Mr Dinsdale –'

'Yes?'

'You did say that after three years I could do the law courts on my own.'

'Did I? I meant perhaps the odd case. You keep going along with the others. I'll leave it to Magnus to decide when you're ready to tackle something on your own. He'll judge what's a suitable case for you to handle. You go by what Magnus says, there's a good lass. Now run along.'

Back in the reporters' room, Randy was triumphant. 'Look, Polly, the Juvenile Elocution Competition's been cancelled tonight. I was down for it. Yippee!'

'Not cancelled,' Sid pointed out. 'Just postponed.'

Randy shrugged.

'Maybe next time, somebody else will get it. Dammit, I did it last year. Fifty renderings of *The Boy stood on the Burning Deck*, I recall.'

'You're wrong,' Polly said. 'I did it last year, and it was six verses of the *Ancient Mariner*. Yours was the year before.'

'Really?' He shrugged. 'Shows what a scar it left,' he said.

'Polly, the tea tastes very odd. What have you put in it?'

'It's not the tea,' she explained. 'It's just that the fog gets into your mouth and makes things taste funny, like when you've got flu.'

'You haven't been trying to clean the teapot again?'

When she first came she had tried to scour the brown stains from the inside of the elderly tin teapot with some newly-invented detergent designed for cleaning drains. The brown had come off, but a curious taste had hung about the tea for days afterwards.

'No, I leave in a good layer of protective brown tannin now,' she said.

She studied the Bible.

'A terrible lot's been cancelled,' she said. 'However will we fill the paper?'

'Don't worry, there'll be more funerals and obituaries than usual. And you'll find when you do your hospital and fire brigade calls that there are many more accidents due to the fog.'

'Did you know,' asked Randy, 'that they stopped *La Traviata* in the middle of a performance in London last night? The fog was so thick in the theatre that the singers just couldn't go on.'

'How feeble!' Polly exclaimed. 'They didn't give up in *Dear Octopus* and I bet our fog is worse than in London.'

'You can't really expect Sadler's Wells to be governed by the same rules as Brigthorpe Thespians,' Randy objected.

'Oh yes she can,' Sid put in, emphasizing his Yorkshire accent. 'Our lot have got stamina, not like those softies down south. A bit of fog wouldn't stop opera singers up here. If we had any.'

'Spoken like a true Yorkshireman,' Magnus said, smiling. 'Years ago, Polly, a disaster was reported in a Yorkshire paper as "Earthquake kills two thousand people. No Yorkshiremen involved", or words to that effect.'

'Aye,' Sid said. 'I've heard that one before. But I've never understood why it's funny.'

He and Randy got back to their proof reading.

'Mr Harry Wills,' Sid intoned, 'brother of Mr T. Wills of Backhouse Lane, wrote home recently from his place of employment on a desert survey in East Africa that he had been taken to hospital for treatment for a tropical disease. Imagine his surprise when in casual conversation he discovered that his doctor was the great nephew of the late Theodore Samson who lived in Ward Street, Brigthorpe.'

Magnus glanced across at her.

'See what I mean, Polly?'

She nodded.

'Magnus,' she said, going across to him. 'About this review. Don't you think I might just put in a bit about the fog? You see, I think it could be quite a theme in the paper. Why don't we have an editorial about the need for a clean air act? We could campaign –'

'Because we're not a campaigning paper. And as for supporting laws to enforce clean air, what about all our readers who get free coal? Mucky, but free. That's where a lot of the pollution comes from. And the factories too. The editor knows better than to risk losing half his readers and a lot of advertisers.'

'To say nothing of our own beloved fire,' Sid cut in, looking up from the auction mart proofs he had been droning out to Randy.

They all looked at the sullen fire smoking away in the little black grate.

'Actually,' Magnus said, 'I doubt if much of that goes up the chimney. It's been blocked for years. The smoke just comes back into the room. Are you nearly ready to go, you two?'

'Half a minute and we're through this lot,' Sid said and began to gabble, 'There was a good show of three hundred and thirty-seven attested newly-carven cows and heifers. Cows made to ninety-eight guineas, heifers eighty-four guineas, young pigs seventy-eight shillings, strong pigs ten guineas, sows and gilts in pig twenty-four pounds ten shillings.'

'All right,' Polly was saying to Magnus, 'I'll just put in a little reference right at the beginning.'

Magnus smiled at her. 'You're a determined young woman, aren't you?'

'Well, it *is* news. It's what everyone's lives are being altered by this week, it's caused deaths, and it affected the production of the play I'm reviewing. We're supposed to be a newspaper and we jolly well ought to put the news in.'

'All right. Not more than two lines, though. I'll check the review for you when I get back. Sid and I are burying the alderman this afternoon.'

Sid looked at his watch. 'We'd better go and get a bite then,' he said. 'Can't bury the alderman on an empty stomach.'

'There'll be a good tea after, mind.'

'What about floral tributes? We'll never be able to read them.'

'We'll get a list from the verger. Thank goodness the new one can read.'

They got up. 'You coming, Randy?'

'Yes, then I'll go straight on to the council meeting. That hasn't been cancelled, more's the pity.'

'You're not coming, Polly?'

'No, I've got sandwiches.'

Actually it was only a penny bun that she had bought on the way to work this morning. Even on her increased wages of twenty-five shillings a week, she couldn't afford much food. Her mother had been so outraged when she started at *The Chronicle* that she had quite expected to be turned out of the house.

'I can't get over you, Polly,' she kept saying. 'Leaving a well-paid job like you've got now, to go and work on a newspaper for almost nothing.'

'When Sid and Magnus started,' Polly had told her, 'they had to pay for the privilege of being trained. They think I'm lucky to get twelve and six.'

'But why do you need to be trained? You could stay where you are at the building society.'

She could have replied that Jim wouldn't be earning anything for years and her mother didn't object to that; indeed she was proud of him. But she knew that her mother would only say it was different for Jim; he was a boy. Besides, she couldn't drag Jim into it somehow. She was proud of him, too. Anyway, she mustn't quarrel with her mother. She couldn't afford to live anywhere else. She must just stick it out at home. Eventually they agreed that she would pay just for her room and heating and get her own meals out, which suited her as she usually had evening engagements and wouldn't have gone home for lunch anyway.

They co-habited, her mother and she, because it was mutually convenient, but they lived like strangers. They shared nothing of each other's lives, they would never be close. Only when Jim came home from college was there any laughter or argument in the house, and even then Polly felt that it was a kind of act they were putting on for his sake, like an unhappily married couple keeping up a pretence in front of the children.

She managed to add to her wages an extra sixpence or shilling a week in expenses, by charging up a bus fare and then walking to wherever the engagement was, or putting down for soup and a sandwich at the agricultural show while actually only eating a bun and going away ravenous. But she never for one moment regretted the choice she had made. She knew that she would put up with any hardship rather than give up her present ill-paid job, for she was a different person here, easy and trusting, quite unlike the tense and prickly girl she could feel herself turn into the minute she entered her mother's house and stepped back into the past.

Simon came back often at first, as he had promised, even though she worked at weekends and sometimes hardly saw him.

'It's a waste of your time and money,' she had pointed out on his last visit. 'Coming all the way, just to take me out to dinner.'

'No, it's not,' he had told her. 'Anyway, it's my time and money and I shall spend it as I like.' He grinned at her. 'Besides, it's the only way I can be sure you get a decent meal once in a while. Don't tell me you don't enjoy it.'

She had to admit that it was true, she thought as she tucked into the cutlets. It was lovely to be taken out to an expensive restaurant and fed with rich food. Being spoiled and pampered was nice. Of course there was no future in it, but on the other hand there was no particular reason to stop him coming if he wanted to. Besides, it was useful to be able to refer vaguely in the office to a boyfriend. It helped to keep Randy at bay. Randy was funny, unconventional, not particularly clean and liable to make sudden and unpredictable assaults on her if they were left alone together. She didn't take him seriously, but laughing at him only seemed to make him worse. Mockery stimulated Randy. It was safer to refer in a staid kind of way to her boyfriend from London.

'I'm organising a new canteen for the staff,' Simon said as the waiter ladled fruit salad out of a cut-glass bowl on to their plates and then poured cream over it. 'It's good that they should get together socially, people of different levels of responsibility. But I had a hard time convincing the board. To me it's quite obvious that a happy staff will be more efficient and productive.'

'Really, whatever you say, it's all about profits, isn't it?'

'What's wrong with that? Newspapers have to make profits too.'

'Yes, but it's not what they're *for*. They're not just about money. They're about people.'

'We're in business to help people too, Polly. People need to borrow money to buy houses. Others need to lend money to invest their savings.'

'I know all that, Simon. But the everyday work in your office isn't concerned with it. Don't you see? On *The Chronicle* it's about people all the time, not just the way we all work together, but being involved with our readers and –'

'I want to get our staff involved in the same way, Polly. I'm starting a house magazine to keep all the staff, however, junior, informed and involved. Involvement, that's the keynote in personnel work. I worry about it a great deal.'

Across the white table linen, the shiny cutlery, the sparkling cut-glass, she observed that his face was plumper.

'It suits you,' she remarked, 'all this worrying about personnel.'

He began to object, but then burst out laughing instead.

'Oh, Polly,' he said, leaning across the table and taking her hand, 'you're so good for me. I wish you'd marry me.'

'Why am I good for you? Because I've said you look well on it?'

'No. Because you see things clearly. You're so honest. You're a natural debunker.' He sighed. 'You know, when I look at some of my business colleagues, and listen to them, I have to admit that pomposity is an occupational hazard.'

'Go on, you'd never get pompous.'

'Not with you around, I wouldn't. Do you want some cheese?'

'What, *as well* as pudding?'

'It's allowed.'

'Yes please, then.'

'You've lost weight since I saw you last time,' Simon said after the waiter had departed, leaving the cheeseboard behind. Busy with the Stilton, she did not reply.

'It worries me, Polly,' he persisted. 'I really do hate leaving you up here.'

'But I belong here.'

'It's not that. I mean, I've got nothing against the north, but –'

'Oh, yes you have. You're just like all southerners. You come up here, have a look round, are surprised it's not as bad as you expected, amazed to find the natives are friendly, then you're jolly glad to get back home safely to London.'

'That's not true. If you only knew how sick at heart I feel when I leave you to go back on a Sunday evening.' He shrugged. 'But there, it's you I want to talk about, not me. If you've finished, I'll order coffee, then I want you to tell me your plans.'

'Plans?'

'Yes. Plans about your work. I mean what are you aiming at now? You must have some rough idea of what you want to move on to after, say two or three years training on *The Chronicle*?'

'I don't know,' she said, suddenly wary.

'There would be so many more openings for you in London. For instance, how about editing our house magazine . . . All right,' he corrected himself hastily, 'I can see that idea doesn't appeal. But think of all the national papers there'd be to work on, as well as the local ones. There are women's pages in the national dailies – I think there'll be much more work around for women journalists soon.'

'What makes you think,' she demanded, 'that I want to write for a women's page?'

'Well, of course I don't know,' he said. 'I'm just throwing out ideas. If you won't tell me what you're aiming at, then obviously I don't know the best way to help you.'

'How can I make you understand,' she burst out, 'that I don't want your help?'

He bit his lip. 'I'm sorry.'

She didn't reply. They sat in silence, her angry words ringing in their ears. Then he said quietly, 'I really did want to talk to you this weekend, Polly. Properly, I mean. About us. And about your plans. I haven't made a very good start, have I?'

'Not very.'

He reached out and took her hand. 'You know, sometimes in London I feel I can only keep going because I'll see you at the weekend. Can't we talk about it calmly? Let's start again. I'll get them to take the coffee into the snug.'

It was a little room with an open fire, off the main lounge. During the week it was full of commercial travellers, but at the weekend it was often empty. They had it to themselves. He pulled their chairs up close to the fire and she poured out the coffee.

'I have learned, you know,' he said humbly. 'Truly I have. I do understand that you want to make your own way. But it seems to me that you're proved that now. You can stop fighting, you needn't be so afraid of sharing your plans. If we got married I promise you I would never try to interfere in your career in any way.'

'You wouldn't be able to help yourself. Management is part of your make-up.'

'Not managing you, Polly,' he said, shaking his head. '*Helping* you maybe, if I could, but that's different.'

'I can't get through to you, can I?' she burst out again. 'I can't make you see that I don't want your help.'

He stared at her, aghast. With her green eyes narrowed with rage and all that red hair, she looked so like an angry ginger cat that he quite expected her to hiss and spit. He waited, watching until she was calmer, then said thoughtfully, 'Are you like this at work? Won't you let anyone help you there either?'

'That's different, you know it is. They've taught me everything I know. Right from the start they've all helped me.'

'So you'll let strangers help you, but not me?'

'I've told you, it's different at work. It's something between equals and nobody is put under an obligation to anyone else.'

'All right, it's a different sort of help. But I still don't see why you can't accept my sort of help, the help of someone who loves you.'

She shook her head. She couldn't explain. She had always done the helping; from being tiny she had been the one who managed, somehow or other. There had been nobody to turn to for help, not when she was little and desperate. She had had to decide everything on her own, any old how, without plans or discussion or even knowing the facts, without anything really except an instinct to survive and see that Jimmy did too.

'I suppose I never got into the habit of being helped,' she said awkwardly.

'It can be learned, Polly, if you love someone. I mean you can learn to accept from them.'

She shook her head again. She didn't want to learn acceptance. In fact learning to depend on somebody was just about the last thing in the world that she wanted to do. But she'd never be able to explain that to Simon; he'd been brought up too soft. Besides, it was too hard to put into words. She just knew that she must never again be made to feel as helpless and despairing as she had as a child, and that was what happened if you weren't independent enough. You got let down.

'You can't be invulnerable, Polly, nobody can,' he said as if reading her thoughts. 'Human beings need one another. You're trying to suppress a part of you.'

'I'm not, I'm not,' she protested, but her voice was high and childish.

'And I'm afraid for you. Please believe me.'

He had taken both her hands in his and as he pleaded with her his face was suddenly naked and vulnerable. Something in her seemed to reach out to him, her anger beginning to melt away.

The door opened suddenly and a man came in carrying a coal bucket.

He paused, embarrassed, then crossed over to the fireplace and got busy with the shovel. Simon didn't move, just turned his face away. It was Polly who was able to smile, make a few light remarks and thank the man as he banked up the fire.

When he had gone, she said in the same casual voice she had used to the stranger, 'Well, Simon, after all these home-truths and this heart-searching, how about another cup of coffee? Then I must be going.'

He covered his face with his hands. 'Oh, damn, damn, damn,' he said.

She felt curiously calm yet elated, as if she had won a victory over herself and was stronger for it. She remembered how she had rejected Miss Capstick's blandishments, resisted the temptation to soften and give in. That was how she felt now as she sat and watched Simon, cradling his head in his hands while she was quite cool and detached. She had been stupid, she realised now, to accept so much from him. She had let him spoil her, let him put her under an obligation to him so that he felt he had the right to say these things to her, things she didn't want to hear, would not hear. That's what happened if you grew dependent on people; they waited until you relaxed your guard, then they struck.

He looked up. 'We can't talk properly here,' he said, 'with people coming in and out all the time. Let's go up to my room.'

'What, waste this lovely fire?' she asked, laughing. 'Besides, only one person's come in and he won't be back. It isn't exactly King's Cross Station, in here, is it?'

'Oh, don't be so hard, Polly. It isn't you.'

She looked at him sharply.

'That's what I meant about being afraid for you,' he went on. 'You pretend to be hard but it's not the real you. You're spoiling yourself. In the end it will weaken you, because it's a sort of false shell, the sort that cracks under stress.'

'I don't see why you think it's your responsibility,' she said.

'Because I love you, and because I can see through this hardness, but other people might not. They could take you at your face value and think you're harder than you are. Then you'd get hurt.'

He was talking disjointedly now as he reached out towards her, tried to take her hands. 'We've been so close, you and I. We know each other's needs, we don't have to pretend. I think you need to get married soon, it's your nature. All right, I'm not saying it should be to me. I'm just afraid that on some impulse you'll rush into marrying the wrong person, or having an affair, because you *are* impetuous and –'

'How dare you talk to me like this? You think you can preach at me just because you come up here and take me out for meals and spoil me. Well, it's finished, this princely act of yours. I don't want you to come up here ever again. I can do without your charity.'

'Polly, you don't mean that! You've enjoyed being with me, haven't you?'

'Of course I have, I'm not denying it, but how'd you like it if it was the other way round and I came down to see you and took you out and then pontificated about your career and your needs?'

He shook his head, baffled by her. 'But I'm not pontificating.'

'Yes, you are, Anyway, let's look at your needs, shall we? You're nearly thirty now and needing to marry, aren't you? What you want is a nice little wife to look after you and support you in your career and have children quickly, because you're getting on a bit. And you want to fit me into this pattern, don't you? I would be very convenient for you. That's why you want me to think I can further my career in London and –'

'Stop it. I wasn't thinking of myself. Can't you trust anyone, Polly?'

She stared at him.

'Can't you?' he repeated. 'Can't you believe you are loved for your own sake?'

No, she realised, I can't believe that. I never was loved and I never shall be. But I won't care. I'll show them all that I don't care. I'll manage on my own.

She felt tears in her eyes. She knew she must not let herself think about it. The past was a dark and dreadful pit that she must not look into. She must not look at Simon either. It was work which would save her; work was her strength and refuge. He was a threat to it and must be got rid of. She was seeing it all clearly at last. She must just get up and say, 'Thank you for this evening, and for all the other evenings. I hope that all goes well, with the house magazine and the new canteen and everything.'

He reached out to stop her, tried to take her hand, but she ignored him and walked to the door, out into the lounge where all the people were. He was too conventional to make a scene there, she knew that. Instead he fetched her coat and called a taxi for her. She let him pay for it but would not let him come with her, afraid that she would weaken. The last she saw of him was his stricken face peering in at her through the window as he stooped to close the taxi door behind her. He was trying to say something, she could see him mouthing the words, but he was soon lost in the mist which swirled about him as the taxi pulled cautiously away. The fog had set in early that year, too.

Chapter 8

The noise of pneumatic drills filled the reporters' room and the table vibrated as she worked. In the street outside, the tramlines were being taken up.

Magnus came in. 'Phew, it's hot in here,' he said. 'I thought Randy got that window open this morning?'

'We shut it to keep the sound out,' Polly told him.

'Well, you didn't succeed, did you?' Magnus remarked as he opened the Bible and began rubbing out initials.

'I saw that,' Polly said, and grinned at him. 'Don't you dare write me in for something you don't want.'

'All above board, Polly,' he said, sitting down next to her and reaching for a pile of reports from local correspondents. 'Sunny Jim wants me to go on Friday to a funeral of a former resident of Brigthorpe.'

She laughed. 'But you spend half your time, you and Sid, going to funerals.'

'Ah, but this is different. It's far away. Sad, really – a chap called Tudor Bean. His family came from here, evidently, but I knew him much later when we were both assistant editors on *The Broughton Guardian*. A dear fellow, he was. Eccentric, but very talented. Suddenly he upped sticks and went off to the country to start a magazine. And of all times, just before the war. We didn't think he'd a hope of succeeding. It was an impossible time to start that kind of project, but he made a go of it. Been a great success. And now after fifteen years of toil – what is it, Polly?'

She couldn't answer. She was back in the ramshackle house, books and papers everywhere, the ceiling bulging overhead, Tudor kindly and philosophical, printing her article, telling her she could be a journalist one day, proposing the utterly impossible as if it was easily within the grasp of an evacuee child from the slums, without an examination pass to her name, the despair of everyone who had to deal with her.

She owed everything to him and she'd never thanked him, never even written. Now it was too late.

'Polly, love, what have I said? I've upset you. What is it?'

'I knew him,' she managed to say.

'Really? Up there in Sidgewick?'

She nodded. She had never spoken of her past at the office. Nobody had pressed her. Suddenly she needed to tell Magnus.

'I was evacuated there,' she said. 'And after a while I was put in a house with two old ladies. The Beans lived next door. I used to go round with eggs and then I helped with odd jobs like wheeling the magazine down to the post office and sticking on stamps. She was lovely too, Mrs Bean, very vague and artistic. She let us mess about. I'd never known people like that. It was Tudor who –' Her voice broke. She covered her face with her hands and, sitting there at the table, began to cry.

Magnus came and put his arms around her. She leant against him. 'I cut myself off from them all – I never even thanked him.'

He held her to him. 'It's all right, Polly. Tudor wasn't the sort who noticed if you thanked him or not. I knew him too, remember.'

She grew calmer as they talked about him. It was wonderfully comforting that Magnus knew him, too. He sat there telling her stories about Tudor when they were working on the same newspaper and soon she was telling him about the day the ceiling nearly fell down, laughing and crying at the same time.

The door opened. Randy came in and stopped, taken aback by the sight of them.

'Right, my lad,' Magnus said, 'this time you're going to make the tea. Run along now and put the kettle on. And make sure Flinders has the best cup – the one without the crack.'

Next day the editor asked her to go up and see him.

'Shut the door, Flinders,' he said. 'I want a chat.'

Surprised, she tried desperately to remember what she'd done wrong.

'I had a talk with Magnus last night,' James Dinsdale began. 'As you know I want a really good article on this fellow Tudor Bean. He's a son of Brigthorpe, even if he did leave when he was six months old. Furthermore, he's a newspaper man, one of us. Finally, he did an unusual thing with that magazine.'

She nodded. 'Yes,' she said. 'Magnus did tell me he was going to write about him.'

He hesitated, then he said, 'We think you should do the article. Can you get up there for the funeral on Friday? I'll make sure you're free. You could stay up over the weekend and research him, then write him up. Plenty of time for next Thursday's paper.'

She was stunned.

'But Magnus could do it better, Mr Dinsdale. I mean that's all that matters. I couldn't do it as well as Magnus.'

'It was his idea,' the editor told her. 'It was Magnus who persuaded me, actually. He said it would be your way of saying thank you to the man.'

She was astonished at how short the journey was; sixteen years ago it had seemed endless. She remembered the delays, the shunting backwards and forwards, the sense of being lost, of being moved about like a parcel, of not belonging. Even as she sat here in the corner of the empty compartment, outwardly calm in control of her own life, she could feel again the bewilderment she had felt then.

Soon she was travelling out of the town, through the sidings and warehouses and the little back gardens with their lines of sooty washing, and into the open countryside. She gazed at the green fields, dotted with grey boulders and with sheep which looked up from their grazing as the train passed by, their jaws pausing momentarily before returning to their rhythmic chewing. She watched the telegraph poles slip by, the wires going up and down, up and down. How peaceful it all was, how friendly, she thought, yet every now and then she felt a sudden unexpected pang of fear as her old childhood dread returned with its sense of loss and bewilderment and anxiety for Jimmy. Then involuntarily she would move her hand as if to take hold of his.

When she reached her destination the station looked smaller than she remembered, and the hills not so high. The grey stone walls too were less forbidding as the bus rattled into the village.

She had already rung the post office the day before to enquire about lodgings, so Mrs Patmore was expecting her. She had promised to arrange somewhere for Polly to stay. Quite a few people in the village took in paying guests now, she had said.

'Oh, there you are,' she greeted her now, as if Polly had never been away. She looked just the same as she stood there stolidly behind her counter, her hair rolled up round a black ribbon band as it had always been, after the fashion of her youth, her plump little hands resting on the polished wood. Polly glanced surreptitiously down at them. The mole was still there and it still looked as if it might roll off at any moment.

'You haven't changed a bit,' Mrs Patmore said. 'It seems like yesterday you used to come in with Mrs Bean and all those envelopes. Oh, we had good times in them days, didn't we?'

Polly was surprised. Mrs Patmore had usually been pretty grumpy when they brought in the envelopes. Presumably hostility towards Tudor had diminished as he became more successful and would be changed to reverence now that he had died.

'Well now, Polly, Miss Emily came in just after you rang and when I told her you were coming, she wouldn't hear of you going anywhere else to stay in lodgings. She said your old room was waiting for you whenever you wanted it. The bed's made up.'

'Oh.'

She couldn't think of anything to say. They didn't have to offer. They actually wanted her back, awful though she'd been.

'I'll be off then,' she managed to say. 'I expect I'll see you before I go, Mrs Patmore.'

The sun was shining. She stood blinking for a moment, for it was always dark in the post office. She had forgotten how quiet the village was. She had forgotten, too, how clean and fresh everything looked. Nothing had changed. She could remember each house, the different grey stones of them and the higgledy-piggledy way the roofs fitted together under their stone tiles. Even the bushes in the gardens were the same. The great tree by the church had not changed either, its branches still reaching out to cast the same shadows on the road, which divided here to encircle the village green. In the evening it would be noisy with birds, this evening as in the summer evenings of her childhood.

She had forgotten how fresh the air up here was; it was sharp against her cheeks, despite the sunshine. She breathed deeply as she passed the village hall where they had been auctioned that first evening. Again her hand seemed to reach down of its own accord as if to comfort that other small, frightened child.

There was nobody in the high street and when she reached the school the yard was deserted, the children all indoors. She paused by the gate, listening to the chanting sounds – tables, perhaps, or the words of next week's hymn – that issued from the tall windows. She remembered the feel of the ropes in her fingers when she was told to pull on them to open those windows which were too high to look out of. But from one corner you could just make out the distant hills. She remembered staring at them while Miss Capstick talked to her. Why had she been so obstinate, why? She would talk it over with Miss Capstick, accept now the help which she had refused then, she thought as she opened the gate and hurried up the flag-stone path to the porch.

Miss Emily came to the door. She too was unchanged. She gave Polly her old familiar look: disapproval masked by good manners. Polly felt herself grow ten years younger, turn clumsy and untidy under that assessing stare, and didn't know what to say.

'Mrs Patmore told me – I mean, it's very kind of you –' she began awkwardly, suddenly resenting having to be grateful and wishing she was paying to stay in lodgings elsewhere.

Miss Emily pecked her on the cheek. 'I'm very glad you've come back to pay your respects to Mr Bean,' she said. 'He was always very kind to you, you know.'

It was the simple truth, but Miss Emily turned it into a reproach.

She led the way into the hall. The same cool, brown and cream hall, though a bit smaller than it had been.

'You could have come back any time, you know. Now go upstairs and leave your case and I'll make a cup of tea.'

She disappeared towards the kitchen. Polly crossed the hall, her heart quickening as she approached the little bookcase which still hung in the alcove. The books were slightly loose on the shelf still. Slowly she went upstairs, her hand trailing along the banister, following the familiar curve of the polished wood until she reached the landing where once she had watched a bonfire burning. The bedroom door was open. Nothing had changed. She walked about the room, touching the blue and purple bedspread, resting her hand on the marble washstand. The curtains moved gently in the breeze. She hoped Miss Emily would take herself off so that she could talk to Miss Capstick. Or perhaps they could have a walk together after the funeral. She took a deep breath. She would tell Miss Capstick about the book. It would be a kind of atonement. Miss Capstick would understand. It would take the sharp edge off her ingratitude. Serpent's tooth, that's just what it had been.

'I always think a cup of tea is what you need after a journey,' Miss Emily said as she poured it out. 'We'll have supper later. How was the journey, Polly?'

'It seemed so short,' Polly said, laughing. 'Do you know, I remembered it as lasting all day when I was little.'

'Well, wartime journeys were very slow, Polly. But now that you've discovered it isn't too far you'll perhaps be able to come back more often than once every ten years.'

She said it with a laugh, but there was that edge of reproach in her voice all the same.

'I'm sorry I haven't been before,' Polly said. 'I really did think it was a very long way – Sidgewick was like a different world really.'

'It would have been nice to keep in touch all the same.'

'Yes, I should have gone on writing. I meant to.'

'Well, you did write twice. You wrote good letters. I think my cousin appreciated them. I found them amongst her things.'

The tea in her mouth turned bitter. It was difficult to swallow. She almost choked.

'She's not – You don't mean Miss Capstick has –'

Miss Emily looked at her in surprise.

'Surely you knew that my cousin had passed on?'

She shook her head.

'I'm sorry, Polly. I should have told you sooner.'

She did sound genuinely sorry, but whether it was for wounding Polly or merely for committing a social solecism, it was impossible to tell.

'I just assumed you knew. Because you knew about Mr Bean, I assumed you knew about my cousin.'

'It was only through work that I knew about Mr Bean,' Polly managed to say. She struggled to get a grip on herself, say what was expected of her. She could not find the appropriate words any more than she had been able to find them for Mrs Biddle when her own father died. She could only picture Miss Capstick as she stood in the schoolroom, hear her voice saying, 'But I would help you, if you would let me.'

'It was only this spring,' Miss Emily went on, 'that she died.'

'You must miss her.'

'Yes.'

It was a statement of fact.

'It was quite sudden. Not like poor Mr Bean who dragged on.'

'No. I'm glad it didn't, I mean she didn't –'

Her voice trailed away. They sat staring out of the window across the village street, not seeing it.

'Well,' Miss Emily said, and Polly could feel the effort she was making to pull herself together. 'As I say, she did appreciate your letters, Polly.'

'I wish I'd written more.'

'It was a strange thing. I found them in a large envelope which contained something quite extraordinary: a copy of Dickens' *Great Expectations*.'

Polly stared at her.

'When I say extraordinary I mean the state it was in. It was all burnt and charred at the edges. She had wrapped it in a big linen handkerchief and kept it with your two letters. Can you imagine why?'

115

Polly shook her head and didn't reply. There were only two people she could have told, and they were both dead.

The church was packed for the funeral. Journalists and other visitors outnumbered the villagers. Afterwards they all walked behind the coffin up to the cemetery, the outsiders somewhat ill at ease, uncertain of village procedures.

Mrs Bean was calm. She seemed much older, the long dark hair streaked with grey, but she spoke to everyone, presided over the funeral tea as if grief had subdued the confusion that usually prevailed in her.

For she was desolate, Polly knew. She saw it in the bruised, hurt look in the gentle, deep-set eyes which once used to watch Tudor so anxiously; in the drawn look of the careworn face, however calm it now seemed. Afterwards Mrs Bean refused all offers of help, but let Polly stay.

'I don't mind you somehow,' she said, as they washed up cups and saucers and plates in the old stone sink in the scullery where once they used to wash out their paintbrushes. 'I can talk to you. I don't know why. I suppose it's because I still think of you as a child and you can tell things to children. Children don't seem to count somehow. And, after all, as far as Tudor is concerned, you are still a child. Always will be now.'

'What will you do? Will you carry on with the magazine?'

Mrs Bean shook her head. 'No.'

'Don't you want to? I mean you both loved it.'

'No. He loved it and I loved it because he did. I didn't love it for itself.'

'But after all those hard years. Couldn't you give it a try?'

'No. While he was ill we were approached by a big group. They want to buy it now. They might change their minds if I delay.'

There was a pause.

'You don't approve, do you, Polly?'

She sighed. 'I don't know. It isn't for me to approve or disapprove. It's just that I thought you would keep it going. I suppose it's because it was part of my childhood. Selfish of me, really.'

'It would be silly you see, Polly, to think I could keep it

alive. You can't do things like that. When a mould is broken, it's broken. I shall try to paint again. Maybe I'll move to a smaller house, have a studio. I don't need much. I'll stay here for a while.'

'Won't they want the house for an office?'

'No, they'll move all the publishing into their main office in London. It will be merged with their other magazines.'

Polly shivered. All its individuality would be lost.

'It would have lost its character anyway,' Mrs Bean said gently, reading her thoughts, 'with Tudor gone.'

'Yes.'

'We have to accept the inevitable. There is no other option.'

There was a ring at the door bell. Mrs Bean pulled a face. 'That's the relations back,' she said. 'They took a walk up to the grave to look at the flowers.'

'I'll go out the back way,' Polly said. 'If that's all right.'

'Do. We went on cutting "Polly's Way" in case you came back,' Mrs Bean said, as she went to let in the relations.

She slipped out by the back door, as she had so often done, and crossed the yard into the paddock. The grass was long, uncut except for the path which bore her name. She walked down it, the hay brushing against her skirt, sweet-smelling. Oh, how that smell brought back the summers of her childhood. She stood, overwhelmed by the sweetness and pain of it. On those gentle summer evenings how often had she walked back tired but somehow calmed and contented by her day's work, almost at one with herself and her surroundings. Yet even as she had walked across the paddock anxiety used to return, the feeling of unease, of not knowing what would happen to them, that nothing was safe or permanent and that anyway she would soon be at odds again with everybody and everything and that it was all her own fault. Now, after all these years, she felt again the same confusion, except that the pain and anxiety were still pressing and real, but the feeling of contentment belonged only to the past and was anyway embittered now by regret.

She made herself go on across the paddock, over the corner of the field, through the gap in the fence and into the Capsticks' back garden. The door was open. Once inside the kitchen she turned, for it was time to lock up, and instinctively reached up towards the bolt.

A man had appeared by the back door. She recognised him immediately.

'Are you going to lock me out again, Polly?' Captain Quigley asked.

Chapter 9

'Come to think of it, Polly,' Randy said, 'that article on Tudor Bean did you quite a bit of good.'

She nodded, without replying. It was a typical Randy remark; what he said was true, but there was something about the way he phrased it which made it highly objectionable, and somehow lessened the truth of it.

'I mean the fact that he died when he did, when he'd become not exactly a national figure but at least well-known in the publishing world, meant that there was quite a bit of interest in him. On the other hand, he wasn't well enough known for them all to have their stuff prepared in case he died. So when they all wanted copy in a great rush and you were there with an article that was spotted straight away it was your chance to corner the Bean market, as it were.'

Magnus put his head round the door. His eyes and nose were red, the rest of his face very pale.

'I've checked the last page,' he croaked, 'and it looks all right. Fred can manage now with the lad to help him deal with the formes. The other two comps can go home. We should be ready for the press in about an hour – I'd go down and see Fred just before that, anyway by nine o'clock. Are you sure you can manage, you two?'

'Quite sure, Magnus,' she said. 'Do go off home. You look awful.'

'I feel awful. I probably won't come in tomorrow.'

'Good,' Randy put in. 'Then if we make a mess of things tonight at least you won't be here to know about it.'

'Oh, Randy, for goodness' sake,' Polly interrupted. 'Of course we shan't make a mess of it. Please don't worry, Magnus. Just go home and get to bed. Forget all about the paper.'

'Thanks, Polly.'

After he had gone, Polly turned on Randy, exasperated. 'Honestly,' she said, 'why go raising doubts in his mind? You could see he was worried about leaving just the two of us in charge.'

'Well, it's so stupid. We're just as capable of putting the paper to bed as he or the others. In fact I reckon we're better at proof-reading than the oldies.'

'All the same, you know how he worries. It is the most important night of the week and if anything unexpected happened, we wouldn't know how to cope.'

'What could happen? Even if war broke out at this stage of the evening we wouldn't be expected to mention it. Especially if it was only something global like a war between Russia and America. Of course, if it was something really important like a riot in Brigthorpe High Street then we might have to change the front page.'

She laughed. 'You're right, I suppose. All the same it's the first time they've trusted us and we're jolly well going to show them. Let's try to make sure there isn't a single mistake for Mr Dinsdale to have convulsions over tomorrow morning.'

'Oh, he'll be in a rage anyway.'

'Do *you* know why he gets in such a state, Randy?'

Randy's thin, bony face turned thoughtful, the deep-set brown eyes speculative. 'I have a theory,' he began slowly, 'that it's because he came to Brigthorpe via Fleet Street. In his mind, he's still working there so when he opens the paper on Thursday a bit of him hopes it will be *The Times* and when he finds it's still the same old *Brigthorpe Chronicle* he's furious.'

Polly burst out laughing. 'I always thought you were mad,' she said.

'All right. How do *you* explain it?'

She shook her head. 'I don't know,' she said. Then she

went on thoughtfully, 'Perhaps it's something to do with aiming high and feeling let-down. The first thing I had published was an article I'd written at school. I was so thrilled and thought it was something special but when I saw it in print, I realised it was quite ordinary. I was bitterly disappointed with myself. Maybe that's how poor Mr Dinsdale feels every week. Frustrated, and angry with himself more than us really.'

'Just what I said a moment ago and got called mad for my pains.'

'Nonsense. You exaggerated. Besides, I think it must be a lot more fun working on a local paper than in London.'

'It's certainly better for training. Isn't that why you came?' Polly shook her head. 'I'd no choice,' she said.

'Oh, I had. But everyone who knew about it said it was best to get on to a small local paper. You see, you do everything here. On a big paper everything's specialised. Here we do the lot, from writing headlines to proof-reading, re-wording advertisements and re-writing all those awful reports from local correspondents.'

'To say nothing of going to funerals and weddings and chivvying the Fire Brigade.'

'And, God forgive us, the bereaved.'

'Yes. I almost refused at first. It just seemed so awful to go and call on some stranger whose husband or wife or whatever had just died. And then I went and found they welcomed me, wanted to talk to me.'

'That's what I mean, Polly. If you hadn't worked on a local paper like this, you would think it was an intrusion, but we know, you and I, that they're delighted to talk about the dear departed.'

'It's strange, all the same. I'm sure I wouldn't want to. And the way they insist on taking you to see the body, too.'

Randy pulled a face. 'I try to get out of that bit. I always remember a pressing engagement when they start showing me the way upstairs.'

'They mostly look as if they're asleep,' Polly said.

'Let's not get morbid, not as night approaches. Let's think of something funny. Did I ever tell you about the time, about a year before you came, when I had to go to see that woman whose husband had had a very narrow escape when the steam roller nearly squashed him against the wall?'

'No, but I remember reading about it. Missed him by something like an inch, didn't it?'

'That's right. Well, when I called round the next morning, I knocked on the back door and she opened it and she hadn't a stitch on. Nothing! There was just this huge, pink lady standing there.'

'What did she say?'

'That's what was so odd. She didn't seem to notice. She just said, "Oh, I thought it was the milk", then I went in and she put something round herself and we talked about the accident.'

'Maybe she thinks the press are blind, like love and justice.'

'Or just don't count, like doctors?'

'Like Mr Spratt. Did I ever tell you about Mr Spratt?'

'Who's he when he's at home, Polly?'

'I was talking to his wife. What was it about? Oh, yes the daughter, Susan. She'd won this drama prize and Mum was very proud. In the middle, Father, who was working nights, came downstairs and joined us. And, Randy, all he had on was this very short vest. It came to where his waist might once have been. I thought he was just very absent-minded and that his wife would die of embarrassment because I was there, but she didn't bat an eyelid – just went on talking about Our Susan.'

'And what did you do?'

'What could I do? I just kept trying not to look for the rest of the interview.'

Randy laughed, 'Oh, but we see life on the *Brigthorpe Chronicle*, don't we, Flinders?'

'Time we went to see Fred, too,' she remarked, getting up and stretching.

'And his unfortunate new assistant,' Randy added, following her out into the corridor.

She shook her head. She was sorry for the new lad. He was very strong but appallingly clumsy. Fred, usually sweet-natured, was forever on at him and really only made him worse with his nagging. They could hear him shouting now as they went down to the basement which housed the press.

'Now for that last forme on the trolley,' he was saying impatiently. 'Don't push it by yourself. Wait! You'll never manage it like that.'

'Oh, I'm strong, Mr Fred, Sir,' the lad assured him.

They were approaching the doorway, Randy just behind her. Afterwards she remembered it all vividly. It was suddenly very quiet in the corridor – there was always something still about the air in those subterranean passageways – so she heard the first little warning sound like a twig cracking underfoot. It was followed by a terrible crash then a prolonged, slithering kind of clatter which seemed to go on and on. It was the sound of hailstones rattling down on to a tin roof, or pebbles on a beach stirred and pounded by ceaseless waves. It was the sound a lorry-load of gravel makes when it is tipped on to concrete. Except that it was a metallic sound that it made, the sound of Brigthorpe's news disintegrating. It was the sound of thousands and thousands of little lead letters which had been painstakingly arranged into words and sentences, into paragraphs and columns, which had all been checked and corrected. Those fiddly little characters had been picked up by tweezers or eased into place by Fred's fingers with endless patience and much spit. And in a few seconds it was all undone.

Polly didn't want to see it. She couldn't, anyway. She realised that she had instinctively covered her face with her hands. Slowly, she forced herself to look.

On the floor, by the great steel table that was called the Stone, lay the empty forme and a great pile of type. The lines of information, the notices, the advertisements, the reports of meetings, the tales of Brigthorpe's citizens, all mixed up in a great printer's pie. Next to it stood the lad and Fred, unmoving. Through the door at the far end of the room she could see the three men in the little foundry which housed the printing press. They had been waiting for the last page. They too stood frozen like figures in a tableau. She was aware of a sharp pain in her shoulder. It was Randy's hand gripping her hard.

Nobody moved. Nobody spoke. Would they stay like this for ever?

Then the lad said cheerfully, 'I'm ever so sorry, Mr Fred, sir.'

She saw Fred's fists go up. Fred, the gentle giant, was actually going to clout the lad. She shot forward to stop him, and was almost between them when the fists were slowly lowered. Which was just as well, she thought afterwards, because Fred had fists like station bumpers and getting in the way of them wouldn't have done her face any good at all.

'Just go home,' Fred said, white-faced but in control of himself.

'Oh, no, I'll stay and help you put it all in order, Mr Fred, sir.'

Fred glared at him.

'I want you out of my sight,' he said. 'Now.'

The lad looked at him, and went.

So did Randy and Polly. Like frightened children they crept quietly away and up the stairs. Back in the safety of the reporters' room, they stood, leaning against the mantelshelf, staring at each other.

'What are we going to do, Randy?' she asked in a whisper.

'We are going,' he said with quiet determination, 'to get the paper out on time and into the newsagents tomorrow morning as usual.'

She heard herself sigh with relief. She hadn't realised how much she had feared that he might say something different. She could have hugged him.

'Where do we start?'

'Well, when I've got my courage up I'll go and make sure they're getting on with melting all that lead down.'

'And I'll check we've got the galley proofs of that last page in order, so that they'll be ready for Fred to work from when he starts typesetting again.'

'Yes, but give him a little while to calm down first.'

'All right. I'll take him a cup of tea.'

'Treat him carefully, Flinders. If he decides to walk out on us now –'

'He'd never do that,' she said, shaking her head. 'He's a real professional, Fred is.'

'I've just remembered that one of the foundrymen – Joe, the oldest one, you know? – used to be a compositor until he damaged his right hand. He might be able to help Fred a bit. I'll have a quiet word with him when I'm down there.'

'I wish *we* could help Fred. But we wouldn't know where to start, would we? All that reading upside down. It's quite beyond us.'

They stood for a moment, remembering. A few hours ago they'd been so authoritative and in charge, and now they felt like a couple of kids, trying to clear away the traces of crime. It was the grown-ups downstairs, the men in leather aprons, who had the skills they needed.

'What about the newsagents?' she asked.

'Ye gods, I'd forgotten! We'll have to ring them and tell them not to go out to the pick-up points tonight. Thanks, Polly, I'll do that now. They'd have been pretty furious if they'd turned out at night and found no papers.'

'To say nothing of the explosions from Sunny Jim tomorrow if he found we'd upset all his newsagents. What will you tell them, Randy?'

'I suppose I'll have to take a wild guess about when we'll actually be ready. Sometime early tomorrow morning?'

'Why not just tell them what's happened and ask them what they'd like us to do? I mean they may prefer just to come here and collect the papers themselves. I'd discuss it with them rather than just tell them what you think. After all, they've been in the trade a long time, maybe it's happened before. There must have been delays for various reasons in the past.'

'Right. I'll go and ring now. Could you check the foundry?'

'Yes. I'll see about it while I'm down there.'

'Look, Polly, we're going to be here all night. I'll go round to the pub after I've finished phoning and get us something to eat, so at least we're not fainting by the time the new proofs are ready for pulling.'

'How will Fred organize it, do you think?'

'I expect he'll set up each column again and let us have the galley proofs as he goes along. At least you and I did the make-up of the page, so that's something we can help with.'

'I've just thought of something.'

'What?'

'Well, the state Fred's in . . . I mean if he does make mistakes, we shan't dare tell him, shall we?'

'It depends how bad they are, doesn't it?'

Some of them were very bad.

'We can't leave shitty for shifty,' Randy said, as they went through the first galley-proof an hour later.

'Nor this wrong caption. Everybody notices wrong captions.'

'Never mind everybody. Let's just think in terms of what the editor will notice.'

'He'll notice everything.'

'I'm not chickening out, Polly,' Randy said, looking down at the heavily marked galley-proof, 'but I think it would be better if *you* took this one back to Fred – gentle feminine touch and all that.'

'All right. I'll take him another cup of tea as well.'

The atmosphere in the basement was grim. Fred didn't even look up when she approached him. He just indicated with two brief nods where she was to put the proofs and the tea. She'd meant to say something about the corrections but 'There's more in the pot, if you want it' was all she dared to murmur. He grunted.

Through the door she could see the printing press crouching, immobile. By now it should have been eating up the great roll of paper, printing all the words which were not yet even set. There was an impossible amount to do in such a little time, she thought in sudden panic. All except one galley was still to be typeset, the page matrix still to be made, the metal print taken – all this before the printing press could get rolling. And it was coming up to midnight. Normally by now the pages would have emerged in their quires, been checked and tied up in bundles with hairy string and left ready for delivery. She was trembling as she went back upstairs.

'It's awful down there,' she told Randy. 'You can go next time.'

'Want a drink? I bought some beer and cider back.'

'No, thanks. I'd rather stick to tea until we've finished the galleys.'

'Perhaps you're right,' he said, pouring himself another cup of the orange-coloured brew, and ladling sugar into it.

'I wish I could help Fred,' she said, thinking of him sitting there, grey-faced, at the typesetter. 'It makes you realise how little we really know, doesn't it?'

'Dammit, it wasn't our fault,' Randy said suddenly. 'Let's

forget it for a bit, there's nothing we can do now anyway until the next galley-proof appears. If Fred had only let the lad stay, at least he could have helped with the corrections.'

Polly shook her head.

'No, he'd only have got on Fred's nerves. He's better out of the way.'

'We're not going to think about it, I tell you. Now let's talk about something else.' He began shovelling coal on to the fire. 'Are you going to stay on this paper for ever, Polly?'

'Not for ever, but for quite a time. And you?'

'Maybe another couple of years. After that I reckon it'll have taught me all I need. But you ought to get out. I can see you doing much more free-lance work now that you've got launched. You can earn a bit, you know, as a local correspondent for a London paper. You could do articles of the kind you did about Tudor Bean.'

'Oh, that was special, Randy. A one-off job.'

'Admittedly you were lucky, but all the same it was a fine article.'

'Thank you.' She hesitated, then added, 'The editor said something about starting a women's column.'

'How did you react to that?'

'Not very enthusiastically. I'd rather not be lumbered with knitting and recipes. I don't see why I shouldn't deal with hard news like a man.'

'Well said, Flinders. There's no reason why you shouldn't. It's a very equal-minded profession, ours is.'

'So you told me when I first came.'

He laughed. 'Oh, yes, when you were so tight-fisted you wouldn't pay your NUJ subscription.'

'Then you told me that they'd always insisted on equal pay, so I coughed up.'

'Other professions are following suit now. Did you see women teachers are going to get equal pay – mind you, in instalments spread over seven years, but it's a sign of the times. But we were the ones to show the way. I'm proud of that.'

'You're a funny mixture,' she remarked. 'You talk about equal pay as fervently as any career woman.'

'Well, it's so ridiculous to say that men should be paid more because they have more domestic responsibilities. Since when have people been paid according to their domestic responsibilities? You might as well say married men should be paid more than bachelors. No, it was just an excuse.'

'Mm.' It wasn't what she meant. What she found strange was that while he was so completely in support of equal pay and opportunities for women, his attitude towards them as individuals was totally unchivalrous. Yet Simon, who was always considerate and kindly, never even thought in terms of equality at work.

'I know what you're thinking, Polly. You're thinking how odd that a cad like me bothers about the rights of women.'

'Mind-reader.'

'Well, it's all part and parcel of the same thing. If you really think of women as being as resourceful and clever as men, of course you expect them to stick up for themselves. It's an insult to do anything else. I agree with the chap who said he didn't give up his seat on the bus to women any more, now that they've got equal standing.'

'Nonsense. You can still respect people's needs just as people, and care about them. I mean if I stand up for an old person or a pregnant women it doesn't mean I don't think they're equal. It just means I recognize they have a special need which I don't happen to have. There's nothing insulting about courtesy.'

'Courtesy,' he repeated. 'That's an old-fashioned word.'

'I owe you for the pie,' she said, reaching for her bag.

'My treat,' he told her, waving the offer aside.

But she made him take the sixpence all the same. She who had had no qualms about accepting whole meals from Simon.

The galley-proofs got steadily worse. They let more and more mistakes go through, terrified of upsetting Fred, until in the end they were only correcting mistakes which might be libellous.

'We can't leave "awful wife" for "lawful wife", Randy, we just can't. Mrs Brainstock will sue us.'

'Or sew us, as we nearly wrote in the previous paragraph,' Randy said, marking the proof. 'Well, that's the lot, Flinders. Is it your turn or mine to go down to the torture chamber?'

'You go. I'll put the kettle on. Tell Fred there's another brew on its way. We all deserve it, I reckon.'

But when Randy came back he insisted on opening the cider and beer.

'Too much tea is bad for you,' he told her. 'Besides, we need something stronger to keep us going. There's still a lot to do, you know.'

'How are things downstairs?'

'Fred's just finishing off and the foundrymen are getting ready to pour the lead for the plates. I've said young Tony can go off once we start rolling. His wife's expecting a baby any moment and she'll get anxious if he's much later home than he said, and he's no way of letting her know. You and I can help with the papers.'

'Oh, yes, I love that part. I helped when I was here with Magnus once. I think it's so clever the way the machine does it all, all that folding and cutting, as well as the printing. And the way it can even chuck every twenty-fourth paper forward when it's throwing them out at the end. It's like magic.'

'Yes, the rotary's all right. You know, I've been thinking, Polly. I wonder if we could use what's happened this evening to try to persuade Sunny Jim to get a decent linotype machine for typesetting?'

'How do you mean?'

'Well, with linotype at least the lines would have been left intact. All the papers are going over to linotype now. Monotype's old hat, and I'm going to tell him so.'

'I shouldn't, Randy. I don't think it's quite the right time to start badgering Mr Dinsdale about his machinery. I'd just keep away from him, if I were you, anyway until the effects of reading that last page have worn off.'

Randy glanced at his watch. 'Well, we'll soon see our first newspaper, Flinders.'

It was three o'clock before the paper got rolling. They stood watching as the great reel of newsprint was seized by the machine, pressed against the inky surface of type, passed across, cut into sheets, folded down the middle by a rod, folded again. Nonchalantly the men pushed aside the first few copies, always too poor to use. Polly couldn't wait to grab one. Then she and Randy dashed upstairs with it.

Silently they perused it, spreading it out on the table and turning the pages without comment.

'Not bad,' Randy said at last. 'Honestly not so *very* much worse than the other pages.'

'It's a pity about the Mayor being called the Major.'

'It's not libellous, Flinders. He was a private in the war, so I expect he'll be quite chuffed.'

'I wasn't really thinking of him, more of Mr Dinsdale.'

'He should be jolly grateful his blessed paper got published at all.'

'At least he can't mistake it for *The Times* this week. Do they ever make printing errors, the really great papers, I mean?'

'Not often, but if they do it's a real howler. When Queen Victoria opened the Albert Bridge, *The Times* described the ceremony very solemnly and concluded, "Then Her Majesty pissed over the bridge." '

'I don't believe it,' Polly said, snorting with laughter.

'It conjures up a wonderful picture, doesn't it? All those skirts too. But it is true. One of the places I worked had a book of newspapers' howlers and it was in there.'

'Come on,' Polly said, recovering. 'Better get back. It must be time for the reel change.'

The great reel of newsprint was hoisted in place by block and tackle worked by the two remaining foundry men and Fred and Randy. Then once again the press began to roll. Polly stood watching, her eyes prickling with fatigue, her body aching, as the paper rolled and crossed and folded, then slid out at the end. It was hypnotic the way it went on and on, wave after wave. Nothing would stop it now. Please God let nothing else go wrong.

Nothing else did go wrong. Two hours later the six of them were tying up the newspapers in bundles, wrapped in last week's papers, ready for the shops.

'I'll go and ring Mr Garside,' Randy said. 'I promised I'd let him know and he'll arrange for the vans.'

He went upstairs and the two foundrymen followed him out, leaving Fred and Polly to tie up the last few bundles. She was wide awake now, could hardly believe they had worked all day and all night. Fred was looking more human, too. He even smiled as he tied the last knot in the last piece of hairy string.

'Well, I'll say good night,' he remarked as Randy returned, 'Or rather good morning. And thanks, the pair of you. You'll be all right as editors one day.'

Then he went out before they could reply.

'He's an odd fish,' Randy said, as they listened to his footsteps on the stairs. 'Starts the night be nearly committing murder and goes off meekly at dawn, practically touching his forelock.'

'Well, I think he's wonderful,' Polly said, looking down at the mountain of newspapers all bundled up and ready. 'Absolutely wonderful.'

It was quiet in the basement now, the great press silent and still like a powerful but dormant animal. She was suddenly aware of the smell which had so fascinated and excited her as a child, the special newspaper smell of ink and leather and melting lead. She took a deep breath of it and shut her eyes.

She opened them suddenly as Randy took hold of her.

'Stop it, Randy. Don't be silly.'

'Why not? We deserve a bit of silliness after this ghastly night.'

'It hasn't been ghastly. It's been very exciting. And we've got the paper out. That's all that matters. Honestly I've enjoyed it.'

'You could enjoy this even more,' he said, tightening his hold on her and kissing her hard.

She couldn't decide afterwards whether it was the cider on an empty stomach, or the excitement of the night, or the special smell of newspapers being printed, or the overwhelming effects of exhaustion, or just plain lust. Whatever the reason, she let Randy go on kissing her, let him press her back and down, let herself slither gently on to the mound of newspapers.

'What would you do if the editor came in now?' was the only objection she raised.

'I'd tell him I'm putting the paper to bed, of course,' Randy said.

'You're not altering those In Memoriams, are you, Randy?' Sid asked suddenly.

'Well,' Randy admitted, 'some of them are pretty bad this week.'

'Get it into your head, m'lad, that we sub-edit everything except those. They are printed exactly as they come in, OK?'

'OK, but just listen to this: "Mrs Binns sincerely thanks relatives and friends for sympathy in recent bereavement and all floral tributes sent, special thanks to doctors for services rendered, Mr Bell for efficient funeral and the employees of the Gas Board." '

'So?'

'Well, it'll just make readers laugh.'

'It doesn't make me laugh,' Sid said. 'That's what she wants to put in, so you just put it in.'

Randy shrugged.

'All right. Though just because something doesn't make *you* laugh doesn't mean to say it isn't hilarious.'

'Does anyone know anything about angling?' Jeff asked.

'I thought you and Sid were experts on every sport ever mentioned in the paper?'

'Everything except fish,' Jeff said. 'We can give you expert advice on cricket, rugby, football, hockey, snooker, billiards –'

'Darts, dominoes, golf, tennis –' Sid went on.

'All right. We get the general idea – you don't know anything about fishing.'

'What's the trouble?' Magnus asked.

'It's this account of the club outing sent in by our angling correspondent. All good clean stuff about eddies and heavy water, but it ends up, "Roach were pretty well on the move and a few bream and chub of fair size, but minnows were a nuisance." *Can* minnows be a nuisance? Does anybody know? At least I *think* it's minnows. His writing is worse than any of ours. It could be willows, I suppose.'

'Or widows,' Randy suggested. 'I mean they might be a bother to anglers on sultry evenings.'

'Thank you, Randy. You can always be relied upon for helpful suggestions.'

'No trouble. Any time.'

'You'd better check with the correspondent, Jeff,' Magnus said. 'He's on the phone, that one. How's your report going, Polly?'

Polly had the Remington. She had been allowed it for her first case at the magistrates' court. She pulled out the paper. It tore. For typing they used the ends of the rolls of newsprint, and since the huge reels of paper which were delivered each week had to be manhandled off the lorry and then rolled across the rough ground outside the office, collecting gravel and dirt in the process, the offcuts were invariably grubby and pitted with holes which tore during typing. Still, she preferred them to the backs of press hand-outs and other pieces of scrap paper which was what they had to use for writing reports.

'It's the case about the bull,' she said and cleared her throat.

'Oyez, oyez, listen for Polly's First Case,' Randy said.

She ignored him. She'd done quite a bit of ignoring Randy this past five days.

' "Ashley Mills, aged 28, farmer, pleaded guilty to allowing a bull to be at large in a field carrying a public footpath. He was fined ten shillings with eight shillings costs. Superintendant Malcolm Stubbs said that on October 14th Miss Fairclough was walking along the footpath from Portway to Easthill when, halfway across a field, the bull came at her. She managed to climb a fence to safety but was dazed and frightened when she reached the nearest house. Mr James Cotterill, of Jones, Scott and Cotterill, solicitors, appearing for the defendant, said he was sorry it had not happened before–" '

'Do you mean that?'

'No. It should read, "said he was sorry *and* it had not happened before. The bull was being fed in the farm-yard and must have got out into the field without anybody noticing. He hadn't given any trouble before." '

'Bravo, Polly,' Randy said, 'but was it the bull or the farmer who hadn't given any trouble before? And, by the way, that bit at the beginning about the bull carrying a public footpath. I wasn't quite clear –'

'Shut up, Randy,' Magnus said. 'It's only a first draft, isn't it, Flinders?'

'Yes,' she agreed, though actually she had retyped it twice already.

Fred came in with a pile of galley-proofs.

'I'll take them,' Magnus said.

Randy looked over his shoulder. 'Good lord, he's early with his editorial.'

'Yes, he asked me to check. He's not in tomorrow. But he's coming in on Wednesday to put the paper to bed himself.'

'Why?' Sid asked.

'After what happened last time,' Magnus said evenly. 'But we won't go into all that again.'

'Why not?' Randy said. 'I think we made a jolly good job of it. Polly's marvellous at putting the paper to bed, aren't you, Polly? You might stay and help Sunny Jim on Wednesday.'

She ignored him and began thumping the Remington.

'Well, the editorial won't be exactly stop press, will it? Full of sweet nothings, is it?'

'He's having a go at masons,' Magnus said, glancing down the paper.

'What, freemasons? Attacking the Brigthorpe business mafia, is he? I don't believe it. What about his readership and –'

'No, the monumental variety. He says they canvass the bereaved for trade.'

'Can't say I've ever noticed that at funerals.'

'Well, they'd hardly tout for custom at the graveside, would they? No, he just means they put pressure on people to spend more than they can afford. He's got a bit about florists, too, advertising by putting their names on the cards attached to funeral flowers.'

'It's a long time since he covered funerals,' Randy remarked. 'They don't have flowers any more. Just floral tributes.'

'His second article's about television. Apparently there are three thousand sets in the town and last month three hundred new licences were issued.'

'Fascinating,' Randy said.

'It's all very well to be sarcastic,' Magnus told him, 'but Sunny Jim is right to point out the dangers.'

'Dangers to whom?'

'Well, to the local cinemas, for a start.'

'Oh, people will always want a night out at the flicks.'

'Then he talks a bit about sport. As he says, who will travel to Headingley in the hope of getting into a test match if they can be sure of seeing it on their television screen?'

'Newspaper correspondents will,' Randy told him promptly.

'Isn't it time for Polly to put the kettle on?' Sid asked.

'Somebody else's turn,' Magnus began.

'No, I don't mind,' she said getting up. 'I've just ripped the paper again. I need a break.'

When she came back she stood for a moment looking for somewhere to put the tray among the piles of copy and newspapers, of cuttings and proofs. Sid was reading proofs to Jeff, and Randy was poring over the entertainments page of last week's paper. He looked up when she handed him his cup.

'I've got a free evening,' he said. 'Want to come out, Polly? Good things at the flicks. Look, Danny Kaye in the *Inspector General*, James Mason in *East Side, West Side* and Clifton Webb in *Cheaper by the Dozen*. Nothing much at the Alhambra or the Gaumont, though. Or there's wrestling –'

'No, thanks. I'm going to represent the paper at the Independent Methodist Women's Auxiliary, and then I'm going on to the dance organised by the Egg Producers' Association in aid of the Lynmouth Flood Disaster Fund.'

'Are they still collecting? I thought the fund was closed by now.'

'Well, if it is, nobody's told the Brigthorpe Egg Producers' Association.'

'Come another night to the flicks.'

'No, I've no money. I've got to save for a coat.'

'Dingley's are selling off woollen gaberdine coats which are normally £10 for a mere seven guineas. Look,' Randy said, handing her a sheet of newspaper.

'If you've nothing to do, Randy,' Magnus said, 'check this.' He handed him the proof and began to read the copy. 'A record £700 was raised by the Parish Church Annual Bazaar –'

Polly settled down at the Remington. On her right, Sid was droning, 'In a scrappy game on Saturday at Plinney's Ground, Magnates Old Boys proceed to the next stage of the Rugby League Challenge Cup competition. The long touch-finding kicks of Geoff Luxford and Simon Goras were a great asset to the home side. Alan Corners was a constructive forward and –'

She rolled in a new piece of gravel-impregnated newsprint.

'The handicraft stall,' Magnus was intoning, 'flourished in charge of Mesdames Hardwick, Hiscock and Twiddle.'
'I don't believe it,' Randy murmured.
'Ashley Wills, aged twenty-eight, farmer, pleaded guilty to allowing a bull to be at large,' Polly muttered to herself as she began to type.

'Polly,' Randy said, catching up with her on the tow-path, 'can you bear to talk to me, or are you going to spend the rest of your life pretending I don't exist?'
She didn't reply.
'Because we do have to work together, you know. In the same office. People will notice. Our work will suffer, won't it?'
She walked on.
'I realise that what happened on Wednesday night has made you pretty mad with me, but I can't really understand why.'
Still she walked on.
'I mean if you hadn't enjoyed it, I could understand you'd be cross. But –'
'Shut up, you pig.'
'That's better, that's more like it.'
He put his arm around her and walked in step with her.
'Now tell me why I'm a pig.'
'Because you're so off-hand and arrogant and – Oh, I don't know. I don't blame you. It was my fault just as much as yours. But at least I was taking a risk with myself. You were risking somebody else. It was just a bit of luck that I was due to get the curse at the weekend anyway. You didn't know that.'
He shrugged, then 'It was unplanned,' he said more humbly. 'One doesn't calculate these things, Flinders.'
'I suppose you'd have been utterly astonished if I'd got pregnant, wouldn't you? You're like the heroes in modern novels by angry young men. They have these great torrid loves scenes and people live together for weeks and then the men are always absolutely amazed when the girls get pregnant. Stunned and shattered, they are. They make such a pose of being sophisticated, but they're stupid and ignorant and don't even know the facts of life.'

'You're right, Polly. Come and sit down and let's talk about it.'

They sat on a rather damp wooden seat facing the canal, and he took both her hands in his.

'Let's forget about Wednesday night for a bit, Polly,' he said thoughtfully. 'Let's just think about us and the future. I reckon we get on jolly well. Look how we worked together that evening to get the paper out. We complement each other in a way. We've got the same views about work and all the important things. I reckon we could make a go of it together. Anyway, I'd like to try, if you would.'

She was astonished. And after she'd been so awful to him, too. Of course, it was a crazy notion, but she was touched that he had even thought of it.

'Randy,' she said, 'it's sweet of you, but truly you mustn't think that you have to marry me just because of what happened on Wednesday night. It was my fault as much as yours. And I don't want to get married anyway. I want to be a journalist.'

He looked at her in amazement. 'I wasn't asking you to marry me,' he said. 'I just thought we might shack up together.'

She jumped off the bench.

'Hey, steady. You'll be into the canal if you leap about like that.'

'You make me quite physically sick, Randy Turnbull. Just let me go, will you?'

She hit out at his hand.

'Why, Polly? What's so criminal about my suggestion?'

'It's so bloody irresponsible, that's what's criminal. I can look after myself, but lots of girls can't. They're taken in by chaps like you and the next thing they're pregnant and the chap's telling them to have an abortion and – Oh, you make me sick.'

'Polly, dear, there is something called contraception.' He said the word slowly, as if spelling it out to a child. 'The safest way is for you to go and get yourself a cap fitted.'

'Shut up, Randy. Apart from anything else, you know jolly well that they're not allowed to fit caps on to unmarried women.'

'*In*to, Polly, not *on* to. You always need sub-editing when you get cross. I've noticed that before.'

'Go away.'

'And all you need to do is wear a wedding ring when you go to the clinic. That's what the other girls do.'

'Goodbye.'

'No, Polly. You're going to tell me why you're so furious.'

'I've told you. You make me sick.'

'No, I don't. I made you very happy. And you made me very happy, too. Be honest.'

His arms were round her again and even as he spoke she felt a quiver, a little jab of remembered pleasure. It made her even angrier with herself. Simon had been right: she was just the stupid sort of person who would let herself be hurt by someone like Randy. She thumped her fists against his chest. It wasn't fair, there was no way of hurting back. In every way, physically and emotionally, men like Randy were stronger. Because they didn't care.

Chapter 10

'Well,' Magnus said, 'here's your chance, Polly. Sunny Jim says you and Randy can both come to the Kirklington Assizes tomorrow. Sid can't make it.'

'Oh.'

Magnus laughed. 'Is that all you've got to say?' he asked. 'I thought you'd be over the moon.'

'I am.'

'Good. Well, I'll be going by bus to Kirklington –'

'Oh, you're coming too?' she said with obvious relief. 'I didn't realise that.'

'Of course. There are several cases going on. I'll give you the background of yours on the journey tomorrow.'

He was touched that she had been relieved that he was coming too. Poor little kid, he thought, she must be more nervous than she lets on. Not such a toughie as she looks, our Flinders.

'We'll meet at the bus station at eight-thirty tomorrow morning,' he told her.

The three of them spread themselves along the back bench of the bus.

'The young couple in the dock,' Magnus said after he had bought the tickets and made a note of the expenses, 'were found guilty yesterday, so today you'll have the sentencing.'

'Oh, is that all? That won't take long, will it?'

'It could. There'll be probation officers' reports and so on. There are all sorts of extenuating circumstances, so I think they'll get off with a conditional discharge.'

'What happened?'

'Briefly, this chap Terence Stokes married young and had two children, then his wife left him –'

'How old were the children?'

'Oh, they were quite little when their mother went. Maybe about two and three.'

Younger than she and Jim had been. Did that make it better or worse, she wondered.

'Anyway, he struggled on for a bit. The only person he had to help him was his mother who lived nearby, but she was an invalid and couldn't do much. So in the end he had to give up his job and stay at home to look after the children. He's been a good father to those kids, no doubt about that. After a year he married again, a girl called Irene.'

He paused.

'What was she like?' Polly prompted.

'Only nineteen. Very idealistic and impulsive. One gets the impression that she rushed into the marriage thinking she was saving the family.'

'Which she was. Presumably Terence could go back to work then?'

'Yes. But what I meant was that she somehow glamorized the situation, saw herself as a saviour, didn't realise what hard work it would be, and lonely, too, for a young girl to be tied down at home all day with two little children.'

Yes, Polly thought, she could imagine that. Somebody else's children, too. And no time to enjoy just being a bride, alone with her husband.

'Go on.'

'How she loves a story, our Flinders,' Randy put in and yawned.

'At this stage,' Magnus said ignoring him, 'I have to explain, Polly, that before she was married, and moved away and lost touch with them, she used to baby-sit for a family called Carsons. This chap Carsons used to make passes at her. He's middle-aged, older than his wife. He's a creep, talks big, all out to impress, really flashy –'

'Magnus doesn't like him,' Randy remarked.

'Do you?'

'No, he's a loathsome sod if ever I saw one,' Randy said.

'To return to the case. One day when Irene was feeling rather fed up with life, Terence took the children to his mother and sent Irene off to the coast, to Knaresby for the day, to give her a break. And as she walked along the pier whom did she meet but our friend Carsons, who enquired kindly after her welfare and listened while she poured out all her woes. Carsons was very sympathetic and understanding and said he'd like to find a way to help them, and invited her back to his hotel for lunch. So at midday she goes there and they have cocktails and a big meal with plenty to drink. The hotel is very grand, she's never been in such a place before, so when Carsons says they're having coffee and liqueurs in his room so that they can talk more easily, she thinks that's quite normal and trots upstairs with him.'

'She was a bit naïve, wasn't she?'

'Yes, and quite a bit drunk, too. Well, you can guess the rest. After an afternoon in bed, she sobered up and felt pretty mad with herself. All might have been well if he hadn't offered her £5. She was furious, so he said he'd make it £10 if she stayed for the night. She really went for him then, and he turned nasty and said she must have known all along that that was the way he intended to help Terence and her. And he let slip that he hadn't really been staying in the hotel at all. After he'd met her on the pier, he'd nipped back and booked a room.'

'But why did it end in court?'

Magnus shook his head. 'Oh, the stupidity of it,' he said. 'After she'd stormed out, she went and walked along the shingle trying to think of some way of attacking Carsons. And the more she thought, the more it seemed a good idea to scare him with blackmail. More than anything she wanted to give him a fright, put him down, get her own back.'

Polly recognised that feeling: wanting to hit back at life, but not knowing how.

'Anyway,' Magnus went on, 'Terence came and joined her and they walked backwards and forwards along the shingle and she told him everything that had happened. He said that the best thing they could do was to forget all about it, just accept that she'd made a mistake and it was all over now. He told her they loved each other enough to weather a storm like this. He didn't at all like the blackmail idea. But she talked him into it, said it was the only way she'd ever feel better about the whole thing. In the end he agreed.'

'That was a bit feeble of him, wasn't it?'

Magnus shrugged. 'Well, they were upset and he obviously loves her. She wanted to do this thing, so he went along with it. I think she felt it was some sort of atonement. She was so ashamed of herself, and so angry that she just had to do something. There didn't seem to be any other way she could hit back at Carsons.'

'How did they set about it?'

'Oh, it was the most amateur, messed-up job you can imagine. She wrote a note to Carsons saying she'd tell all if he didn't send her £250.'

He stopped. The inspector was coming round. Magnus found their tickets, handed them to him, waited while they were scrutinized and took them back. Polly watched the ritual impatiently.

'Go on,' she said, as Magnus stowed the tickets away again in his wallet.

'Oh, she's so simple, that girl, Irene. I mean, you only have to look at Carsons' smug face to see that he wouldn't be scared of publicity. He wouldn't mind the whole world knowing he'd seduced a girl in a hotel in Knaresby. He'd be quite proud of himself. He went straight to the police, of course. Irene had told him to put the money into a brief-case and leave it in a hedge, in a country road. She said in court that she knew the police would be waiting for her. She walked along that dusty, tree-lined road and knew she was walking into a trap, but she kept on walking because she couldn't think of anything else to do. The brief-case was lying in the hedge. She picked it up and stood there, literally stood waiting, until the police came out from where they were hiding. The police statement bears this out. So they took her to the police station and charged her. She wasn't even surprised to find there was only newspaper stuffed inside the brief-case. She'd expected that, too. It was all so childish and silly.'

'And all this is established already?'

'Oh yes, they don't deny anything. She tried to take all the blame but Terence insisted that he'd been equally involved, so they're both in the dock and yesterday they were both found guilty.'

'But you think they'll get a light sentence?'

'I should think a conditional discharge in view of their past good behaviour and the fact they're no danger to anyone. They've had this case hanging over them for eighteen months and anyone can see they're scared and sorry. They've learned their lesson all right. Anyway,' he added, getting up as the bus drew into the bus station, 'that's the background to your case, Polly.'

'Thanks, Magnus. I feel as if I'd been there myself.'

He smiled at her as they stood waiting to get off the bus. 'That's a great compliment, Polly,' he said. 'It's a reporter's job to make you feel you were in court, too.'

She nodded, though that wasn't what she had meant. She'd meant that she felt as if she too had walked up and down the shingle at Knaresby, resentful and confused, as if she too had later walked along that dusty, deserted road, between the trees which hid the watchers, aware that she was walking into a trap, but not knowing what else to do but go on walking.

The pomp and ceremony of the Assize court was very different from the informality of the magistrates' court she was used to. They watched as the judges' cars drew up and the high sheriff waited on the steps, flanked by two trumpeters in full rig.

'That's the origin of the expression "Going upstairs", meaning to be committed to the Assizes,' Magnus whispered as they listened to the clarion call as the judge ascended the steps to the court.

'Never heard of it,' Polly said.

'Doesn't mix with the criminal classes, doesn't our Polly,' Randy said. 'A model of virtue, aren't you, love?'

'Shut up,' she said, walking away.

'I'm coming with you to the blackmail case. Didn't you know? Magnus thinks you need someone to hold your hand.'

She ignored him.

'I'll be no trouble. Not a word. It's all very solemn and hushed in there.'

He was right. Into the court processed the judge in his scarlet robes and the high sheriff in his black velvet knee breeches, satin blouse and medals, followed by the chaplain. Here, she thought, justice will be seen to be done. The cases she had reported in the magistrates' court and petty sessions always seemed to her so hopeless and pathetic. The crimes sounded exciting, words like deserter and bigamist conjured up visions of desperate men, but the accused all looked so shabby and sad and incapable of anything, including the crimes they were accused of. Crime, it seemed, had more dignity here.

The judge was a sharp-featured little man, his face yellowish and red-veined. His ears, which were large and paper-thin, were likewise threaded with little red veins. They stuck out from the sides of his head and were so thin that she could see the light through them as he sat in front of the tall windows. The effect, under this wig, was goblinish.

He was sharp and impatient. When the probation officer was called he reprimanded her and her department for being so slow in producing the reports that the court had requested. He brought out the words The Court as if its power was absolute. Polly, who knew from other cases how over-worked and harassed the probation officers were, wondered if the judge realised the conditions in which they worked, often without a proper office or secretary. If he did know, he didn't sound as if he cared or thought it was any of his business.

Flustered after the reprimand, the probation officer began

hesitantly but then made a good job of outlining the history of the couple in the dock. Irene had a poor background, was fostered several times, but had never been in trouble. She had wanted to give these children a proper home because she had never had one of her own. She was idealistic about it but inexperienced in managing children and a home. She was very low and cast down at the time of the crime. Since then things had gone better. During the eighteen months that had elapsed, Terence had got a better job, had just passed his driving test and had been promoted to van driver, both children were happy and well looked after. The marriage had stood the test, even been strengthened by the months of anxious waiting, of not knowing if a case would be brought against them, then the uncertainty and delays. She was quite sure from her knowledge of them that they were genuinely sorry and had learned their lesson.

The couple in the dock listened carefully. The girl, Irene, slight and fair, was surreptitiously holding the young man's hand. He was a nice-looking chap. When the probation officer stressed their repentance and anxiety for the children, you would see it mirrored in their faces, Polly thought. They did look sorry, they did look anxious, they did look as if they would support each other and care for their children. One thing they did not look was criminal. He kept glancing down at her, giving her the faintest smile of encouragement, and the warmth was instantly reflected in the girl's eyes as she momentarily relaxed. Even from the other side of the court, Polly could feel the understanding between them. She took rapid shorthand notes, not only of what was said but of the people involved, the court, even the judge's ears.

When the probation officer had sat down, the judge prepared to pass sentence. He repeated yet again the sorry tale, stressing that the defendants were of previous good character, that the crime was not premeditated. Irene had acted on the spur of the moment. In no way had Carsons been set up. She had acted foolishly but without malice aforethought. She was young and inexperienced and had been impressed by the sudden luxury she was offered. Her husband had been very unwillingly involved. If a custodial sentence was imposed on her, the children would suffer as there was no-one else to care for them. If a custodial sentence was imposed on the father then they would be without money and he would have small prospect of a job when he came out of prison. The court saw before them a young couple whose whole future was at stake. What they did not see, he added, were two little children who would lose the only people who could look after them. The sins of the fathers – and mothers, the judge said, updating the law of Moses – are visited upon the children.

As he spoke the couple in the dock visibly relaxed, even nodding assent at some of his remarks. The whole court was with them. They had been punished enough, for the case had been twice postponed. Now the end was within sight. Even the jurors looked relieved, Polly noticed, reflecting that it must have been hard for them to find the pair guilty, knowing the sentence which that might incur, but they had no alternative. The couple had never denied the crime.

Suddenly the judge's voice changed, his face darkened. 'But blackmail is an ugly thing,' he said. 'The very word is ugly and rightly inspires fear and contempt. We must never give the impression that blackmail,' and his voice lingered on the word as he repeated it, 'that blackmail goes unpunished in this land. Therefore the sentence of the court upon you and each of you is that you be imprisoned for a period of two years.'

There was a gasp from the court and then suddenly a terrible cry of agony from the girl. It was inhuman, that sound, it cut through Polly and everyone in court. And as she cried out, she fell. The young husband caught her and for a moment Polly saw them clutching at each other, two despairing figures, dreadfully changed from the vision of hope they had presented only moments before.

It only lasted for seconds. Then officials rushed forward and hustled them out unceremoniously, dragging them away to their separate prisons, now when they most needed each other's comfort. Their departure, robbed of all human dignity, made a striking contrast to the manner in which Justice had arrived, robed and heralded, in court.

Everyone, Polly observed, had been shocked into immobility by the sentence and the terrible, desolate cry which followed it. The jury sat so still that they seemed like twelve figures carved in a single frieze. The probation officer was leaning forward, her forehead on her hand, posed like a statue. Polly saw the whole scene as if it were a painting in which an artist had caught for all time a single moment in their lives and fixed it so that afterwards, when she looked back and relived that day, as she did many times, she could see again that picture of the court in all its living detail.

Only the judge seemed unconcerned. He turned to speak to an officer behind him, his arm resting on the back of the bench, perfectly relaxed. Then he laughed.

The sound broke the spell. There was a shuffling as people began to move. The frieze which had been the jury broke up into its component parts, twelve individual men and women. The probation officer began to gather up the pages of the report which had been so peremptorily requested and so totally ignored. Polly wondered what was going on in her mind.

'Randy,' she said, and he jumped when she spoke, for he too had been lost in the scene. 'Shall we go and talk to her?'

'She hasn't any power, Polly,' Randy said, watching the chastened figure of the probation officer move towards the door.

'We could at least let her know that we saw it all, heard it all. I mean we're witnesses of what happened –'

'Better wait and ask Magnus. He's in for a shock. Anyway they're on to the next case.'

They sat through the next case, observing a young man get four years for rape. Two other cases of rape were taken into account, and a third of assault. The assault was really rape, too, but the victim had not wanted to give evidence about it, only about her damaged face, for as he raped her he had put his fingers into her mouth and ripped it wide open, tearing into her cheeks. It was all part of the same attack, but of what else he had done to her body, the girl refused to speak.

'My God, I'm not surprised,' Polly burst out when they were sitting with Magnus in the snack bar during the lunch recess. 'In front of that judge and all those officials. How could she?'

'Do you realise,' Randy put in, 'that that dangerous maniac only got the same four years as those two kids who had a childish go at blackmail? And they've never hurt anyone and are never likely to. What price British justice?'

'I must say, I'm amazed at that sentence,' Magnus agreed. 'I never thought it would be anything except a conditional discharge. Maybe at worst a few months' custodial for her.' He shook his head, baffled. 'No, I never foresaw this.'

'What can we do, Magnus?'

'Do? Nothing Polly. If you wanted to influence the course of justice you should have been a barrister, not a journalist. Did they appeal against the sentence?'

'No,' Randy said.

'Everyone was too stunned,' Polly added.

'Well, they've still time. A lot depends on their lawyer. Meanwhile, Flinders, your job is to report what happened, not try to alter it.'

'Of course.' Her face lit up. 'That's what we can do. I mean it wasn't in the least democratic was it? It's all very well having a jury to try you, but in this case what mattered was the sentencing and that was quite arbitrary, just one man's decision. I'm sure it wasn't what the jury wanted and it wouldn't be what the public would want, if they'd been there. It's up to us to tell them what went on. I took lots of notes. I can describe just what the atmosphere was like in court and how horrified everyone was and –'

'Flinders!'

She had expected Magnus would give her his blessing, offer help. Instead he looked alarmed.

'Now, Flinders, don't be silly. We must do what we always do: give the outline of the case as succinctly as possible, report the verdict and the sentence, get everyone's name right. Check how MacIlroy spells his name by the way. We got it wrong once, I remember.'

'But Magnus, that's not reporting the truth of it,' Polly burst out. 'Carsons was the real villain of the piece. *He* ought to have been in the dock. If all we give are the bald, outward facts, we could give the readers an impression of a pair of professional criminals intimidating some poor helpless chap. I mean that's the opposite of the truth.'

'It's how it must be reported,' Magnus said evenly.

'Not by me, it won't be,' Polly retorted.

Magnus looked at her.

'Time to get back into court,' was all he said.

On the bus going home he refused to discuss it with her and found a seat for himself apart from the pair of them. But when they arrived at the bus station he was more conciliatory. 'Look, Polly,' he said, 'I know the day hasn't turned out quite as you expected and that you're upset. But it's time you grew up. Everyone goes around saying British justice is marvellous but that's only because they rarely see it in action. There comes a moment of disillusionment for everyone and yours was today, I think. Accept it, Polly.'

She shook her head.

'Anyway,' Magnus said briskly, 'let me have your copy tomorrow sometime.' Then a note of warning came into his voice as he added, 'And remember this is your first Assize, so the editor will be looking at your copy very carefully.'

He left them to catch his bus home.

Suddenly it began to rain. Polly and Randy made a dash for the bus shelter, an open-sided affair through which the wind gusted. Polly shivered. She had worn only a thin cotton dress for the July Assize.

'Come on,' Randy said. 'I'll treat you to a pie and a pint at the pub.'

He took her arm and propelled her through the drizzle to the pub on the corner. She felt too tired and miserable to object. Besides, her rage against Randy had abated. Her quarrel with him seemed trivial compared to the dreadful scene they had witnessed together in court.

While he queued at the bar, she sat at a corner table. The grandmother would know by now, she thought. Was she at this moment telling the children? What would she tell them? How on earth do you tell two small children that both their parents are in prison? If it had been only one parent, the other could have managed, concocted something, kept the family together. But both! On the other hand, if she didn't tell them the truth, those children would think their parents had left them for no reason. They'd maybe think it was their own fault, something they had done to make their parents stop loving them. They would listen for odd references, try to fathom it, in the helpless way of children who can't possibly understand the ways of the adult world.

I know something about you, Polly Adams. Your Mam's

run off. I saw her go out earlier. She was carrying a suit-case. She's gone for good. That's the sort she is.'

'Penny for them,' Randy said, returning with the food and drink. 'Though I think I can guess.'

'I was thinking about the children tonight.'

'Yes. I was, too. That judge has smashed four lives today, hasn't he?'

'I could understand it if he didn't know about the children and everything. But he did, he went through it all, raising their hopes because he seemed to understand.'

Randy nodded. 'Yes, I think that's what shocked everybody. That, even more than the actual sentence. It was that long rehearsal of how bad a custodial sentence would be and then, wham, he imposed one on both of them.'

'I couldn't see the sense of his saying that people mustn't get the idea that blackmail goes unpunished –'

'It's called an exemplary sentence. To discourage the others, you know.'

'Yes, I know the theory of it. But who was there to be given an example to? Really and truly, who would ever know about this case beyond a few locals? I bet there won't be one potential blackmailer stopped in his tracks because he's happened to read about Irene's feeble little effort being punished like this. Yet in the vague hope that there might just be such a person, the judge has broken up a family and inflicted all this misery, created all these problems. Not just may have done, but certainly has. It's wicked.'

'I suppose he would argue that sparing a family isn't his concern. He'd say his job was to administer the law, not worry about real justice, as we understand it.'

'Then why did he go on about the children at all?'

'I don't know. Unless it was to add to the punishment by raising false hopes. But actually I don't think the law can be administered impartially. It's administered by people, so personal feelings and prejudices are bound to enter into it. Like, well, who you identify with.'

'How do you mean?'

'Well, from the start I think they all identified with Carsons. You imagine it: he goes to the police, all injured innocence with his story of having this brief fling with a girl at the sea-side and now the wicked bitch is trying to blackmail him. Of course they all identify with him.'

'The policeman looked as sorry as anyone else in court,' Polly objected. 'When the sentence was given.'

Randy shrugged. 'Oh, by the end of it they could see the reality, couldn't they? But it was a bit late by then; the wheels of justice had turned and crushed Irene and Terence and two children in the process.'

'But the judge,' Polly said. 'He's meant to be impartial.'

'He's a man,' Randy pointed out. 'He could identify with Carsons, could imagine such a thing happening to himself, or at least being tempted. It was his sort of human frailty. But look, Polly, if you're as ambitious and tough and logical as a judge must be, there's no way you can identify with Irene, a helpless kid trying to hit back at the world so stupidly. He would never have been even tempted to behave like she did. He'd have known better ways to get justice for himself if he'd been damaged. You and I and a jury could understand her, but he couldn't.'

He sat back and took a long drink.

'That's what I meant,' he concluded, 'by saying that the system may be perfect, but it's people who administer it. People, not gods.'

'I don't think the system is all that good anyway,' Polly said suddenly. 'Think of that rape case. The girl didn't bring evidence against the man simply because the system makes it impossible for her to do so. It's always happening. It's a rotten system. And then again, the system lays down sentences, but the same sentence is different for different people. For some people going to prison is just that, but for Irene, don't you see it's much worse? She passionately wanted to make a home for those children, because she didn't have one herself. All her troubles have stemmed from that. And now she's been forced to betray them. She's had to abandon them for two years, do the same dreadful thing to them that was done to her when she was little and her parents deserted her. She'd been made to inflict the same misery on two quite innocent children that she loves and wanted to help.'

She was near to tears.

'This won't do, Flinders,' Randy said with sudden firmness.

'Do you think that the judge is sitting weeping about that family tonight? Do you really think that as he pours out his first glass of claret, he's worrying about those children and who's putting them to bed?'

He held her half pint of cider up to her lips.

'Drink,' he ordered.

She drank, but it felt like treachery.

'More,' Randy insisted, putting the glass into her hands. 'No, Polly, he's sitting there feeling quite satisfied with the way justice has been administred in his court today. He's done his duty, bless him. He's made England a safer place for middle-aged adulterers.'

Polly spluttered.

'Come on,' Randy encouraged. 'Get the pie inside you, too, and then we'll be able to think better. Have you noticed how difficult it is to get good ideas on an empty stomach?'

'Artists and novelists in garrets are supposed to manage it,' she said, trying to respond to his attempts to cheer her.

He took a bite out of his pie and then stared at her, chewing.

'Flinders,' he said at last. 'Do you think you're in the right job?'

'What do you mean?' she asked, alarmed. 'I love it. I really do. It's just the injustice of this one case.'

'It's not that, Flinders,' he interrupted. 'It's the way you write, too. You need more space than journalism gives you. You remember we talked about it when you did the Tudor Bean article?'

She remembered that night well.

'We talked about us both moving on.'

'It's different for me. I shall work my way up, and if on the way I can have a crack at injustice, so much the better. But you –' He stared at her, assessing. 'Your style's different. You write from the inside. I just feel it's not a journalistic approach. I don't want to sound discouraging,' he said with unusual gentleness.

She shook her head. 'Oh, you're not,' she said.

He was the only one since Tudor Bean who really cared about what she did with her life.

'Well, then, it seems to me that you put so much of yourself into what you write, so much of your heart, and you write something really good and all that happens is that it gets cut back to the bone and ends up being wrecked as creative prose and not really being particularly good journalism. That's what I'm afraid of – that you'll go climbing steadily up, I don't doubt that, but that it'll be the wrong ladder you're climbing.'

'So?'

'Well, it could be that you should give up the idea of saying everything in a thousand words and give yourself something more like seventy thousand.'

She laughed for the first time that day.

'You're mad,' she said. 'Seventy thousand words is a novel.'

'Exactly.'

He was serious, she realised. She thought about it.

'I don't think I have that sort of imagination,' she said.

'Novels aren't about making things up, they're about finding things out. Your sort of novel would be, anyway.'

He went to get more drinks, accepting her money to do so. She sat and thought for a moment about what he had said, but then decided to put it away until later; at the moment she had more urgent things to think about. The first phrases of her report on the Assize case were already taking shape in her mind.

It was Magnus who was sitting in the editor's room on Monday morning, her report on the desk in front of him.

'You're lucky, Polly,' he said, 'that Mr Dinsdale is away today and I'm in his chair.'

It wasn't just his voice or the way he called Sunny Jim Mr Dinsdale; everything about him spoke of anger barely kept under control.

'I made it quite plain to you on Friday evening, Polly, the kind of report we wanted.'

'But, Magnus, I reported it as it was. Is there anything in that which isn't true?' she asked, pointing to the papers on his desk.

'We're not talking about the truth, Polly. Don't be so naïve. You're an intelligent girl and you knew perfectly well what I meant. This is not a campaigning paper. I've told you often enough that our job is to serve the local community –'

'But I *was* doing that, trying to anyway. Irene and Terence and the children, they're all ordinary local people. We should be on their side. A great injustice was done and –'

'But, Polly, life *is* unjust. Look, some children are born healthy, others are born deformed, so right from the start there's injustice. Some children come from happy homes, some from broken homes and –'

'Oh, shut up, Magnus. As if I didn't know that life's unfair!' she exclaimed, her eyes filling with tears.

'Sit down, Polly,' he ordered. When she had moved a pile of books from the other chair and sat down, he added, more in sorrow than in anger, 'It doesn't help to be rude and childish, you know.'

'I'm sorry,' she said hopelessly. 'I really *am* sorry, Magnus. I shouldn't have told you to shut up.'

His mouth twitched.

'Oh, Flinders, what shall we do with you?'

'I don't know.'

'Look, the editor hasn't seen this yet. My advice to you is to let me tear it up and then you write a proper report for me. We'll just forget this one, shall we?'

His kindly face was full of concern as he spoke. It was awful; she'd much rather he was angry. She remembered how wonderful he'd been when Tudor died, how he had persuaded Sunny Jim to let her go to the funeral in his place, how understanding he had been of her need to pay tribute to her old friend. Of all the people in the office it was Magnus whom she most wanted to please. How comforting it would be, she thought now, to take his well-meant advice, creep back into favour.

She shook her head, but said nothing.

'What I don't really understand,' he said, 'is why you're so upset about this case. Frankly, I think you're over-reacting. If, as you say, you are well aware that the world's an unfair place, why do you take this example of injustice so much to heart? Why are you prepared to risk so much for it? Because you are taking a risk, you know.' He paused to let the warning sink in. 'I hope you realise that,' he added pointedly.

There was silence, then she said slowly, 'I've always known life's unfair, but I've always thought that the law was meant to redress the balance, and the awful thing about this case is that the law has simply added to natural injustice. Made it worse, don't you see? That little family had to bear all sorts of problems from the start. Irene never had a home or parents, Terence was deserted by his wife, the children haven't much security, and the law has just piled on more injustice – that's why it's all so dreadful. And apart from all that, legal injustice *is* worse than the other sort. It sets the seal on all injustice. It makes it official.' She paused for breath, then added, 'So that's why I have to write it down as it really was.'

'Why you? Isn't it rather arrogant of someone as young and inexperienced as you are to take it upon yourself to reprimand a judge? Why you?' he repeated.

'Because I was there. I heard it and saw it all. So I have to bear witness. Yes, that's it,' she repeated, suddenly aware of the truth of it. 'I feel obliged somehow or other, to bear witness.'

He looked at her thoughtfully then said, 'There is a possible way out, Polly. I wouldn't normally have mentioned this to you, I'd have left it to the editor. But he has been thinking of giving you more scope –'

'Scope? Me?'

'Yes, a women's column. Maybe eventually a whole page.'

'In order to keep me off the hard news, you mean?'

'Well, it might be a solution, if you really can't conform. I'd do this report for you now, and in future you wouldn't deal with this sort of thing.'

'No, thanks.'

His face hardened. 'Then I must point out to you, Polly, that if you don't want to work in the way we require of you, there are other people who would be eager to take your place. We'd be sorry to part with you, but we'd really have no choice.'

'You mean you'd sack me?'

'Yes.'

Of course she'd known all along that it could lead to this, but to hear it actually put into words was a different matter. To give it all up, this world were she'd been so happy, where she felt she belonged, as she had never belonged anywhere else, ever. She felt sick and dizzy at the idea of it. She couldn't speak.

'Polly,' Magnus said gently, 'don't rush into doing anything silly. As I've told you, the editor hasn't seen this yet, but I know what his reaction will be. Why not let me tear it up? Then I'll cancel all your engagements in the Bible today so that you can be free to rewrite it.'

Still she didn't reply.

'I do wish, Flinders,' Magnus went on, 'that you could believe that I'm not some sort of enemy. I'm on your side. I'm trying to help you. I always have. Can't you believe that? Can't you trust me?'

Simon had used those very words to her, she thought. She had told him it was different with people at work, that she could accept their help, give them her trust. It reminded her of how much they had all helped her; Magnus, above all, had surely earned her trust.

'Very well,' she said. 'I'll rewrite it.'

'That's a sensible girl!' She could hear the relief in his voice. 'You've made a very wise decision, Polly, really you have.'

He got up, beaming at her. She beamed back, momentarily sharing his relief, full of joy at being taken back into the fold. But the feeling didn't last; it began to ebb away even as she followed him down the stairs and along the corridor. Back in the reporters' room all she felt was shame as she settled at the table to rewrite her report, while Magnus made his necessary little alterations in the Bible.

Chapter 11

'You never told me you'd met Captain Quigley again,' Jim remarked unexpectedly as she handed him the tea. 'You never said.'

She shrugged. 'I just didn't think to mention it. Do you want breakfast now or will you wait till you're dressed?'

'I'll wait.'

He stretched and yawned. 'I'd been awake for ages,' he said. 'Then I heard you crashing about so I thought I'd come and drink cups of tea with you and watch you eat. I don't often have you to myself nowadays.'

She smiled, remembering the breakfasts they used to have together, bread and jam, the kettle on the gas, the sound of Mrs Biddle clearing out her fire on the other side of the thin wall. There was no torn lino in this kitchen, the fittings were modern and everything shone. Only the old teapot and cosy were the same.

'How old do you think he is, Polly?'

'Who?'

'Captain Quigley, of course. Well, Major now.'

'I suppose he was in his early twenties when he came to the farm and that was fifteen years ago, so maybe he's in his late thirties.'

'He doesn't look that old. He's very fit. Army life, I suppose. But I wish you'd told me you'd met him again, Polly.'

'It was only by chance after Tudor's funeral. Does it matter?'

'No. It was just that I felt a bit stupid when he talked about you and I didn't know you'd set eyes on him since we were vaccies. It was at the training camp, you know. I suppose he picked me out because I was older than the other National Service chaps and then recognised the name.'

'Do you ever regret doing your National Service after you went to university instead of before?' she asked to deflect the conversation.

'No.'

He got up and brought the teapot over to the table and poured out more tea for them both. 'Some people said it was good to have a break between school and university, made them more mature, but I can't say I noticed it. They used to say the girls at university didn't like chaps straight from school as much as the older ones.'

'And didn't they?'

He smiled, a lazy, reminiscent sort of smile and shook his head. 'I can't say I ever found it a disadvantage,' he said.

She watched him, standing there in his dressing gown, trying to think of him playing the lover. It was impossible. Handsome he certainly was, very appealing in his dressing gown and with his thick hair uncombed, but only Jim all the same.

'Interview me, Polly.'

She pushed her plate away and cleared the table in front of her. Then she pulled forward imaginary papers, sorted them a bit, glanced down at them and said, looking at him over non-existent spectacles, 'Well now, Mr-er-Adams, tell me why you want to teach?'

He burst out laughing. 'Do you remember doing our catechism? If you look like that, I'll start reciting, "Wherein I was made a member of Christ, the Child of God, and an inheritor of the Kingdom of Heaven." '

She sniffed disapprovingly. 'Just concentrate on our discussion Mr Adams, if you please. This is a serious matter, you understand. You may only be choosing a career, but we are choosing a history master for Cuddlethorpe Grammar and may be saddled with him for a very long time.'

'Well, sir, – or madam, of course – I think it is largely because I enjoy dealing with children and –'

'How can you know that, Mr Adams? This is your first post. You are, I imagine, more accustomed to the company of your peers than of your juniors?'

'Oh, come off it, Polly, they won't talk like bloody dictionaries.'

'And you won't get the bloody job if you swear at the interview. Oh, honestly, Jim, I don't think it's possible to practice an interview. I should just listen very carefully to what they have to say and try to answer as honestly as you can.'

'Tell them I'm impressed by the pay, the security and the long holidays?'

'No, it's as silly to blacken yourself as to pretend to be more idealistic than you are. Why don't you forget about it, relax and have a good breakfast? You've masses of time. The train isn't till 11.40, is it?'

'Mam wanted me to practise. You know what a state she's in about this interview.'

'Well, let her have a go at training you then. I'm off.'

She got up and carried her dishes over to the sink.

'I thought you were going to court this morning, our Polly?'

'I am.'

'It doesn't start till ten, so you can stay here and help me to keep calm.'

'No, I'm going early so I can sit and work in the press gallery until the court opens. I often do that. Nobody minds. And I won't get anything done if I stay here – you'd see to that.'

He pulled a face.

'You're so strict nowadays, Polly,' he grumbled.

'I have to be,' she said, drying the dishes and putting them in the cupboard. 'I've a story to get written up before the court opens.'

'A good one?'

'Yes.' She smiled. 'You'd like it,' she said.

'Come on, tell.'

Again the beguiling smile as he pulled her chair out from under the table. She let herself be made to sit down.

'There was this retired signalman called Flaggit,' she began.

'I don't believe it.'

'And he'd gone back temporarily to do duty at the level crossing. Last Thursday he had just closed the gates of the level crossing and gone back to his cabin when he heard a crash and saw a car right across the line. The train was due in three minutes. Without a thought for his own safety, Old Flaggit dashed down the line waving a hand light and so averted disaster. When he came back the car had gone.'

'You don't say he'd imagined the whole thing?'

'No, I don't. The barrier was broken. Well, the police were alerted, of course, and spent the night searching the roads for a battered car.'

'No trace of it?'

'None. But in the cold light of next dawn they spotted it parked in a field with its owner, one Harry Gowers, asleep at the wheel, and a smell of alcohol which the constable described as "overpowering".'

'How could they be sure it was the same car?'

'By the tyre tracks. Also Mr Gowers didn't exactly deny it. He said he was driving along the road at night and saw the red lights of the signals in front of him and mistook them for the rear lights of a parked car, so naturally accelerated to overtake it. When he came to a halt, he was on a railway line with a barrier in front of him, so he reversed back up the road and was on his way home when he mistook a turning and found himself in a field. So he went to sleep. He could only assume that the smell of whisky arose from the fact that somebody had broken a bottle of it in his car recently.'

'It'll make a lovely story, Polly. Full of human interest and nobody actually hurt. Funny, too.'

'Oh, I mustn't be funny, Jim. It's got to have a suitable ring of solemnity and perhaps a reminder about taking care at level crossings.'

Jim yawned and stretched.

'I love to hear your cases, Polly.'

She smiled at him indulgently. It was true, he did love a tale. She had relayed most of her cases to him. Not the blackmail case, though. For some reason she had not told him about Terence and Irene and Mr Carson's. Perhaps she cared too much about it to use it for entertainment, she thought. Or maybe she just felt ashamed of the way she had given in. There was a feeling of unfinished business too, as if one day she would come back to it, and didn't want to find the waters muddied with idle chat. Meanwhile she had a feeling of not being trusted at the office as she used to be; something was spoilt. Magnus especially was less at ease with her.

'It's not so much that I disagree with you,' he had said recently, 'but it's the way you set about getting things done, Polly. It puts people's backs up, and that really won't do on a local paper like ours.'

She knew that he was trying to warn her. Oh well, she thought, I suppose something will precipitate a crisis one day, a similar court case will have to be reported, similar threats will be made. She didn't know when it would be or how she would react. She tried not to think about it.

'I must go, Jim,' she said, getting up from the table. 'If you want to be useful, you might take Mam a cuppa when you go upstairs.'

'I thought she was going to lie in and try to get rid of that cold today?'

'Yes, but she might want a drink. I looked in earlier, but she was asleep.'

'All right. But I shan't sit and hold her hand. I don't want her germs, thank you very much.'

As she walked to court, taking all the quiet back ways, she let herself remember her walk with Martin Quigley, the memory of which she had refused to share with Jim. It was a memory which she took out now and then and relived, but only when, as now, she knew she would not be interrupted. That evening, after she left Mrs Bean, she had meant to work on her article about Tudor. Captain Quigley, after visiting his aunt, had intended to go and see friends in the village. Instead it had seemed the most natural thing in the world that they should set off up the dale together in the late afternoon. It was a perfect day; it would be light and warm for many hours yet.

It was the time of day when she and Jimmy used to walk back to the farm after school, the time of day when the lambs began to frisk, even when they were a few months old and looked bigger than the newly-shorn sheep. It was the time of day when the sun had lost its midday intensity, when the air would soon begin to cool and the dry-stone walls give back the warmth which they had absorbed during the day. She paused, as she walked, to touch the stones and feel their warmth as she used to do when she was little, letting her hand slide over the smoothness of some, fingering the rough, lichened surface of others.

As they walked, Martin Quigley told her that the Braithwaites had left, retired to somewhere far away and the farm was empty now, awaiting new tenants at Michaelmas. She was relieved to hear it; she wouldn't have to think up an excuse not to call on them. Even now, after all these years, the hurt was as fresh as it had been when she was nine years old.

When they reached the farm, the gate into the yard creaked eerily as they opened it, the house looked deserted, no dogs barked.

They stood by the pump and he said, 'Of course, you weren't here long, you and your brother, were you?'

She shook her head, unable to reply. He looked at her curiously. 'It hurt,' she managed to say, 'being sent away from here.'

She turned her face away, holding back tears, and put her hand on the pump for reassurance, trying to get a grip on herself. But the familiar feel of the lumpy metal under her fingers only brought her childhood rushing back more strongly, as if the pain of their dismissal from the farm was contained in the very metal of the pump. She had been dry-eyed and resentful then but to her bitterness against the adult world, time had added pity for those children so that now she could weep the tears she had not shed then. She just stood there, her hand on the pump handle, as she had so often done years ago, and cried quietly and without fuss.

Martin Quigley did not fuss either. He led her out of the farmyard and up the lane to the place where the stream flowed under the ground. From there they climbed up to the source and all the time she was talking quietly, telling him how it had been. As they sat on a boulder by the stream, she even told him about Miss Capstick and the book and he understood and did not pretend that rumours of her awfulness as an evacuee had not reached him from his Aunt Emily. Somehow the way he let her talk and did not take advantage of her distress was more comforting than any embrace or demonstration of sympathy would have been. Then she fell silent and they sat companionably on their boulder as the sun began to set.

As they watched, the shadows lengthened and the stillness of evening moved gently into the dale, taking quiet possession of it until everything that belonged here, even the sheep and little streams, seemed to submit to it, while the distant hills and the green slopes near at hand were alike subdued. Then they got up and walked quietly home, as if afraid of disturbing the evening stillness.

She did not see Martin Quigley again; he left early the next morning and she was herself immersed in work. But the memory of that walk remained, a quite separate thing from other memories, which she could uncover and enjoy whenever the time was right. She knew that she would never forget it, or let it blur. It would always be clear and vivid, a reminder that peace was a real and powerful thing, not just the absence of strife. She had been taken aback when Jim asked her about Martin Quigley. He did not belong in the everyday world. He belonged in that memory and was part of that peace.

She was almost at the magistrates' court. She decided to take a short cut down an alleyway, which led through the yard at the side of the police block where the cells were. She could go down there and in by the side door of the court.

She set herself to thinking about a headline for the level crossing case. There was the Bartropp Paternity case to be written up too, she thought as she pushed open the gate that led into the yard. At first she couldn't make out what the noise was. It sounded like a mixture of an unruly school playground and a heavy rainstorm. Odd on a peaceful spring morning. Then she stood in the gate way, unable to move, staring.

On the far side of the yard a naked man was standing, his back to the wall. Not exactly standing, for he was jumping, dancing up and down and screaming with pain as if the ground was burning hot under the soles of his feet. But it wasn't the ground that was torturing him. It was a policeman with a high pressure hose. He had his back towards her, his sleeves rolled up, and he was playing the hose up and down the man's naked body but mainly on his genitals, which the man tried in vain to protect with his hands or by leaping out of the way. But with great skill the policeman used the lashing water like a whip to control him.

Vomit rose in her throat, then she turned and ran.

She ran all the way to the telephone box and dialled Mr Dinsdale's number. Almost in tears she poured out what she had just seen. In England. In their own town. Here.

He heard her out in silence. Then she said, 'I don't want to know about this, Polly. Put it out of your mind.'

'Of course I can't put it out of my mind! I'll never get it out of my mind, never! I can't describe what it was like. You *must* do something. We must tell people what is going on.'

'I decide what we must tell people on our paper, Polly, not you. Besides, why should anyone believe the tale of one girl with no witnesses?'

'But the man will say what happened to him.'

'Will he? And risk something worse happening next time? Oh, Polly, be your age. He's most likely a drunk, an old lag. The police would get him in again without any trouble, he knows that. He won't complain. I've never known any prisoner in a case like this who's complained twice.'

'A case like this? You mean it's happened before?'

'Not exactly like this, but similar things happen. The police are human, like the rest of us.'

'If you won't print my story, then I shall send it a national newspaper.'

'Do that and you're fired.'

He put the receiver down.

She was trembling as she walked away from the telephone box. Inside her head she could still hear the sounds that the man had made. Once, in the war, she heard a correspondent on the wireless reporting on what had happened in a Russian village which the Nazis were punishing. They assembled the villagers to watch as their leader was burned to death. But they burnt him by a very gentle flame which they played on him for hours so that he did not burn or suffocate, but simply melted very slowly, the fat from his body dripping from him until he was dancing in a pool of it, slipping in it. It was like watching a piece of meat cooking very, very slowly the villagers said, and the sounds that issued from his tortured lips were like no sound that they had ever heard a human being make.

It was not the same here in Brigthorpe. The man in the yard would not die, but it was part of the same thing. The hose, the tormentor. Men are made in the same image and the same evil can take over any of them if it is allowed to grow. She could not pass by on the other side.

She retraced her steps back to the telephone box. The chief constable was courteous and listened to her more patiently than her own editor had done. She decided it was best to be honest and told him exactly what happened and that her editor had refused to print her story. Afterwards she regretted that; he might have taken more notice if he had feared publicity.

'Well, Miss Adams,' he said, when she had finished. 'What you tell me is highly regrettable and I shall certainly look into it. Did you by any chance see the police constable's number?'

'No, he had no jacket on. He was just wearing trousers and a shirt with its sleeves rolled up.'
'But you saw his face? You would recognise him again?'
'No, he had his back to me all the time. I don't think either of them saw me. There was so much noise going on. I don't think the man looked up at all. He had his head bent right down, trying to protect it. He couldn't use his hands to cover his face, you see.'
'Yes. It must have been a very distressing sight, especially for a young lady. But you must understand that cleaning up drunks is a pretty unpleasant business, too. I think you wouldn't find that very enjoyable either. Sometimes they do have to be hosed down.'
'No,' she insisted. 'It was a pressure hose and it was not being used just to clean him. I saw it all with my own eyes.'
'Well, you leave it with me, Miss Adams. Thank you for letting me know. I'll certainly look into the whole matter, you can rest assured. Now you do as your editor suggests and forget the whole incident.'
She would never forget it, never. She knew that. She knew, too, that there was only one person who would understand, see it as she did. Loathe him as she often did, he was the one she had to talk to.
'Randy?' Magnus repeated, surprised. 'He's still off sick.'
She'd forgotten all about Randy's 'flu.
'Anything I can do?' Magnus asked. 'You look upset.'
She hesitated. It would be good to pour it all out to Magnus but instinct told her that his sense of duty to the paper would make him take the same line as the editor.
'No, thanks,' she said.
'Actually, if you want to see Randy, the editor's looking for someone to take a letter to him. It's urgent. The Cleghorn business, you know.'
She groaned.
'It's serious, Polly. Mr Cleghorn was in again this morning. Apparently he's having all kinds of adverse reactions to his speech. Or rather what Randy reported as his speech. Mr Cleghorn says it's the flat opposite of what he was trying to convey to his audience.'
'It's not like Randy to get it wrong.'

'True. Randy has his failings, but deafness isn't one of them.'

For a moment, as she stood on the doorstep of his lodgings, she wondered if Randy had simply run away, the place seemed so deserted. Maybe he wasn't ill at all, just too scared to come into the office and face the music. She was turning away when she heard a sound from the other side of the door and saw the knob turn. The door opened and Randy stood there in his pyjamas. He had put on, but not fastened, an old tartan dressing gown and was carrying his slippers. He was a bad colour, his eyes had black circles round them, but his face lit up when he saw her. 'Flinders, what a lovely surprise. Come in. And I nearly didn't bother to come down. I think everyone else must be out.'

He led the way upstairs, still carrying his slippers. His ankles were bony and as white as peeled potatoes, she observed, as she followed him up the stairs, across the landing and into his small attic bedroom, which was stuffy in the summer heat. He got back into bed, exhausted even after so little exertion, and she sat down on the only chair.

'Have they sent you to sack me?'

'I don't know.'

She handed him the letter which he tore open clumsily.

'Well, it's not the sack, yet,' he said, when he had read it. 'But Sunny Jim says he requires an explanation acceptable both to himself and the Chairman.'

'Can you explain to me?' she said.

He looked around the room, as if to make sure nobody could hear. 'I'll try,' he said. He paused, as if trying to make sense of it in his own mind. 'You see, Sunny Jim was dead keen on getting full reports of all three speeches by the candidates last Wednesday. Set the scene for the by-election and all that. They chose to make them in outlandish places, needless to say. I mean God knows why Cleghorn has to make a major policy statement at the County Show. Anyway, I was feeling more ill than I've ever felt in my life. I couldn't stop shivering and I had this pneumatic drill boring a hole in the top of my head. Just to complicate things I had to be back here at midday and then cycle out to Naunceton for the second speech and then on to the showground for Cleghorn. Somewhere along the line I lost my pad and had to take it down on loose sheets. I didn't eat all day, but kept going on aspirin and alcohol. I had two brandies before I cycled out for the last run. They took all my life's savings, but I couldn't have got there otherwise and I knew the editor really wanted those speeches.'

'So?'

He shook his head and groaned. 'I can't describe what it was like trying to write that night. I'd got the first speech down fairly well, the second was pretty rough and the third was frankly unfathomable. I couldn't make out my own shorthand and I'd got all the pages confused. And you know how usually you've got the gist of the thing in your mind anyway? Well, I hadn't. I just had no idea what he'd said. The meaning hadn't reached my brain. Anyway, I put down what I thought each of them was likely to have said, and handed it in. The rest, Polly, is history,' he concluded solemnly.

He was putting a brave face on it, she thought, but she knew how serious it would be for him to be sacked. He had no other income and no parents to turn to. He wouldn't get much of a reference from his editor either.

'I get the impression,' she warned, 'that Sunny Jim wants your head on a platter.'

'I don't think he's too fussed about the platter.'

He lay back, shut his eyes for a few moments, and then said, 'What would you do, Flinders? Confess all?'

She shook her head. 'No, I'd lie low for a bit. It's lucky you're ill. I'll tell them you're too feverish to reply now, but will when you're a bit better.'

'Yes,' he said more cheerfully. 'Tell Sunny Jim I'll write when the delirium has left me.'

'Well, words to that effect. And you never know . . .' She shrugged. 'At least it gives us a day or two for something unexpected to happen.'

'Like Cleghorn dropping down dead? He's not the sort. At the moment I feel as if I'm locked in a nightmare and the only possible solution is to wake up. It would have to be Cleghorn, wouldn't it? I mean I have to pick the candidate who's chairman of the directors of the newspaper which employs me, don't I? And which employs Sunny Jim too, which is even more important.'

'Look, Randy, there's no point in thrashing it all over in your mind now. You might as well relax. There's nothing you can do. Lie there and swallow aspirin and I'll come back tomorrow evening and give you an up-to-date report on the Cleghorn situation. Then we'll concoct some sort of letter together.'

'Thanks, Flinders. You're a pal.'

'That's all right. See you tomorrow about eight.'

She delivered the message to the editor the next day. He listened, grim-faced and silent. Randy and she were both in disgrace.

'I'm going to collect a reply for you this evening,' she added.

'It had better be a good one,' Sunny Jim said ominously.

She was in the reporters' room reading proofs for the Local Wills column to Sid when Mr Cleghorn's letter came. Magnus, who was making the preliminary selection of letters for the correspondence page, opened it.

' "Mr Albert Potter of the Manor House, Springfield Terrace, rag merchant, who died on April 3rd last," ' Polly intoned, ' "left £9,664 3s 10d gross (£8,896 7s 2d net). Duty paid £354. He left £100 to his housekeeper, Mrs Lavinia Stoker, if still in his employ, his masonic effects to Donald Hirst of 22 Moorcroft, Brigthorpe . . .' But all the time she was watching Magnus, observing his swift reaction to the letter, his sudden exit.

' "£2,000 to his wife's niece, Caroline Ash of Totnes, and the family Bible to his sister Harriet Potter," ' Polly went on until he was out of ear-shot. Then, 'I wonder what Chairman Cleghorn had to say in that letter?'

Sid shrugged. 'Probably told the editor to sack the lot of us.'

But when Magnus came back he said cheerfully, 'Well, that's all over.'

'All of us for the chop?'

'No. Apparently Mr Cleghorn has been rereading the report of his speech very carefully and realised that it was a pretty good speech and so he's written a long letter for pub-

lication in this week's paper justifying the stand he took and answering all potential critics.'
'But –'
'Yes, Polly?'
'Nothing.'
'Oh, and Polly, the editor says there's no need for Randy to reply to his letter, but please will you call just the same and give him best wishes for a quick recovery? And here's half a crown to buy him a bottle of Lucozade.'

When she told Randy that evening, he sat on the edge of his untidy bed and roared with laughter.

'Do you know, that's one solution I never dreamed of,' he exclaimed. Then he calmed down and, looking at her solemnly, said, 'Let it be a lesson to us both. Never underestimate the power of the press, Flinders, to influence the policy of our masters.'

'Fool,' she said amicably. 'Have some Lucozade.'

'Thanks, we'll celebrate on it. You have the tooth mug and I'll have the jam jar.'

As they drank he said, 'And how are things at work, apart from *l'Affaire* Cleghorn?'

She hesitated. 'Well, there was something I wanted to talk to you about, Randy. That's really why I came yesterday, but then I thought you had trouble enough already.'

'Out with it. Tell Uncle Randy. He's better now.'

'Yes, you look better.'

'Back to work tomorrow. Phew, but I've been lucky. Go on.'

She told him what had happened in the yard next to the courts, what she had seen and what she had heard. She repeated to him her conversations with the editor and the chief constable.

'What we need,' Randy said, when she had finished, 'is another witness. I suppose they'll be a bit careful after this, but it could be worth a try. We'll go through the yard together next time and see what we can see.'

'I wish I hadn't rung the chief constable now, and most especially I curse myself for telling him that the editor wouldn't print the story. Publicity was the only weapon I had and I chucked it away.'

'Oh, don't you worry, he'd have been on to Sunny Jim himself anyway and made sure of his silence.'

'Do you really believe that? I mean, I thought that journalism was about revealing the truth, not hiding it. That's what we're for, isn't it?'

'So long as the truth isn't inconvenient to the establishment, yes. If it is, they'll put every possible difficulty in the way.'

'But how can you say that so calmly? It's awful.'

He looked at her. 'Not once you've accepted it. Then all it does is make the job a bit more difficult and challenging. I believe what you told me, Flinders love, and I believe people should know about it. It's a bit of news that's a lot more important to our readers in the long run than who was the speaker at the Women's Institute last week.'

'So what do we do now?'

'We go to court together next time, and I'll take the camera. And if we can collect evidence, we'll see this through, you and I, and nothing will stop us, even if we both get the sack.'

'Oh, thank you, Randy.'

It was heartfelt; she was no longer alone. What she had seen had been shattering enough, but what she had heard from an editor and a chief constable had shattered her even more. And now in this grotty attic bedroom where Randy lodged, she felt her faith a little bit restored. Randy had only just escaped being sacked and yet here he was, ready to risk his job again for a matter of principle.

'Randy,' she said suddenly and in surprise. 'You're a good person.'

He stared at her for a moment, then began to laugh.

'But you are,' she insisted. 'Don't pretend. You care about what's right. Isn't that what being *good* means?'

'Oh, Flinders, you are so funny.'

His arms were around her. 'It's not at all what you were calling me last time we discussed my morals,' he went on, steering her towards the bed.

'Well, maybe there are different sorts of goodness – stop that, Randy.'

'Oh, no, my lovely Flinders, I'm going to take advantage of

your new opinion of me. I'm going to seize my moment,' he murmured, kissing her. 'Besides, if anyone ever needed comforting it's you. So just relax. Leave it to Randy. And, by the way, since I know you didn't do as I said about the wedding ring and the clinic, Randy's seen to all that, too.'

It seemed right, the two of them united against the world in the attic bedroom.

Next week they went to court together. It was sunny as they entered the alleyway which led to the side entrance of the court.

'Good for photographs,' Randy said.

When they reached the yard, however, the great gates were locked.

'That's the first time I've known that happen,' he said. 'We'll just have to go in the front entrance.'

There they talked to the young constable on duty.

'By the way,' Randy remarked to him casually, 'I always come in the side entrance – you know, down the alley. Much quicker from my side of town. But it's all bolted and barred today.'

'Yes,' the constable said. 'I don't know why. Did no harm, the press coming in that way, but the Chief says it's to be closed. I think they had a bit of bother with intruders or something. Anyway, troublemakers of some kind or other. Shame when that happens. It spoils it for everyone else.'

She didn't tell Randy what she had done; there was no point in involving him, she thought as she posted her letter off to the national newspaper. She was the one who had been there, so she must be the one to bear witness. It all seemed inevitable now; she realised that she had been waiting for something like this to happen ever since the Assize. She had expected it to be another court case, that was all.

Everything that Sunny Jim said was inevitable too when he summoned her to his room that Wednesday morning, after the telephone call from his fellow editor in London.

'So he will be in touch with you,' he concluded coldly. 'He will be returning your article and giving his reasons for rejecting it, no doubt.'

She should have realised that they would gang up against her; on impulse she had sacrificed everything and achieved nothing.

'Do you remember what I said to you on the phone when you rang me that morning, Polly?'

Her chin went up defiantly as she waited for sentence to be passed upon her, but she said nothing.

'Do you?' he insisted.

'Yes.'

'But despite that you went ahead, didn't you, and wrote to a national paper?'

'Yes.'

'So you're fired. Do you understand why?'

'Yes.'

'Have you anything to say? Any explanation?'

She realised that he wanted her to try to explain, would prefer an argument.

'No,' she said.

'Then you'll be paid until the end of the month, but need only work for the rest of this week.' He reached for the Bible which he had brought up to his room. 'Your last engagements will be the Conservative Bazaar on Saturday morning and the Rotary dinner that evening. Drop the copy in by Sunday evening, will you?'

He leaned back and looked at her. It struck her that his present controlled rage was quite unlike his usual Wednesday furies. This was the real thing.

'I'm sorry we have to part like this, Polly, but really you give me no option. I am prepared to let you have a good reference. You're an intelligent, hard-working girl. You write well. But I'm not prepared to put up with insubordination from you or anyone else.'

He waited as if expecting some reply. When none came, he added, 'Well, I'll see you before you leave. Oh, and ask Magnus to come up, would you?'

'Anything wrong?' Randy asked when they were alone together in the reporters' room.

'No, nothing,' she said lightly. 'Bit of a headache, that's all.'

She had decided that she would tell nobody. Magnus and the editor knew, of course, but nobody else needed to. She would work on as usual, right up to the end. It was her way of managing.

But she had to tell her mother.

'Well, I can't pretend to be sorry,' she said, a note of triumph in her voice. 'If you ask my opinion it was the silliest thing you ever did, leaving the building society and going in for newspaper writing. Long hours and rotten pay –'

She stopped. Perhaps it was something in the expression on her daughter's face that gave her pause. Whatever the reason, she went on more gently, 'Well, don't worry, Polly. Things are easier now that Jim's got a job. I can manage without taking any money from you while you look around.'

She made as if to put an arm round her daughter's shoulders as she sat at the kitchen table, but Polly stiffened and moved out of range.

'I'll make a cup of tea,' her mother said.

Polly said nothing. As her mother busied herself at the sink she sat silently at the table, resenting being beholden to her even for a cup of tea.

'There,' her mother said, putting the tray down on the table. 'You know what I've been thinking? They might take you back at the building society. Really that's the sort of job for you, Polly. Better paid and a nicer class of people to mix with.'

She is trying to be kind, Polly thought, she is holding out an olive branch. She wants to sit here and drink tea with me and plan my future.

'Do you mind if I take it upstairs?' she asked, getting up. 'I've an awful lot of work to do. It's going to be very busy, this last week at the office.'

Chapter 12

'Suez Crisis,' the telegram said, 'arrive Brigthorpe station midday stop Please meet if possible stop Quigley'

She only just got there on time. The Conservative Bazaar dragged on. They kept saying they'd do the raffle but didn't, and she had to stay to get the names of all the winners. Then the chairman launched into a long political speech. She was still frantically trying to take it down in shorthand when the train was due in at the station.

She was lucky – it was late. In fact, she bumped into Martin Quigley as she ran across the forecourt. He caught her by the arm and steadied her. 'I'm so glad you could come,' he said. 'Have you time for lunch at the Station Hotel?'

'Oh, I've nothing urgent until a dinner to report this evening.'

'Good, then we've plenty of time to talk.'

The Station Hotel was old and grand and dusty. It wasn't very warm either. She kept her coat on as they sat as near as they could to a small and smoky fire.

'You'd think they could pinch a bit of coal from the stoker,' she remarked.

He laughed. 'You don't change,' he said, shaking his head at her.

'From what?' she asked, surprised. 'I mean you haven't known me long.'

'I've known you fifteen years,' he said. 'And that's just the sort of thing you might have said when you were – how old were you when you locked me out and then we had tea together?'

'Nine.'

'Yes, I've known you since you were nine, Polly.'

'On and off,' she pointed out.

'And you always had a direct way with you, even then.'

Although the dining-room was almost empty, the service was very slow. Elderly waiters crawled across a great acreage of thick, red carpet to deliver them food that was almost cold, moving dishes with great deliberation and lifting the cutlery as if it were very heavy.

Martin Quigley was apologetic.

'It's not your fault,' she reassured him. 'Maybe we should have sat nearer the kitchen, then the food wouldn't have had such a long journey.'

They chatted and laughed and were so much at ease with one other that she almost forgot about being sacked. She almost forgot about the telegram, too. It was towards the end of the meal that she asked him what it was all about.

The waiter was struggling with the trifle, trying to persuade thick and adhesive custard to leave the serving spoon by shaking it up and down with rapid jerks of his mottled brown hand. At last he succeeded in dolloping it on to their plates and moved slowly away.

'I've decided to leave the army,' Martin Quigley said. 'I shall apply, when this lot's over, for an administrative job in the Ministry of Defence.'

'That's a very sudden decision, isn't it?'

'In a way, yes. I was approaching the age when I'd have had the option of doing that, but this Suez business has made up my mind for me. I really can't see how our Government can feel justified in attacking Egypt on the grounds that she's already been invaded by Israel. And I don't believe the politicians anyway – I think there's been collusion all along the line. Most of us think that. So while I obviously have to go ahead and obey orders now, I just don't want to be involved in any repeat performances.'

'Oh, just like me!' she exclaimed. Then she, who had not even told Randy that she had been sacked, poured the whole story out to Martin Quigley.

'What will you do?'

She shrugged. 'I'd like to find another job on a newspaper, but there'd be nothing local and I can't afford to live away. I suppose I'll just have to look for an ordinary office job.'

'What would you really like to do, if you could choose?'

'Free-lance writing,' she said, surprised at herself for being so forthcoming. Maybe it's always easier to confide in strangers, she thought.

'Randy, the other reporter of about my age –'

'What an extraordinary name.'

'He's really called Randell, but gets called Randy. He thinks I could get free-lance work. Actually he thinks I'd be better at non-journalistic writing.'

'You could give it a try. That's the only way to find out if you can do anything, Polly.'

She shook her head. 'No, I need the pay packet. I can't do without that even for a short time.'

'Even living at home?'

She shook her head again; she couldn't explain. She would never take anything from her mother. Every bit of heat she used, every crumb she ate, she would pay for.

'You can't take from people you don't love,' she said abruptly.

He didn't reply. Afraid that she had embarrassed him, she said, 'I interrupted you just now. You were going to say something about your plans.'

He hesitated.

'Let me pour out the coffee first,' he said.

'Thank you. What time do you have to leave? I suppose it's the 2.45 to London?'

'No, I'm just going back where I came from.'

'Oh. You've something to do here in Brigthorpe then?'

He looked at her. 'Yes, you could say that.' He paused and then went on, 'What you were saying just now wasn't really an interruption. It may well be connected with what I was going to say.'

'How?'

'I was going to say – or rather ask – would you marry me?'

She dropped her coffee, the whole cupful, all over the seven guinea gaberdine coat from Dingley's. He jumped up and dabbed at her with paper table napkins.

'I'd better go and wash it,' she said. 'I mean it's waterproof, isn't it?'

She was trembling as she sluiced the coat down in the Ladies' Room. It must be some sort of joke, she thought, soaking herself as well as the gaberdine as the water sloshed over the side of the basin in a great tidal wave right down her front. He scarcely knew her, probably thought she was still a silly kid to be teased. She looked for something to dry herself on. There was nothing but a roller towel hanging in a great loop far too high up. Of course she'd made a fool of herself when they first met, so maybe he'd always think of her like that. She managed to arch herself up and rub her front with the edge of the towel, then lifted up the skirt of her dress and rubbed that too. Thank goodness she'd got a decent frock on under the coat, she thought, as she hoisted up one leg to try to dry it. It was lucky too that nylons dried easily. Her foot got tangled up in the loop of the towel and suddenly she skidded on the wet, slippery tiles and sat down hard. She wasn't hurt but could have cried all the same, sitting there on the wet floor.

She made a great effort and got up, biting back tears.

'Pull yourself together, Polly Adams,' she told her reflection, 'And no blubbing, mind.'

Her face stared back, a bit puffy. The green eyes were full. She sniffed and took out her comb. She combed her hair carefully, and powdered her cheeks. They were pale. She pinched them. She put on lipstick. Martin Quigley, she told herself, is not one who would tease like that. He's a mature man, quite grown-up and responsible. The Suez crisis had made a lot of people take sudden decisions. There was that friend of Jim's who was getting married in a great rush because he'd been called up. And it was true: they had known each other fifteen years and she felt just as much at home with him as if they had been together most of that time. And if she did marry him she wouldn't need to worry about money any more. And she'd be able to go free-lance.

Of course Martin Quigley was serious, she was convinced of that by the time she had taken off her shoes and dried them on the roller towel, watching the door in case anyone came in and caught her at it. It wasn't as if he was a silly ass like Randy. Randy . . . he wouldn't be a problem any more. He was only a problem because he satisfied a physical need and yet she didn't like him, not really. Well, she didn't respect him, anyway, not enough to marry him. She had realised over the past year that she couldn't live celibate. Simon had been right when he said she was ripe for marrying, and here was Martin Quigley asking her to do just that. And she did respect him. Marrying Martin Quigley would solve all her problems and make him happy, too.

But he's a stranger, all the same, she thought as she arranged the dripping coat over the radiator by the basin. I don't really know him at all. But, in a way that only made it more exciting.

'Oh, I don't know, I don't know,' she said aloud, taking one last look at her reflection before bidding it farewell.

Martin Quigley did not see her come back into the dining-room. He looked very lonely sitting there surrounded by empty tables, she thought as she walked the length of the room to join him. Off guard, he quite lost his strong, self-contained, soldierly look. His expression was wistful as he stared in front of him, his chin cupped in his hand. For a moment she saw in him the little boy he must once have been, and was reminded of Jimmy.

'Oh, I'm sorry,' he said, jumping up. 'I didn't see you coming.' He held out her chair for her. 'And I mean I'm sorry, too, because of how I – I mean, I sort of sprang that on you in such a, well, thoughtless way. So clumsy –'

He shook his head, not knowing how to go on, and looked at her helplessly. Again he reminded her of Jimmy. He had that look, frightened and upset, of a little boy who has done everything wrong. Instinctively she wanted to reassure him, make it all right for him.

'No,' she said, 'I was the clumsy one.' She waited until they were both sitting down and then smiled across at him. 'And thank you, yes, I will.'

He looked at her and swallowed.

'I'm sorry, Polly,' he said with some embarrassment. 'But I don't know if it's the coffee you're accepting, or me.'

'Both,' she said. 'I've had a long time to think in there, and I've decided it's a good idea – to get married, I mean.'

Chapter 13

'Welcome to the colony, Mrs Quigley,' Mrs James said, crossing the veranda to greet her at the top of the stairs. 'How are you?'

'Pregnant,' Polly told her. 'Thank you.'

'Oh, yes, well, so I see. I mean, how nice.'

She was a tall woman and imposing with it. Polly noticed that she sailed rather than walked as she led the way across the veranda and into the drawing-room.

'Now let me introduce you to the ladies, while the maid brings your coffee. Or would you prefer lime juice?'

Having chosen lime juice, Polly was presented in turn to Mrs Baxter, a tiny mouse of a lady with a thin, pink mouth and fine whiskers, who held out her limp little hand like a paw. By contrast Mrs Shotter, who gripped her hand hard, was solid and tough-looking with busy black eyebrows under a thatch of wiry hair. Polly didn't catch the name of the third lady who looked ill and kept fanning herself with a straw fan.

They sat, the five of them, dotted about an enormous room, separated from each other by what seemed acres of polished floor which made the subsequent questioning more like an interrogation than conversation. During the proceedings an African girl moved silently between them filling up cups and glasses, offering biscuits.

'Mrs Quigley's husband,' Mrs James began, 'is working here for the Ministry of Defence.'

They nodded.

'Very hush-hush, is it?' Little Mrs Baxter asked, turning to Polly, her mouth and whiskers twitching nervously. 'Not to be talked about?'

'Oh, no,' Polly reassured her. 'He talks about it all the time. They're busy with the piling now.'
'Piling?' Mrs James repeated. 'How fascinating.'
'Are you connected with the Kent Quigleys?' Mrs Shotter asked abruptly.
'I don't know.'
'I ask because my husband is connected with them on his mother's side.'
'Oh.'
There was silence. Mrs Baxter sipped nervously at her lime juice, Mrs Shotter dipped her great eyebrows over her coffee cup and the one who looked ill sighed and wielded the fan.
'Do you have any brothers and sisters?' Mrs James asked.
'One brother. He's a teacher.'
'Really? My nephew is a schoolmaster too. He teaches mediaeval history at Eton.'
'Our Jim teaches history at Cuddlethorpe Grammar.'
'How nice. I must tell my nephew to look out for him.' There was a pause, then she added, 'What is his name, may I ask?'
'Adams. Jim Adams. I was Polly Adams before I was married.'
'We know a Brigadier Adams in Cumberland,' Mrs Shotter told her. 'Is there any connection, I wonder?'
'Shouldn't think so,' she said. 'My mam and dad come from Brigthorpe since way back.'
'Ah.'
'And are you settled in?' the lady with the fan asked, her voice faint and plaintive. 'Have you settled the servant problem?'
'We don't seem to have a problem,' Polly said, puzzled.
'The Quigleys are in the Matthews' house and the servants were included,' Mrs James explained on her behalf.
'How sensible. It's always difficult to know what to do about the servants if you go on leave. We always throw them in with the house.'
'And are they any good, Mrs Quigley?'
'What?'
'The servants. The servants the Matthews left for you.'
'Oh, Lily and Mavis? Oh, yes, they're ever so nice. The

only trouble is they don't leave anything for me to do really.'

'Surely in this heat, and in your condition – ?'

'Yes, it's all right when you're pregnant, but what do you all do with yourselves when you're not? I mean do you have jobs?'

There was a shocked silence.

'Jobs,' little Mrs Baxter repeated and twitched nervously. She glanced at Mrs Shotter, whose eyebrows had disappeared into her wiry black hair so that her features were now concentrated at the top and bottom of her face and there seemed to be a blank area in between, pink and roughened, like blotting paper. The one who looked ill fanned herself gently and gazed down at the floor, in whose highly polished surface were reflected the huge ferns which hung in baskets from the ceiling.

'Well, you see,' Mrs James began, recovering first, 'we feel we *do* have a job. Running a home and seeing to everything is a job, as it was for our mothers and their mothers. And of course when the children come out from England for their long summer holidays, we're very busy indeed.'

'But the servants do all the work,' Polly pointed out.

'Ah no, they have to be told everything. You can't trust them with decisions. You'll soon find out. We have a busy social life, too. Most mornings there is a coffee party at one or another house, then the menfolk come home for luncheon. In the afternoon it's wise to have a rest and in the evening there's nearly always a cocktail party or dinner or reception. Something of that sort.'

Polly shook her head. 'It's a funny way to live,' she said.

'And of course the younger ones go down to the new swimming pool,' Mrs James put in, as if that was some sort of a job, too. 'You must join them. You'll find it very useful when you have the baby.'

'Yes. They say that if you throw babies into the water they swim even though they've never been taught.'

'It may be true of native children,' Mrs James said, 'but not ours.'

Having done their duty by the newcomer, the ladies of the compound fell to talking among themselves, about people and topics that meant nothing to Polly, so she sat, watching them and listening but not joining in, until it was time to go.

Contrary to what Mrs James had said, Martin didn't come home to lunch; he preferred to take sandwiches and a flask of iced drink with him to work. Lily was sitting waiting for her on the back steps to the kitchen.

'Madam's back,' she said, and grinned.

'Hello. You should have gone, Lily.'

'Everything's ready for madam's lunch, all in refrigerator,' Lily said. 'But I stay for the wash up.'

'No, there's no need. I'll do it. You go home.'

'Thanks, madam,' Lily said, and made her way down the steps.

Polly watched her go, the wide, black feet treading confidently down the rough steps and across the stony path. How tough the soles of her feet must be, she thought. Lily hated wearing shoes. She put them on for good manners sometimes in the evening and walked awkwardly in them, as wary as Polly would be if she went bare-foot on stones. At the gate she turned and waved. Polly waved back, and then went indoors. She took her salad and fruit out on to the veranda and sat rocking herself in a cane chair, nibbling at the green peppers and tiny lettuce leaves, at the mangoes and pawpaws and juicy fresh pineapples which Lily's uncle grew.

Whatever would she have done with herself, she wondered, if she hadn't been expecting this baby? It had been strange enough in England when she got married and was suddenly deprived of all the office gossip and friendship, to say nothing of work. She had never thought she would miss it all so much, the company, the ceaseless jokes and excitement of getting the paper out on time. She had ached to be back there. They had moved three times in the year between getting married and coming out here so she hadn't been able to get a job. Martin was away at least twelve hours a day, and when he was at home he wasn't exactly companionable.

He wasn't interested in people, she realised. She remembered the first time they went out to visit one of his colleagues and she came home ready to mull over the evening, but he refused to talk about it. He never wanted to chat or discuss anything. They made arrangements quite amicably. He didn't seem to think there was need for anything more. He won't

change, she realised very soon, it will always be like this. I shall always be lonely.
Why hadn't she realised, she often asked herself. In all the excitement of getting married it had never entered her head. Of course they'd rushed into it because of the Suez business. Silly really because the Suez thing had fizzled out in no time. All that stuff about Egypt having a stranglehold on our lifeline. Well, nobody bothered about that now. Politicians seemed to make and abandon enemies as some people do friends, to suit their own convenience. But even if they'd waited it wouldn't have made any difference. She'd have wanted to marry him just the same.
They'd said all along they'd start a family soon, because he was nearly forty. Not that it happened straight away. It took a year. Not surprisingly really. She hadn't realised that not all men were interested in sex. No, she had realised, but she'd thought that they wouldn't be bothered with women at all, certainly wouldn't want to get married. Often at night she lay and thought about Randy and even Simon and then guiltily pressed up against Martin's body as he slept and told herself not to think wicked thoughts.
Altogether it was a relief to find she was pregnant even if it did mean she was going to give birth in a faraway island inhabited by strange natives like Mrs James, Mrs Baxter, Mrs Shotter and the lady with the fan. She rocked and dozed and the baby moved about companionably inside her.

'How was this morning's outing?' Martin asked her that evening.
'Very funny. It was called a coffee party.'
'You must have been to a coffee party before?'
'Well, I've had coffee with people, of course, but a coffee party here is different. It's all very stiff and polite and they cross examine you, as if you'd committed some crime or other.'
'What about?'
'Things like you,' she told him. 'By the way, is your work – what did she say – *hush-hush*?'
'No. I wouldn't have told you about it if it had been.'
'Oh.' She thought about that for a moment. 'Not even me?'

'Of course not.'

'But surely it's all right to tell a wife? I mean wives are different.'

'No, they're not. Not as far as work is concerned. If it's confidential, it's confidential.'

She didn't argue. She rarely did. There was no point. He was so sure about everything that he left her no openings. At first she had found his decisiveness reassuring: it made him seem mature, dependable. But now it seemed to press her down, stifling thought. As she sat now in silence she found herself resenting his oppressive certainties.

'And how have you been feeling in yourself?' he asked formally.

'That's confidential information,' she told him.

He didn't think it was funny.

'Oh, I'm fine,' she said, relenting. 'I'm seeing that Mr Funchu tomorrow evening.'

'I'll come home early and pick you up.'

'Thanks.'

Mr Funchu was the only gynaecologist in the colony. He was surprisingly big for a Chinaman, she thought at that first visit, but he had tiny hands. Which was a great advantage, she decided as he examined her; having great fists moving about inside you, pushing against this and that, would be really very nasty. Worse even than being treated by a dentist with halitosis.

A week before the baby was due she went for what she hoped would be her last check up.

'Well, maybe next time I see you, I'll be having the baby,' she said to Mr Funchu as she was leaving.

To her surprise he looked dubious.

'I'll be available if I can,' he told her.

'But I thought it was all arranged. I mean – that you'd deliver the baby?'

'I hope so, but I'm a very busy man, Mrs Quigley. It is just possible I won't be available.'

He sounded so off-hand, she couldn't reply. She was horrified at how panic-stricken she felt. She was almost in tears when she got back to the car where Martin was waiting. At first she couldn't speak, but then managed to tell him.

'Soon deal with him,' Martin said, reversing the car.

'But how? If he's too busy? But he's never said anything like that before. He's always said to contact him in good time when I start having pains and – '

Martin got out of the car. She followed him into the hall. He went into the office where Mr Funchu was preparing to leave. The walls did not reach the ceiling. She could hear every word.

'I gather you may be too busy to deliver my wife's baby, Mr Funchu?' she heard Martin say.

'That is so.'

'How much will it cost to make sure you are available?'

'A hundred dollars, Mr Quigley.'

'Right. I'll make out the cheque now.'

'Thank you. Today is the 12th.'

There was a pause, a little rustling of paper, then Martin said, 'So we'll contact you as arranged.'

'Certainly. Good night Mr Quigley.'

Sometimes Martin's certainties were wonderfully comforting, she thought as she leant up against him gratefully in the car.

He didn't even understand her gratitude.

'Well, it was obvious. He just wanted a bit more money,' he said. 'No problem.'

'I wish he'd said so. Why didn't he ask for more in the first place?'

'Well, it's not like England, Polly. In England medicine's still a profession. Here it's a business, like in America, where Mr Funchu trained. So just as a tradesman might ask for a deposit in advance of supplying goods or services, Mr Funchu expects a down payment to ensure he'll be available when you go into labour.'

Mr Funchu was available and made a good job of delivering the baby which they called Timothy after Martin's long-dead father, Miss Capstick's nephew.

Timothy was plum-coloured when he was born, and wrinkled like someone who has stayed too long in the bath. He only had one eye open, which gave his face a lop-sided, bemused look. She was astonished at how she felt. She could not take her eyes of him; she wanted to gaze at him for ever.

He lay there facing her, his one open eye not yet focused on this world. How alarming it must have been for him to be suddenly torn away from his peaceful floating world inside her, where everything was done for him, and be pushed out into this strange land where he had to learn to breathe and suck and get used to daylight and alien sounds. No wonder he looked a bit battered.

'It's all right,' she whispered to him suddenly. 'I'm your mother and I'll never go away and leave you.'

Timothy was nearly three when they left the colony, Sarah was eighteen months and Polly was expecting her third child in September.

'It seemed the most sensible thing to do,' she explained to Jim on their first day back in England. 'I mean there was nothing else to do in the compound apart from having babies and looking after them.'

'So long as it's not habit-forming,' Jim said. 'At this rate you'll have a cricket team in no time.'

She didn't reply. Mr Funchu had explained that this must be her last child.

They were making the supper while Martin unpacked and her mother read a story to Timothy. She hadn't wanted to come here, but her mother's invitation had been very pressing. Then Jim had written to say he would meet them at Heathrow and didn't mind sleeping downstairs on the couch so that the children could have his room, and Martin had said it would solve the problem of where to stay for the few days until their house in Marston was ready. So there were three of them against her, all with logic on their side. But she bitterly resented being forced to take favours from her mother.

Her mother's desertion of them when they were little, never mentioned and never forgiven, was incomprehensible to Polly now that she had children of her own. She thought of Timothy and Sarah and tried in vain to imagine how anyone could leave their own children, abandon what they themselves had brought into the world. She didn't like being parted from them even for a few hours; it was unthinkable that she should ever risk not seeing them again. She shivered at the thought and at the fiendishness of a mother who could inflict such pain on her own children.

Her mother, when she came in with Martin, was looking cheery and not fiendish at all.

'Timmy's ever so good,' she said. 'Reminds me of Jimmy when he was a little lad. He was ever so good was Jimmy. Timmy's like him in looks as well. I've thought that from when he was tiny.'

Martin had been meticulous about sending her photographs of the children. She had kept them all. They were dotted around the house on mantelshelves and tables. They got on well, Martin and her mother.

'What can I do to help, Granny?' he asked now.

Polly stiffened at the name. So she who had shirked the responsibilities of being a mother was to have grannyhood bestowed upon her unearned, she thought resentfully.

'Nothing, thank you, Martin. It's all ready,' her mother said as she sat down. 'Help yourself. I only wish you could stay longer than three days.'

'We can't,' Polly said shortly. To be beholden for three days was three days too long.

'You'll have had enough of us by the time we go,' Martin said. 'And we really do want to get settled up in Marston before I start work.'

'Well, let me come up and help when the new baby arrives. At least I can look after the other two. Or they could come here, if it's easier.'

'That's a very kind offer, isn't it, Polly?'

Polly thought it was a bloody cheek and nearly said so. Her irritation was spreading to encompass Martin. She tried to check it; after all, she had never told him what her mother had done – she could not bring herself to speak of it – so she shouldn't blame him for going along with this new-found perfect granny business. But she did.

'We mustn't wear you out,' he was saying. 'You're the only grandparent our children have, so we must take care of you.'

'That's quite a responsibility for me,' her mother said, smiling at him. 'I'll do my best to be a good one.'

'I'm sure you will,' Martin said, smiling back.

Polly felt like getting up and going back to the colony. The ladies of the compound might have been pretty awful but at least they weren't relations.

'If you two want to go off shopping or anything tomorrow,' her mother said later as she poured out tea, 'I can take care of the children. You just go off and don't worry. I'll hold the fort.'

What a vision! As if she'd ever trust her children to her mother's care.

'We might take you up on that,' Martin said. 'Polly's got her nest egg to squander, haven't you, darling?'

He never spoke in this teasing way if they were alone together. It must be something to do with having a granny around.

'Where did the nest egg come from, Polly?' Jim asked.

'It was a mistake. Martin used to pay an allowance into my account every month. He told the bank to cancel the standing order when we went abroad but they forgot, and just went on paying it although there was no money coming into his account. The first we knew was when they wrote about the overdraft.'

'That was a bit careless of them, wasn't it? I mean, I thought banks never made mistakes.'

'Oh, yes, they apologised and cancelled the charges, but it did mean that Polly had this tidy sum put by, so we thought it would be best to keep it intact for expenses for the next baby. You could go and spend some of it tomorrow, Polly. You'll need warmer maternity clothes this time.'

Polly shook her head. She had other plans for the money. She'd use it to pay someone to look after them all when she had the next baby. She had only just decided.

'Now you sit and rest while we clear up,' her mother said, when the meal was finished.

'Oh, we've done enough sitting on aeroplanes,' Polly said, getting up.

'Then come for a stroll with me,' Jim said. 'It's a lovely evening.'

They walked slowly through the park, she and Jim, arm in arm, and for the first time since she got back, she felt glad to be home.

'Let's go into the Lamb and Flag for a drink,' Jim suggested suddenly.

'No alcohol for me.'

'You can have a fruit juice. Come on, let your baby brother treat you.'

She settled herself on a stool at a little round table while he went up to the bar. She watched him as he chatted up the barmaid. Soon she would view him as just Jim, but after an absence of three years she could see him in a detached kind of way, through a stranger's eyes. His face had filled out and he had gained weight. He was strikingly handsome. They were very conventional, his good looks, rather glossy, like a man in an advertisement or a hero in a second-rate film, but good looks all the same. Heads turned when he passed.

He had a rueful grin, too, which he was using to good effect at the moment. It showed his very white, perfect teeth. He came towards her carrying the drinks.

She glanced at her watch. She didn't really like leaving her husband and mother together. She didn't know what schemes they might be devising.

'Sorry it took so long,' Jim said.

'It's all right. I was watching you chatting up the barmaid.'

'Oh, you get better service if you turn on the charm a bit,' he said. 'Cheers.'

It was nonsense, she thought. He only needed to do it to bolster his confidence, which had been shattered when he was little.

The pineapple juice tasted strange and tinny. She sipped it. His eyes were watchful over his beer mug. He put down the mug carefully.

'Polly,' he said, 'I'm in a spot of bother.'

He spoke slowly and then gave her his sudden, white-toothed smile, a bit shame-faced.

'It's this girl,' he said.

'What girl?'

'Mandy. Her name's Mandy.'

'Yes?'

'I've got her pregnant.'

She stared at him.

'That's why I need your help – financially, I mean. Only a temporary loan, of course.'

'But surely you earn enough to get married on? And you've been teaching five years. You must have saved something?'

'I wasn't really thinking of getting married,' he said, as Randy had once said to her. 'More of her having an abortion.'

'Abortion?'

Instinctively her hands moved to cover her womb, as if her own baby was threatened.

'Yes. And of course it costs a lot and I don't know why but I never seem to manage to save. So when you were telling us about your nest egg at supper, I thought maybe I could borrow it? I'd pay you back, of course. Probably by the end of next term, if that's all right. I mean, I expect Martin makes enough to keep you going, doesn't he?'

'Oh, Jim, for goodness sake! You do realise it's illegal, don't you? She could go to prison, and her abortionist, too.'

'Yes.'

'And it's dangerous. I mean it isn't as if you can check up on the qualifications of these abortionists. They're criminals, so there's no way of telling if they're any good at their job.'

'I know.'

'And what about Mandy? Does she want to have an abortion?'

'Well, yes, I think so. Now.'

'You mean you've persuaded her?'

'In a way.'

He sighed and then burst out suddenly, 'It wouldn't do, Polly, I know it wouldn't work. Everyone says it's wrong to rush into marriage in circumstances like these.'

'You should have thought about that before,' she said, but she spoke gently because she was thinking that she, too, had rushed into marriage with a stranger and with less reason than this.

'I know, Polly. You don't need to tell me. Of course I shouldn't have got us into this mess, but I have.'

'And now you think you can just pay up, rub the baby out of existence and – '

'Please, Polly, I'm desperate or I wouldn't ask.'

It was the real thing, this desperation. There was nothing rueful about it. It rendered him quite plain, as if the handsome features were too soft to bear such strong emotion and had crumbled under the weight of it.

'Mandy must be pretty desperate, too,' Polly said, 'if she wants her baby.'

'She doesn't. She says – '

'Go on.'

'She says she'll either marry me or have the abortion plus £100 for herself.'

She stared at him, stunned.

'However did you get involved with someone like that?'

'The usual reasons. Oh, you'll never understand, it's no good. You're stronger than I am. You can resist temptation.'

She shook her head. 'It's not true,' she said.

Hadn't she behaved the same with Randy? She hadn't any regard for him, not really. If she'd got pregnant, he'd probably have told her to have an abortion. And he didn't even have a sister to cadge money off. What would she have done? Well, for a start she wouldn't have asked to be paid £100 to kill her own baby.

'I'm sorry, Jim,' she said. And then, when his face fell, added quickly, 'I mean it's all right. You can have the nest egg.'

'Oh, Polly.' He leaned forward and reached for her hands. 'You're a sister in a million, you are. You've saved me, really you have. I'll go and see her tomorrow and we'll make arrangements. I'll tell you all about it when I get back, I promise.'

He squeezed her hands. The baby in her womb twisted and turned. She withdrew her hands and rested them there. Some babies are luckier than others, she thought. Some wombs are safer than others. Even before you're born, there's no justice.

'No,' she said. 'I don't want to hear about it. Just take the money.'

'In my opinion,' Martin said, 'You should ask your mother to come and look after things so that you can rest.'

'No. I can manage.'

She was adamant; she would not be beholden to her mother.

'You're very independent.'

'I've had to be.'

There was silence. Only the rustling of newsprint as, sitting one on each side of the fireplace in the house provided by the Ministry of Defence, they divided the paper between them, page by page.

'It isn't as if she'd mind,' Martin persisted. 'She'd love to be asked.'

Oh yes, she'd jump at the chance to come. Polly knew that.

'And we're not going to make habit of asking her, Polly. It is the last time, after all.'

'Yes, it's the last time.'

Tears suddenly filled her eyes. Foolish really. Three babies was enough. But the certainty of it hurt her. And the way he remarked upon it, as if it wasn't sad. She brushed the tears away. It was just that she was tired, very, very tired. She never would have imagined in the days when she worked round the clock on *The Chronicle* that she could have felt so utterly worn out. It was an effort even to get up and walk across the room.

'After all, your poor mother had to part with you and Jim because of the war. It would be kind to let her – '

'She didn't *have* to part with us.'

She stopped. She could not tell him. It was still a raw wound. Fresh as yesterday was the memory of that sunny afternoon when she sat in the back garden with Jimmy, eating jam sandwiches. She even remembered the feel of the pips embedded in the bread and margarine and sensed again the foreboding she had felt then.

'Well, it's true that the evacuation wasn't compulsory, but she would have been risking your safety if she'd kept you with her. People really did think that the northern industrial towns would be flattened.'

'I suppose so.'

Weary day followed weary day. Timothy was restless and bored and difficult. There was talk of setting up a play group run by parents but it came to nothing, and anyway she knew she wasn't strong enough to help. It was as much as she could do to drag through the daily routine of dressing the children, feeding them, washing nappies, heaving them in and out of prams, lifting them into the bath, getting them upstairs, carrying Sarah, dragging Timothy along. If only she'd had the nest egg she'd have used it to pay someone to come and help. Universal Aunts, she thought, with a sudden vision of a capable somebody or other taking over everything while she lay, in a great cumbersome heap on the bed until it was all over and she could cope and be herself again.

'Mothers only qualify for hospital deliveries if it's the first baby or anything after the fourth,' the doctor said.

For a moment she didn't understand and thought he meant the fourth of July.

'My baby's due at the end of September,' she pointed out.

'That's true,' he said, puzzled but reassuring. 'And as I was saying, yours will have to be a home delivery.'

She was pleased. She wouldn't have to leave the other two. It would all be much easier. No need now to regret the nest egg and the help it might have bought.

'The midwife and I will look after you.'

'Thank you.'

But when she showed him Mr Funchu's letter, he sent her to a gynaecologist who examined her and said the birth would have to be by Caesarian and he would sterilise her at the same time. She thanked him, holding back the tears.

'So it's hospital after all,' Martin said. 'Well, you'll have to ask your mother to come now. You can't rely on me to be at home.'

True. She knew she could not rely on him.

'I'll talk to the doctor about it when I go for my next check,' she said. 'We're going to make all the arrangements then.'

Anything to postpone the decision: procrastination seemed the only way, just plod on from day to day because anything else was too tiring. Only three months to go, she could manage that surely?

But she didn't. She went into premature labour the following month, during the night when Martin was away. The doctor was on holiday and a young locum came, looked briefly at her and said it was too late to try and get her into hospital. The baby could arrive at any moment; they would just have to cope, the two of them.

There was something theatrical about him, but soon she ceased to take any kind of intelligent interest in the proceedings. After what seemed an eternity she heard him ringing the midwife. She was aware of the midwife arriving, heard her say that it would be a long time yet and that they must get the patient into hospital, heard herself shouting that she couldn't leave Timothy and Sarah. There was a nightmare journey in an ambulance and a nightmare delivery in hospital and then it was all over and she heard them say that she had had a little girl but be brave, Mrs Quigley, she is dead.

Her mother and Martin came to see her.

'I'm staying two weeks,' her mother said, 'at least. Martin asked me and I agreed.'

'Oh.'

It didn't matter any more.

'It's to help him as much as you,' her mother said, a note of defiance in her voice. 'He has a very responsible job and we mustn't add to his worries. So you just lie there and get yourself better.'

'Sarah and Timothy are fine,' Martin said. She didn't care. It was almost impossible to believe but she felt nothing for them.

'You are suffering from shock,' the gynaecologist told her. 'But of course we did try to warn you that this might happen.'

Had there been warnings? She had not heeded them. They had not said there was any danger to the baby, only to herself, but she should have guessed; of course they would play down the danger to save her anxiety. She should have been more suspicious of their reassurances. She would have been if she hadn't been so determined to manage on her own. More rest, just for a few weeks, and the baby would have been safe. There was nothing wrong with the baby except that its mother had let it down. Her poor baby had been as unlucky as Mandy's. Mandy had killed her baby, but she, Polly, had neglected hers and let her die because she had been obsessed by the need not to be beholden to her mother. She had intended no harm to it, but as far as the baby was concerned it came to the same thing: no life, no life at all.

Her mother, who was well installed when she got home, had dressed the children up in their best clothes to welcome her. For a moment she didn't understand, thought they were celebrating. She couldn't bear to look at them, groaned as she stumbled past them and up the stairs. In bed she lay facing the wall, willing time to go into reverse, back to the days when the baby was moving inside her, give her a second chance. There are no second chances, Polly Adams.

The midwife visited her.

'That young doctor's going on a course of obstetrics next month,' she said. 'Pity for your sake that it wasn't last month.'

'It wasn't his fault,' Polly said wearily. 'It was mine, I knew I wasn't fit.'

'Your mother would have helped you. She's ever so nice, your mother. I had a chat with her on my way up. Shame she wasn't here before really. Might have saved you, bed rest might.'

'Yes.'

'Oh, there's a card for you. Your mother said it came by the second post.'

It was a Get Well card from Jim. In it he enclosed a cheque for the nest egg he had borrowed.

Chapter 14

'We're doing the war in history,' Timothy said. 'Has Dad got any of his stuff that I can have?'

'What sort of stuff?'

'Uniforms and so on. I've picked the army. We've all got different projects, you see. Some chose the airforce or the navy and some are doing things like rationing and gas-masks and evacuees.'

You're thirty-four, Polly Adams, and it all happened twenty-five years ago. It may seem like yesterday to you, but already it is history to your son.

'I'll ask him,' she said, 'when he rings up tonight.'

'There's plenty of stuff of mine in the attic,' Martin told her that evening. 'I'll see what I can look out for him at the weekend. I'll be home late on Friday, by the way.'

'Oh, but you know Tim! He always wants things yesterday. Well, for tomorrow morning at the latest.'

'Then you'd better try that big brown case with the straps. It's got the uniform in and there are medals, too, in a smaller case inside it. Near the bottom, I think.'

'Medals! He'll love that.'

'It's not as heroic as it sounds. Only service medals. Everyone got them.'

'Anything else?'

'I'll look myself at the weekend. It's time we started clearing up the attic anyway since we've got to move.'

She was sad to be leaving this house. It was the first they had ever bought. It was only an investment, Martin had said, and didn't mean that they were settled. All the same, the fact that they had bought it did make it seem more like home, more than the rented houses had done, or the ones provided by the Ministry of Defence.

It was a tall, narrow, Victorian terrace house, the cellar too damp for storage but the attic ideal. Too good really, she thought as she surveyed it that night, with its trays of apples at one end and its array of trunks and cases, boxes and tea chests and cardboard cartons tied with string. They were both hoarders. She still had the trunk of baby clothes untouched. She averted her eyes from it.

She soon found the case with the straps. A treasure trove for Timothy, she quickly realised, lifting up layer after layer of khaki uniform, complete with Sam Browne belt and holster, forage cap and shorts. And here were the medals in their separate box. Another case nearby, inscribed Lt Martin Quigley, provided more and different material. There were photographs, all carefully labelled, with each soldier's name and rank. She lugged both the cases over to the trap-door.

It occurred to her suddenly that there must be other relics of the war which might be useful to the rest of Tim's class. Her gas-mask, for instance. Surely she'd seen that not long ago? She remembered noticing how the rubber had perished. Had she therefore thrown it away? Or put it back into one of the mixed boxes? She tried a few but they were all full of more recent acquisitions. She yawned and glanced at her watch. Nearly eleven. One last look and then bed.

She opened an old leather case, covered with labels. Nothing much in here that would help. It was all pre-war, pre-history for Timothy. School pictures of Martin, rows and rows of little boys, all looking well-scrubbed and subdued. There was something sad about them, unnatural, uprooted from home. There was one of Martin and the rest of his dormitory, none of them looking much older than Jim had been when they were evacuated. Martin was in the middle of the front row, one of the smallest, his chin defiantly up. There were several of a cherubic little boy, unlabelled, presumably Martin, but she couldn't be sure. More boys, one called Alistair, and then there was Colin and Barney. Distant cousins, perhaps. They ought to be put all together in an album. She prised up what looked like a big album at the bottom of the case and opened it to put the loose photographs in.

But the photographs in the album were altogether different. Young men, some in pairs, all posing suggestively, obscenely. She drew back, repulsed, then stood quite still, her heart thumping. What were they doing here, hidden in this attic? Gingerly she made herself approach the case again. There were books underneath, paperbacks with pictures and few words. She glanced at the meagre text: descriptions of the pleasure of giving and receiving pain. In the pictures men and women were beating and being beaten, with hands, slippers, canes. There were whips, too. The expressions on all the faces were knowing, salacious. Why should he have books like this? Thank God she hadn't let the children help her in the search. What would she have said to them?

There must be a simple explanation, she told herself. Maybe someone had handed them in for a jumble sale, or they'd been seized from a bookshop or some kinky soldier or other. Maybe someone had given them to him for a sick joke, or just to embarrass him. But all the time, as she was conjuring up these explanations, a part of her recognized and made sense of it all. It fitted in with the feeling she had had from the start of their marriage that something was wrong, that he did not want her as Simon had done, as Randy had done. Something mechanical in his touching of her, sometimes a roughness, as if he wanted to hurt rather than caress. Sometimes she had felt an instinctive fear, as if her body sensed this and recoiled. Maybe her mind had only now discovered what her body had known all along.

Maybe her mind had got it all wrong, though. It was dreadful to jump to conclusions, disloyal. Besides he wasn't violent to her or the children. On the contrary, he was quiet, reserved. But then didn't the men whose curious tastes were catered for in back street establishments carry on their everyday life quite normally, their wives ignorant or loyally mute? She thought of the number of times murderers and rapists were described as quiet and gentle by family and friends. Isn't it always a surprise to find out what is hidden underneath?

Oh, God, what was she doing weaving such fantasies? Pull yourself together, Polly Adams. Go downstairs and act normal. It's Tuesday and you won't know the truth of it until he comes home on Friday. So you might just as well go through the familiar routine, lock up and go to bed and forget all about it for now.

But downstairs nothing seemed normal. All the familiar objects looked strange as she went around the house, locking doors and drawing curtains. And as she walked from room to room a curious tension began to creep over her, taking hold of her body and refusing to relax its grip.

She took sleeping tablets but lay awake, her mind busily recapping the past, looking for clues. She tried to stop, told herself to disbelieve. But of course she would refuse to believe it, wouldn't she, she thought, just as mothers refuse to believe that their child is retarded or husbands and wives refuse to believe that their partners are unfaithful, against all the evidence. And if it turns out not to be true, then their disbelief is loyalty, but if it is true then their disbelief is mere stupidity. Was she being loyal or stupid? Perhaps self-preservation requires disbelief, at least until you get conditioned.

She began to shiver; she couldn't stop the violent shaking. She banged her head against the pillow to try to break the spasm, make her body relax, but the pillows were too soft. She got out of bed and banged her head against the wall instead. Thump, thump. If only she had been the crying sort, maybe she would have relaxed after tears. She had cried when she was on that walk with Martin after Tudor Bean's funeral. She had cried at the pump and he had been gentle with her. It was nonsense to think of him as violent. All the same, she thought now with hindsight, he had not reacted to her tears as a man normally reacts to a woman who is weeping. He had not put his arms around her, drawn her to him. He had let her talk, but had not tried to comfort her.

It was nearly three o'clock. She went downstairs and across the hall into the kitchen. Now everything seemed not just strange, but unfriendly, watching her with hostile eyes. She found that she was watching herself, too: a woman walking about in the middle of the night, her long red hair loose down her back, her face tense. A woman pouring milk into a pan, lighting the gas under it, walking round the kitchen while the milk warmed. Stop it; she mustn't go on like this. She went to the telephone in the hall. Again she stopped herself. You're going mad, Polly Adams. Imagine it: Can I speak to Mr Quigley, please? Hello, darling, are you a pervert of some kind, a sado-masochist perhaps? Oh good, well that's all right. I just wondered, you know.

The milk boiled over.

She was tense and sharp with the children the next day, had to force herself to go up to the attic with Tim and bring the cases down, pretend to share his enthusiasm as he snatched eagerly at each and every item. She seemed to be acting a rôle all the time, acting taking him to school, acting playing with Sarah, observing herself, hearing herself talking normally to Martin when he rang. If I knew the truth, I could bear it, she thought. It's this limbo of not knowing that I can't bear. If he prevaricates, shall I stay in this semi-mad state for ever? He must not be given the chance.

She waited until late on Friday night when the children, always excited when he came home, were at last asleep and she and Martin were alone in their bedroom. He was sitting up in bed, his hands clasped behind his head, preparing to tell her his arrangements for the following week.

'I've something important I want to talk to you about,' she interrupted him.

'Fire ahead,' he said and smiled at her in that rather condescending way he had, as if to reassure her that he would deal seriously with anything that seemed important to her in her little domestic world.

His expression changed abruptly when she handed him a couple of the books and said, 'I want to know all about this.'

He looked directly at her as she climbed into bed beside him.

'I wanted you never to find out,' he said. 'I didn't want you to know.'

Thank God he was honest about it. She loved him at that moment more than she had ever done. She could bear anything now.

'I was bound to find out,' she said gently, 'sooner or later. And besides, I knew there was something. It would have been better if you'd told me from the start.'

'I didn't think you'd take it so calmly. I thought you'd be disgusted.'

For the first time, he was talking to her directly, as an equal, without reserve.

'Well, tell me now. Tell me everything about it.'

He lay back, his hands clasped behind his head again. 'It began long before I went to school,' he said. 'My father, as you know, was an army man, posted abroad where my mother lived with him until he died. Then she died on the journey home. So I was brought up by my aunt. I had a nanny, of course. She used to smack me. I enjoyed it. It was the only time anyone made any physical contact with me, I suppose. And she made a little game of it, a ritual. So I'd do something naughty to get smacked. I think she enjoyed it, too. She smacked me rhythmically and quite hard, so there was fear as well as the pain. And that was exciting. I was very upset when she left, which she did, of course, when I went away to prep school. They took me early because I was an army orphan, as it were. Most of the boys there were sons of army people.

'There were little rituals of beating there, too. We had to queue up outside the headmaster's study and he always kept us waiting. It was very tense, the waiting. We'd hold on to each other, almost suffocating with anticipation. Then there was the pain, as well as this feeling of sharing with the other chaps, a sort of animal comfort.'

No mother to turn to, Polly thought. No natural comforter, just a great emptiness to be filled somehow or other. How wicked are the things that we do to children.

'When we went into the study, the canings always took place on a little dais at the far end of the room, farthest from the window, that is. It was very dark, almost like a cubbyhole, because there was a kind of partition which had a big Union Jack fixed to it and some regimental flags. So the beating became all tied up in our minds with patriotism and the army.

The headmaster used to tell us that if we looked at the flags first it would help us to be brave and not to cry. He really did seem to want to help us to bear it, to be sorry for us even.'

'But didn't you think it was odd? Didn't you ever talk about it among yourselves? I mean some of you must have wondered why he should beat you if he loved you, and why he didn't just tell you off if you'd done something wrong?'

'No. It wasn't like that, Polly. We simply didn't dream of questioning it. We accepted that it was the way life was and we had to put up with it. I doubt if more than a handful of the boys had parents in England anyway, or if the parents would have taken much notice if they had complained. You've got to remember we were very little. I went there when I was six.'

She thought of Jimmy at that age. Who would he have turned to if he hadn't had a big sister aged eight?

'And then, you see, Polly, the headmaster was a sort of god to us, so I suppose we thought that it must be all right, because he ordained it. And in chapel he used to preach a lot about God inflicting on us punishments that we didn't understand, but that were for our own good. That's what earthly fathers have to do, he'd say. Then he'd smile and add that headmaster too sometimes had to be cruel to be kind. But I suppose the real reason was that he enjoyed it.'

'And later? Was it the same at public school?'

'No. We got caned sometimes, but it wasn't the same kind of ritual any more. But by then, of course, it was all part of me. I suppose it was for some of the others as well, but I didn't realise it at the time. I thought I was the only odd one. And soon they all seemed to be talking about girls, about necking and petting and all that sort of thing,' he added with distaste. 'I didn't want anything like that. I wanted –'

He stopped.

'What did you want?' she prompted after a while.

He shrugged.

'I suppose I wanted to punish them,' he said slowly. 'I wanted to do to them what had been done to me. The idea of it excited me.'

'And did it ever excite any of them?'

'No. Once there was one girl I think might have enjoyed it.

She was a great lump of a thing. A horsy sort of creature, she was,' he added contemptuously.

She could understand what he was saying with her mind, but somehow could not believe in this strange, loveless world.

'But surely, in all those years when you were growing up, there must have been somebody, sometimes, that you liked and wanted to put your arms around, maybe just affectionately or to comfort them.'

'No,' he interrupted her almost fiercely. 'Never.'

'You mean you never fell in love with anyone?'

'Once. With the wife of my commanding officer. She was unobtainable, of course.'

'So you never made love to her?'

'Of course not. I've told you, she was unobtainable.'

She hesitated. 'And what about me?' she asked.

'You were different. You were such a funny little waif of a thing, Polly, that first time I saw you, with your great green eyes and that incredible hair. And scared. I suppose I liked that. Scared because you thought I was a Hun, then scared I'd tell on you. Maybe that was why I was drawn to you later on. And you were still vulnerable. I couldn't hurt you, when we got married, yet I didn't really know any other way.'

'I understand,' she said simply. 'I didn't before, but I do now. I only wish you'd told me right at the beginning.'

'But I've explained that. I was afraid you'd be horrified, and anyway I was ashamed.'

'You didn't trust me much, did you?'

'I was afraid of losing you,' he said.

She took his hands and pressed them to her face, loving him because he had feared to lose her. Suddenly it had all become quite ordinary; not a terrible, secret thing any more, not something to be labelled by a psychiatrist and generalised about, just a part of Martin's life, a sad event which had left a scar, something which they could talk about, deal with together. After the torments of the past few days, she felt light-headed with relief.

For a moment she stroked his hands gently then laid them on her breast and reached up to put her arms around his neck.

'We'll solve it together somehow,' she said. 'You'll see.'

He took her arms and carefully disengaged them from his neck.

'There's nothing to solve,' he said.

'But of course there is!'

'It's in the past. I promise you that.'

'But nothing's in the past. It's all part of us, our past is. It's built into us for ever.'

'Oh, I don't agree. I've quite crushed this thing. I can cope with it now.'

'No, Martin. These things can't be crushed. They've got to be faced.'

'So you're an expert on "these things", are you?' he asked, giving her a sheepish little smile. 'I didn't realise.'

'I didn't say that. But I do know that you can't run away from problems. You've got to face them.'

She felt the trust, the easy understanding that they'd had only a few minutes ago slipping away. She didn't know how to hold on to it, so resorted to argument.

'If you'd really crushed it, you wouldn't need these books, would you?' she said.

'Well, I admit I find them helpful sometimes. Especially when I'm feeling lonely and tend to think about these matters.'

'But you needn't feel lonely. I can help you, better than any old books, I can.'

'It's kind of you, Polly. You've shown great tolerance. I am only sorry that you had to find out.'

'But I'm glad I did. Now it's in the open, you're not carrying this burden of secrecy any more, and I can help you –'

'Thank you, but there's no need. I've managed all these years. As I say, I appreciate your understanding –'

'Oh, stop talking to me as if I was a public meeting!' she burst out.

'I'm just trying to keep the conversation as reasonable and unemotional as possible in the circumstances.'

'But that's what you always do! You can't face anything emotional, so you just hide behind these silly rationalisations.'

'We all have own ways of dealing with things,' he said.

Then he added, as if defying her to contradict him, 'It's my problem, I shall deal with it in my own way.'

'But it's *not* just your problem. For God's sake, we're married. It's my problem as well as yours.'

'No, I don't want to be involved. There's no need for it to affect you.'

'But I'm your wife. Of course it affects me.'

'It didn't before you found out.'

'But it *did*. All right, I didn't know the cause before, but I knew the effect. It stopped you having a normal relationship with me.'

'Well, that depends on what you mean by normal, doesn't it? Most people would say that a marriage like ours, with a son and a daughter and a nice house and garden and a steady income, was quite normal. It isn't as if we had rows or argued about money. I'm sure most women would find it quite satisfactory.'

'But you don't know about most women, do you?' she remarked, surprised that it hadn't occurred to her before. 'You don't even like them very much.'

'It's true my working life has been spent among men.'

'Do you miss the army?'

Taken aback by the suddenness of the question, he was silent for a while, then, 'Yes,' he said sadly. 'I didn't realise how much I would miss it, until after I left. The comeraderie, you know. At least, I did realise how difficult it would be in civvy street –'

'Is that why you married me?'

'Well, yes, I suppose so. I don't mean you in particular, but I knew that if I left the army, I must marry, I must have a base. I've always thought family life looked very nice, from the outside –'

The ache to comfort him returned as she thought of him as he had been then, wistful and lost, looking in at the windows of other people's marriages like a homeless child. And what he had seen was not the reality of marriage at all. He had seen only a picture of what he had wanted to see. Just as she herself had done. They were both equally to blame.

She turned to him. 'Martin,' she said, 'please let's try. Let's try to work it out together. There must be a way.'

'No,' he said. 'I'm sorry you've found out. Now I want you to be a good girl and forget all about it.' And he looked at her upturned face and planted a dismissive little kiss on her forehead.

It was the dismissiveness that did it. All the suppressed rage and pain at being rejected over the years suddenly boiled up in her.

'I'm no longer a girl,' she told him angrily, 'and I've never been good.'

'Oh, Polly, Polly –'

'And I'm not going to go on being so bloody tolerant if you won't even try to help yourself.'

'What are you going to do then?' he enquired matter-of-factly.

'There's not much I can do if you just pretend there's nothing wrong. You're just shutting yours eyes to it, because you daren't face it. So you're making it worse, more secret and sinister and powerful, don't you see?'

She desperately wanted to put courage into him, as she had once done with Jimmy.

'It's all right for you,' he said with sudden petulance. 'You're stronger than I am.'

'I've had to be. And you could be now if you'd just act responsibly and let us face this thing together.'

He was silent for a while, as if weighing up her words, but in the end he only said wearily, 'I think it's rather late to make sensible decisions tonight. We should settle down now and perhaps we shall see things more clearly in the morning. I've had rather a long day, you know.'

He pecked her on the forehead again, gave an apologetic little shrug of his shoulders and turned off the light.

She lay mute and furious while he slept, angry with herself as much as with him, for she had let the golden moment slip, had handled it clumsily. It had been stupid to resort to argument, he would always hide his weakness behind a barrier of counter-arguments. But what else could she do? The other approach, instinctive to her, evoked no response in him because he was made differently. Or rather he hadn't been made differently, not from the start. It was people who had damaged him, people who were paid to care for him when he was little. They were the ones who had damaged him.

Suddenly she felt a great surge of hatred for them, for the unknown nanny with her rhythmic smacking, for the faceless schoolmaster with his dais and his flags. And her rage spread to all others like them, including parents, who damaged little children and never saw the harvest of the seeds which they had sown, never knew what they had done. Forgive them, for they know not what they do? Never. She, Polly, would gladly hang the contradictory millstones round their necks.

Chapter 15

Ship Lane, in the centre of the town where they now lived, was known locally as Fleet Street because it housed the offices of the weekly newspaper, as well as the two local evening papers. Two of the national papers also had their Northern offices there, side by side. Polly stood looking in the window of one of them now, wondering, as she pretended to study the photographs, if she could screw up the courage to walk in and ask if they had any sort of job for her. That's what you did when you were seventeen, Polly Adams. Where does all the courage go?

She was here with Martin's blessing. It was he who had said that when Sarah started school in September she ought to find a job. She had been thinking the same thing herself, but the fact that he suggested it now, made her suddenly see all the difficulties. Besides, he was suggesting it for the wrong reasons.

She had been making one of her periodic efforts to get through to him yesterday evening, recapture the closeness of the night they had talked about this childhood. As usual she had succeeded only in irritating him.

'What are you complaining of?' he had asked. 'Don't I provide for you and the children? You may not believe it, but

I do strive to make you all as happy as possible,' he added, answering a criticism she had not made.

He would never understand, she thought despairingly, only turn what she was trying to say upside-down and make her feel guilty. Other people would easily understand what she meant. But then he wasn't other people. He was the one she had chosen to marry, on an impulse with a bit of calculation thrown in. You made your choice, Polly Adams, made your bed, and must lie on it. Alone. For in this new house he had made himself a study-bedroom so that he could read late into the night. He was studying military history, Nazi history to be precise. He collected Fascist memorabilia too; just a few bits and pieces to bring the period alive, he explained. In the attic of the new house he had crates of Nazi documents and maps and plans and pictures.

It was yesterday that he had made the suggestion that she should go back to work in September. 'I think,' he said, 'it would take your mind off what you see as our domestic problem. You tend to be obsessive about this in my opinion. It would be excellent therapy for you.'

She shrugged. She cared too much about journalism to treat it as therapy, as a distraction or a substitute. Besides, to take a job in that spirit would set the seal on the marriage as it was; she wanted it to be different. Hers was not the way of acceptance.

'I have no doubt at all that it could be arranged,' he went on, 'with careful planning. I am quite prepared to fit in as regards meals and so on. I hope I have never been unreasonable about domestic matters.'

'No, of course you haven't.'

He had talked at some length. She stood leaning against the wall by the window, her head cushioned on the thick fabric of the velvet curtains which they had bought with the house. A bit shabby but the real thing, heavy old-fashioned velvet, she thought as she rubbed her cheek gently against them, only half-listening to Martin's calm, measured tones. More and more he addressed her like a public meeting, so that she felt as if she was at one of the gatherings she used to report for *The Chronicle*. Increasingly, she listened to him as a reporter might, detached, observant.

When he had finished his speech, and gone up to sort out documents in the study-bedroom, she stayed gazing out of the window and fingering the thick pile of the curtains. It was a gentle evening, the sun setting over the garden. Oh, for comforting arms to creep into; oh, for a shoulder to cry on, someone to lean against and feel safe.

Pull yourself together, Polly Adams, you never felt like that when you were younger. Maybe having children weakens you, makes you need support so that you have extra strength to give them in turn the support they need. Yes, she had let herself get too weak in these childbearing years; perhaps that was the price women had to pay, in return for all the joy. And this cold, unnatural marriage had weakened her too, dispirited her somehow. Courage, Polly Adams, start fighting back. The dance must go on, the children must be cared for, the house managed, and you will keep your reason by finding a job.

She repeated these instructions to herself, now, as she stood outside the newspaper office in Ship Lane, gazing at the photographs in the window. Here was Jane Smollett, the mayor's daughter, receiving a bouquet of flowers from little Belinda Jones on the occasion of the opening of the new wing of Drinkley's Primary School, and stout Mrs Clackton in a tweed coat and felt-and-cardboard hat proudly holding the end of a lead at the other end of which seemed to dangle a bundle of wool which was in fact her prize-winning Pekinese. Even Polly, distracted as she was, her mind full of other things, other pictures, could see that it wasn't a very good photograph.

Suddenly, as she stood there irresolute, a man dashed through the big swing doors and crashed into her, clutching her close to him before he realised who it was. When he did recognize her, he clutched her even closer.

'Flinders!' he exclaimed. 'What a lovely way to meet.'

He was still holding her very close.

'Let go, Randy,' she ordered.

He laughed and relaxed his arms very slightly, but only so that he could hold her back a little way from him and inspect her.

'Not much damage,' he pronounced, 'in – how long? – seven years?'

'Eight,' she said.

'Where shall we go to celebrate?' he asked, releasing her and then taking her arm. 'I'm starving. I can afford something a bit better than a pork pie nowadays, by the way. The Rendezvous would do, I think. It's quiet. A good place for the long talk we're going to have.'

'Are you married?' she asked as they walked arm-in-arm towards the restaurant.

'Ever our direct little Flinders,' he said. 'Yes and no.'

'What does that mean?'

'I was. And the divorce goes through next month.'

'Oh, is that sad for you? Do you mind, I mean?'

He shrugged. 'Not much,' he said. 'We've been separated for years. We only lived together for six months.'

'Randy!'

'But we'd known each other for a very long time before we were married. It was a genuine case of marrying at leisure and repenting in haste.'

She laughed and shook her head at him as they stopped outside the restaurant. He took her hands in his and said, 'And you, Flinders? You married in haste, didn't you?'

'Yes,' she said, suddenly wary. 'Suez crisis and all that.'

'I remember. But there were other crises too, I think. Well, in we go and we'll talk about it as we eat.'

It was, as he had said, a quiet little place. The sort you might call intimate, she thought, and certainly very expensive. He settled her into what looked like choir stalls for two and ordered their drinks while they studied the menu.

'Don't stint yourself,' he said. 'This is on expenses.'

'I don't believe it. We couldn't even get a cup of tea on expenses in the old days.'

'Times have changed, Flinders. And not just for me because I've become a chief reporter, nor because we've been taken over by a huge national group. The whole atmosphere has changed. These are the roaring sixties and we've never had it so good, the Prime Minister says so, no less. All that old stuff that we grew up on, you and I, about austerity and not consuming too much at home because the nation must pay its way by exporting, has gone clean out of the window. We live in the age of the consumer now. So you just get consuming like a good little capitalist. Go on, have the steak.'

'It's a different world,' she said, shaking her head. 'But I still don't see how I count as expenses.'

'Because we're going to talk business, aren't we?' he said, suddenly serious. 'You were loitering with intent outside the office, weren't you, Flinders? It calls you back, doesn't it, the smell of newsprint, like the whiff of grapeshot to an old soldier?'

She couldn't deny it.

'But before we talk about that,' she said, 'tell me about you. When did you leave *The Chronicle*?'

'About two years after you went.'

'Was it friendly? Your departure, I mean?'

'Very. I wanted to go and they were glad to see the back of me. So it was all very amicable.'

'And the others? Are they all still there?'

'Yes. You ought to go in and see them, Polly. It's not very far from here.'

'I might do that. I have to go to Brigthorpe to see my mother next week.'

'She still lives there?'

'Yes, but she's in hospital at the moment so I'm going over to visit her and make arrangements to bring her back to convalesce with us. That could make going back to work difficult. I'll just have to see how she gets on.'

He looked at her, puzzled.

'Won't it be a bit of a strain?' he said. 'I thought you never got on very well, you and your mother.'

'Yes, I mean no, we weren't close. I never wanted to be beholden to her. But it's different now, I'd be looking after her.'

He thought for a moment, looking at her.

'Yes, I can understand that,' he said slowly.

She was surprised at his understanding. Martin had found it incomprehensible. He had been perfectly happy for her mother to come to stay, he said, but found it amazing that Polly, who had not wanted her to come when she could be a help, should ask her now when she might be a burden. Polly had tried to explain, but soon gave up. They seemed to talk on parallel lines nowadays, she and Martin, their ideas never meeting.

She saw that Randy was watching her. Before he could ask any more questions, she said, 'Do you think it's all right, then, if I just call in at *The Chronicle* on Monday?'

'Do that. Surprise them all. At least Sunny Jim won't be on the rampage.'

'Does he still do that, after all these years?'

'Of course he does. People don't change their ways. Polly, love, just because we take our leave of them for a few years. Why should they? He probably won't remember that you've left. I can just see him telling you to put the kettle on and handing you some proofs.'

Polly laughed. 'Alternatively he may remember that there were, as you said just now, one or two crises just before I left. Rows, in fact.'

'Lord, yes, the Cleghorn affair, the police business and the Assize case. Come on, let's finish up this bottle. I expect they've got plenty more in the cellar.'

'What happened to Irene?'

'Who?'

'Irene. The girl in the blackmail case.'

He looked puzzled for a moment, then, 'Oh, *her*,' he said. 'I lost you for a moment. I don't know what happened. I suppose she's out of prison years ago. Why do you ask?'

'I often think about her. Well, all of them,' she admitted. 'And wonder about them.'

'Really? You do surprise me, Flinders. Do you remember all the cases as clearly?'

'No, just some.'

She spoke reluctantly. It was another world, which she kept apart and did not speak of. Some instinct, which she did not understand, banned discussion. In this inner world, she had imagined a childhood for Irene, something to explain why she was as she was, why she had done what she had done.

'You could follow it up, Polly,' Randy said, filling her glass. Then he put the bottle down and looked at her, his face brightening with sudden professional interest. 'There might be a story in it. A nice piece of human investigative journalism. Have the strawberries and cream.'

'They're ten shillings extra, Randy.'

'Never mind. It's on expenses, now doubly justified if you're going to do this piece about the effects of prison on Irene and her family. You've set my professional antennae flapping. Or we might dig out some other similar case, but more recent. What do you think?'

'Antennae don't flap,' she said, taking a long drink of wine.

'Come on, don't quibble. Are you interested in doing this story and others on a free-lance basis?'

'Oh, Randy. It was just the sort of thing I'd been thinking about. Sarah starts school in September and then I'll have free time.' She hesitated, then added, 'And for all sorts of reasons I *need* work.'

'Well, don't go getting pregnant again.'

She flinched. 'No,' she said. 'I won't do that.'

'Sorry.'

A quick glance, a touch of her hand. He had picked up something just from the tone of her voice, the look on her face. He was strangely perceptive, he who could be so brash. It had puzzled her long ago and it puzzled her still. She drank and he watched her and said, 'Well, what do you think, Flinders?'

'I don't think I could do what you suggest about Irene. It's too complicated to explain, but I couldn't do it what way. I'm sorry. But other work, yes, I should love that. Would there be a chance, do you think, of a part-time job, something to fit in with the school holidays?'

'No,' he said. 'Definitely not. You should know the newspaper world better than that. Even if you did free-lance work you'd have to be available all the time. Stories aren't going to crop up conveniently just when you happen to be free to research them, Polly. If you want a job that fits in with school terms, you'd be better to teach.'

'Don't be silly, Randy. You know I'm not a teacher.'

'Then employ someone to look after the kids. Get a childminder. People do.'

She thought about it, of Sarah and Tim coming in from school and her not there. She thought of all those afternoons when she and Jimmy had come home to an empty house. She thought of the holidays. She thought of the unfatherly Martin.

'No,' she said. 'I can't work full-time. It wouldn't be fair to them.'

'Polly,' Randy said. 'You're really being a bit exasperating. How serious are you about work?'

'After the children, I suppose it's the most important thing in my life.'

He handed her the liqueur that he had ordered for her without asking if she wanted it.

'Then your best bet,' he said, 'is to be a novelist.'

She smiled at him.

'Just like that,' she said.

'Yes, Flinders, just like that.'

'It's all right, Polly,' her mother interrupted her quietly. 'There's no need to find excuses.'

It was one of those remarks that cuts across a conversation ending all possibility of going on as before. Polly said nothing.

'You didn't want me moving in on your children, because you've never forgiven me for moving out on you and Jim.'

Polly could think of no answer to such a bald oversimplification. It was somehow too terrible for mere assent, but on the other hand she could not deny it, this awful truth which she had never framed.

'Why,' she asked instead, 'are you saying this now?'

'Because I'm dying,' her mother said matter-of-factly. 'Don't worry – I'm not going to ask you for forgiveness. I know I would never get that. I'm just going to try to get you to understand, so that eventually, perhaps –'

Her voice trailed off. Her strength came and went in spurts. She would regain it.

In the sickroom a breeze moved the net curtains, and the setting sun shafted in through the other window, throwing a bright triangle of light across the bedspread.

'Does the sun bother you?' Polly asked. 'I could draw the curtains.'

'No. I like it.'

Her mother's voice was firm again. She was going to talk; there was no stopping her now. Polly was suddenly aware of everything in the room, sharply defined. She felt she could see round the polished rungs of the chair in the corner, feel the patina of its wood as it stood there, isolated, observant. Behind the door hung her mothers pale blue candlewick dressing gown, soft and fluffy, except for a patch above the pocket where her mother's entering hand had worn it thin. She had not noticed before the sweet smell of the roses on the window ledge, faint but pervasive, nor the insistent ticking of the little gilt travelling clock on the bedside table. Now they were all sharp and clear and attentive as if the room and everything in it were waiting for her mother to speak.

Very deliberately her mother took a drink of water, then settled herself back against the pillows. Her hands, thin now and white, slightly rearranged the sheet as if she was arranging her narrative.

'After my father died,' she began, 'my mother put me into a home and I never saw her again. It was by the canal, the home was, not far from your office at *The Chronicle*. It's been pulled down long ago, of course. Sheep Street, it was in, at the back of the market. After nearly two years, her sister took me. She was fifteen years older than my mother, and her husband was even older than she was. They were more like grandparents really. They'd no children of their own. I expect they thought I'd be useful when they were old.

'When I was sixteen my aunt died. I was scared of my uncle. He was a violent sort of a man. He never hurt me, but he always seemed to be seething with rage underneath. I'd have left if I could, but I'd nowhere to go and no money. I had a job in a café, but it didn't pay much. It was in the café that I met your father. When he said he wanted to marry me, I couldn't believe my luck. He was older, but so different from my uncle, none of the violence, and he didn't drink. Very quiet he was. He offered me a home, a home of my own. I thought it was the most wonderful thing that had ever happened.'

Her eyes were dreamy with the remembrance of it as she reached again for the glass and drank.

Polly said nothing. She had never heard her mother talk so. Who would have thought she had so many words in her?

'It was all right at first. I had you and Jimmy –'

She stopped suddenly and for a moment Polly thought she was going to break down. Then she went on, 'I was the happiest I had ever been, I suppose for about two or three years. Then he got more and more silent. Taciturn, that's what he was. Then more grumpy and critical. Perhaps it was his lungs. He was gassed in the first war. In the end he didn't seem able to stand the sight of me. I'd try. When you two were in bed and we were alone in the evenings, I'd try to chat, try to get through to him. "Must you be so bloody cheerful?" he'd say.'

She looked at Polly thoughtfully. 'Perhaps he resented my good health,' she said, and added ironically, 'Well, he wouldn't have much to resent now, would he?'

Polly shook her head; she had no words. She had come to visit her mother, expecting to find her in a hospital ward. She had not at first grasped the significance of this quiet little room in a special house in the hospital grounds, nor of something different but hard to define in the attitude of the staff, as if they had abandoned the bustling struggle against illness and accepted it if not quite as a friend at least as a necessary companion in their scheme of things.

'It was when you both started school,' her mother went on, 'that I realised I couldn't stand it any more. He was suffocating me. He only had to come into the room and I felt I couldn't breathe. I just knew I had to get out, as if he was a gaoler and I had to escape. It was all unnatural and I couldn't explain because he wouldn't talk to me. I tried, but he wouldn't answer. A row would have been better. Anything would have been better. You can't understand it – you've got a normal marriage.'

Polly made no comment.

'You can't imagine the difference it made when I got to know Fred. To have someone I could talk to, just a normal, ordinary man. His wife had been killed in an accident and he was lonely. He was so kind and warm and thoughtful. Oh, so loving and he could, and I mean we –'

Polly knew what she meant. Even in her present mood, her mother did not put it into words.

'We got on well together,' she said.

She was silent for a moment and then burst out, 'It wasn't you and Jim I left, Polly, it was your father. Don't you see?'

'No. It was all three of us.'

'It wasn't. I tell you it wasn't. I loved the pair of you. I always planned to get you back somehow or other. Fred wanted you, too. We'd have given you a proper home. I thought I'll just get my strength up, then I'll get the children somehow or other. I couldn't stay with your father, Polly. He would have finished me. But I did try. That morning after I got back from taking you to school I decided I'd talk to him straight. He was just going off to work. He didn't want to listen so I stood leaning against the door so he couldn't get out of the room and I said that if he would even try to love me a little bit, I'd stay. I begged him. At last he spoke. "You'd never leave the kids," he said. And I looked at him and I heard myself say, "You're forcing me to", and I was surprised really because I hadn't meant to go and didn't know I would say such a thing. If he'd said one kind word, I'd have stayed, but he just said, "All right, go if you must", and pushed past me through the door and out of the house. So I packed up a suit-case and went.'

Polly remembered the suit-case. She remembered Sarah Biddle, saw again the iced cake on the table and Jim's greedy little face.

'I remember,' she said.

But it was the wrong word. She more than remembered, she lived it again, heard it all, saw it, felt it all again. As she had many times before. It was with her now, the emptiness, the great, aching emptiness of knowing that her mother had gone.

'Oh, you never forgot,' her mother said bitterly, 'and never forgave. Not like Jimmy. He didn't bear a grudge.'

'It was different for him,' she heard her own voice burst out. 'He had me. He had me for comfort.'

'Yes,' her mother whispered, almost under her breath. 'That's true. You looked after him. You were his mother.'

The sun had gone out of the room now. The last of its rays touched the roses on the window sill so that they seemed to belong to the glowing world outside and not to the shadows within. She could not see the expression on her mother's face.

'When you came to us when your father died,' the voice in the shadows was saying, 'I knew you'd never forgive me. Implacable you were. I shall never forget your little face, hard as stone. And I'd see your eyes on me, condemning. They followed me, your eyes did, accusing me all the time. Yes, you condemned me from the moment you came in the door.'

How leaden her feet had been as she dragged herself down the street towards that house, Jimmy running ahead. She felt again the dread, the hanging back while he went mad with joy because he had not seen his mother for a year. Was it really because he had not been bereft of comfort for a year, as she had? Or was it just that he had a more forgiving nature?

'I couldn't have taken you with me when I left your father, Polly. The law was different then, and he'd probably have kept you out of spite. But it could have worked out after he died. We could all have been happy together then, but you wouldn't have it. You put some sort of ban upon it.'

'It made no difference that he'd died. It didn't alter the fact that you'd left us a year before. The damage was done.'

'If only he'd died a year earlier.' She said the words quietly, almost casually, and they sat in silence for a while, trying to imagine how it might have been. Then she went on, 'When you were evacuated and Jimmy wasn't happy and I came to see you, I hoped – oh, I don't know what I hoped. Not to bring you back, of course, but to get in touch with you again, be your mother again like I used to be. When you were a baby you'd lift your arms and I'd swing you up in the air, and when you were a toddler you'd run to me, but now you always looked away.'

'I couldn't bear the sight of you,' Polly heard herself say.

'Oh, I know. It was the price I had to pay. And because you disapproved of me, I did everything wrong.'

She smiled suddenly. 'I could feel you willing me to go away and leave you alone with the Braithwaites. God, how I envied that woman.'

'Envied Mrs Braithwaite!' Polly repeated, astonished. Mrs Braithwaite who had not left her own little girl, but had lost her all the same.

'Yes, envied her,' her mother repeated savagely. 'Can't you understand that? But I knew she was better for you than I was and later when you went to Miss Capstick, I knew she was better for you too, because she was good with education. They gave you more than I could, even if I hadn't been in the munitions, Mrs Braithwaite and Miss Capstick did.'

'Since we're speaking the whole truth,' Polly said, 'Mrs

Braithwaite got shot of us pretty quickly, and we didn't want to go and live in the village with Miss Capstick either. Jimmy cried all the way.'

Her mother was taken aback. 'Did you know why she sent you away?'

'No.' She shrugged. 'It must have been something I did, I suppose, without realising.'

Her mother looked at her hard. She was very still on the bed. The outline of her body might have been a wrapped effigy, so still she lay.

'Polly,' she said slowly, 'did you also blame yourself because *I* went away?'

Polly stared at her, at the pale face with dark shadows under the eyes which watched her across the shadowy room. From some unknown source the truth was drawn.

'Yes,' she said. 'Yes. I always thought it must be my fault. Not just something I did, but what I was. That I didn't deserve to be loved, so you went away.'

'And yet you blamed me, Polly.'

'No, I didn't, I didn't,' she cried out, her voice high-pitched and childish. 'I thought it was all my fault.'

She hadn't worked it out. She hadn't even known it until now. But now that she was out of control, was crying, it was all clear, as if the truth could only be heard when reason was silenced. 'I thought Jim and I weren't worth anything because first of all you left us and then Mrs Braithwaite sent us away.'

'But I've told you, it wasn't like that. I left your father, not you.'

'But we didn't know. Children just see things from their own point of view, from low down. Everything stems from themselves. And they think life's fair, so that if something like that happens there must be a reason, that they're being punished for being – oh, I don't know, just bad.'

'But it wasn't like that,' her mother said again. 'I had to save myself. It was some instinct of self-preservation that forced me to get away from him.'

'But it was like that *for us*. How could we know what grown-ups were feeling? We never thought of you as his wife anyway. You were just our mother. We didn't know anything about your marriage so it was different for us. I mean the truth of everything is different for different people, but especially for children.'

The storm of tears was over. She lay back in her chair, as still as her mother had been, who was now leaning forward, animated.

'I want you to understand, Polly. It was nothing to do with you, nothing you'd done wrong. I did love you both and I'd have stayed if I could.'

'But you didn't stay.'

'Only because I'd stopped feeling I was doing any good by staying with you. He made me feel I was no use to anybody. I just felt you'd be better off without me, I was in such a bad way. And I knew you were safe with him. He'd never hurt you. It was just me he hated.'

Exhausted by the effort of so much speaking, her voice faltered, but her face remained animated and the eyes which raked her daughter's face for any sign of understanding were bright as she managed to summon up the strength to finish her appeal. 'It seemed the only thing to do, Polly. Don't you see?'

Polly knew that if her mother could have got off the bed she would have done so now. She would have come over to her daughter, put her arms around her and they would both have cried and been reconciled before she died. But she was too ill to get off the bed, wasn't she? If anyone was to make the move it had to be Polly. For a moment she was tempted; the thought of it was very sweet. She had to force herself not to look at her mother, force herself to a stare across the room, at the chair, at the roses, at the dressing gown, at anything except her mother's face, so that these inanimate witnesses of the scene could give her strength to resist, never to betray the past, the children in the garden.

They did not fail her; she was soon able to turn on her mother a blank, uncomprehending stare, which extinguished the sick woman's animation as abruptly as a storm cloud, driven across the night sky, obliterates the light from a thin slip of a moon. Hopeless now and wan, the only sign of life in her lay in the one hand which plucked feebly at the bedclothes. Then, as if she felt obliged to make one last forlorn effort, she said in a voice that was not much more than a whisper, 'I'm not making excuses, Polly. Don't think that. I just wanted you to understand. For your own sake, I want you to understand.'

'I do,' Polly said wearily. 'You made a choice, that's all. I'd have made a different one, but then we're different people. Whatever I felt then, I certainly don't blame you now.'

'You still don't understand,' her mother said with equal weariness. 'I had no choice. Not that it matters now.'

She closed her eyes, exhausted. Polly watched her. She was right, this figure on the bed, this effigy who was her mother and would soon be dead. She was right. It made no difference at all what she, Polly, thought now. It was what had happened in the past that mattered, and that was built into her for ever, buried deep, far beyond the reach of talk or reason. Even the truth could not touch it now.

Chapter 16

'He never told me you were beautiful,' Jim's girl friend said, climbing on to a chair to reach the bowls and vases on top of the kitchen dresser.

Polly, who was sweeping out the cupboard under the sink, got off her knees and tipped the contents of the dust pan into the bucket on the draining board.

'He probably doesn't think I am,' she said. 'Look, don't keep climbing up and down, just hand them down to me and I'll pack them straight into the Oxfam box. Unless you'd like any of them?'

Marie-Louise scrutinised the various containers on the shelf.

'This one, I like,' she said.

'Actually it's a celery jug, but you're welcome to it.'

'For celery, you have a special jug in England?'

'Yes, made of glass and fluted like that. Everyone had them before the war. Well, my mother didn't because she didn't have much of anything, but later on she took to collecting the sort of things she'd have liked to have had when she was younger. Like that cake stand and the silver condiment set.'

Marie-Louise had already said that she would like the cake stand for the flat when she and Jim were married. 'We shall be very English with our afternoon tea,' she said, 'and our three cakes on the cake stand.'

'Except that nobody does that now. You'll be like expatriates keeping up traditions that went out in England years ago.'

They got on well, she and Jim's girl. It was only after the funeral that he and Marie-Louse had told her they were getting married next month. She assumed that Marie-Louise must be pregnant but was delighted at the news all the same. When Jim had first talked about the new French mistress on the staff, Polly had imagined some young *assistante* straight from college who had taken his fancy, a passing affair like all the others. She had not looked forward to having the help of such a girl in clearing up everything in her mother's house. Now she wondered how she would have managed without it. For she had got it all wrong. Marie-Louise turned out to be nothing like Jim's other girl friends. Not conventionally beautiful, or even pretty, she had a very expressive, attractive face and was warm and friendly. Furthermore she turned out to be very practical when it came to sorting out everything in the house. She was strong, too, which was a bonus.

'I'm awfully grateful to you for your help,' Polly said. 'You and Jim have worked terribly hard.'

'We're on holiday. We've plenty of time. Really it is I who am grateful to you for letting us have so much that will be useful in the flat.'

'Well, it will save you having to buy everything at once when you're in such a rush.'

'Yes,' Marie-Louse said, and shrugged. 'We needn't have rushed after all.'

'How do you mean?'

'We decided to get married quickly so Jim's mother could come and live with us when she came out of hospital.'

Polly almost dropped a tray of glasses from the top shelf, she was so surprised.'

'Live with *you*?'

'Well, he knew she would not be able to live alone again.'

'But I'd have looked after her. He knew that. I told him.'

'Yes, but he said it wasn't fair. He said it was his turn to take responsibility now. So –' she shrugged – 'we were going to get married anyway and he asked me if I'd mind getting married sooner so that we could look after her together when term started. The flat is very near school. Between us we could have managed very well.'

'But Marie-Louise, what a way it would have been to start married life, with a resident invalid mother-in-law!'

Marie-Louise shrugged again. 'I liked her,' she said. 'And, anyway, it's often easier to get on with other people's mothers rather than your own.'

Yes. Because you only have to live with what is there, see what is there to be seen. With the end product, you live only in the present. Polly nodded, but said nothing.

'We talked to the headmaster about it last term. Apart from him, nobody on the staff knows. They'll all be very surprised when we come back married next term.' She laughed and added, 'I expect they'll think I'm pregnant.'

Polly made reassuring noises of negation and felt ashamed of herself.

'Take this silver rose bowl,' she said, by way of apology. 'It'll look nice with the cake stand in the flat.'

The front door slammed. It was Jim returning from the Oxfam shop. Sarah and Tim ran in ahead of him.

'Next load,' Tim requested authoritatively.

'You can tell there's army blood in that lad,' Jim said. 'He almost had the Oxfam lady saluting, he's got us all so organised.'

'We mustn't waste time, Uncle Jim, because she says she shuts the shop in half an hour.'

'It's all ready, Tim, in cartons in the hall,' Polly told him. 'Oh, and there's this lot of china and glass.'

Jim took the box from her.

'Any more?'

'We haven't quite finished. Marie-Louise, I suppose you and Jim couldn't bear to take the entire contents of the dresser to the flat and sort it out later, could you?'

'Yes, we'll do that, then you can lock up here tonight and know it's all finished.'

'Any chance of a cuppa when we get back?' Jim asked, opening the kitchen door with his shoulder as he carried the carton out.

'Yes, we've left some mugs out.'

'Don't pack the kettle again,' Tim warned.

'Come on, bossy boots,' Jim said, 'they know what they're doing.'

He led them out and there were sounds of cartons being dragged across the tiled floor of the hall, of the front door opening and closing a few times, then the car drove away.

'Yes,' Marie-Louise went on, continuing the conversation as if they had not been interrupted, 'it was very sad, the way it worked out. I told Jim we need not rush the wedding now, but he wants to go ahead all the same.'

'I had no idea,' Polly admitted, 'that he was planning all this. I mean, to take our mother to live with you. He never mentioned it.'

'I think he wanted to present you with a *fait accompli*. He knew you would feel it was your duty to look after her, and you already have your husband and two children to care for. No, as I told you, I think he was determined to take the responsibility this time. He felt he owed it to you.' She smiled suddenly. 'He may have forgotten to tell me you were beautiful, but he thinks the world of you, Polly. I know that. He has told me how you looked after him when he was little.'

'In the war, you mean?'

'And before that, when your mother left you.'

'He told you about that?'

'Yes, of course. Should he not have done?'

'Oh, no, it isn't that. I mean I just thought maybe he wouldn't want to talk about it. It was a bad time for us.'

'Oh, but to one's wife one can talk of anything, even the bad times.'

'That's how it should be,' Polly said, and on a sudden impulse crossed the kitchen and hugged her. 'I'm so glad it's you Jim's marrying,' she said.

'Were some of the others so awful?'

Polly laughed. 'Actually, yes,' she said. 'But whatever they'd been like, I'd still prefer you. I hope you'll be very happy.'

'With Jim it shouldn't be too difficult.'

'I hope not, I do hope not.'

'He's a credit to you,' Marie-Louise said. Then, because Polly looked astonished, she added, 'You say that in English, do you not?'

'Yes, we say that. It's just the thought that surprises me. I somehow never imagined that he owed anything to me, if you see what I mean.'

'Oh, but he feels he does. I know that he does.'

Polly shook her head, baffled.

'You're tired,' Marie-Louise told her. 'Never mind, only that kitchen dresser left now, then we sweep the floor and all is finished.'

It was extraordinary, Polly thought as she handed down plates, tipped kitchen gadgets into carrier bags and began to wipe the inside of the drawers, how close it had brought the three of them, this working together on the strange task of sorting out the belongings of the dead.

In each room the pattern had repeated itself: you opened the door and stood there and the room stared back at you, full of someone else's possessions which were suddenly your responsibility because their owner was no longer there. Yet they weren't yours, these things. You had no right to handle them. You apologised under your breath to some unseen presence as you opened each cupboard, each private drawer, looking in boxes, feeling in pockets. And all the time, despite the guilt and memories, you had to get on with the sorting and clearing, with the practical arrangements, with sensible discussion, because there were other priorities, other obligations. Oh yes, there was justification enough for all this prying. So gradually the room was cleared and sorted and swept, and its door was closed upon it. Another room was dead.

For it did seem that when somebody died, their belongings died too. All these little everyday things, once so needed, touched, used, put away carefully in their own special place, all gathering meaning from one ownership, had now become haphazard things, unlinked, without anchorage, ready for scattering. Later on it would be different: they would take on new life in new places with different owners. They outlive us.

But now, for a little space, they had lost all significance, these material things, they offered no reassurance. Only people did that. That was why the three of them, as they worked together dismantling the house, had grown closer to each other, like survivors. Disencumbered by the brief death of material things, they were simpler, more direct with each other, could say things they would not normally have said. Or they could work together in weary but companionable silence, as she and Marie-Louise were doing now, as if the understanding between them had stood the test of something other than time, for they had known each other less than a week.

Jim came in before they were finished, but he kept the children outside, to help him tidy the garden, he said. She knew it was just to keep them occupied, keep them from bothering her. For the first time, Jim seemed protective, older than she was, Polly thought, or at least of an age. From the moment their mother had died, he had taken control, seeing to all the arrangements, the forms and everything. It was he who had found a home where his mother's clothes would be useful, he who had located the Oxfam shop and taken there all the oddments they had no need of, he who looked after Timothy and Sarah, giving them tasks just within their limits, so that they were kept busy and felt important. For the first time in her life she had a sense of leaving things for him to decide, even of leaning on him. Could be always have been like that and she hadn't noticed? Or was it Marie-Louise who had changed him? Or his mother's death? Whatever the reason, he seemed at last, her baby brother, to have grown up. She left her mother's house that night with a weary but contented sense of a long and arduous task finally accomplished.

It was a humid August evening, the air sticky and still, and Polly was smothered in tiny black harvest flies as she walked slowly down the garden to where the children were playing weddings under the weeping ash tree. Or rather Sarah was playing weddings; Tim joined in with ill grace, in return for the half hour Sarah had spent bowling balls in his direction earlier in the day.

'You open the taxi door for me,' Sarah ordered him now.

Tim opened an imaginary door and with great dignity Sarah climbed into the cardboard box, lifted the old net curtain in after her, adjusted the hair band which attached it to her head, and arranged the rest of it round her knees, smoothing it like satin.

'I've jammed your fingers in the door,' Tim said, 'you left your hand hanging out.'

'No, I didn't and you haven't.'

'Yes, I have. You'll have to go to hospital,' and he made wild gestures with an imaginary steering wheel to show how fast he was going.

'I won't go to hospital,' Sarah shrieked. 'I'm going on my honeymoon like Auntie Marie-Louise. I'm going abroad to a big hotel.'

She was near to tears. Polly judged it the right moment to interrupt.

'Bedtime,' she said, and took Sarah's hand and kissed it. 'There, I've kissed your fingers better. Goodness, what have you done to your face?'

'It's my make-up.'

'She rubbed sand on it,' Tim said in disgust. 'She spat on the sand and rubbed it on her face.'

'Brides do that,' Sarah told him.

'Huh, more like an Indian squaw, you look.'

'Tim,' Polly said, 'you go and feed the hamster and I'll take Sarah to have her bath. Come on, Sarah.'

'Oh, *please*, Mum. I haven't thrown the bouquet yet.'

'All right, go on.'

'You stand there, and be bridesmaid, Mum. I'll throw it into the crowd and you try to catch it.'

She hunted around in the box, found the limp bunch of assorted weeds held together by an elastic band and, smiling graciously, threw it out. Polly caught it.

'Now,' Sarah told her, 'you'll be the next one to be married.'

'She's married already, stupid. She'll be a bigamist and go to prison.'

Sarah's lip began to tremble ominously.

'The hamster, Tim,' Polly prompted.

'Oh, all right.'

'Oh, Mum, I didn't tell you,' Sarah said, 'Susan's hamster had babies and the father hamster ate them all up.'

'I expect,' Tim said callously, getting his own back for having to play weddings, 'that if Auntie Marie-Louise has babies, Uncle Jim will eat them.'

Sarah shrieked and began to howl in earnest. She stood in the box, the tears making little clean runnels down her sand-encrusted cheeks, the net curtain all awry, twisted to one side to expose the grubby pink T-shirt and the navy blue shorts which had slipped to reveal an expanse of plump, childish tummy. Polly picked her up and swung her in an arc above her head. Sarah looked down at her, surprised out of her tears by the way the blue sky and great curved branches of the weeping ash had suddenly tipped and lurched and turned upside-down.

'Silly girl,' Polly said, kissing her, as Tim went off to the shed where the hamster lived. 'He only said it to tease you. If you didn't cry he wouldn't bother.'

As she carried her up the garden, the sobs subsided into a muffled snuffling which gave way to a prolonged yawn. Sarah's head lolled against her mother's shoulder. She was almost asleep. Polly rubbed her cheek gently against the warm, sweet-smelling hair, and held her close.

She heard him come in as she finished settling the children. Tim was sleeping, as he always did, flat on his back with both hands above his head on the pillow. In the room next to his, Sarah lay, curled up as usual, with her thumb in her mouth, sucking even in her sleep. Polly gathered up all the discarded bits and pieces of clothing, shirts and shorts and sand-stained socks, shut both bedroom doors quietly behind her and went downstairs.

Martin had put down his brief-case on the kitchen table.

'Children in bed?' he enquired, as he gave her the small, ritual kiss.

'Yes, both asleep, thank goodness. How was your day?'

'Not bad. I had lunch with the Minister's side-kick, so I'm not hungry. Don't bother to cook much.'

She nodded, though in fact, having only had a sandwich for lunch, she was starving.

'I'll go and have a wash then,' he said. 'Give me a shout when it's ready. I'll be in my study.'

'All right. It'll be about an hour,' she said.

When he had gone upstairs, she began to sort out the children's clothes in the scullery, putting the dirtiest ones to soak, pushing the rest into the washing machine. It was only when she came back into the kitchen that the silence struck her. Here I am, she thought, this Friday evening, in this empty kitchen, the children asleep, Martin no doubt already settled in his study, and suddenly I can't stand it any more. I thought that I could just detach myself, be independent of him, but I can't. I cannot live like this.

The realisation was so unexpected that she had to sit down to think about it. She needed a drink. She helped herself to the nearest available alcohol, which was the cooking sherry, poured herself a glass and sat down again. It was something to do with its being Friday. Weekends were always worse. At weekends you couldn't help longing for a proper evening together, a night out together, or just an early night together. Especially an early night together.

It's no good saying you can't stand it any more, she told herself as she drained the glass. You've got to talk to him. That's what sensible married people do, talk their problems over. But I've tried, she argued back wearily. Oh God, I've tried. Have another glass of cooking sherry and try again then, Polly Adams.

He was sitting at the desk when she went in, bending over a cardboard carton which he was about to unwrap. He looked up with ill-disguised irritation at being disturbed.

'Supper already?' he asked. 'That's quick.'

'No, I – '

She stood in the doorway, staring. She hadn't been up here for a while and was amazed at how much his collection had grown. The study seemed to be filled with iron crosses, Nazi helmets and buckles, with S.S. armbands and shoulder flashes. There was even a photograph of Hitler.

'It's horrible,' she exclaimed. 'Horrible!'

'What? My collection?' he asked, half ashamed, half gratified. Then he laughed and shrugged. 'It's no worse than the weapons they collect in most museums,' he said.

'But when you think of the things they did, the people who wore this uniform – '

'Just because you study something, Polly, it doesn't mean that you approve of it.'

He gave her a crafty little smile, like a child pleased with its own cunning. In fact there was something about the way he looked around the room that reminded her of a small boy, shame-faced but defiant, trying to hide his weakness behind a show of cruelty. He is trying to prove how manly he is, she thought. It's really got nothing to do with military history.

'You see,' he said, 'I might just as well have studied Napoleon and collected memorabilia of the *Grande Armée*. Only this is more recent. Of course, it's easier, too, because there's so much more stuff available.'

He glanced down at the box on the floor.

'Take that, for example,' he said. 'Gerard gave it to me today. It was part of a job lot he bought at an auction.'

'Gerard?'

'You know, I've mentioned him. My mate from army days.'

She shook her head, certain that Martin hadn't mentioned him. Certainly she'd never heard him refer to anyone as a mate before. It was not the sort of expression he used.

'Well, if supper isn't ready – ' he hinted, obviously keen to get on with unwrapping his box. He was like a child being kept from opening his present.

'I came up because I wanted to talk to you,' she said, ignoring his appeal.

'Oh, what about? Not about my collection?'

'No. Well, I suppose that does come into it. It's the whole way we live, really. It struck me suddenly this evening, I don't know why. You know, the way you come up here and shut yourself off from the rest of us – '

'Oh, there's nothing odd about that. I'm sure a lot of chaps feel the need to unwind after a day's work.'

'No, Martin, it's not just that. Please do try to be honest about it. Really, if you think that the marriage was a mistake and you don't love me, I'd much rather you said so.'

'Polly! Really, what a thing to say! Am I the sort of person who would marry someone they didn't care for? It isn't as if

227

we were both in our teens when we got married. Come on, you don't mean that, do you?'

He put his head on one side, smiling, trying to coax her out of it. He had a triangular-shaped face, the blue eyes wide set. He had changed since they were married, she thought. Without the uniform, and now that he was less bronzed, his features seemed more delicate and sometimes, like now, they had an ambivalent expression, like a Leonardo angel.

'Please take it seriously, Martin,' she said. 'I'm not joking. Truly, I can't go on like this.'

'Like what? It isn't as if we throw plates at each other.'

'Like we are, just co-existing. Oh, I can't describe it, we're like ships that pass in the night, not touching, moving in our separate ways. You know what it's like.'

He looked at her uneasily.

'You're trying to tell me you're unhappy?'

'Yes.'

'And you think it's my fault? You're blaming me?'

'No, I'm not saying that. I'm just saying we should discuss it.'

'All right, let's have a discussion. Sit down.' He moved a chair forward for her, pulled up his own, fidgeting to hide his embarrassment. 'What proposals do you have?'

When she didn't reply, he said, 'I'm quite prepared to discuss any reasonable proposals. Or even unreasonable ones,' he added, with a self-conscious little laugh.

'It's not a matter of proposals.'

'Oh dear, I'm sorry. I misunderstood. I thought you wanted a discussion.'

She should have known it wouldn't do any good, she thought hopelessly. Keep calm, she told herself, go on trying.

'Have the children been difficult today?' he asked with sudden kindness. 'Is that the real trouble?'

'No,' she said fiercely, annoyed that the onus was being shifted on to the children. 'They've been fine.'

'Good. You know, I think you ought to get out and about a bit more. You'll enjoy the air show tomorrow. Being tied in with little children is bound to make you a bit fed up and frustrated.'

Frustration. Was that what it was?

'And as for my coming up here, I assure you it's perfectly normal.'

What is normal? she wondered. Over the years she seemed to have lost track of what was normal and what wasn't. Suddenly she realised she would have to get away from him for a while to rediscover normality.

'Would you mind,' she asked, 'if I went away for the weekend? You take the children to the air show tomorrow. They won't miss me. You can just tell them I need a little break. They'll understand that.'

The clear blue eyes widened with fear.

'Why?' he asked sharply. 'And where would you go?'

'I don't know. I've only just thought of it. Somewhere like Knaresby, maybe. I just want a chance to sort things out in my own mind.'

'Is there a man?'

Her hands flew up to her face. For a moment she didn't speak, then she said in a low voice, 'No. I want a break. I told you the truth when I said that.'

He didn't reply.

'The shopping's all done,' she went on. 'You'll find supplies of everything in the fridge. Just explain to the children simply in the morning, won't you? They're looking forward to the show, so it won't worry them. I'm sure it won't.'

She hesitated for a moment and when he still did not reply, said, 'Well, goodbye then. 'I'll just go and put a few things together.'

In the doorway she stopped.

'Martin, if you don't want me to go, you've only to say so.' She waited. 'I mean, if you love me and want me to stay, please tell me, and I won't go. You only have to say, Martin. Please, Martin.'

He looked at her blankly and then turned back to his desk.

She waited for a moment, then turned and left him.

In a daze, because it had all happened so quickly and unexpectedly, she gathered up her night things and put them in a case, put on her coat, checked that she had the car keys and went downstairs. She didn't know where she was going, just that she must get away, have a break, breathe freely and think. Above all, think. She didn't know what had made her say Knaresby, but it would do. In some simple, anonymous room in a Knaresby guest-house, she would have quietness and time to think. But all the time she was listening, hoping that he would say a word to keep her here. Only one word, but he would not say it.

In the hall she heard his voice. She stood, the case beside her, her bag hanging on her arm, ready to run upstairs to him. But on the point of moving, she realised that he was not calling to her, was not asking her to stay, was not going to say he loved her. His voice was stern as he ordered the children, 'Wake up. Put on your dressing gowns. Your mother's going.'

Frozen, she stood in the hall. She seemed not to be made of flesh and blood any more. She could not move, but she saw them. He pushed them to the top of the stairs. They stood on the landing in front of him: Tim in his maroon dressing gown, Sarah in her blue, rubbing the sleep out of their eyes.

'So you'd better say goodbye,' he said.

They looked at her, puzzled, still half asleep, and as they realised what was happening the bemused expression on their faces changed to horror and fright. She saw herself as they must see her standing there, dressed ready for a journey, her case alongside her. Then Tim began to cry. Tim, who never cried, began to shake with sobs, while Sarah, the cry-baby, shed not a tear. She simply went whiter and whiter and her eyes seemed to get bigger in her face, great pools of dismay, but still she made no sound.

It was like a nightmare, the way she could not move. Then suddenly, as if she had woken, the paralysis lost its grip. In a few bounds she was up the stairs, had her arms around them. They clung to her, both sobbing now: 'Please, please don't go. We'll be good.'

'It's all right,' she said. 'Of course I'm not going. Come on, back to bed.'

But they did not trust her, they held on to her, pulled at her coat to take it off, took hold of the skirt of her dress, clutched at her hands, at her hair, as she knelt there. Then, somehow or other, the three of them made their way to Sarah's bedroom, because it was nearer, and they pulled her down on to a chair, her children did, and took off her coat, struggling with the belt and the heavy metal buckle. Tim took her bag, which was still hanging on her arm, eased it down over her hand and then surreptitiously, when he thought she wasn't looking, hid it in the cupboard.

Then they sat one on each knee and she rocked them gently, all three of them crying.

Martin came in.

'I'm sorry, children,' he said. 'It was my fault. I upset your mother.'

'You'll stay, won't you? Please stay. He's said he's sorry,' Tim said.

'Whatever he did, he didn't mean it. And we're sorry too.'

'And we all say things we don't mean sometimes.'

'It's all over now, isn't it? Can't we just start again?'

She was amazed at them. They might have been twice their age, the way they spoke. All the arguments she had used to assuage childish disagreements were being presented to her now.

She could not look at Martin. How could he have done this to them? It was their quarrel, his and hers, and had nothing to do with the children. How could he have used them like this, as a weapon against her, rather than ask her to stay himself, say he loved her and wanted her to stay? He had made her inflict on her own children the terror that had once been inflicted on her. And for no reason except to save himself from talking to her.

She soothed them, rocked then in her arms.

'I was only going for a couple of nights,' she told them. 'But I won't go if you don't want me to. It's all right.'

She saw it, the little flicker of satisfaction on Martin's face. She wanted to shout that she hated him, would never forgive him. Instead she held them close, the children who had been upset enough already, and then gently persuaded them back into bed. She left her coat lying over the back of the chair and her bag hidden in Sarah's cupboard: their childish logic would tell them that she couldn't possibly leave the house without these things, and they would feel safer for it.

'Go to sleep now, children,' Martin said. 'Or you'll be too tired to go to the air show tomorrow.'

She was trembling as she followed him downstairs, trembling with anger and shock and guilt.

'How could you?' was all she could say when he steered her into the kitchen.

'Well, I thought you were going, and it seemed the best way to stop you. And you have to admit that it worked.'

'If you wanted me to stay, couldn't you have asked me on your own behalf?'

He shrugged. 'It might not have worked,' he said. 'And I was a bit desperate. As I say, I thought you really were going. Don't worry about Sarah and Tim. They'll get over it. Children are very resilient.'

'That's a very convenient lie,' she said angrily. 'People who hurt children always say they're resilient. Of course children bear things. What else can they do? The suicide rate among little children isn't very high. They bear neglect, or bereavement, or being abandoned. But that doesn't mean they're resilient, just that they have no option.'

'Well, I can only say I survived without either parent, so I suppose it must be possible. Anyway, let's forget it and have some coffee.'

It was pointless to argue. He was living proof of the fallacy of his own argument; it was just because he had not been resilient that he now deprived his wife not only of passion but also of tenderness and affection. He would never understand it. In the face of such incomprehension her anger drained out of her. For he, too, was a victim. She felt only a weary kind of pity for him, almost love, but a love which had in it none of the respect she had once felt for him.

'I'll come back in a minute for the coffee,' she said. 'I'll just go and tidy myself up.'

What a sight she was, she thought, as she looked at herself in the glass, with her face stained and her hair all rumpled from the children's frantic caresses. As she dragged a comb through it, weariness and acceptance crept over her. If fighting him was going to involve hurting the children then she couldn't do it. There was no sense in generation after generation inflicting on their children the hurts that had been inflicted on themselves. There was no end to it. She knew that her explanation to the children that she was only going away for a night or two, although true, had been rendered false by what Martin had done. She knew that they would pretend to believe but would go on worrying, though they would probably never mention it again. All she could do was provide extra reassurance and love and hope that time would do the rest. Somehow she had to go on, even though sometimes, like this evening, she felt she couldn't bear it. At least she knew how her mother had felt.

She paused, taken aback by this realisation, as she stood in front of the long mirror. The last of the evening sunshine slanted in through the window, making a triangle of light on the bed and carrying with it, on a gentle breeze, the scent of late roses. The room seemed suddenly watchful, as she stood there, just as that other room had done when her mother lay very still on the bed, like an effigy, only the pale fingers moving as they plucked at the sheet. She felt the sudden chill of an unseen presence and glanced behind her at the bed. She told herself not to be silly, the effigy had never been there, and anyway it had been lifted up from that other bed long ago, carried away and burnt. She, Polly, had witnessed it. Yet still she crossed over to the bed now and, gently stroking the linen cover, whispered, 'Forgive me, forgive me,' to whatever might remain when all else was destroyed.

Chapter 17

It was a perfect autumn morning, the day Sarah started school. Polly walked home feeling light-headed with relief, for Sarah had run into the school without shedding a tear, clearly delighted to have caught up with her big brother at last.

It was a long time, Polly realised, since she had walked at her own pace and alone, knowing that the rest of the day was hers to do as she liked with. She felt curiously disencumbered, free at last to plan her own life. She would wash up and make the beds quickly and go straight into town, she decided as she turned into their row of Victorian terraced houses. She wouldn't postpone for a single day the business of finding a job. She was ready to compromise, too, accept Randy's advice, find someone to help her look after the children in the holidays. It was an absolute priority now, a good job which would provide the companionship she needed if she was to bear the loneliness of being Martin's wife.

Because she had to bear it. She must never again break down, inflict on the children appalling scenes like the one on that black Friday evening. It was an adult problem, created by herself and Martin, to be solved in an adult way, not lumbered on to children who could not understand. She would not be guilty, however inadvertently, of visiting the sins of the father on the children. She remembered, for the first time in years, her argument with the vicar in the catechism lesson, saw again the tall black figure with the teeth like tombstones, and felt again the relief she had felt when she realised that the stalwart Miss Capstick was on her side. She savoured that memory for a moment as she stood on the doorstep, the front door key in her hand.

The sun was just beginning to make itself felt. Suddenly she did not want to go into the empty, childless house, but walked instead around the side and stood looking down the long back garden. The mist hung over it still, the sun was not much more than a dispersed glow, bringing a touch of warmth all the same. It was very quiet. She stood entranced. It was a perfectly ordinary town garden really, with bushes and beds on each side of the grass and a concrete path dividing them. But this morning it had a magical feeling. It wasn't the excitement, the promise of a spring morning; it was a different kind of magic, speculative and strange.

She began to wander down the path, letting herself drift in the wonder of the morning. The grass was long and wet with dew and between its blades the spiders had spun fine webs which lay in little pools of gauze across the lawn. The bushes, too, were netted with cobwebs. She looked at them with wonder as she walked along the path. At the end of the garden was a huge weeping ash tree which swept the ground with long trailing branches. In front of it was a bench. A spider had swung a web between a branch of the weeping ash and the end of the bench. The sun shone through it, lighting up the perfection of it, the intricate patterns, the symmetry, all finer than the finest crochet work. She put her anorak on the bench and sat down gently, fearful of breaking the web. But, insubstantial as it looked, it was strong and only quivered a little, then steadied itself and was still.

Polly, too, sat very still, gazing down the garden, letting it cast its spell over her. She remembered the other garden when she was little, the garden with the clothes-line and the old pile of rubble which had once been a henhouse and was now overgrown with pink, flowering weeds. It was still overgrown and always would be, for it was as real to her as this garden, as clear in her mind as Miss Capstick had been just now, and the crowlike vicar with his approval of visiting the sins of the fathers on the children, shared all those years later by the judge at Irene's trial. And he was real, too, the judge was. He still sat there in front of the tall window, the light shining through his red-veined, papery ears. And Irene, too, in the dock, only now Polly did not hear that terrible desolate cry with her ears; it was there in her head and always would be. And the children she had never seen, she could see them in her mind's eye, not clearly but dimly in outline as if they were waiting in the wings.

The sun was higher in the sky now; she could feel it on the side of her head as she sat there on the bench in the quietness of the garden and thought about Irene and the children, as she often did nowadays. Only nowadays she didn't think of her as Irene any more. In her mind she had become somebody else, she didn't know why, only that she was beginning to take on a life of her own and that whenever Polly was able to detach herself from everyday preoccupations, as she was now, so that her mind floated free, she seemed able to enter the world of this woman who was not Irene but who had nonetheless grown out of her, because it all seemed to stem from that moment of the terrible cry in the dock. She knew that she had to discover that life step by step and in some strange way that she didn't understand, take it into herself, relive it and shape it and write it down because that was the only way to make it real.

In these moments she saw it very clearly, the task seemed quite simple. But the confidence never lasted, for the world of this woman who was not Irene but had grown out of the desolate birth cry, might seem strong and real when it was within her but it could be instantly shattered by the sound of the telephone bell, a knock at the door, or the cry of a child. It had no substance and it could not be recalled at will. Sometimes it just faded away for no reason and she was back in the world of everyday things, governed by other priorities.

But she knew that it was still there, that other world, because it always came back, reassembling itself, presenting problems as fresh as when she had last pondered them. It was she herself who had been absent. That was what made her feel guilty: she had a feeling that she had failed in some duty, failed to give life to the woman who was not Irene, failed to give substance to this other world because she had not found the words. She had excuses, of course. It needed uninterrupted time, which she had not had before today. And she was afraid of getting it wrong. Courage, that was what she lacked. Today she had the time, the uninterrupted time, but still she lacked the courage. It would be easy to chicken out, set herself some easier task, like taking a job on a newspaper, for example. Nobody would know that she had chickened out. It would seem a sensible thing, to the outside world, to return gradually to her career. They would not know that she had failed, even if she told them. It was a curious sort of failure that nobody could comprehend except herself.

For a moment she was tempted, as she had been this morning when she walked home from school, before this other world had once again, unasked, asserted its authority, its different priorities. What sense did it make to give up the chance of going back to a job she enjoyed, knew that she could do, to try to do something she didn't understand, didn't seem to have control of and could never explain, because it was a secret thing? She could not do all three: not run a home, go out to work, and try to write this book which was asking to be written. Perhaps she could just try, and if she found she couldn't manage the book, then go back to journalism? But some inner voice knew better and told her that once started, she would not give up. It would be a commitment, like a child is a commitment.

She laughed suddenly, out loud, in the misty silence of the autumn garden. That was it; it was quite simple. You don't know anything about childcare or even giving birth when you start a baby. Either by conscious decision or in a moment of passion you commit yourself. Then there's no going back. So commit yourself to this thing, Polly Adams, and work it all out afterwards. This sense of obligation wouldn't be so strong, if there wasn't some way or other of fulfilling it. Trust to that, and commit yourself.

So she got up and, walking in a daze, made her way into the house. Ignoring such things as the dishes on the breakfast table, she went over to the kitchen dresser and found, in the drawer where she kept scrap paper and crayons for the children, an old exercise book from her own school days and two pencils. Still keeping her eyes off the clutter in the kitchen, she went back into the garden.

It was an old maths book, the right hand page marked with lines and the left one with squares for graph paper. It would do. Only three pages had been used. She turned them over. The last showed a Graph to Illustrate the Cosine. She must have known what it meant at the time because she'd got a B+ for it. She turned to the next page, which was blank, pressed it flat and wrote Chapter One at the top. Then she sat staring at the empty page and felt frightened.

She sat there for a long time, the pencil relaxed in her hand. Then after much thought, she underlined Chapter One, first with the pencil she was holding which was hard and squeaked, then with the other which was soft and made no sound.

She had never given a name to the girl who was not Irene, she realised. She had thought a lot about her, and her early childhood and how she came to be fostered. She had found it all out when she was lying awake at night or in the early morning, or whenever she had glimpsed that other world in uninterrupted moments as she was doing now. But just as in a dream people are real but nameless, so this girl had needed no name. But now she had to emerge from the dream; things were going to have to change. Call her Maisie. Polly was surprised; she hadn't expected a funny old name like that. She wrote it on the outside of the book, on the cover where she had written her own name twenty years ago.

What she didn't know, she realised, was at what point she would break into Maisie's life. When she was born, when she was married, somewhere in her early childhood or when she was first fostered? The ideas swam around in her head. Then the word foster took over. She couldn't think why there was something special about it. Then she remembered. She was sitting with her mother on the back doorstep one afternoon after school, drinking tea. It was the first time she had had proper grown-up tea, as opposed to a cup of milk with a splash of tea in it. Her mother was gossiping to her just as if she really was grown-up and not just five and a half. She was talking about a Mrs Bantam who lived down the street and had three children as well as two others that she took in. 'She treats those foster children just like her own, which is as it should be,' Polly's mother said. 'Not like that Mrs Parker. She never should have been allowed to foster kids, Mrs Parker shouldn't.'

Polly felt again the relief she had felt then that she hadn't shown her ignorance, for until then she had thought that Foster was the surname of the children who came to school with the Parkers. If she had let it slip her mother would have laughed and the grown-up feeling would have been lost for ever.

Betty Parker was her friend and they sat together at dinner time. In the summer they took their sandwiches outdoors and ate them leaning against the back wall of the school, facing down the playground, because that was the sunniest place. Betty Parker always brought a brown paper bag containing two sets of sandwiches wrapped separately in greaseproof paper. She had to be careful she got them the right way round for the ones for the Parker children had butter in them and the ones for the foster children had margarine. Whatever she thought of it now, it had not struck Polly as odd at the time; she had just thought it was the way of things, one of the rules of life. She was more impressed by the greaseproof paper. Her own sandwiches were always wrapped in something second-hand, like the inside of cornflake packages, which she carefully folded and took home with the elastic band, ready for tomorrow. Buying whole rolls of greaseproof paper just to cut up and wrap sandwiches seemed to her very extravagant.

But now she felt it, the significance of it, the hurt to Maisie, who had been rejected by her own natural mother when she was born, then fostered by a kindly woman like Mrs Bantam who couldn't keep her. So she had had to go to someone like Mrs Parker who saw to it that she had margarine in her sandwiches. But unlike the real-life foster children, Maisie was on her own, she was the only foster child in the family of butter-eating Parker children, she had nobody to confide in, she was the odd one out, always.

Yes, Polly realised, that was the point to start. Start with the sandwiches, with Maisie watching her own special packet being unwrapped, Betty taking great care because her mother would be sure to ask. She used to sniff them. How clearly she remembered that little scene now, and the feel of the wall, and the emptiness inside you, because you were always starving by dinner time. And afterwards you lay back satisfied and the stone was warm and crumbly and little bits flaked off and clung to your hair. You could feel them, like you could feel the sun on your face and the nice full feeling in your stomach, as you waited for the bell for afternoon school and hoped that they would forget to ring it, but they never did.

She was there again now, but somehow she was Maisie, and she was thinking of her first foster mother who had never made her feel that she was different from other children and who, it seemed to Polly, looked like Mrs Biddle. Yes, she had Mrs Biddle's springy fair hair and scrubbed red cheeks, rather raw-looking they were, and her eyes were a pretty blue, but watery and pinking round the rims. It was a long time since she had thought of Mrs Biddle.

Sometimes Mrs Biddle put powder on her face when she was going out. She chucked it on any old how, so that Polly's mum said she thought she just stuck her head into the flour bin. She must have done it to try to subdue the bright pink of her cheeks, but in no time the skin shone through unabashed.

As she leaned against the wall Maisie was thinking of her foster mother putting her face in the flour bin and of the way her kindly face shone through, whatever silly things she did to it. She was kind all the way through. You trusted her because nothing was hidden; you could see her thought processes working themselves out in her watery blue eyes and across her pink, scrubbed face with its anxious, rather puzzled look. She was the first person Maisie could remember and she had loved her. Yet this same kind woman, who was always worrying about what to do for the best, had sent her away and Maisie never knew why. That was the question which filled her mind now, as she ate her bread and margarine sandwiches and listened to the others chattering, as they leaned against the rough wall of the school, the sun on the faces, waiting for the bell to ring.

Polly paused before starting to write, staring round the garden, not seeing it. She hadn't thought of these people and places for years yet the memory of them must have been there all the time. Suddenly she realised that it was from this, from deep within herself, that she would find what she needed to create Maisie's childhood and write her life, the life of the woman who was not Irene. Somehow their two worlds would meet and combine, somehow characters would grow out of other lives and take on a life of their own, although she didn't understand how. But she knew that all her past was there, all of it, not just the consciously remembered events, especially not those, but everything she had ever felt or puzzled over, misunderstood, or seen or heard and been moved by, all the people and the places and tastes and sounds and smells, all the hurts, all the funny and odd things, all of it was there, undiminished, unchanged. Yes, it was beyond the reach of change, waiting to be revisited.

But she herself had changed, she had grown up, so while she could still feel what she felt then, she could also look back, with a different kind of understanding. It did not diminish anything she had felt, indeed it made it more poignant. But it added a new dimension, by distancing her from herself. It had to be like that, she realised now; she had to see it with an observer's eyes if she was going to describe it. Otherwise it would be all haphazard, as life is. But she had to find a key, retrieve just those things which she, or rather Maisie, needed. It was all there within her, but it needed this outsider's vision to select, to shape and transform. A pattern will emerge, she told herself as she began to write, just give it the chance, Polly Adams.

She was lucky that first day. Beginner's luck, she often thought later. The more she wrote – and she wrote rapidly with the soft, quiet pencil – the more she felt convinced that this was the right path, if only she could manage not to muddle it all up by interfering. Somehow she had to let Maisie find her own way through this landscape which she, Polly, had enabled her to enter. She must not let her own mind intervene or even be critical. The time for criticism would come later, she was aware of that, but she must not frighten it all away by being critical now. If she could just obliterate herself, the other world would be free to exist and into it would come the people and scenes in Maisie's life, things long forgotten, things she had not even known she knew. They came unheralded and unsought, as if they has been waiting their moment, and all she had to do was recognise and accept them. It was as if the whole story was there already for her to uncover, like finding the statue within the stone, but working very quietly and carefully, never imposing her will. Randy had been right when he said that novels were not about inventing things but about finding them out. But it was not easy, for she herself was the barrier, it was she herself who got in the way, blocking the light of her own imagination. And if for one moment she let herself be conscious of herself sitting there writing, it all faded away. *Let me not be*, she prayed as she wrote that morning, *let me not be*.

Yet all the same time, part of her had to keep watch, overseeing it all. She had to be intensely aware, ready to see the possibility of a pattern, while never forcing it. She had to listen to what her characters were saying, but never push words into their mouths. It was a special sort of watching and listening, secret even from herself. She was a spy, an eavesdropper. She was so afraid of drawing attention to herself that after the soft pencil had worn flat and her writing was all fuzzy, she dared not use the other one because it was hard and squeaked obtrusively.

Then, quite suddenly, she was cold, aware of her body shivering. She seemed to be back inside herself and uncomfortably chilly. She looked up, expecting clouds, but the sun was still shining. It was just that it had moved inexplicably across the sky, leaving the bench in shadow. It was shining on the other bushes, the ones against the western wall. Definitely the sun was lighting up the variegated leaves of the holly on the wrong side of the garden.

She looked at her watch. It couldn't be! Not three o'clock. She had to fetch the children from school in half an hour and she hadn't even washed up the breakfast things.

But for a moment she did not move. You will get through it, she told herself, you will rush around like a mad thing later, but for now, just for a little while, savour it, this special moment. Some instinct told her that it might not easily be summoned up again, that elusive other world, so real, yet insubstantial, which she had just left; it might resist a deliberate attempt of her will to bring it back. Therefore savour it, Polly Adams. So she sat for a few minutes, feeling drained yet satisfied, and relaxed. On the end of the bench, where the big spider's web had linked it to the branch of the weeping ash, all the intricate tracery was gone. Only the strong outer framework remained.

Chapter 18

'Do stop prowling about,' Randy said as she reached the window. 'You're so restless today.'

She looked back at him, smiling.

'It's a beautiful flat,' she said. 'When you told me it only had two rooms, I imagined something tiny. You forgot to mention they were each as big as a small house.'

'Yes,' he agreed, lying back in his armchair and surveying the high ceiling, the cornices and tall sash windows. 'When the estate agents said it was spacious, for once they weren't exaggerating.'

'Well, you're pretty big yourself. You need plenty of space,' she remarked absently, busy with the shutters. 'They really do work, don't they?'

He watched her as she first carefully unfolded them across the window, secured them with the iron bar, then released it and fastened back first one shutter then the other so that the sun, momentarily locked out, suddenly jumped back into the room, lighting up the gold in her hair, the expression of childish concentration on her face.

'Do you remember,' she asked, turning towards him, 'the last time I came to see you at home? In your digs? In that attic in Union Street?'

'Do I remember? Silly Flinders. Shall I ever forget it? Come here, you're like a woman with child, you're so restless. I think,' he added thoughtfully, 'that you must be with book.'

Suddenly wary, she stopped walking towards him and changed direction. She went across to the bookcase, where she stood examining the titles.

'Come here, Flinders.'

She shook her head.

'You *are* with book,' he said. 'All right, don't look so alarmed. I shan't start asking questions.'

She relaxed and began to walk slowly towards the fireplace. Then she stood, leaning against the marble mantelpiece, observing him, puzzled as always by the way he understood.

'How do you know so much?' she demanded. 'I mean, how did you guess about the book? I haven't breathed a word about it, not to anyone.'

He hesitated. 'The usual signs, I suppose,' he said. 'I've noticed them in other writers. A sort of suppressed excitement. A kind of secrecy.'

'I'm sorry I can't talk about it even to you, Randy. But you're right. It *is* a bit like having a baby. Once it's born, everyone can understand and talk about it, but when it's still inside you, nobody can feel about it the way you do yourself. I suppose that's why when you lose a baby people don't understand what you've lost. A book unformed is vulnerable, too.'

'It's all right, Flinders, you don't have to apologise,' he said, getting up. 'I do understand. You see, it isn't like journalism where it helps to talk things over, and everything's on the surface anyway. Fiction's got to be dug out from somewhere deep within you and nobody can help with that, not really. You trust your instinct, Flinders, and don't talk about it if you don't want to. Later on, when it's taken shape, you may feel differently. And I'll be here.'

'Thanks, Randy. I thought you'd be cross because I wasn't trying to get a job any more. I was almost scared to come and tell you, you know.'

'Silly Flinders. As if I wouldn't understand! You've made the right choice, of course you have.'

'But the funny thing was that it didn't seem like a choice at all. I'd actually just decided to go and get myself a job, then I found myself sitting on a bench writing a book instead. I still can't really believe it.'

'Well, choice or not, it's what I've always hoped would happen.'

'And, Randy, if I was going to talk to anyone about it now, it would be you. It's just that it's not clear yet, it's all still a mystery and I'm dead scared that if I talk about it, it'll all disappear.'

'I've told you I understand,' he said, crossing over to her and putting his hands on her shoulders. 'So I shan't say any more about it. Except, oh my darling Flinders, I am very pleased for you. It's quite the best thing for you to do.'

He was kissing her and it was as it used to be. She forgot all the stress and rejection and misery of the past few years. It melted away from her in the sudden warmth. Her body behaved as it used to do, responding to his. It was all so simple and right and natural and somehow good. She laughed for joy.

'I never thought,' she said afterwards, as she lay in his arms in the double bed in the huge bedroom, the telephone lying unhooked on the bedside table, covered with a pillow, 'that adultery would seem so, so – '

'So what, Flinders?'

'So innocent,' she said.

The children would be at the party now, at Jeremy Thwaites' house. Mrs Thwaite would have collected them all from school and taken them home. They would be having tea and, as they ate their jelly and sausages and crisps, she was lying here committing adultery. It was really very odd that she didn't feel guilty.

'Should you put the phone back on the hook?' she asked.

'No, I told them I wouldn't be available after my business lunch.'

He stroked her damp hair off her face. 'Your breasts are all pink and flushed,' he said. 'We'll stay like this always, won't we Polly love, now that we've found each other again?'

'Yes.'

She was warm and relaxed and happy. He held her even closer, her head against his chest.

'I can hear your heart thumping,' she said, wriggling away and putting her head on the pillow.

'Don't you like that?'

'No. It sounds like a radio sound effect. You know, thump, thump, woosh, thump. And it sounds as if it might burst. A bit alarming, really.'

'It would be a lot more alarming if you couldn't hear it,' he said, kissing her. 'I don't mind hearing your heart beating,' he added, putting his head against her breasts. 'It's a lovely sound, my Flinders' heart.'

She said nothing, but lay cradling his head. He had a big head. His face was a bit too long, she thought, as she gently traced the outline of it with her fingers. His eyes were dark brown, almost black now, the pupils were so big. Her finger followed the line of his mouth and he nibbled it. She laughed and he kissed her breasts. She lay back with her eyes closed, her fingers in his thick dark hair, and all the familiar old feelings caught her up and carried her gently along on the current.

'You didn't laugh that time,' he said, teasing her.

She clung to him, afraid of losing the sweetness of it.

'It's odd,' she said later, 'how different the same thing can be, isn't it?'

'Mm. Happy?'

'Mm. Thirsty, too.'

'It'll wear off.'

'You mean you're too lazy to get up and make me some tea?'

'That's right. And you don't want me to anyway. Not really.'

'No. Not really.'

She just wanted to stay like this for ever, at one with him and herself and the whole world. And still she didn't feel guilty. In fact she felt as if she had made amends. For she had condoned too much Martin's rejection of what he disparagingly called the physical side of their marriage. It was every bit as bad to reject one's animal nature as it was to concentrate too much on it. It was worse really, for it was a denial of life. Besides they are inseparable, the emotional and the physical. Even as you feel compassion, your hands reach out to comfort and to touch. Love is indivisible, she thought, as she lay in Randy's arms and gently stroked his back, touching him with her fingers but feeling him in her heart. That was what the self-contained, untouchable Martin would never understand. Suddenly she knew she did not love him any more. Rejected, her love had withered. Maybe it had never been very strong. But it had been there, alive once. It would have grown if he had nurtured it.

'A penny for them?' Randy said.

She shook her head, said nothing but held tightly on to him, realising for the first time that she was in danger of falling in love with him, but refusing to admit it even to herself. It didn't fit into her scheme of things, not that entire sort of love.

At five o'clock he made her tea and brought it to the bedside, wrapping his dressing gown around her.

'Now, my darling,' he said, 'we've got to start being practical.'

'You mean get up? There's no hurry.'

'No, I mean talk. Talk about the future. About the divorce. I know it's difficult now, but the law's going to be changed soon.'

'I'm sorry. I'm not with you. I thought your divorce was almost through.'

'I mean *yours*, Flinders. Drink some more tea. It will clear your mind.'

'Divorce?' She put the cup down and turned to face him. 'Randy, what makes you think I'm going to get a divorce?'

He stared at her. 'Well,' he said at last, 'all this.' He waved his hands about helplessly. 'And you've just said you want to stay like this for ever.'

'Well, we can – I mean, be like this for ever. We can arrange it. The school holidays will be a bit tricky, but we'll manage.'

It was his turn to put a cup down. Deliberately he took both her hands in his. 'Flinders,' he said, 'what the hell do you mean? You must have understood I wanted to marry you.'

'*Marry* me?'

'Oh, God, what did you think of me? Of course I want to marry you.'

'But you've just been married and it didn't work.'

'Oh, that.' He shrugged impatiently as if it was irrelevant. 'That was just a stupid mistake right, from the start. I married on the rebound.'

'Oh,' she exclaimed, for a moment distracted. 'Who from?'

'You, of course.'

'Me?' She lay back, baffled. 'But you never wanted to marry me. You positively told me you didn't.'

'All right, I deserve that. I acted like an idiot. But I grew up pretty quickly after you'd gone. I realised when you went off like that what an utter fool I'd been. But it was too late. Oh, why did you do it? Of all the crazy, impetuous things, just to come into the office on a Monday morning and announce that you were getting married and going off, just like that, on the spur of the moment? The months after you'd gone were sheer hell. I loathed myself. I promise you, Polly, however much you loathed me, I hated myself even more. I kept going back over everything I'd said and done, realising how stupid and blind and selfish I'd been. I'd never treated you as you should have been treated, never tried to win you – '

'Would I have let you? I don't think old-fashioned ideas of wooing and winning fair ladies were part of our creed, were they?'

'Deep down, yes, they should have been. Fair ladies do happen to be more vulnerable than unfair men. I didn't take that into account, though you did tell me a few home truths at the time. I thought about them afterwards, when it was too late.'

'I still don't see why you got married.'

'I was so furious with myself that I just had to do something, even if I knew if was stupid. You know, like people suddenly decide to sell their house because their marriage has gone wrong, or rush off to work abroad as if they can somehow leave their problems behind. Anyway, I compounded one mistake with another. But I was lucky. She's a nice sort of person and she let me off the hook. Now we have to unhook you.'

'My case is different,' Polly said.

'No. You acted on impulse, too. You took a risk. Now you've got to have the courage to unravel your mistake.'

'Oh, no, no. It's utterly different. I have two children.'

'Well – '

'I warn you, Randy, if you say children are resilient I shall hate you.'

'All right, spitfire, I wasn't going to say that. I was just going to say that if we take it very gently, step by step, the children will come round to it.'

She shook her head.

'Look, Polly. Are you really saying you'll stay with Martin rather than risk upsetting the children?'

She thought for a moment. 'Yes,' she said. 'That's what it amounts to.'

'But they could visit him, keep in touch with him – '

'No. Parents aren't people you visit. Parents are people who are there at home, part of the fabric of the place, like your own bed and the hamster.'

How could she describe it? The whole world, a single thing to a child. You couldn't pull down a wall here, remove a ceiling there, without putting the entire building at risk. Nothing would be certain any more.

'It can't be done without hurting them,' she said. 'People deceive themselves who say that it can.'

'Right, Flinders,' he said with sudden anger. 'What are we supposed to do? Wait fifteen years or so until they're adults? And what about the hurt to us?'

'It was our choice, Randy. But Sarah and Tim had no say in it. They were born to the pair of us, Martin and me. They don't know anything else. There is no way they can escape damage if the only world they've known since they were born is broken up.'

He spoke more gently now. 'I know, my darling,' he said. 'But I think we have to accept that there are greater evils even than that. Like your unhappiness with Martin.'

She didn't reply.

'I know,' he went on, 'that you're too loyal to talk about it and I'm not going to press you, but what is wrong is something pretty basic, isn't it?'

She nodded, but still said nothing.

'Think about it, Polly, whatever it is, and just ask yourself if you still think you have to bear it rather than risk a temporary upset to the children.'

'Nothing is temporary to children.'

She spoke hopelessly. Soon she would have to go home, face again the coldness of her wintry marriage, shut out from the one who should be closest to her, yet living together as man and wife. All unnatural and wrong.

She clung to him. 'I can bear it, I *can*. If we can just be like this sometimes.'

It would warm her, tell her that she was not abnormal, that human beings were meant to love and be loved, if she could just cling to him, cling to normality.

'You're saying, are you, Polly – I mean let's get it quite clear – that you'll go on being married to Martin and just have me as your little bit on the side, eh?'

She flinched but she couldn't deny it. She pressed her head down on to his shoulder.

'Yes, I suppose I am saying that,' she whispered.

'Well, I don't want that. I love you and I want all of you and I want you all the time. I want you to be my wife.'

'Don't, please, don't. It's no good. We've got to make do with second best. Can't we? Like this?'

He was silent for a moment, then he said, 'Flinders, if you knew of a man who suggested this arrangement, that he'd be a good family chap and just keep a mistress on the side, would you approve? I bet you'd be the first to say he was one hell of a hypocrite, using both wife and mistress because he was too feeble to choose between them and preferred to hurt them both.'

She didn't say anything. Soon she would have to go. It was seven o'clock. In half an hour she would be knocking on the Thwaites' front door and the children would be rushing around holding balloons and there would be from the hall a glimpse of a littered dining-room, paper napkins in crumpled heaps on the table, potato crisps on the floor and poor Mrs

Thwaite exhausted but determinedly cheerful as she handed out parting gifts to the children, offered sherry to their parents and longed for everyone to go.

Polly would find their coats, Sarah's and Tim's, and remind them to say thank you and drive them in the dark to their wintry home, where the light would be shining from Martin's study as he sorted out his maps and documents and Nazi memorabilia.

'You'd say,' Randy was going on, 'that he was just using the mistress for sex, wouldn't you, excluding her from the rest of his life? Yet that's the rôle you're happy to cast me in.'

'It's not true. And I wouldn't say that anyway.'

'I bet you would.'

'I wouldn't because I wouldn't know the circumstances, or what the wife was like, or anything. How can you judge when you don't know all of it? Who knows what goes on behind closed doors? I've learned that, Randy, truly I have. If nothing else, I've learned not to stand in judgement.'

'Well, that's very convenient,' he said bitterly. 'But I haven't. As far as I'm concerned it's a totally wrong way to live.'

She was tired and full of foreboding. With equal bitterness she replied, 'Your sudden morality's a bit unexpected, too. I don't remember your having any qualms like that in the old days.'

'We've both changed,' he said. 'Let's just leave it at that.'

They dressed in silence, said goodbye briefly and politely, then she went to pick up the children from their party, bracing herself to listen to all their chatter.

Chapter 19

'Whatever are you doing? Writing a book?' Jennifer asked.
'No, just sorting out papers,' Polly lied, shutting the dining-room door and leading her friend into the kitchen. 'Coffee?'
'Yes, please. You're not moving, are you?'
'No. We're here for another three years at least, Martin says. Milk? Sugar? How was school today?'
'Exhausting. I can't think how people manage to teach little children all day. Mornings only are quite enough for me.'
Polly laughed. 'Stay and have a sandwich lunch,' she said. 'I was just going to have a break anyway. Or is James expecting you at home?'
'No, he's at a diocesan meeting. I'd love to stay. I haven't seen anything of you for weeks.'
'I've been busy,' Polly said vaguely, then went on, 'I hear enough about *you*. Every word you utter is taken as Holy Writ by Sarah and Tim. We get these great pronouncements, ending, "Mrs Dawson says."'
Jennifer Dawson laughed.
'How you must hate me sometimes,' she said.
'Sarah came home last week and said, "All the mummies have to wear brown knickers for the concert, Mrs Dawson says."'
Jennifer spluttered into her coffee.
'She's lovely, your Sarah, she never listens properly. She's such a dreamer. And Tim's so organised. They really are incredibly different. What I actually said, Polly, was that she and all the other little ones who are animals in the play, should wear brown knickers – you know, the sort they wear for P.E.? – and a brown sweater, then we'll make them all different heads and – '

'It's all right. I didn't take it seriously. I mean I didn't rush out and buy a pair.'

She liked Jennifer Dawson. She was direct and unconventional. She was also minute. She sat now, diminutive, on a stool by the Aga, her tiny feet in their buckled shoes not reaching the ground. She had, Polly thought, an elfin look as she perched there, bright-eyed, fresh-cheeked, her neat little legs crossed at the ankles. At other times, especially when she was tired and looking a bit drawn, her head seemed too big for her body, giving her the look of an attractive witch. Either way, the one thing she never remotely resembled was the traditional picture of a vicar's wife.

Her husband, James, had been vicar of St. Chads, next to the school, for six years and had, so Polly had been told, transformed it from a run-down, unwelcoming place, with a regular congregation of about half-a-dozen elderly gentlefolk, into an active community who packed into the church every Sunday. She had seen that for herself when she had taken the children to a family service soon after they arrived and found that there was standing room only. Actually it was not so much a service as a pantomime with mildly religious overtones, the aisles being used for charades and processions by teenagers playing percussion instruments, while babies loudly had their say and toddlers crawled around among the choir stalls, James himself frequently lunging to gather up a stray child which was endangering either itself or the church fabric.

Polly had thought, at that first service, that it was maybe rather hard on the half-dozen elderly gentlefolk who had kept the place going over the previous years, but she had been won over and now always brought the children, or rather they insisted on coming. Martin, who had hitherto been the only one to be on parade, as he put it, on Sundays, disliked the family service intensely and now stayed at home on Sunday mornings, busy in his study.

'That's pretty,' Jennifer remarked, after they had eaten. 'I had a dress a bit like that years ago.'

She was looking at a frock which Polly had hung on the kitchen dresser.

'It could be the same vintage,' Polly told her. 'I had that one long before I was married. I came across it when I was hunting in the trunk this morning and thought it might do for Sarah for dressing up.'

'You can't let her have it! It's lovely. Does it still fit you?'

She shrugged. 'I don't know,' she said. 'I shouldn't think so. I was really looking for something to wear for a ghastly do Martin and I have to go to.'

'What sort of a do?'

'It's the centenary of the contractors who are doing work for the Ministry of Defence. They're inviting some of their clients, so that includes Martin among others. It's a dinner with maybe some dancing afterwards, Martin thinks, but he's a bit vague about it all.'

'How do you know it'll be ghastly then?'

'Because I've been to similar functions. I can guarantee its ghastliness, I promise you. Anyway, the pressing problem is what to wear. I've got two long dresses that would do, but Martin seems to think it won't be very formal.'

'If I were you, I'd wear that one. Go on, Polly, try it on.' Jennifer jumped off her stool and slid the dress from its hanger. 'Goodness, how lovely these old materials feel after modern synthetic fabrics,' she exclaimed. 'Come on, put it on.'

For the first time in years the Horrockses cotton rustled over Polly's head and her fingers fiddled with the row of tiny buttons. It still fitted her perfectly. Jennifer was entranced.

'Feel the quality of it,' she said. 'It's a sort of glazed cotton, isn't it? But silky, too. And just the right length. Nobody would think it was New Look from way back, would they?'

'Well, you do, for a start.'

Jennifer laughed. 'Only because I was trained as a designer. I don't think you need worry that anybody else would notice. And what would it matter if they did, anyway? I bet that in a few years' time people are going to be paying huge sums for some of these old dresses and blouses, so hang on to any you've got. Hasn't it worn incredibly well? The material looks almost new.'

'Oh, I always kept it for best. Then dresses went short just about the time we were married, so I put it away and forgot all about it till this morning.'

'Well, don't you dare let Sarah get hold of it. It really suits you. The colour does something to your hair and skin. It glows. You must wear it, Polly. Promise. I won't go until you do.'

'All right, I promise,' Polly said, for much though she liked Jennifer and enjoyed her company she wanted her to leave now so that she could get on with sorting out the papers in the dining-room. She had only an hour left to remove all traces of her secret activity before the children came in from school so Jennifer had to be somewhat abruptly dismissed. Writing books, Polly thought as she shut the door behind her, doesn't really go with cultivating friendships.

She had been checking her typescript against her final draft before she was interrupted. The chapters were spread out in piles across the table and chairs and overflowed on to the floor. She had, rather late on in the book, decided to alter somebody's name, but had not realised how many odd references there were to him, scattered throughout the pages. She kept coming across ones that she had missed. That was a mistake she wouldn't make again, she resolved. Next time she'd get the names right, from the start.

How tidy the final typescript looked, she thought, admiring the finished pages. It had a neat, inevitable look.

But it wasn't in the least bit inevitable, any of it. Over the past eighteen months she had rewritten it three or four times. When she had sat under the weeping ash tree all those months ago, writing in her old maths book with the squares on one side and the lines on the other, she had no idea that Maisie's life would turn out like this, or of the other people who would come into it. There was that do-gooding lady, Mrs Follett, for example, who had appeared from nowhere, interfering in the plot. She, Polly, had tried to keep her out, but she kept barging in, sometimes bringing her hen-pecked little husband with her.

Mrs Follett had taken it upon herself to help Maisie, winning much praise from her friends for undertaking such a thankless task. Mrs Follett was very energetic and clever. She was also childless, had an unsatisfactory husband and came of a generation and class whose parents refused to allow their daughters to have a career. Had she been trained she might have been very successful in any profession which would have given official blessing to her penchant for interfering in the lives of others. As it was, her interference was unskilled, lacking in self-knowledge and very damaging to the recipient.

Poor Maisie suffered a great deal as the object of Mrs Follett's attentions, and indeed the whole theme of the book developed from that lady's misdirected energy, for with hindsight Polly could see how she exemplified the way in which adults use children to satisfy their own needs and how vulnerable children are to being manipulated by adults, whom they may instinctively distrust but lack the experience to understand and fend off. And yet she had tried to keep Mrs Follett out of the book; she shook her head in disbelief that she could have been so blind.

What she really needed, she often thought, was to have some godlike figure at her elbow as she wrote, telling her when the plot was taking a wrong turning, or which path to choose when she reached a fork in the story. Or, failing that kind of divine guidance, she wished she had gone to university and got herself a degree in English Literature so that she would know how to write books. As it was, she realised, she was on her own and would just have to learn as she went along. Besides, nobody could have understood it all well enough to advise her not to try to shut out Mrs Follett. And maybe, in fact, Mrs Follett had gained by having to fight her way into the book, just as people in real life are made stronger by adversity.

Real life. What did it mean? The people in the book were as real to her as the people she met in shops, or the mums waiting outside the school. Sometimes she even forgot, when she thought about them on her own, which were characters in the book and which lived down the road. It was all rather frightening, she thought as she gathered the typescript together and prepared to send it off to the first publisher on the list of six which, with Randy's help, she had chosen after a careful perusal of the *Writers' and Artists' Year Book*.

It had become her Bible, the *Year Book* had, she realised as she checked through the section on how to prepare a manuscript for sending to a publisher. Yes, she had used double spacing and wide margins and the same size paper throughout. Damn! She hadn't got the return postage to enclose. It was evidently very important: publishers got angry if you didn't send the wherewithal to post your offering back to you. In the end she took the manuscript, plus brown paper and string and scissors and sellotape, and wrapped it up in the post office, after it was weighed. She walked the extra half mile to the main post office, too, in order to avoid Mrs Stubbs, who kept the local shop with a sub-post office at the back, noticing the address and making comments. She was surprised, as she handed over this work of eighteen months, at how light-hearted she suddenly felt, as if a burden had been removed from her.

They won't accept it, she told herself, as a kind of insurance policy against disappointment. It will plop back through the letter box in a month of two.

But of course it did not. It was far too big to go through the letter box. The postman had to ring the bell and hand it to her in person. Six times. Each time she immediately sent it off again to the next publisher on her list, stopping only to remove the letter of refusal and tear off the tell-tale label. She took the *Year Book's* advice and retyped the first two pages of her script to freshen it up when it began to look a bit dog-eared.

They wrote her nice letters, the publishers did. They did not fob her off with rejection slips. Promising, they called her. They implied that if they had been looking for this type of book, hers would have been the very one they would have chosen. But unfortunately at the moment they were not seeking this kind of book for their list. She decided to hasten the process of rejection by sending copies to two publishers, simultaneously, then worried for weeks in case they both accepted it. She need not have been anxious. By the sort of coincidence which she would not have allowed herself in fiction, they were both returned on the same day.

Meanwhile other characters for another book began to worry her. She did not really want to know about them. She felt, that spring, that she didn't have the strength to breathe life into them, and the loneliness of the whole business depressed her. But they would not let her alone. They opened doors into her mind, they peered at her through little windows, those characters that she did not want to have to create. They plagued her.

At night she lay awake, anxiously testing ideas, trying out this scene and that, letting her mind float, letting if whiffle about like a dog after a scent. She thought sometimes of Mrs Bean. When she was little and they went for walks together, Mrs Bean would stop, make a frame of her hands and look through it at the view beyond. She was trying to see if it would make a picture, she said. It had puzzled Polly, though she accepted it, as she accepted everything about the Beans. She herself could look at the old tree that leaned across the beck, or at the dry-stone wall, badly in need of repair, by the side of the packhorse bridge, and just like the look of it. But Mrs Bean couldn't. Mrs Bean was an artist, so she had to try to take the old tree or the dry-stone wall, take it and make a picture of it. And now sometimes Polly felt that she, like Mrs Bean, was obliged to take something in life, some experience, or feeling, or person, take it right into herself and make it into a kind of picture. She had to weigh it up, see if it would do, only she could not frame it with her hands but had somehow to test it in her mind, balancing it all to see if it would make a book. Sometimes she envied Mrs Bean for it seemed to her that it must be much easier to paint a picture than to write a book, because you could use your hands to make a frame and see it there all at once before you. But envy was silly, she knew that. You have to do what you have to do.

That's what Randy had said, the day they sat over lunch selecting likely publishers from the *Year Book*. She had kept her promise to show him the finished typescript although they had not met since that afternoon in his flat, the afternoon the children had gone to Jeremy Thwaites' party and she and Randy had loved and quarrelled and she had ended up hating him. And still did, but a promise is a promise and he did know a lot about writing.

That's what she had told herself when she delivered the parcel to his office, and told herelf again when she went to receive it back from him over lunch. He had approved of the book, made a few minor suggestions about it, and then talked about getting it published. At that level all was fine, but the moment he mentioned, even obliquely, the subject of divorce, she felt fear and resentment rising in her. Soon she was calling him obdurate because for him it was all or nothing, and he was calling her obdurate because she wouldn't even discuss the possibility of leaving Martin. She thought how stupid it all was, for they were both lonely and needed each other and could be friends, but he wouldn't have it, he was so obstinate. It was all his fault, she thought resentfully as she left him. And when he asked her to let him know how she got on with the publishers, she said she thought there wasn't much point in keeping in touch now.

Jason and Groves were the last of the really big publishers on her list. Their rejection was different from the others. Somebody called Peter Falconer wrote to her to say that they were afraid her manuscript was not suitable for their list at the moment, but that if she happened to be in London and would like to call in, he would be glad to talk to her as they considered her work interesting. She could collect the manuscript at the same time. If, however, a visit was not possible, then he would return it to her under separate cover.

She read and reread the letter. Sometimes it seemed almost as good as an acceptance. Sometimes it struck her that he was just being kind and rather condescending, or just plain economical, saving postage. She replied immediately saying that she happened to be coming to London on Thursday week and would be free towards the end of the morning. Then she rang Jennifer and asked her to have the children after school. Jennifer's children, as she had hoped they would, begged that Tim and Sarah should stay the night. Martin was away all week, so she was now entirely free.

Jason and Groves' offices were ancient and warren-like. A secretary guided her down what seem like miles of corridors and tunnels, some so narrow that you had to go in single file and not be too fat. She was taken down ramps and stairs and along more passages until she lost all sense of what floor she was on, let alone which direction she was going in. She began to wonder what would happen if they left her unattended in these catacombs and if she would ever get out. She should perhaps be unwinding a thread to guide her back, or, like the rich squaw who went to stay in a grand hotel, chip a trail in the panelling with a small tomahawk. But suddenly the secretary opened a door and she was ushered into the presence of Peter Falconer. Taken aback, Polly had to force herself to walk towards him, this impressive-looking man who could decide the fate of her book.

He was middle-aged, his face saved from being handsome by the long upper lip which somehow elongated it and gave it a look of self-mockery, like a sad monkey. All this she observed as he rose, uncoiling himself from his chair behind the desk, for he was very tall and bony and seemed to have to crank himself up in segments. They shook hands aross his desk, fingers meeting just above her manuscript.

She found herself staring at it. It seemed so odd to see it in this strange place, its top pages retyped in what suddenly seemed a very obvious ploy. For a moment they both stood there, leaning awkwardly forward, hands clasped, and then sank back into their chairs on either side of the desk.

'Tell me,' he said, 'who taught you to write?'

'Nobody.'

'I mean, how did you know how to set about writing a book?'

There was no way in which she could describe how it had felt that autumn morning in the garden, writing quietly with a soft pencil, fearful of breaking the spell, the fragile web.

'I didn't,' she said. 'I just began at Chapter One.'

He suppressed a smile. She saw it flicker across his face, barely perceptible but certainly there. She flushed.

'I only ask,' he began, speaking slowly and kindly, obviously doing his best to put her at her ease, not wanting to make her even more tongue-tied and stupid, 'because it is rare for us to be sent an unsolicited manuscript of this quality. I suppose you realise that we are sent thousands every year, of which I suppose about ninety-nine per cent go back without comment, just a rejection slip?'

'But where do all the published books come from, then?' she asked, surprised.

'Oh, from our own established authors. Many are commissioned too, of course.'

'But they must have all started sometime?'

'Yes. And of course we do take the occasional unsolicited work.'

He paused and looked at her gravely. He was more like a lion than a monkey, she thought, the subdued, world-weary sort of lion, not the sort that roared at you at the start of the pictures.

'A few years ago,' he said, tapping the manuscript, 'we'd have taken this. I tell you in order that you won't feel too discouraged. Indeed, if it were up to me I'd have taken it even now. I don't like to think of losing you to another publishing house. I must in fairness say that you might get a different answer from another publisher. They might accept it and do very well with it.'

Was she really sitting here, Polly Adams, hearing such things? Was this important, Dickensian-looking man, with his great leonine head and battered good looks, and kind sad eyes and silver grey hair, rather too long, but clean-looking and silky, really talking to her as if she was a proper writer?

'But the truth of the matter is that during the past few years, we've had some disastrous losses with first novels of this kind. And our accountants won't stand for another first novel losing us money.'

He shrugged helplessly, giving her at the same time an apologetic smile. 'We have to make ends meet,' he said.

There was silence. There seemed nothing she could say that would not sound like begging, for she desperately wanted to plead with him to find some way of making ends meet that would include publishing her worst-selling novel. Then perhaps she would become professional and find how to be a proper writer.

'One thought did occur to me,' he began, and stopped.

She waited, observing him. He was hesitant; she had the feeling he was going to say something he was vaguely ashamed of.

'You may not like the idea, Mrs Quigley. I'm not sure I do, but it might just strengthen my hand against the accountants.'

He gave her a shame-faced, conspiratorial look.

'You see, my dear, there are fashions in publishing. We have to try to foresee what they will be, catch the tide, as it were, Usually the tide starts in America nowadays and arrives here a few years later. It seems likely that the next wave of fashion will be for novels about the pop scene and about feminism.'

He spoke of both genres with equal distaste.

'The cognoscenti tell us that within a decade all our rivals will have a statutory feminist on their list. Just before I wrote to you I was speaking to young Chaytor, a fellow who has recently joined us – appointed, I may tell you in confidence, to polish up our image – and he was very keen that we should have such a one and so, if you will forgive the change of metaphor, put ourselves ahead of the field. It seems that the feminist mob would otherwise keep clear of us, our list being too conservative for them. In the same way, an agent with a best-selling novel about a pop group on his hands would not immediately think of offering it to Jason and Groves. You will have guessed what I am leading up to.'

She shook her head. It was all very remote from her and her book.

'It seemed to me that there were elements, something in your style, which might fit you to write such a book. With admittedly a great deal of rewriting this might perhaps become a feminist novel.'

She could think of nothing to say.

'The very impressive central scene, for example, with Maisie in court, now there would be a chance to give her a tremendous speech. A modern Portia, don't you know?'

'But she wasn't very articulate,' Polly said. 'That was one of her problems.'

He waved her objection aside.

'You'll find it much easier to make that sort of change than you as a beginner imagine,' he told her.

'But it's a major change, it's changing her character.'

'Of course. I think we should want her to be much more forceful, more successful. Yes, it would be a success story. That's what the readers want in the 1960s. If you do decide you can go along with the idea, I think we'll bring young Chaytor in on the act. He's really more *au fait* with this sort of thing. To tell you the truth, I haven't much use for this feminist trend myself.'

'But – '

'Yes?'

She couldn't explain. If he didn't believe in it, how could he want to publish it? And he wasn't seeing it from Maisie's point of view at all. He was imposing ideas on her because it was convenient to his trade. The motive seemed all wrong. She shook her head. 'Nothing,' she said.

'As I see it,' he went on, 'you could keep the bones of your plot but re-write the central character. Make her more of a fighter, an Aldermarston marcher, maybe, make her a campaigner. Make her a liberated lady.'

'But the point is that she's been weakened – '

'Oh, I accept that. The point would have to be altered.'

'But it was the point I was trying to make, at least I realised it was as I went along. It kind of emerged.'

He nodded, Then he paused, looked at her in some embarrassment and said, 'And of course she would be more sexually liberated. I think that some of the love scenes could be, well,' he paused, searching for the right word, 'expanded,' he concluded.

The telephone rang. He picked it up, spoke briefly, put it down, glanced at his watch and said, 'I think the best thing is for you to go away and think about all this, go through the manuscript and see what alterations you could make along the lines I suggest, and then send me in the revised script. Oh, and one other thing,' he paused and gave her a kindly little smile, 'if you'll forgive me for saying so, I don't think that *Maisie* is quite the ideal name for a 1960s heroine, do you? More suitable for a Victorian parlour maid, don't you think?'

He pressed a bell and the same secretary who had brought her here appeared through what Polly had assumed to be a cupboard door.

'Find an envelope for Mrs Quigley's script, Prudence, would you?' he asked.

Then he got up and held out his hand to Polly.

'Keep in touch,' he said, dismissing her. 'Can you find your own way out?'

'No.'

Without her thread or little tomahawk there was no hope of retracing her footsteps.

'Prudence will take you,' he said. 'Goodbye, Mrs Quigley, and thank you for letting us see your manuscript. It has great merit. I am truly sorry we cannot give you the answer you must have been hoping for.'

He held on to her hand in a kindly way, smiling his charming smile, then he released it and sat down. She followed Prudence to the door. As she turned in the doorway and looked back at him, he seemed older and sadder as he sat there, the smile quite gone from his face, a look of gloom, of petulance even, having replaced it. Yes, his face in repose had a petulant, disenchanted look.

The winter sunshine struck warm when she emerged from Jason and Groves. It blinded her for a moment after the dimly-lit corridors. She walked down the street without thinking where she was going. She was furious with herself. She'd made a real mess of that interview. She groaned as she remembered. Somehow, fool that she was, she hadn't managed to take the whole thing seriously from the start. It was something to do with all those winding corridors that triggered off idiot thoughts of Ariadne's thread and the squaw's tomahawk. She should have used all that marching time to prepare herself so that she would be calm and dignified when she went into his room. Instead of that she'd been tongue-tied and stupid. She hadn't even concentrated. She had let herself slip into seeing it all as an outsider; it had been like watching a play with Falconer taking the lead. She'd become a kind of fall guy. But, be fair to yourself Polly Adams, there really was something theatrical about him, as if he saw himself acting the part of the great and powerful publisher, encouraging the new writer. Then at least you should have played your rôle a bit better, Polly Adams. Oh damn, damn, damn.

It wasn't just today, she realised. She was always doing this. She was developing a terrible habit of observing things, not participating. She might have known it would be a disaster, that she'd mess up her one chance. In her rage she thrust her hands deep into her pockets. Her fingers struck cardboard.

She drew out a visiting card. It must have been there all the time, she realised, turning it over in her hands, since that awful evening at the contractors' centenery celebrations. Had she really not worn this coat since then? Probably not. It was her black coat, reserved for special occasions such as this one visit to London, when she had intended to make a good impression on the publishing world.

She had slowed down; she was crossing a London square with a little garden at one side. She went into it and sat on a bench, still holding the card in her hand. She stared at it, remembering.

She had worn the coat over the Horrockses cotton dress, of course. Martin had approved of the dress. So had their host, she could see that. He had looked her up and down appreciatively as they drank sherry before dinner and he told her about the people she would meet. 'Mostly they are our own staff,' he had said, 'but we have several of our clients here as guests. There's your husband from Defence, of course, and Mr Blenkinsop from the Outward Building Society who has travelled up from London with his wife to be with us. And Mr Holroyd from the County Council.'

Appalled at the mention of Simon's name, she had not heard the rest of the list though she did her best to look interested. It was not so much the idea of meeting him again that horrified her as the fact that she was wearing the same wretched dress. She could have strangled Jennifer Dawson for persuading her into wearing it tonight. She thought wildly of escaping home to change into something else, but oh, what a thing to have to explain to the babysitter, she thought.

Then she saw him, Simon, crossing the floor towards them. He had put on weight. He looked very important, not to say pompous. No, that was unfair. It was just that he seemed to be encased in some rubbery layer of protective confidence. Perhaps it helped him not to show too much dismay at the sight of her. True his expression did glaze over, like something set in aspic, but he said smoothly enough when they were introduced, 'I don't expect that Mrs Quigley remembers, but we met years ago when she was working for a branch of our company in Brigthorpe.'

'Of course I remember,' she heard herself say. 'You were in charge of the typing pool.'

There was an embarrassed silence, nobody quite knowing how to take this remark. Then the chairman said, 'Well, you've gone a long way since those days, I'm sure,' and led the way into the dining-room.

She sat between Martin and the chairman, a jovial little man, distracted throughout the meal by the prospect of making what turned out to be a very long speech, giving a blow by blow account of the not particularly interesting history of his firm. Polly filled in the time by observing Simon's wife, who was sitting opposite to her. She was a pretty, plumpish woman in blue lace, obviously very used to supporting her husband on such occasions. She listened to the speech with an air of rapt, almost regal, interest. Pleasant, attractive and unexceptional, she was exactly right, Polly thought, for a successful businessman like Simon. She would never embarrass him, never let fall silence-provoking remarks, and there was that touch of stoicism about her that seemed to say In Time of Adversity, I Will Stand By Him. Polly imagined her, pale but calm, alongside him in the dock. Supporting, not shrieking.

The fantasy was interrupted by the end of the chairman's speech and the need to clap and murmur felicitations. Afterwards there was a little gentle, middle-aged dancing in the course of which she moved sedately round the floor in the encircling arms of the little chairman, then of Martin, and finally of Simon.

'You haven't changed a bit,' he said.

'You mean the dress hasn't.'

'What dress?' he asked, genuinely baffled.

Of course, she should have realised that men don't remember clothes. But *she* did. She had this awful vision of herself perched on his knee in this self-same dress, the bodice folded back from the waist.

'And I never was in charge of the typing pool,' he said, grinning at her and looking suddenly like his old self. 'That was Mrs Jones.'

'Well, I couldn't think of anything else to say.'

'I know. I was taken aback, too. There, never mind, it's all a long time ago.'

He smiled across at his wife, who was dancing with Martin.

'We've three children,' he said. 'Two boys and a girl. What about you?'

'One of each,' she said.

'Fair enough.'

It had seemed a curious comment to make on two human beings he had never seen. But then who was she to be critical about curious remarks, she who had wildly attributed to him the management of the typing pool for no reason whatsoever?

'You must look us up, if ever you're in Surrey,' Elizabeth Blenkinsop said as they waited to collect their coats at the end of the evening.

'Here's my business card,' Simon said to Martin, offering it to him. 'I've put our home address on the back.'

Martin was holding the black coat open for her, so Polly took the card and a moment later put it in her pocket.

She sat on the park bench now, looking at the card, and suddenly the address of the Outward's Head Office registered in her mind. So that was the great modern building she had passed as she walked to Jason and Groves. What a contrast the two neighbouring offices were, the publishers and the building society. There wouldn't be catacombs in Simon's domain: she could imagine it, all the concrete and glass of the 1960s, great open-plan offices with tropical plants in a foyer the size of a car park. She fingered the card and thought about it. Why not ring him? There was a telephone on the corner. It was exactly the sort of distraction she could do with, to help her forget the mess she had made of the interview with Peter Falconer.

'If only you'd rung five minutes earlier, Polly,' Simon said, 'I could have taken you out for a proper lunch, but I've just booked an appointment for two o'clock. Still we've got half an hour. There's quite a good Italian coffee shop just round the corner. They do sandwiches and so on.'

'I know. I saw it. Something like Marco's, isn't it?'

'That's right, Liugi's actually. See you there, then, in a few minutes.'

She arrived just before him. It was crowded, but Simon still had the knack of finding a table. People seemed to make way for him, she noticed as she followed in his wake. He looked a bit too prosperous for the coffee shop, though: Expense Account Man personified, Simon was.

'And what brings you to London?' he asked as they settled down.

'Oh, just shopping,' she said casually, sipping her coffee.

'I see you've been writing a book,' he remarked.

She stared at him, amazed. He nodded towards the parcel on her knee. The big brown envelope containing her manuscript had a huge blue and white Jason and Groves label stuck in it.

'Oh, that,' she said, confused and also furious with herself for not noticing the label before. 'Well, you see – '

He laughed aloud. 'Come on, Polly, admit it. You've been visiting J & G, haven't you? That's your manuscript, isn't it? And that's how you come to be alongside my office. Q.E.D.'

She hesitated, then realised it was too silly to deny it when the evidence was so obvious. 'All right,' she said, and told him, briefly, about the book and the interview.

'But Polly,' he said, 'that's marvellous. All you've got to do is a bit of work on the thing and it'll be a best seller in no time.'

She laughed. 'No, I don't think that,' she said. 'But seriously, I don't see how I can alter it, Simon.'

'Rubbish, of course you can. You must. If you get in with Jason and Groves, you'll be all right. They're making money hand over fist, I can tell you than. Shares rising, too. I know; I've got some.'

She shook her head: they were different worlds, the world of her book and the world of his shares.

'I'd get on with altering it right away, Polly. How long did it take you to write the book? As it now stands, I mean?'

'About eighteen months.'

'Then at the most it would take you about nine months to alter it, wouldn't it? Get on with it, Polly. I don't see what's holding you back.'

'What's holding me back, Simon, is that it would really be a question of altering the whole point of the book.'

'Ah, well, then, that would take a bit longer. Maybe more like a year.'

She ate her sandwich and didn't reply. Different worlds, different wavelengths, different everything. As it was in the beginning.

'You could do it, Polly,' Simon said encouragingly. 'I always thought you were very talented.'

'Thank you. But it's not that, not the hard work, that's worrying. You see, you've got to be true to the book, haven't you?'

'Well, it depends what you want. If you want to be published you can't have scruples like that, can you? Actually you can't have too many scruples in any business. It's a tough old world, you know, Polly.'

'I know. That's why parts of it have to be kept honest.'

He looked puzzled for a moment, then said, 'Well, all these things are relative. But my advice to you would be to try to do exactly as they suggest.'

'I shall have to think about it,' she said. 'Certainly I shan't dismiss the whole idea out of hand.'

'I should think not! Most people would jump at the opportunity. Mind you, it must be jolly hard to write books with children about. Why not pack them off to boarding school? It's amazing how they settle. Our youngest never wanted to go. He used to be sick, physically sick, all night long before he went back to school for the first three terms, then he just seemed to accept it.'

'We're lucky in having an excellent school nearby,' she said. 'The children are very happy there.'

'Well, yes, and I suppose you have to look at the cost, too. Fees never go down, do they? But I know Elizabeth finds she's quite enough to do coping with them in the holidays, never mind term-time as well. It gives her a chance to have a bit of life of her own, bless her.'

He glanced at his watch.

'Give her my love,' Polly said mechanically.

'And remember me to Martin. I've got to dash now, but let me get you another cup of coffee before I go.'

She sat, after he had gone, thinking about what he had said. It was sense, she could see that. But it was the sort of sense that belonged to this outside world. It didn't make sense in terms of the book itself. It wouldn't make sense to Maisie or Mrs Follett. On the other hand, she thought, stirring her coffee, enjoying the way the brown sugar made darker whorls in the creamy cappuccino, maybe the fact that she herself had lived in their world for so long unfitted her for seeing anything about the book objectively or even from acting in her own interests. Certainly Simon had given advice which he thought was in her interests. His goodwill was patent. His view was simple, too, in the naive way of the wordly-wise. But all the same his advice was of the sort you would give an acquaintance; it wasn't necessarily the same advice as you would give somebody you really understood and cared about. They need harsher truths. The coffee was now a boring, uniform beige. Fit only for drinking. She drank it.

The train was packed. It was the fast one, the one the businessmen used, only tonight it was late and slow. Polly had no sooner settled in her seat, having walked the length of the train to find one, than she realised that the dining car was at the other end and she was starving. The sandwich lunch had long ago worn off. So, bumping and swaying, she made her way back, telling herself that the journey took three and a half hours and a meal would pass the time. She would drink wine and reach a decision about the book, she resolved, clutching her manuscript and squeezing past people standing in the corridor.

But the dining car was full. She stood looking down it, every table taken.

An attendant came up to her. 'One, miss?' he asked. 'You can have this table at the end here. It's reserved for staff use really, but I'll soon lay it up.'

'Thank you very much. I'll just put this down to reserve the place and go and have a wash.'

So she put the manuscript in its big brown envelope on the seat and left the attendant clearing away account books and tin boxes from the table in readiness for laying it.

In the lavatory she peered at her face in the grimy looking glass. She looked awful and hoped it was something to do with the mirror. She wiped away a few smuts, washed her hands, combed her hair, powdered her face and felt better. When she got back to the dining car the manuscript had gone.

She stood in the doorway to the dining car, swaying with the movement of the train, staring at the empty seat in disbelief. Perhaps she had never left it there? She went back to the lavatory, but it was now occupied. She returned to the dining car. There was still no manuscript. She could see the back of a man's head on the near seat, opposite where she had been going to sit. He turned round as she approached. It was Randy. He grinned at her and held up the envelope.

'Looking for this?' he asked, standing up to help her into the seat opposite him. 'It wasn't magic,' he went on before she could say anything. 'I saw you from the other end of the dining car. They'd just told me there were no more places, but I saw you work wonders on the waiter with those great green eyes of yours.'

'No, I did not,' she said indignantly. 'He just offered to lay the table for me. It's where they usually add up the money.'

He laughed. 'I'm not complaining,' he said. 'I grabbed the seat opposite straight away. Have a drink. You look awful.'

So the grimy mirror had not lied. She accepted. There was no way of avoiding him now. Every other place was taken.

'I'm a regular on this train,' Randy said. 'I recommend the halibut. The cheeseboard is excellent, too. And they have a good wine list.'

She resented the way he was taking over. When the waiter came she ordered the beef.

The train was elderly and trying desperately hard to make up time. It rocked and swayed, so that the soup swirled about and splashed out of the bowls. Randy grinned at her. 'If we're going to be shipwrecked,' he remarked, 'we might as well be friends.'

'Idiot,' she said, trying not to smile.

'That's better. I always worry about your health if you're not insulting me, Flinders.'

He waited until the main course arrived before he said, 'Are you going to tell me about this manuscript, Polly?'

'Later,' she said, 'eating's a full time job on this train.'

It was over the cheese, which was, as Randy had foretold, excellent, that she recounted to him, as exactly as she could, the interview with Peter Falconer.

He listened carefully, then he shook his head. 'It's a non-starter,' he said. 'It's the sort of rubbish he would come up with.'

'Do you know him?'

'Well, I know *of* him,' Randy conceded.

'That little preposition makes a lot of difference,' she pointed out.

'All right, let's say I know him by reputation then, and he doesn't have a particularly good one among writers. And notice, Polly, that he hasn't committed himself, has he? You could wreck this book and he still wouldn't take it.'

'Do you think that? That it would wreck it?'

'Of course,' he said, surprised. 'Don't you?'

'Yes, but then I thought perhaps I was just being lazy, not wanting to work any more on it, and I know writers have to be prepared to make alterations to manuscripts.'

'Well, there are alterations and alterations, Polly. He's not suggesting changes that would strengthen the book, he wants a different book. In that case you might try to write such a book, if you want to, but not muck this one about.'

'I wish you'd been there and actually heard him,' she said, and sighed. 'He was quite convincing, Randy.'

Then she wondered if that was true. No, Peter Falconer hadn't sounded really convinced himself. 'I don't know,' she said, shaking her head. 'I don't know what to think.'

'Here, have some celery,' he advised, pushing it towards her and then taking a stick of it himself. They sat chewing companionably, dipping the rough and stringy ends of the celery into a little pile of salt on her plate, making patterns.

'If I'd known the cheese board was like this,' she said, 'I wouldn't have bothered having the rest of the meal.'

'It isn't always quite like this,' he told her, filling up her glass. 'It's just because you've bewitched the waiter. That's why we've got all this vitamin C.'

Not only had the waiter left them the tin of biscuits and all the cheese, but a jug of celery, a bowl of radishes and a dish of watercress as well.

'Maybe they're just using this table as a sort of sideboard,' she suggested.

'No, it's all for love of you. I saw it happen. You stood in the doorway, Flinders, in your black coat, a tall dark spire you were, with your hair shining like a beacon of light gold and – '

'You told me I looked awful.'

'Well, you did, by your standards. But by normal ones you were so lovely that all he could do was offer you tributes of Stilton and watercress, celery and radishes. I'd have done the same myself in his shoes. As it is – '

'As it is,' she interrupted impatiently, 'you're supposed to be offering me advice about my book.'

'Right.'

He pushed his plate aside and, leaning forward, looked at her intently.

'Seriously, Flinders,' he said, 'I think that rather than making a mess of the book, in the hope that he might publish it, which probably isn't up to him anyway, you'd do better to try one of the smaller publishers.'

'That's not what you said before. You said the bigger ones had more outlets and better distribution.'

'All right, I did say that. But all that has happened is that you've got the same reply from all the big publishers you've tried. What they're saying, in their different ways, is that the book has literary worth but it isn't commercial. Now if you take a smaller publisher, like Bernard Barrack for example, he doesn't have to worry so much about that. All right, he has to make a profit, obviously. But he doesn't have the huge overheads and he doesn't have accountants breathing down his neck all the time. He's still in the business of taking a manuscript he likes and publishing it.'

'Yes.'

It seemed simpler, clearer now, isolated on the train, cut off from the pressures of the outside world.

'As for telling you to expand the love scenes,' Randy was saying, 'that's just a euphemism for telling you to put in some dirty bits to help the sales.'

'You thought they were all right as they were?'

'Yes, they were fine.'

He put a radish in her mouth. It was cool and sweet.

'I think food tastes better on the train,' she remarked.

'Quite right,' he told her solemnly. 'It's nonsense about fresh air. If you really want to enjoy things like radishes, you should eat them in a nice smoky tunnel.'

'We've both had too much wine,' she said and yawned.

The waiter came and cleared their table, sweeping the cloth, making everything tidy. Then he put big white cups in front of them and filled them with steaming black coffee.

'And there's another thing, Polly,' Randy said, when the waiter had left them. 'At the moment you just want to get this book published. But if you do a wrecking job on it you'll have to ask yourself if in the long run you'll be glad you've had it published. You might come to regret it later. You've got to see it as part of your whole work.'

'It might not be. It might be the only one.'

It scared her to think that by not cooperating with Peter Falconer she might be missing her one big chance.

Randy shook his head.

'I don't believe that,' he said.

He had more faith in her than anyone, she thought, including herself. In a funny kind of way he cared more about her writing, truly cared, than the man Falconer. Tears pricked her eyes. He saw them and took her hands in his.

'Darling Flinders,' he said. 'Marry me, you silly idiot.'

She sniffed and laughed despite herself.

'You know I can't,' she said.

'The word should be *won't*, not *can't*. It's only a very small printing error I know, but it does rather alter the sense.'

Then his expression changed and, abandoning his teasing manner, he said quietly, 'Look, Flinders, I know you're not happy with Martin. I'm sure of it, I feel it in my bones, that you're deeply, profoundly unhappy. I don't know why or what it's all about – '

And she would never tell, never.

'Only that it's something almost beyond what you can bear. And I know you have this thing about not upsetting the children. I don't know why you have such an obsession about it – '

'Life is full of great unmentionables,' she said as lightly as she could.

Alarm bells were ringing loudly in her head, reminding her that the price of happiness for Randy and herself would be misery for the children. She would never betray them, never. It was unthinkable. She stared out of the window. It was black dark outside and her reflection stared back at her. The effect was even more devastating than the image in the grimy mirror had been, for it hollowed out her eye sockets, turning her into an old woman.

They were hurtling into the night now at breakneck speed, the coffee ebbing and flowing in their cups with the swaying of the train. The dining car emptied but they sat on, tolerated by the staff, not wanting to go to their separate compartments. The attendant brought more coffee.

'He's really taken a shine to you,' Randy said.

'Rubbish.'

'I'm enjoying all the perks thereof,' he said. 'I've never been offered all these extra cups of coffee when I've been alone.'

'Do you come often?'

'At least once a week, I spend the day in London.'

They talked sporadically until the train approached the station.

'Are you being met?' he asked. 'Or can I run you home? I've got the car in the car park.'

'No. Nobody's meeting me.'

It had been raining heavily up here while the sun shone in London. The water lay in dirty pools outside the station yard, and in the car park there were oily lakes on the uneven ground.

The car wouldn't start.

'It doesn't like the damp,' he said, after trying several times. 'Give it a few minutes and I'll try again. Sorry.'

'It's all right,' she said, and shivered.

He put his arm around her and opened his coat to share it with her.

'Will they be worried about you at home?' he asked.

'There's nobody at home.'

'I see.'

The rain began to beat down hard, noisy against the roof of the car. It was good to be enclosed. They sat in silence, wrapped up in his coat. It's like it used to be, she thought, cuddling up against him. But no, not really, just a little hint of warmth, a reminder of how things can be. The reality of her life now was Martin's study, his collection of Nazi memorabilia, the children asleep at the Dawsons, her hollow, hollow marriage. That was her world now.

But just for one night she could forget it with Randy. Then she must return, learn the way of acceptance.

Next time he tried, the car started.

'Flinders,' Randy said, as they moved slowly out of the car park, 'shall we go to my flat and have a nightcap and negotiate about this divorce of yours and this marriage contract we might have, you and I?'

'We can go to your flat for a nightcap,' she said, 'but there's no negotiating to be done. I've told you that.'

'In that case I'll take you straight home,' he said brusquely.

It was like a slap in the face. For a moment she said nothing, numbed. Then she just wanted to get away from him, get out of his car, but she looked at the driving rain and thought better of it. Instead she sat trembling with rage and spat out the necessary instructions for getting her home. Even before the car had stopped outside the house she had opened the door.

He reached over and took her hand.

'I do love you, Flinders,' he said quietly.

'I hate you, Randy,' she replied, getting out.

'Do you want your manuscript?' he asked, picking it up off the floor and handing it to her. 'Or do you hate that, too?'

She snatched it from him and without another word turned and walked into the house.

It had been a rotten day, she thought angrily, as she switched on the hall light. The house struck cold. A waste of time and money, that's what it had been, a bloody waste. All she wanted was a hot bath to thaw her and wash the grime away. But in the bathroom she found she had forgotten to turn on the immersion heater and there was no hot water.

I really hate him, I hate him more than anyone in the world, she thought, furious with herself for being deprived of a hot bath through her own carelessness. He's far worse than Martin, who at least can't help his problems. How can he say he loves me? He doesn't love anyone except himself. He just enjoys humiliating me, that's all. How typical of him not to want me to alter the book to please Peter Falconer and maybe make a success of writing. Typical!

All the same, next morning she took his advice and posted the manuscript to Bernard Barrack, enclosing a polite little note and the return postage.

Chapter 20

The swings were all taken; Sarah ran over to the slide instead and Polly sat down on the bench to watch her. Sarah was quite plump still, she thought, observing the podgy little legs toiling up the steep metal steps. She still had that roly-poly baby look which Tim had now quite lost. At the top of the slide she sat down, carefully arranging herself in the prim lady-like manner she sometimes put on, settling her dress carefully in place. But once she had launched herself down the slide, she forgot all about being grown up. Her skirt blew up in the air as she abandoned herself to the joy of speed, a grin of delight on her face. At the bottom she waved to her mother, and then ran round to climb up the steps again. Suddenly there was a queue of children for the slide and half the swings were empty. It was always like this; they moved around in shoals, the children at the park.

'Nice to see the kiddies,' the man next to her remarked. He was a good-looking man with very clear blue eyes and thick, fair hair. She nodded.

'Which is yours?' she asked.

He shrugged. 'None of them,' he said. 'I just like to watch them.'

'Yes.'

Conversations were always like this at the park: sporadic, most of one's mind occupied with other things as hers was now as she watched Sarah and thought about fictional characters, worrying about them as if they were her children.

'Your little girl not at school yet?'

'Sarah? Yes, but she's been off with a cold. She's better today, but it didn't seem worth sending her back just for Friday.'

'Lovely day like this, too. Fresh air do her good.'

'Mm.'

The idiot lullaby of the ice cream van, soft but carrying, wafted across to them from the other side of the park. Sarah was instantly at her side.

'No,' Polly said. 'It'll spoil your tea.'

'Oh, please, Mum. All the others are having one. It's only sixpence.'

'I'll treat you,' the man said. 'Come on.' And before Polly could say anything, he had led Sarah off to the van.

Polly watched, annoyed. She was even more annoyed when she saw that they didn't come straight back, but went around the field, Sarah licking her ice, the man walking beside her. Well, at least he was looking after her, she thought, her eyes following them as they walked though her mind was still on her book.

All the same, when they got back she said sharply, 'When I said no, Sarah, I meant no.'

Crestfallen, Sarah went off to the slide.

'Just one more turn,' Polly called after her.

Ashamed of her mother's rudeness, Sarah didn't reply. Polly was a bit ashamed of it herself. 'I'm sorry,' she said, turning towards the man, 'but you know, it's very difficult to stop them eating sweet things all the time.'

He didn't hear her. He was watching the slide intently, a curious expression on his face. What was that word it made her think of? Lycanthropy. That was it: turning into a wolf.

Suddenly, before she could collect her thoughts, Sarah was alongside saying virtuously, 'I've had my one turn and come straight back.'

'Oh, aren't you a good little girl,' the man said, leaning forward and poking her in the tummy.

Sarah giggled and squealed and pretended to run away so that he chased her and she ran back to the seat. She sat down between them, folded her hands on her lap and prepared to make conversation.

'I've got a guinea-pig,' she said.

'What's he called then?'

'He's called Paddy and he's lovely. He's black and brown and has got long hair with rosettes in it, like curls. He's really pretty.'

'Guinea-pigs aren't pretty. Only little girls are pretty.'

'Hamsters aren't nice,' Sarah said, adding primly, 'they have bad habits.'

'Dear, dear,' he said, feigning shock. 'What sort of bad habits? Do they bite? Like this?'

He took the plump, baby arm, and, holding it by the wrist and elbow, lifted it up to his face and pretended to bite.

'They don't just bite,' Sarah said. 'They eat their babies all up.'

'Oh? Well, you're just a baby, so I shall eat you up.'

He lunged at her. Sarah laughed and jumped away, tugging to get her arm free, but not trying very hard. She was teasing him, flirting, enjoying fighting with someone she was sure wouldn't hurt her.

He was laughing, too, but Polly saw that his blue eyes were cold and intent. Suddenly horrified and scared, she jumped up.

'Come on, Sarah,' she said.

'Come to the ducks,' Sarah said to the man. 'Come on, we've brought bread.'

'No,' Polly said. 'We must go home now. Come on.'

'But you said –'

'I didn't realise how late it was. We've got to get home before Time comes in from school.'

'But –'

'Be quiet, Sarah, and don't argue. That's enough.'

When Sarah refused to budge, Polly took her by the wrist and dragged her off.

'But why, Mum? It isn't late. He said it was half-past two not long ago. He said I could call him Uncle Tom –'

'Listen to me, Sarah. He isn't a nice man and I don't want you to talk to him ever again. Do you understand? If he does, you come to me straight away. Do you hear?'

'But he *is* nice. He bought me an ice-cream. It's just *you* that's horrid and –'

'And you mustn't talk to any other men either, not to anyone you don't know, however nice they seem. Do you understand that?'

Sarah began to cry.

'I'm sorry, pet,' Polly said. 'I know it's hard for you to understand and most of them *are* nice, of course they are. But the trouble is you can't tell the few that aren't, not just by looking at them. Nobody can.'

'How could you tell then?' Sarah sulked.

'Well, you just get to have a better idea when you're older. But even I can't be sure, Sarah. It's better to be on the safe side. Just try to trust me, love.'

'Oh, all right,' Sarah said, suddenly bored and hungry. 'What's for tea?'

'There's real honey in the comb. And crumpets.'

Sarah relaxed and let her mother's hand slide down from her wrist so that they were holding each other properly by the hand. It was a sign of forgiveness. They walked amicably together, not talking, fingers intertwined.

'Look, there's a parcel,' Sarah said when they got back. 'The postman's left it in the porch.'

Recognising it, Polly overtook her and picked it up.

'Papers for Daddy,' she said, holding the side with the Bernard Barrack label against her body. 'I'll put it in his study.'

'Paddy must be starving,' Sarah said. 'I'll go and feed him.'

She ran off and Polly took the parcel indoors and pushed it into the bottom drawer of her desk. That's that, she thought, I'm not going to try any more publishers. She was trembling. She was much more upset than Sarah had been by the man in the park. It was all her fault. She should have realised much sooner. She would have done if she had been concentrating, but she had been thinking about the book. She had drifted off into that other world, observing but not really seeing what was going on in front of her eyes. She could see it now, the plump little forearm, marbled pink, like little washerwoman's arms, Sarah's were. And the man's head bending over it, his mouth pretending to bite. God knows, there'd been enough publicity about men like that, and she'd let her child go wandering off with him to buy an ice cream. She shivered at the thought of it. And she'd made an awful mess of trying to explain to Sarah about it afterwards. She would have to try again, try to get through to her, without making her frightened and suspicious. Without making her too wary of people. She pushed the heavy drawer shut, determinedly closing her brief career as a writer, and went to get the tea.

'He's too fat, Paddy is,' Tim told his sister when he came in. 'Guinea-pigs shouldn't be as fat as that.'

'No, he's not, he's just right.'

'He's bigger than a Chihuahua.'

Sarah thought about it.

'Good,' she said at last.

She's learning, Polly thought, she's growing up.

'Bert Siddon had a Chihuahua and the cat ate it,' Tim counter-attacked.

Sarah's lip began to tremble.

'Come on, wash your hands. The crumpets are ready,' Polly said.

Sarah stopped in mid-howl and came to the table.

'When's Dad coming home?'

'Not till tomorrow lunch time,' Polly said. 'The conference goes on till late tonight, so he'll drive home during tomorrow morning.'

Tim was outraged.

'But he said he'd mend my puncture,' he objected. 'He said he'd show me how. He said we'd buy the stuff in the morning and mend it, and now he won't be back until the shops are shut.'

'It's all right, Tim, we'll buy the puncture set tomorrow morning, then it'll be ready for him when he comes back.'

But he didn't come back in the afternoon, nor did he return on Sunday. She told them he must have been delayed and it was nothing to worry about. Actually the children weren't in the least worried; they were used to his not being there. It was she herself who was worried. She imagined car accidents, heart attacks, sudden loss of memory. She considered phoning the police and ringing round the hospitals, but feared to alarm the children and anyway knew that if there'd been an accident they would have contacted her already: his pockets were full of papers by which he could be identified.

'I expect he's gone straight to the office,' she said on Monday morning.

'Oh well, it doesn't matter now,' Tim told her. 'We've mended the puncture anyway.'

She waited until they had gone to school and then rang his office.

'He's got a week's leave,' his secretary said, without asking her who she was. 'Would you like his home number? That's where he'll be.'

'Thank you,' Polly said automatically and found herself writing down her own telephone number, slowly, at dictation speed.

Then she sat, staring at the paper with her own telephone number on it. At least that ruled out an accident. He'd planned this, whatever it was. But why hadn't he told her? And where had he gone? Had he decamped abroad? Spy. The word jumped at her from nowhere. Ministry of Defence secrets? It was possible he had knowledge somebody might want to buy. She should go and look for his passport. Or there might be something else in his study, some clue. Stop it, Polly, there's a perfectly normal explanation, of course he isn't a spy. His work has to do with construction, not policy, there's nothing secret about that, not really secret.

Maybe, she thought, going slowly upstairs, he's joined some neo-Nazi group. Maybe he's in South America. Lots of Nazis had gone there after the war. She had once hear him say that they were used to advise police states there on torture. But he would never have said that, would he, if he had been planning to go there? He'd have kept quiet about the fascists in South America if he'd been thinking of joining them. It didn't make sense.

She stood on the landing. She couldn't force herself to go into that room. She realised that she had always thought of it as quite apart from the rest of the house, something black and secret in the midst of everything normal. She couldn't face it, not now, the evil of it. She told herself not to be stupid. She made herself take hold of the knob and turn it. The door was locked.

She ran downstairs. She must get out, get out of the house. Get out, among normal everyday things for a while. She went as she was, without a coat, and walked quickly to the park. Deserted it was, the slides and swings empty this Monday morning. Mothers would be busy with the washing, children indoors, kept happy with promises of the park this afternoon. Just walk quietly, Polly, and think, think calmly. Remember all the ordinary everyday things as you walk through this familiar park, down to the pond where the ducks are. And please God don't let that awful man appear.

But only the German woman was there, feeding the ducks. They had talked before, in the haphazard way of conversations in the park. She looked like an old woman, the German woman did, white-haired and drawn, with very deep-set eyes. But from what she had said about her youth before the war, Polly thought she couldn't be more than fifty at the most, maybe less.

She greeted Polly cheerfully. 'Today,' she said, 'is my twentieth anniversary in England.'

Polly smiled and congratulated her.

'Yes, I came here in 1947,' the German woman said.

'Alone?'

'I was the only one left.'

Did she mean the only one left of her family, or in the concentration camp, or what? How had she survived, this woman? Polly knew from the scraps of talk they had had before, inhibited by the children, that she was a survivor. She had wanted to know more of her history, but not today. What a curious mischance it was, Polly thought, that today, when she just wanted to try to find some peace, some normality, they should be alone and undisturbed together, herself and this survivor of the holocaust, now when she wanted to get away from the thought of it all, from the room with its Nazi memorabilia and all it stood for, that evil place in the heart of the house. But here was the woman in the park talking about it, domesticating it, even.

'Hitler was very respectable,' she was saying in her curious, ironic, broken English. 'Oh yes, I know you British always think he was an obvious devil and the wicked Germans fell for him, but it wasn't like that at all.'

She shook her head and threw some bread on the water. The ducks squawked and fought for it.

'When I was growing up in Germany', she said, 'it was the right thing, the respectable thing, to be in Hitler's party. If you didn't join the Party, if your families didn't go to the rallies, you were thought – well, a little bit leftish, maybe. Otherwise you'd have joined the Party, wouldn't you? So respectable people sent their children to join the Hitler

Youth, they attended the rallies, cheered the leader. It was good and proper and patriotic. Some things, of course, we didn't like. I remember my father being anxious when they formed a national police force. He was afraid how it might be used, but then they said it would be more efficient, a national force. They called it the Gestapo.'

The ducks were waiting. She threw them more bread. They uptailed, they dived and splashed. Overhead the sky was blue with soft white clouds. Polly thought of Martin's study and the woman spoke of Hitler.

'And you see, there were trouble-makers, we heard a lot about them: Jews and communists. And gradually it came to seem that socialists were communists, and liberals were socialists and they were all trouble-makers so the police couldn't be too soft, could they? That was their reasoning, and they had to maintain law and order, so they said. Others said they did it in ways which were worse than no law and order. Some said it was better to risk attack in the street than being dragged into a police cell and beaten up. But not many. Well, the trouble-makers weren't our sort of people, were they? I hadn't read the words of Bonhoeffer then, but I have since. Do you know them?'

Polly shook her head.

'It goes something like this,' the German woman said. 'They came in the night and took away my neighbour. But he was a communist. I'm not a communist, so I said nothing. They came in the night and they took away my neighbour. He was a Jew. I'm not a Jew, so I said nothing. They came in the night and they took away my neighbour. He was a socialist. I'm not a socialist, so I said nothing. They came in the night and they took away my neighbour. He was a liberal. I'm not a liberal, so I said nothing. They came in the night and they took me away. And there was nobody left to speak for me.'

She staved out across the park, seeing nothing that was there.

'That man was my father,' she said.

There was silence, then, 'It built up so slowly,' she went on, 'until it seemed inevitable, the way everything was taken over by the Party, everything patriotic, everything respectable. And abroad all your superior people seemed to think Hitler was all right, so what doubts we had, we suppressed. Your wealthy, influential people supported him for the same reason that ours did, because he was anti-communist. If the communists were bad, then the fascists must be good. People thought they had to choose between one extreme and the other. Except for the very clever people of course, but then they disagreed among themselves. And besides, who trusts the very clever?'

'We've been so lucky in this country,' Polly said. 'Not having to make a choice. We always seem to find a middle way. We don't like either extreme, the majority of us anyway.'

The woman shook her head.

'You've never been tested,' she said. 'In America, I think it could happen. Just remember that Hitler didn't even have television to spread his propaganda. And here, too, it could happen, only not yet.'

'Why not yet? If not now, why ever?'

'How old are you?' the woman asked suddenly.

'Thirty-six.'

'You grew up in unnatural times, you who grew up after the war in England. For twenty years or so, for a generation, people remember what it was they were fighting against. But now they are beginning to forget. Perhaps I am sensitive about it, but I hear them say things now that they would not have said even ten years ago. Soon they will have forgotten altogether. They will still fear the left but they will have forgotten the danger of the right, forgotten the kind of monster they fought against in the war. And America will lead the way, because she did not witness it as Europe did. And in Europe they do not tell their children how it was.'

'But it can't be right,' Polly protested, 'to go on telling children what happened. How can you ever stop bitterness and hatred if you go on remembering what was done in the past? Besides it's instinctive to protect children from horror.'

'That's what ensures that memory only lasts a generation, and that lessons are never learned. So we will go on making the same mistakes until we destroy ourselves.'

'But could you ever make them understand? Children see things simply. Tell them about the Nazis and it might just make them hate all Germans. Would you tell your own children?'

The woman shook her head. 'I have no children,' she said. 'The women in our camp were all used for experiments. When they had finished with us they sterilised us.'

Polly did not speak. She felt an innocent child herself in the presence of this woman, only a few years older than she was, but white-haired and grey-faced with suffering.

'It is why I don't go and sit by the swings where the children play,' the woman said softly. 'It is why I prefer to come here on my own in the morning.'

She took Polly's arm.

'The torture came to an end,' she said. 'But the pain of childlessness lasts for ever.'

'How do you stop it all?' Polly whispered. 'The cruelty of men, they way they fight and torture? How do we stop it?'

'We can't. They will always justify it. You know, the doctors who experimented on us were professional men, trained to heal and cure. They were family men, with wives and daughters. Yet they operated on us without even using anaesthetics. Do you know why? Because the anaesthetics were costly and we were not worth the expense. You can't argue with evil, I learned that. They will always find reasons for doing what they want to do. All you can do is teach your children, show them and tell them from very young. Because it all starts here,' she added, tapping her heart.

Then she turned and walked away as abruptly as she always did.

Polly stayed on for a little while, the enormity of it dwarfing her own anxiety, numbing her brain. The world seemed a dark and evil place, as if the sky itself had blackened and the leaves withered. She had a sense of not being able to grasp it, the ugliness of this seemingly beautiful world, the incomprehensible wickedness. Slowly she became aware of her surroundings, of the blue sky and green trees, and of her own body shivering because she had come out without a coat.

Smoke drifted across the park. She half shut her eyes against it as she got up, knowing that she must go home now and decide what to do. It was no use losing herself in global despair; it wouldn't tell her what to say to the children at teatime.

It was pine branches they were burning, she realised as she walked towards the park gate. She had seen them stacked up last week, the day she had hurried Sarah away from the man in the park. Yes, pine branches, she was sure of it; it was the same smell as the fire in the Braithwaites' kitchen, when the chimney smoked because the wind was wet and in the west. The same acrid, pungent smell, it was, which made your eyes smart. But a lovely smell all the same. And it had been lovely, too, playing with Mr Braithwaite by the fire. Something in her softened as she remembered. She saw herself again playing Ride-a-Cock-Horse with Mr Braithwaite by the kitchen fire. She saw again Mrs Braithwaite standing there, watching her with anxious brown eyes. And suddenly she understood why she had been sent away.

The telephone was ringing as she opened the front door. It was Jim.

'Oh, you're back,' she said as normally as she could. 'Did you have a good holiday? Thanks for the card.'

'Oh, it arrived all right, did it?'

'Yes. Last week.'

'Good.'

There was a pause. She could hear school noises in the background, children's voices and footsteps, hollow-sounding in distant corridors. Then he said, 'I didn't ring before because he told me not to, but whatever's going on?'

'Who told you not to ring?'

'Martin, of course.'

'When did he talk to you?'

'He didn't. There was this letter waiting for us when we got back home from holiday. He told us your marriage had broken up and that you might be in need of a bit of support and asked us to ring you, but not until today. Polly, we'd absolutely no idea –'

'Neither had I,' she said.

'You mean –?'

'I mean I didn't know about our marriage breaking up. He hasn't actually mentioned it to me. Did he say where he was?'

'No. Don't you know?'

'I only know that he wasn't at work today and has arranged

a week's leave. At first I thought he might be dead, or injured or something, then I thought maybe he was up to something illegal. Now it all seems a bit far-fetched. Honestly, I don't know what to think.'

'Polly, do you want one of us to come over? I'm afraid I can't stay long. But if it's any help I could come over in the evening after school and stay till early next morning.'

'No, don't think of it. We'll keep in touch. I'll ring you when I have any news.'

'Yes, do that, and don't hesitate to ring if you need help. And Polly –'

'Yes?'

'Take care.'

'I will. Don't worry about me. I'll be all right.'

She sat there, after he had rung off, feeling desperately alone in the empty house. How quiet it was, how cut off. She wished she'd asked Jim to read the letter to her. Perhaps he'd misunderstood it. But he probably hadn't got it with him anyway. Presumably he'd rung from school in order to talk to her when Sarah and Tim weren't around. It showed how worried he was. Made her realise how serious it was, too. No good trying to kid herself any more.

She made herself get up, wash dishes, make beds, hoover carpets. Do everyday things, she told herself. There was something reassuring about routine tasks. Lucky she'd decided last Friday to give up writing. She wouldn't be able to settle to it now. Get a proper job instead. Need the money now. No money in writing books. Just as well Bernard Barracks had rejected her manuscript. If they'd taken it they might expect another. Funny how it all turns out for the best.

Numbed, her mind seemed only capable of thinking in jerks, in shorthand.

The bell rang. James Dawson was standing on the doorstep, having propped his bicycle up against the wall. Wearing jeans and a baggy sweater with leather patches on the elbows, his mop of hair windswept from cycling, he looked, as always, every inch not a clergyman.

'Martin asked me to call,' he began.

'How very kind of him,' she heard herself say, far too brightly. 'Do come in.'

He glanced at her, obviously uncertain how to take anything she said, and she led him into the kitchen. He sat down on the stool by the Aga, making it seem puny and fragile for he was as huge and ramshackle as his wife was neat and tiny. He was like a great untidy Old English sheep-dog, Polly thought. Even now, in all her anxiety, she felt an urge to pat him.

She resisted it and instead went over to the sink and made them each a mug of coffee. Meanwhile he had dropped his head into his great hands; she wondered if he was praying. Deeming it wrong to interrupt prayer with coffee, she sat herself down at the table near him. He looked up, rubbing his face. His skin always seemed rather on the loose side, so that his face looked crumpled when he had finished rubbing it. She handed him the coffee.

'Martin seemed to think you might need a bit of support today, Polly,' he said, as he took it. 'He suggested I should come round and see you. I'm very sorry to hear about the divorce.'

'Really? Thank you. Everyone seems to know about it except me. He has told my brother and he's told you and no doubt many other people. But me he has not told.'

Why was she talking in this ridiculous, stilted manner? It was suddenly difficult to control herself. She wanted to laugh. She bit her lip, fighting back hysterics.

'It's awful for you, James,' she managed to say in her normal voice. 'I'm sorry. What a mission to be sent on. Did he happen to mention where he was going?'

'No. Don't you know?'

She shook her head.

'I suppose you've told Jennifer? Or does it count as parish work?'

He smiled. They had often joked about where the boundaries lay.

'Yes, I told her. I hope you don't mind. I thought the children might be upset at school.'

'They've shown no sign of it. Fortunately they're quite used to their father being away. I've just told them he's working away for a few days. I'll go on saying that until I've got news.'

'On Wednesday, you mean?'

'Wednesday?'

'I'm sorry. I'm making an awful mess of this. He just said in his letter that you might need support on Monday and Tuesday, so I assumed that he was contacting you on Wednesday.'

'I don't know. He's been very thoughtful, lining up friends and relations to look after me in the meantime.'

'You're taking it very well,' he said smiling at her. He had a remarkably sweet smile. It lit up his plain face. It was impossible not to smile back, impossible not to feel warmer, stronger, in the presence of such manifest goodwill.

'You're not just in a state of shock, are you Polly?'

'Well, I'm in a state of surprise, shall we say. But shock suggests something needing treatment, doesn't it? And I'm all right. Truly. Tell Jennifer not to worry.'

He got up from the stool, gave her an unexpected little hug, and said, 'Let us know if you want us. I hope you'll hear something good on Wednesday.' Then he left her.

She did hear something on Wednesday, but it was not good. A letter was waiting for her from Martin when she got back from taking the children to school. He told her that he had felt he needed a little time away from the family to think things over, just as she had once felt the need to get away, so surely she would understand. He had gone to see Gerard and after a lot of discussion, they had decided that it would be best if he stayed there permanently. They had always got on well together and had a lot in common. Also he had come to the conclusion that family life was not right for him. He hoped she wouldn't be too distressed and of course he would continue to provide for the children and she must go on using the joint account until a legal settlement was reached. He left all the decisions to her as far as the children were concerned and would not seek custody of them nor insist on seeing them and perhaps it might be easier for her just to tell them that he was dead. He was sorry for any anxiety he had caused by going away without telling her, but he just had not been able to face talking to her about it and thought that this was the best way out.

She sat motionless, too stunned to feel anything but a vague kind of pity for him. Then she read the letter again, more slowly, trying to make sense of it. As she read, pity for the man gave way to anger at what he was doing. Tell them that he was dead, just like that, as if it didn't matter? Apart from the legal complications, how could she live a lie with her own children, day after day? He hadn't thought about it at all. He, who was so meticulous about trivial things, he had dismissed in a phrase his children's happiness and peace of mind, in an offhand phrase! But she couldn't tell them the truth either. It's all very well to say that children should be told the truth, but the truth may be something they can't understand. Oh God, what was she going to tell them when they came home tonight? She could not tell them the truth, any more than Mrs Braithwaite had been able to tell her the truth when she, Polly, was a child.

Poor Mrs Braithwaite, to have been forced to send them away without explanation. How she must have agonised over that decision, knowing how much she was hurting them, these children she had taken in when nobody wanted them, these children she loved and who loved her. But she had no alternative but to hurt them, fearing greater harm. And she had to bear the knowledge that the source of danger was her own husband, loving and gentle man that he was in every other way. So she had chosen to send them away and she, Polly, had repaid her with implacable, unforgiving resentment, never going back, never sending a word of thanks. The remembrance of what she had done swept over her now, obliterating for a while her own trouble in the grief she felt for the woman she had hurt so many years ago. That poor trapped woman. And now she herself was caught in the same kind of trap. Maybe it was a punishment for her cruelty, maybe our sins are simply visited on ourselves. What was she going to tell the children? She clutched her head in her hands and heard herself moan.

There was someone at the door. She couldn't possibly see anyone now. Go away, James or Jennifer or whoever you are. Just go. I must have a few hours by myself to decide what to tell the children when they come home. Leave me alone. They didn't ring again. But then she heard someone trying the back door. It wasn't locked. She heard footsteps. Then Jim came into the kitchen. She looked at him with disbelief. He was the only person in the world she could bear to see now, and he had come.

She got up, but he came quickly across to her and put his arms around her and she began to cry. He manoeuvred himself and her on to the chair where she had been sitting and held her close to him. She cried for a long time, she who had banned his tears when he was little. She cried for the children in the garden years ago, and for the woman who had walked away from them, carrying her suit-case down the road. She cried for Mrs Braithwaite and the children expelled from the farm because it was no longer a safe refuge. She cried for the hurt she had inflicted on both of them, and they were tears of repentance. She cried for the special pain men had inflicted on those women, forcing them to hurt children whom they loved, and they were bitter tears. She cried for the helpless ones who lash back as Irene had done, hurting nobody but themselves because there is no justice, and they were tears of rage. She cried because she had wanted to show the truth of it, yes, that had been her motive for writing, and she had failed. And they were tears of despair. She cried for all the mindless cruelty that had savaged the German woman and millions of others like her, for the waste and misery of it all when the world could have been so beautiful. She cried for the children who have to be disenchanted, robbed of that wise ignorance which tells them how the world could have been. So that in the end, when her sobs subsided, all she said was, 'What shall I tell them?'

Jim held her close. 'There's plenty of time, Polly,' he said. 'Just relax.'

'How much time?' she asked, dreading his going.

'I can stay most of the day, if you'd like that.'

'Like it? Oh, Jimmy.'

She nearly started to cry again, only now they were tears of relief. Just by being here, he made things seem better. The fact of it, and the love that had brought him, warmed her; it glowed like a little flame in what had been total darkness.

'Would you like to stay here and talk, Polly? Or we could drive out somewhere and walk, or just sit in the garden.'

'Let's stay in the garden,' she said. 'Like we used to.'

So he moved the bench into the sun and she brought out coffee and they sat, not talking at first, just sitting and listening to the sounds of the garden, the distant hum of the traffic and the occasional sharper sounds from nearby gardens. She held his hand and felt strength returning. Until at last he said casually, 'Want to talk about it?'

'You'd better read his letter,' she said and went to get it. 'I'll make more coffee,' she added, not wanting to see his face as he read.

'Did you know?' he asked afterwards.

She shook her head. 'I knew there was something, but not this, too,' she said cautiously, and he did not press her.

'In the long run, you know, it may be for the best.'

'What?'

'That he's gone.'

'But he *can't*. He must come back.'

He looked at her, astonished. 'But, Polly,' he said at last. 'You can't make him. And anyway, what's the point?'

'The point is that parents can't just walk out on their children,' she burst out furiously. 'You ought to know that, you of all people. Honestly, Jim, how can you think it's all right for him to go? He's their father. They need a father.'

'But not an unwilling one,' he said gently.

'Then we must just find a way of making him willing,' she said, chin defiantly up in the air. 'There's no reason why he shouldn't accept responsibility. He's quite good with children really, he's careful when he's in charge of them and he likes explaining mechanical things to Tim. And, another thing, he's never mean about money; he doesn't begrudge spending on them the way some fathers do –'

'Polly, it's no good,' Jim interrupted. 'You've got to stop thrashing around. You've got to accept that he's gone.'

'No, I won't,' she told him. 'I admit that I did feel like giving in at first. It seemed so pitiable and hopeless. But I feel better now, stronger, since you came. I've just got to put things right, Jim. For the children's sake, I must.'

'But you can't put them right, Polly.'

'I can jolly well try.'

'No. Some things are beyond even you. You've just got to accept that.'

'I can't. More than anything in the world I want the children to have a proper home, with both parents. I want them to have peace and security and, oh, all the things that we didn't have.'

Her voice broke. Jim took her hands in his. 'That's an ideal, Polly,' he said. 'But life hasn't worked out that way. You've got to face reality.' He smiled at her. 'Come on, you were always rather good at that. Down to earth, you were. Both feet on the ground. You can accept this, of course you can.'

'I can't, Jim,' she whispered. 'I can't bear it.'

'Yes, you can.'

He put his arm around her shoulders. 'You're a fighter, Polly,' he said. 'You always had an instinct to go in with both fists up. And you've never given in, even when you were beaten. But you can't fight this. You've got to do something which is harder for you than fighting. You've got to accept it. There's no way you can change him. He's as he is. Let him go.'

'But people can change. I could help him, if only he'd try to help himself –'

He shook his head. 'Look, Polly, you can put a bit of spunk into a small boy, as you did with me, but you can't change a grown man. And even if you can get him to come back, do his duty by the children as you see it, you couldn't make it natural to him, couldn't make him enjoy it and the children would realise that. They'd sense it more and more as they got older. It wouldn't be a happy home.'

She sat, her head resting on her hand, her long hair falling forward, saying nothing, not convinced of anything now.

'Oh, I don't know,' she said. 'I don't know.'

Such a picture of despair she looked, that he hated to go on badgering her.

'If Martin wanted to change,' he made himself say, 'there might be some point, but he doesn't, does he?'

He picked up the letter and reread it carefully, as if to make sure.

He was right, Polly thought, watching him. Martin would never change. She had tried to reach him, but he would never admit to any weakness, never face it, never accept her help. Nor would he strengthen himself by trying to understand her needs and weaknesses. He would not change now.

'Polly,' Jim said, putting the letter down.

'Yes?'

'It's a sad letter, but I think it's a brave one. I think he's doing this for your sake.'

'Mine? Oh Jim –'

'Shh, let me finish. I think he recognises it's a hopeless marriage – he's honest about that – but he knows that you'll never leave the children so you're trapped. I think he's offering *you* a way out. I think he does care about the children but he's prepared to give them up because he sees it's the only way to free you, too.'

'Oh, poor Martin. If that's true –'

All the pity she had felt when she first read the letter seemed to surge up in her again; the same pity she had felt when he had told her about his childhood. Suddenly she remembered the night he had woken up the children because he was afraid that she was leaving. She had felt nothing but anger against him then, but now she felt pity for a man who did not value himself enough to ask her to stay on his own behalf and so had used the children to voice his own childish terror.

'So accept what he's offering you, Polly.'

'But, don't you see, I can't. Even more now, I can't, if what you say is true. You see, he was a victim too. It's so unfair. I can't let him give up what little he's got –'

'Polly, there are some natural injustices you can't try to put right. You just have to find your own way of living with them. He's having the courage to do that. You must, too. Pity is no basis for marriage.'

She looked about her as if seeking an answer in the physical world. But the sad autumnal garden seemed to stare back, offering nothing. The dew was still heavy on the grass and a mistiness hung over the shrubs and bushes. In the herbaceous border the great clump of phlox which had glowed white on summer evenings when all the other colours faded, was brown now and rotting. Next to it, the pale blue Michaelmas daisies were straggly and spotted with mildew.

'We shouldn't just take from the strong,' Jim was saying. 'Weak people, flawed people, have the right to make sacrifices, too. Accept what he's offering you, Polly.'

She turned and looked at him, noticing for the first time that his hair was turning grey just above his ears and that his face was thinner, more lined than it had been. For a moment she seemed to observe him in a curiously detached way, as a stranger might. His face seemed pared down, firmer, much stronger, but the eyes which appealed to her now were the same eyes that had looked out at her through softer features years ago, before time had done its work. She thought how strange it was that this man had somehow grown out of that boy, this man who was trying to help her now.

She reached out to take his hand and felt tears pricking her eyes. To stop them falling, she tipped her head back and gazed up into the October sky. It was a pale, milky blue, criss-crossed with the bare branches of the weeping ash whose leaves came late and fell early. The dry seeds hung in their papery cases like little bunches of keys which rustled when the faint breeze disturbed them. She tried to make out a message of hope, but all she heard was resignation.

'Yes,' she said at last to her brother. 'You're right.'

Even as she spoke she realised that although she herself had failed to help her husband, somebody else might be able to. Perhaps with Gerard he would feel safe enough to admit his fears and let himself outgrow them. Hope broke unheralded into her resignation and it was with much more conviction that she repeated, 'Yes. You're right.'

Jim didn't reply, just sat and held her hand, knowing that it was settled.

The sun banished the last faint wisps of the mist. Midges swarmed low, hovering just above the grass. A few bees were busy among the Michaelmas daisies and in the distance they could hear the soothing hum of traffic.

'A penny for them?' she asked at last.

'I was just thinking, Polly, that any moment now we might hear Mrs Biddle shovelling coal.'

'Oh, Jim! Fancy you remembering that.'

'Don't you?'

She shrugged. 'That's different. I don't forget anything.'

'Such as?'

She looked at him, hesitated. There were so many things they had never spoken of, she and Jim. Then suddenly it was easy and she found herself talking to him as she could never ever have talked to anyone else. And never had. They had shared their childhood, they had grown up in the same soil, they belonged to each other. There was so much that they didn't need to explain. They talked now about their mother going and about the auction in the village hall and about the Braithwaites, and although she did not tell him the exact message that had been carried to her on the smoke in the park, the knowledge wafted in the smell of the pine logs, somehow he seemed to understand.

'What I remember best of all,' Jim said, 'was the drive up to the farm in the trap.'

'You were asleep.'

'Not all the time, I wasn't. It was like magic, that drive in the moonlight. Do you remember the time on the roundabout, Polly?'

'When you were sick?'

'That's right. When Fred took us out.'

'Do you know why?'

'Why what?'

'Why he took us out?'

'No.'

'It was so our mam could go to Dad's funeral. I was mad about that.'

'Why? I suppose she'd have to go, wouldn't she?'

'I don't know.'

She shook her head. Talking to Jim seemed to take the power out of memories. They were exorcised, like ghosts.

She stretched and yawned.

'Oh, I feel so much better,' she said, smiling at him. 'So much stronger.'

'Good. You look better.'

'I feel ready to talk about all the practical things now, like what I should tell the children tonight.'

'Just one thing, Polly, before we start. You've worried about the children as far as all this is concerned, but what about you? Apart from wanting him back as a father for the children, did part of you want him back for yourself – as a husband, I mean?'

'He hasn't really been one,' she said in a low voice. 'He didn't like that either.'

She leaned against him.

'However have you borne all this?' he asked. 'And it all looked so happy and normal from the outside.'

She shrugged. 'I suppose I just went on hoping that it would come right. It's amazing how you do. Then I was busy with the children, then I thought I'd get a job –'

'But you didn't, did you?'

She shook her head.

'No, you see, instead –' She hesitated. She had thought just now that she could talk to him about anything. But the writing of books was a different matter: she had to force herself to talk about it, even to him. Besides, she didn't understand it herself. It still amazed her, that she had written, actually written, a book. She, Polly Adams. But she did her best to explain to her brother now.

'And somehow, living in that other world,' she concluded, 'I seemed to obliterate this one. Not consciously, you know, but it just happened.'

'When you were little,' he remembered, 'you used to lose yourself in reading. Maybe books are your salvation.'

She laughed. 'Yes, it's the same sort of thing really. Much harder though. Perhaps the feeling of obligation I had was something to do with repaying a debt.'

He wasn't sure that he understood what she meant, but said nothing, grateful that she had laughed.

'I'm going to bring out some sandwiches,' she said, getting up, 'and after that we'll start planning.'

They had to move the bench again to catch the afternoon sun. It slanted on to them as they sat there, leaning against the sandstone wall of the outhouse, enjoying the warmth on their faces as they ate their picnic lunch.

'I should have cooked you a proper meal,' she said. 'It's awful to come all this way and only have sandwiches.'

'Don't be silly. I don't want you wasting our precious time together cooking.'

She looked at her watch. The children would be home in a couple of hours. She felt the panic building up in her again.

'Oh, Jim, what shall I do? I can't tell them the truth, but I can't do what he says and tell them he's dead.'

'Can't you just fudge it a bit?'

She stared at him, puzzled.

'I mean, maybe you don't have to choose between the truth and lying? You always see choices very clearly, don't you? You always did. Things were black and white so you made quick, clear decisions. But maybe it isn't like that this time. Why not just tell them that he's gone away for a bit? Then next weekend you can all come and stay with us, that'll distract them. Let them get used to him being away, gently, not abruptly. No,' he said as she was about to interrupt, 'I know exactly what you're going to say.'

'What?'

'You're going to say it's no good postponing decisions.'

She laughed. 'Dead right, I was,' she said.

'Well, I think you should. Just let things drift along gently for a bit.'

He hesitated, then said, 'And actually Marie-Louise and I have arranged a little distraction.'

'Oh?'

'We're going to have a baby. At least she is. That should keep the children happy for a bit.'

For a moment she actually forgot about Martin.

'Oh, that's lovely. I'm so glad,' she said, kissing him. 'And very thoughtful of you, little brother, to go to all this trouble for our sake.'

'Goose,' he said, shaking her gently. 'You know what I mean. I'm telling you earlier than we'd normally have done, to give them something new to think about, that's all.'

'I'll leave it to Marie-Louise to tell them next weekend, if you really want us to come.'

'Of course we want you. And –'

'What?'

'Well, it sounds a bit arrogant, but it may be a help to Tim to see a bit more of me now. You know, another chap about the place.'

She leaned against him. There was nobody who would be a better model for her son, she thought, than her brother.

'I'll break it to them gradually then,' she conceded.

'That's right. Just keep everything as normal as possible. Look, Polly, I'd better leave before they come in from school or they may think something's up.'

Again the feeling of panic. He saw it in her face.

'You'll be all right,' he said.

She nodded.

'I don't like to think of you alone all day. But I suppose it has to be like that, writing books.'

'Oh, I shan't be. I'm giving it up. Didn't I say? I'll look for a job in journalism now.'

'You've kept up your old contacts?'

She hesitated, then told him about Randy.

'Does he know that Martin's gone?'

'No, I haven't seen him for ages. Hardly anyone knows about Martin. I suppose they'll have to soon.'

'Why don't you tell him? Randy, I mean?'

'It's nothing to do with him,' she said. 'I shan't go asking him for a job.'

'But he seems to have been very helpful in the past.'

'Actually he's sometimes been remarkably unhelpful,' she interrupted sharply.

'Sorry,' he said, grinning at her and pulling a face.

It was the sheepish, apologetic grin that did it; she had a sudden picture of him looking just like that as he sat up on a chair with two cushions at the kitchen table at the farm while she badgered him to do his schoolwork, cramming him so that he wouldn't get left behind.

'What is it?'

'I was just remembering how I used to make you do your lessons up at the farm,' she said. 'I was an awful bully, wasn't I?'

'Never mind, I've bullied you a bit today, too.' He laughed and shook his head. 'No, I'll never forget those awful sums you used to set me. And the English parsing and comprehension. But I never would have bothered otherwise. I was a natural dunce.'

'No, you weren't. You just gave up because of all the upsets we had.'

'Maybe. I only wish there'd been somebody to do for you what you did for me.'

'You just have,' she said.

When he had gone, she put ready the children's tea and prepared to begin the process of telling them about Martin.

Sarah came in first.

'Our parents can come to the concert, Mrs Dawson says,'

she announced before she took off her coat. 'When's Daddy coming back?'

Not expecting to have to face the question so soon, Polly braced herself. 'Sarah,' she said as calmly, as she could, 'Daddy has gone –'

'Where?' Sarah interrupted sharply.

'I don't know where –'

She stopped in mid-sentence, so dreadful was the look on Sarah's face.

'Well, how do you know then? Why didn't you stop him?' she shrieked, her face contorted. Polly looked at her, horrified. Before she could cross the floor to reach her, Sarah had dashed out of the kitchen, slamming the door behind her and shot off up the garden. Polly followed, but bumped into Tim in the doorway.

'Steady there,' he said, in his form-master's voice. 'What's the hurry?'

'It's Sarah. She's upset.'

'That makes a change,' he said sarcastically. 'What's got into her this time?'

She stood, torn between the two of them, then decided it was more important to talk to Tim.

'Because Daddy's gone away.'

'Well, she shouldn't be so stupid. She hardly sees him anyway.'

Shattered, Polly could only stare.

'Look, Mum, I've got to cover this French book with brown paper. I told you yesterday. And now Mr Mortimer says that if we don't, he'll confiscate them.'

'Yes, I'm sorry, I did look for paper but I couldn't find any. I'll try again.'

'Could you do it now? I'm the only one left who hasn't covered it. Honestly, Mum, he's hopping mad. They're new books, you see, quite new.'

'We'll look in my desk drawer,' she said, leading the way. 'And Tim, about Daddy –'

'The bottom drawer, is it?' he asked, running ahead.

'Yes, that's right. But, Tim –'

He was rummaging around in the drawer.

'There's no paper, Mum,' he grumbled, exasperated.

But the manuscript was there, wrapped in good quality brown paper.

'You can have this,' she said, unwrapping it and giving him the thick brown paper, not caring any more who saw the label.

'Thank's, Mum, it's super.'

Yes, you had to hand it to publishers, they did send back your rejected work in the very best paper, she thought, watching him smooth it out on the floor and place his book in the middle.

'There's plenty,' he said. 'I could do my geography book as well. Where's the scissors? And sellotape?'

'Bring it all into the kitchen,' she said. 'I'm just going out to have a word with Sarah.'

She stooped to pick up the letter which had fallen out of the parcel when she unwrapped it. It was a long letter, a letter of acceptance. The manuscript was being returned to her to check and to consider a very minor alteration to Chapter Seventeen.

Dazed, she went back into the kitchen.

Sarah had just come in. She was standing, looking blissfully happy, talking to Tim. Her guinea-pig was straddled over her arm.

'We've finished all the dandelions in our garden,' she said. 'Do you think the people next door will let us start on theirs?'

'But, Sarah, you were so upset when I told you Daddy had gone –'

'It's all right, Mum,' Tim interrupted. 'She thought you said Paddy. Where's the sellotape?'

Chapter 21

It had seemed a good idea, at first, that they should spend the week at Sidgewick, the four of them. She had thought how lucky it was that the young couple who had bought the Capsticks' house when Miss Emily died should have converted half of it into a cottage which they let to summer visitors. But as she approached the village now, she began to regret it. She felt at first doubt, then panic, then certainty that it was a terrible mistake to come back.

'You're very quiet,' Randy said, taking her hand. 'Would you like to walk the last bit? The children and I can drive on and meet you at the house.'

'We don't know the way,' Tim pointed out. 'It's only Mum that knows the way.'

'Can I walk with Mum then?' Sarah asked.

'No. You two are going to help me find the house. It shouldn't be too difficult in a little village, should it?'

Tim began to object, but thought better of it.

'O.K.,' he said. 'We'll stay with you if you really can't manage.'

So she got out alone and stood for a moment breathing in the air, which was fresh and crisp despite the sunshine. Oh, this air, how it always surprised her, almost tangible in its purity, not a mere nothingness like the air everywhere else. And how quiet it was, how peaceful. As she walked between the high walls which narrowed the entrance to the village, there was no sound except for her own footsteps. Soon the dry-stone walls gave way to houses, grey stone houses with uneven roofs, houses which seemed to have grown there, not been built like houses in the town, but always to have been there, like the boulders in the fields. Then the road divided to embrace the village green, enfolding in its grey arms the green's triangle of grass with the tree in the middle whose spreading branches cast across the road shadows in whose coolness she had once walked on hot summer days.

She passed the village hall and the post office where Mrs Patmore still reigned, for Polly could see through the narrow window the outline of her head and shoulders as she leant across the counter talking to a customer as she had always done.

The school was quiet as she passed, the playground deserted and no sound of chanting from within. Maybe they didn't chant any more, now that learning tables by rote had gone out of fashion. But of course they would be on holiday. There were a few children playing in the street. She recognised one or two of them, then realised it was their parents she was remembering.

By the time she had reached the house where the others were waiting she knew that it was right to have come back.

In the days that followed the children settled in as if it was home. She took them to play down at the beck, they strolled in the evenings along the lanes, they had picnics at Thieves' Way where Tim and Sarah climbed the rowan tree as she had done as a child and ran along the trunk which straddled the river, looking down at the water far below as they clambered among its branches, hiding in the leaves. And now, on their last day, they were walking up the dale, following the lane where she and Jim had walked daily to school from the farm, and where she had once come with Martin Quigley. They had been talking about him, she and Randy, as they toiled slowly up the hill, the children running far ahead.

'You're very tolerant about him,' Randy said, but it was a comment not a criticism.

'I've no right to be anything else.'

All the same she knew that he was puzzled by the way she could so easily forgive Martin for leaving the children in a way that she herself would never have done. It did hurt her that he had left them so casually, it did frighten her that such callousness existed. But she had grown to accept that lack of feeling in him over the years, so it did not shock her. He couldn't help it. You can't give what you have never received; he had not had even a memory of his absentee parents. Then he had been a victim, too, of his nanny, his schoolmaster, his friends. But that was something she could not speak of even to Randy. It belonged to her and Martin, for the night when he had told her about it now seemed the only true moment in their marriage, too precious to be shared. Besides, it couldn't be shared. The thing which had happened to Martin was too complex to entrust to the shorthand of conversation.

So she said nothing, but walked on, one hand in Randy's, the other reaching out now and then to touch the stones on top of the wall, feeling the smoothness of some, fingering the roughness of those which were encrusted with lichen.

'Hurry up, you two,' Tim bawled at them from far ahead.

'Well, you come and carry the pack then,' Randy shouted back.

To their surprise, Tim took this seriously, dashed back to them and insisted on having the rucksack transferred from Randy's back to his own. Then he ran off ahead again, despite the pack, to show how strong he was.

'He's so helpful nowadays,' Polly remarked. 'How he's grown up in this last year.'

'When he was being stroppy this morning, I told him he was jolly lucky to be taken on my honeymoon. And rather to my surprise, he agreed that he was.'

'Oh, bless him!'

'Mind you, Sarah did rather spoil the effect by asking if they could come with me every time.'

She laughed.

'Isn't it odd how they sometimes seem to understand like adults, then suddenly they're such babies again?'

'Mm. But they're growing up steadily, you know.'

'Thank you,' she said suddenly.

'What for?'

'For making it all work out, making me see sense.'

He had been so patient, so uncharacteristically patient, Randy had. He seemed to have had the strength to wait for ever, never rushing her. Gradually he had won the children's trust, never forcing himself on them. From the moment Jim had gone, unbeknown to her, to see him at his office and told him that Martin had left, Randy had been there, her friend, not her lover.

'Maybe it's your brother Jim you should thank,' he said now, as if reading her thoughts.

'Both of you,' she said.

She hadn't been very cooperative, she realised. How unwillingly she had gone with Randy and the children to the pantomime while Jim waited at her house for Martin so that they could clear the study together. It had been against all her instincts not to see to it herself, but to let Jim deal with it for her. She had sat in the pantomime, the children bouncing up and down in their seats alongside, joining loudly in the songs, shrieking with laughter at the Dame, and all the time her mind had been on what Jim and Martin were doing back at home. And she had thought, 'This is what Uncle Fred did, when he took Jim and me to play on the roundabout while our mother went to the funeral.' Jim had said that history didn't repeat itself, but tears of shame had burnt her eyes all the same. It just seemed wrong.

But as they walked home afterwards, through streets bright with Christmas decorations, she realised that for the first time in weeks she was not filled with dread at the thought of going into the house. She felt as if it was somehow cleansed, an evil removed from it, so that when she went indoors she felt light-hearted and from that day on began to think that it was possible, just possible, that she could have a future which included both Randy and the children. Yes, that was the day she had accepted her own weakness, recognised that there were things she could not deal with, and it had in some strange way strengthened her.

'It's going to be all right,' Randy said now, and he stopped there in the middle of the lane and took her in his arms and kissed her. Over his shoulder she could see a sheep staring at them, its jaws shifting rhythmically from side to side as it chewed, its brown eyes like beads of glass as it watched their embrace.

'I tell you it's going to be all right,' Randy said again as they set off up the hill, his arm around her, her head against his shoulder. 'You've got to believe that, Flinders. It's just that your confidence has taken a battering, that's all.'

She did find it hard to believe, really believe, in the plans that they were making. Whenever she had taken happiness for granted, it had been snatched away. Oh, there had always been reasons; there had been reasons for her mother leaving them, for Mrs Braithwaite sending them away, for Martin's rejection of her. But she had only found out the reasons later; at the time it had seemed that simply by being happy, relaxing her guard, she had attracted instant retribution from the gods. It would be sensible to reserve a little bit of disbelief as a kind of insurance policy against disaster.

'Try to believe,' Randy's voice cut in, 'that life could be waiting round the corner with a bouquet, not a sandbag.'

She laughed. 'I'll try,' she said, leaning against him for reassurance, because she was beginning to dread going back, leaving this place where she felt safe. Of course it would be all right, she told herself. There was nothing to feel guilty about, she had got rid of that old obsession, that fear of re-enacting the past. She would set about organising the new house, work out a new pattern with Randy and the children, get on with her writing. The proofs of the new book would arrive soon and the next one was already begun. For there were things she needed to say and must find a way of saying, she must learn how. There was no reason to be afraid of going back. Just a matter of confidence, as Randy said. She knew it all with her mind; it was just that she didn't feel it yet in her heart.

They had reached the brow of the hill where the lane opened out into a different, loftier world. She could see the source of the beck now, gushing out of the hills high up on the left, white and milky against the green hillside. Beyond it, far in the distance, towered the great mass of Old Bear, upon which she had fixed her eyes to give herself strength to resist Miss Capstick's kindness years ago, and down there to the right in that huddle of trees must be the farm. Her eyes filled with tears as she thought of her implacable hostility towards Mrs Braithwaite, of her rejection of Miss Capstick, of her refusal to be reconciled to her mother when she was dying. Who was she to be intolerant of Martin Quigley when we're all in need of mercy?

The children were standing waiting for them at the spot where the stream went under the lane. It flowed swiftly through a grating into the tunnel and reappeared, calm and shallow, in the pastureland on the other side.

'Is this the gate, Mum?'

'That's right.'

'We could put the tent up here,' Tim said as he shut the gate behind them. He stood surveying the flat patch of grass, which still grew greener because the soil here was deeper. 'We'll never drive the pegs in up there. It's too rocky.'

It was a very small tent which Randy had bought them; it didn't take long to set it up, knocking the pegs in with a stone from the stream. Then they left the children playing there and climbed up the hillside, clambering from rock to rock, often pausing to get their breath and look back, as she had done years ago. She was still amazed at the way the stream sometimes flowed so gently then suddenly took off to rush in a torrent so deep and fast that it didn't seem possible that all that water could have come from the placid pool above. Then only a few yards further on it would subdue itself again, diminishing to a quiet stream.

'Phew, that was quite a climb,' Randy said, throwing himself down on the grass at the top where one of the sources of the beck emerged from under an overhanging rock. He took off his jacket and spread it out for her on the short turf, and they sat together watching the water slide gently over the first mossy ridge, mesmerised by the way it folded continuously over the rim.

Randy lay back, his eyes closed, but she sat gazing around her. Nothing had changed. She could make out the same cairns on the hilltops, the same patches of scree, the same precipice of rock on the shoulder of Little Pyke. She smiled at herself; it wasn't surprising really that it hadn't changed in a few years, this ancient landscape. But it wasn't just that. It was the way she could shut her eyes and remember it exactly as it was. She knew, without turning her head, where the little copses would be, and the great boulders brought down in the Ice Age, and where the stiles were in the dry-stone walls. And if she climbed up on to the flat top of Mickleburgh Fell she would still know where to find the crevices where the astonishing ferns grew out of the stone. In her mind's eye she could see the lonely, gale-swept tree which stood, gnarled and bent, on the edge of the precipice, like some wild crone with long hair lashed back by the wind. She looked at the one cloud in the sky and saw that it would soon be casting its shadow on the hill behind her, taking the sparkle out of the patch of scree, turning it momentarily unfriendly, then rippling on, racing across the green hillside. It wasn't just the features that she knew of this familiar face, but every expression also.

I love it, she thought, I love this place more than anything in the world.

'I've been watching you,' Randy said. 'What have you been thinking?'

'I think,' she said slowly, trying to understand it herself, 'that perhaps everyone has a special feeling for the sort of countryside they're brought up in. But if they're unhappy, for any reason – because their parents are always quarrelling, or because they're lonely, or bullied at school or something – they turn to those surroundings for comfort. I don't mean deliberately. I think it's just an instinctive thing for children to do. But whatever it is, walking through woods or on cliffs by the sea, or on hillsides like this, they find a joy there that they don't find anywhere else. They can relax in their woods or whatever in a way that they can't among people because of their unhappiness.'

'Mm. For me it was back streets of towns,' Randy said. 'But it's the same idea. Go on.'

'So when they're grown up, years and years later even, when they walk on those hills or through those woods, they don't just feel the ordinary adult pleasure in them, they feel again all that old comfort and happiness that they felt as children. It comes back, inextricably bound up in their surroundings. Don't you see? They can't help it. They've invested all the sights and sounds and smells of the countryside with that intense love. But they don't remember why. And even if they did, it wouldn't make any difference.'

He had been lying back listening to her, but he sat up now, close to her so that she could lean against him.

'And I've just realised something else,' she said. 'When I walked up here with Martin, after Tudor Bean's funeral, I was really feeling all that joy and comfort left over from being a child here. It was the first time I'd ever been back. It was overwhelming, and I'd no time to work it all out. Martin got caught up in that feeling. I bestowed it all on him, all that love.'

She paused and then added softly, 'And he was – as he was. And he couldn't carry the burden of that love.'

Neither of them spoke, then she went on, 'That's really why I don't blame him. It was my fault. I imagined myself in love with him. I brought it all on myself. I suppose most of our troubles are self-inflicted. But I hurt him, too, as well as myself.'

It seemed to have been drawn out of her; she was tired by it. She lay against him, and he stroked her hair back off her face and gently kissed her forehead.

'And now you're here with me,' he said. 'It's a bit ominous, Flinders. Maybe it's not me you're in love with but the place?'

She smiled at him.

'No, I loved you in the unpropitious town,' she said. 'Mucky and foggy, with no happy memories. Besides, I don't remember falling in love with you. Mostly I remember being mad at you.'

He pulled a face.

'A proper little fury you were.'

'Well, you always mocked.'

'Still do.'

'But in those days I thought people had to be solemn or they weren't serious.'

'Silly Flinders.'

'I know. I've learned a lot since. I don't trust solemn people any more. They can never be really serious.'

'You trust me?'

'Yes.'

'Even with those two?' he asked, nodding down towards the children.

'Yes, oh yes.'

He rearranged his jacket to make a pillow for her against the boulder and she lay back on the sweet-smelling grass. The turf here was so thin that she could feel the rock just beneath it. It was as if her body was pressing down against the bones of the world, so that she seemed to be part of it, part of the hillside, part of this earth. She shut her eyes and felt the sun prickling her face. She could smell the warmth of the grass, hear the ceaseless rippling of the beck which had been flowing here year in year out, day and night, unobserved, while she had been far away, following her own course in different pastures.

Scenes from that life elsewhere drifted, like a series of vignettes, through her mind now; it might have been the life of a stranger, so little did she understand its sudden joys and incomprehensible sadness. How black the world had seemed that day in the park, black and hopeless. It was strange that she could feel so differently now, she thought, looking up into the clear sky, feeling the sun on her face, because it was the same old world, with the same sort of people in it, the same cruelty, the same evil. It was she herself who had changed.

'Make the most of it,' Randy murmured. 'Back to work tomorrow. Back to reality.'

'I'm looking forward to going home,' she heard herself say and was surprised at the conviction in her voice.

Randy was surprised, too; he glanced at her, enquiring.

She shook her head and didn't reply. She couldn't explain that this was her reality and that she was part of it and would carry the feel of it back with her. Instead she lay against the boulder and let her eyes rest on the distant fells, pink and hazy in the heat, and the nearer hills whose green slopes were dotted with sheep and patterned with dry-stone walls. She looked at the farm sheltering in the trees and at the lane which ran like a grey ribbon up the dale and out of sight. She saw the children playing by the gate, where the grass was greener, down there where the stream disappeared under the lane. It foamed as it made its way through the grating, where long ago her forked branch had stuck, looking with its brightly coloured blossom like a stranded doll or a human child. Then she looked back again at the source of the stream as it emerged from the rocks beside her. It seemed to pause, lingering for a while in the placid pool, and then rolled gently over the mossy ledge to flow away from her, sometimes rushed and turbulent, sometimes inexplicably calm.